D1539982

"Mokhtefi was able to reconstruct the sights and sounds of life in his village of Berrouaghia and the constant pressure he felt to be [a 'French Muslim']...moving."
— **ALICE KAPLAN,** *The Nation*

"Mokhtefi's witty commentary illuminates his buoyancy even in the midst of destruction and heartbreak...His story is a page-turner...his colorful portrayal of the character of time, place, and people in colonial, wartime Algeria provides captivating reading, as well as context for the relations between France and Algeria then and now."
— *Markaz Review*

"Mokhtar Mokhtefi's autobiography holds an original position in the panorama of increasingly abundant memoirs of veterans of the war fought by the Algerian Front de Libération Nationale (FLN) against France between 1954 and 1962. For freedom of tone, irreverence, assumed subjectivity, as well as for the elegance of a swift and precise style, the work avoids any eagerness of edifying narrative or systematic theories; what emerges is, in contrast, almost a social history of Algeria during the colonial era."
— **ANDREA BRAZZODURO,** Marie Sklodowska-Curie Global Fellow, Ca' Foscari University of Venice and University of Oxford

"Mokhtar Mokhtefi and I met and became friends in the last year of his life. We spent hours discussing the manuscript of his memoir; it was his reason for being. He had two essential objectives: one was to remind today's youth that under colonialism one was never a citizen but a 'French Muslim,' a subhuman being, treated as such. His second goal was to display how independent Algeria, as other former colonies, became the continuation of colonization, in the form of dictatorship. The colonialists departed but would be replaced by Algerians who in effect colonized fellow Algerians, and it is not over."
—AMARA LAKHOUS, author of *Clash of Civilizations Over an Elevator in Piazza Vittorio*

"A gifted storyteller, Mokhtefi communicates an infectious love of country, yet he firmly dispenses with the pieties of official nationalism by depicting infighting, internal purges, and political ambitions within the nationalist ranks. *I Was a French Muslim* has been brilliantly translated from the French by the person closest to the author—his widow, Elaine Klein Mokhtefi, in her own right a talented writer and veteran of the Algerian Revolution."
—MADELEINE DOBIE, Professor of French and Comparative Literature, Columbia University

"When I read Mokhtar Mokhtefi's memoir, I had the feeling I was discovering my Algerian heritage. It represented the promise of belonging. It made me see how little I had understood colonialism, the war, the people, their resilience, and their humor. It has been a breathtaking adventure. Through

him, I have felt the fear of persecution, the incommensurate anger against colonialism, the salty smell of the streets of Algiers, the electrifying atmosphere of independence, the dreams of a boy and soldier who became a free spirit, and the sounds of laughter and rapture. *I Was a French Muslim* is the gateway to a world so distant today, a world pregnant with promise and fury, of life and joy, of dignity, passion, and utopia. May his words resonate in our hearts and our lives."
—KARIM AÏNOUZ, Brazilian film auteur and director

"Mokhtar Mokhtefi recounts in the first person an intimate page of history that marked him for life...*I Was a French Muslim* tells the story of the battle, not only against colonialism, but above all, for liberation. The personal and the political come together to trace the ideal of emancipation that retains its currency and remains to be achieved, in Algeria and elsewhere."
—WALID BOUCHAKOUR, Algerian journalist

"In chronicling his personal journey from 'French Muslim' to 'Algerian freedom fighter,' Mokhtar Mokhtefi leads the reader, with candor and humor, through Algeria's transition from colonial territory to independent nation. Keenly attuned to the complexities of both colonial society and the nationalist struggle, Mokhtefi's memoir eschews simplistic narratives in favor of a richly detailed, nuanced portrait of Algerian history, and of the men and women who shaped it during these pivotal decades."
—CLAIRE ELDRIDGE, Associate Professor in Modern History, University of Leeds

"For those unfamiliar with the Algerian War for Independence, this historical fresco in the first person offers a gripping account of life in colonial Algeria and a poignant tale of a generation's struggle for self-determination. Expert readers—especially those steeped in the lore of Pontecorvo's *The Battle of Algiers*—will be struck by Mokhtefi's version of events, which sidesteps that perhaps most famous episode of the war, preferring instead to expose the daily grind of logistics and politics that was rural warfare. If Mokhtefi's experiences seem far removed from spectacular urban warfare of an Ali La Pointe, his account of one of the world's longest-lasting liberation struggles is at once more politically complex, and, ultimately, more personal."
—LIA BROZGAL, Associate Professor, French and Francophone Studies, University of California, Los Angeles

"This memoir is history written in real-time, intimate and compelling. Yet Mokhtefi never loses sight of the larger historical importance of his personal commitment and the wider dimensions, and potential dangers, of the Algerian struggle for independence. A book to be read by any serious student of the tangled relationship between France and Algeria, past and present."
—ANDREW HUSSEY, Professor of Cultural History, University of London; author of *Speaking East: The Strange and Enchanted Life of Isidore Isou*

"*I Was a French Muslim* is an intensely intimate account by Mokhtar Mokhtefi of his eight years as courier, radio operator, and official of the Algerian independence movement

[1954–1962]. He describes crossing the desert on foot, the friendships made, and the arrogant and power-obsessed officers in charge. There are major and minor spats as well as love affairs. This is the story of a generation and its struggle for freedom. But Mokhtefi doesn't shy away from a bleak assessment of the future. A personal day-to-day, moment-to-moment recounting—lucidly translated from the French by Elaine Mokhtefi—this book is a page-turner."
—**MANFRED KIRCHHEIMER**, filmmaker

"Neither saccharine nor cynical, Mokhtar Mokhtefi's memoir skillfully depicts the struggle of 'French Muslims' during French colonial rule and the Algerian revolution while also foreshadowing the paradoxes and unfulfilled promises of independence. This graceful translation from French provides much-needed access for Anglophone students of history. His memoir will surely take a central place among autobiographies and memoirs of the era for its balanced and compassionate evocation of the tensions of nationalism and—equally important—for its exploration of a young man's political awakening."
—**ELISE FRANKLIN**, Assistant Professor, University of Louisville

"Dashing and charismatic, Mokhtar Mokhtefi dedicated himself to the liberation of his country, French-occupied Algeria, only to become an exile in France, then in the US, because the post-independence government could not tolerate a man of his integrity and democratic principles. Instead of succumbing to bitterness, nostalgia, or vanity, the sanctuary of many political exiles, he remained faithful to the ideals of self-determination and freedom that had led him into the liberation struggle."

—ADAM SHATZ, contributing editor at the *London Review of Books*

"This marvelous book takes the reader inside the society of Muslim Algeria in the late colonial period, then inside the evolving anticolonial nationalist movement, and finally inside the National Liberation Army (ALN) and its fledgling signal corps, conveying with savory details the particular flavor of each, while recounting the author's step-by-step road to freedom in the process of transcending his original condition of a second-class Frenchman denied citizenship in his own country."

—HUGH ROBERTS, Edward Keller Professor of North African and Middle Eastern History, Tufts University

I Was a French Muslim

I Was a French Muslim

Memories of an Algerian Freedom Fighter

MOKHTAR MOKHTEFI

*Translated from the French
and with an introduction by*

ELAINE MOKHTEFI

Other Press
New York

Originally published in French as *J'étais français-musulman*
by Éditions Barzakh, Algiers, in 2016

Copyright © Éditions Barzakh, Algiers, 2016
Translation copyright © Other Press, 2021

Production editor: Yvonne E. Cárdenas
Text designer: Julie Fry
This book was set in Janson.

10 9 8 7 6 5 4 3 2 1

Library of Congress Cataloging-in-Publication Data
Names: Mokhtefi, Mokhtar, 1935–2015, author. | Mokhtefi, Elaine,
   translator.
Title: I was a French Muslim : memories of an Algerian freedom fighter
   / Mokhtar Mokhtefi ; translated from the French and with an
   introduction by Elaine Mokhtefi.
Other titles: J'étais français-musulman. English
Description: New York : Other Press, 2021. | Originally published
   in French as J'étais français-musulman by Éditions Barzakh,
   Algiers, in 2016.
Identifiers: LCCN 2020056384 (print) | LCCN 2020056385 (ebook) |
   ISBN 9781635421804 (hardcover) | ISBN 9781635421811 (ebook)
Subjects: LCSH: Mokhtefi, Mokhtar, 1935–2015. | Revolutionaries—
   Algeria—Biography. | Algeria—History—1945–1962.
Classification: LCC DT295.3.M66 A3 2021 (print) | LCC DT295.3.M66
   (ebook) | DDC 965.04092—dc23
LC record available at https://lccn.loc.gov/2020056384
LC ebook record available at https://lccn.loc.gov/2020056385

Contents

Introduction *vii*

I CHILDHOOD *1*

II AWAKENING *115*

III SOLDIER IN THE
ALN SIGNAL CORPS *197*

Acknowledgments *401*

Map of Northern Algeria *402*

Acronyms *404*

Algerian Leaders *406*

Glossary of Arabic Terms *410*

Introduction

Elaine Mokhtefi

Mokhtar and I met in Algiers in 1972, by chance. I was driving a colleague, Behja Bensalem, home from work, when she saw Mokhtar coming out of Boubaker's bakery, there where rue Didouche turns left. She asked me to stop and called to him. He came forward, a baguette in hand, slipped his curly-haired head through the passenger window, kissed her on the cheek, and nodded to me. Behja pronounced my name. They hadn't seen each other for some ten years, since they had worked together at the Ministry of Agriculture and Land Reform.

I was pleased to set eyes, finally, on someone I had heard spoken of time and again. Colleagues and friends had often told me about Mokhtar, his intellect, honesty, militancy, his leadership qualities, all on display when he was head of the Algerian national students' association just after independence. Behja had described the power of his public speaking, how engaged she became on hearing him. He represented the future of Algeria. Did he know of me? Perhaps. I was often on national television or the radio as interpreter for English-speaking visitors, generally militants from national liberation organizations in African countries. As far as I know, I was the only American employed by the Algerian government. That in itself was news.

Behja asked Mokhtar to come to dinner, to meet her husband and child. He said, "I'll call you, if the number hasn't changed." No, it hasn't, do that. Horns were honking behind us. We rushed off. Mokhtar called that evening and mentioned that it would be nice if she invited the driver of the car to dinner as well. Why not? said Behja.

That is our story. We met that Saturday night in February 1972 and have been together, even when apart, ever since. Algeria was our meeting ground. We recognized in our souls that we were associated on deep-set planes: the struggle for justice and freedom, the fight against racism and prejudice of all sorts, our belief in the dignity of life, and our love.

Mokhtar was born and raised in Algeria, a colony of France. It was a settler country, something like the United States or Australia. People came from France, from Europe and around the Mediterranean to occupy the land, beginning with a first invasion in 1830. They decimated the population individually, collectively. They killed off tribes, they smothered them wholesale by smoking them out within caves. They colonized the land and indentured the inhabitants.

Algeria became the kernel of a French empire that after

the Second World War began to crumble due in part to France's role as a collaborator of Nazi Germany. Another decade of war ensued in which Indochina (Vietnam, Cambodia, Laos) fought for independence from France and defeated the French ignominiously in battle. The United States actively supported France, footing 80 percent of the war bill, supplying planes, helicopters, and personnel, including pilots. That colonial war ended in 1954, the year the Algerians launched their own war of independence.

During the course of history, France had experimented with various formulas for governing Algeria. In the final analysis, the colonial powers maintained a system of subjugation of the population. They ruled by violence, trickery, by hate. There were one million settlers, the "Europeans," backed by the laws and repressive machinery of colonial France; they bent the nine million Algerians to their iron will.

Upon independence, 132 years after the French first set foot in Algeria, the indigenous population was 90 percent illiterate. They had been governed by the inventors of "human rights," behind the watchwords *liberté, égalité, fraternité* . . .

Algeria went to war for its independence, despite the odds. France was considered the fourth-strongest military power in the world, and, once again, was supported by the United States, both militarily and politically. On November 1, 1954, about a thousand men across the country launched the fight with old rusty rifles, Boy Scout knives, with their bare hands. They attacked both military and civil targets. No one delivered the battle plans to the enemy. Secrecy prevailed.

Algerians understood that their battle for freedom would depend as much on diplomacy as on warfare. They were present everywhere, at international congresses and institutions, in major capitals, in the back rooms where freedom fighters meet. They practiced solidarity actively and, as the war ground on, opened their training camps to the liberation organizations of South Africa, Southwest Africa, Mozambique, Angola, Zimbabwe, as well as from other continents. Nelson Mandela was among those who received training. Thirty years later, when he was released from a South African prison, he would arrive in independent Algeria and proclaim before the multitudes cheering him: "I am Algerian."

Algeria survived the war, eight years of it, profoundly mutilated. Many of the leaders had just a primary school level of education, if that. They had never practiced democracy. Free discussion had never been authorized. Political organizations had been banned by the French authorities, activists were threatened, arrested, their civil rights abrogated. Algerian leaders responded to the methods used to control and maim them by introducing similar constraints and techniques. Many aspects of the climate of war endured after independence. Clandestinity, which had been a necessary tool, became a way of life.

Mokhtar lived and breathed Algeria. The country became his mother, his sibling, his truest and deepest love. He joined the struggle, became an activist in his high school years, organizing a secret cell of the Front de libération nationale (FLN) among the students. His most fervent wish was to bear arms for the liberation of the country. He became a soldier of the National Liberation Army (ALN).

Mokhtar trained to be a signal corps operator. He learned Morse code and how to manipulate sophisticated transmission equipment. The training took place in secrecy in Morocco, the brother country, close to the border. He crossed back into Algeria at the head of a crew with arms, his radio kits, and equipment.

The French were flabbergasted: how could this inexpert, uneducated people, whom they disdained, on whom they cast contemptuous names and expressions, this "nigger" population, invent and actually build a signal corps that allowed them to establish a wartime communications network? The quarantined, the confined, had outsmarted the power brokers. In 1957, in the heart of the war, the operators were in place and active with their illegal American equipment and talking to each other in Morse code, from city to city, field base to headquarters, mountain refuges to desert oases, instantaneously.

It was always Mokhtar's intention to write the story of the men with whom he trained and those who were instructed afterward. It was his duty, he said, to honor those who had come back traumatized, unhinged, those who never returned. May they not be forgotten, may we remember how bravely they had given their lives so that others would one day be free.

"French Muslim," in the title of Mokhtar's book, is not an idle formulation but the designated name for Algerians under the French colonial administration. While Algeria was considered part of France and its million "European" inhabitants were considered French, Algerians' identity cards (*cartes d'identité*) labeled them as "French Muslim," similar to the Vichy regime's introduction of the word "Jew" on French ID cards during the Second World War. Even though France portrayed itself as a secular state, it defined its Algerian subjects by their religion. If we apply this categorization to the United States, our personal ID cards, generally driver's licenses, would carry the label "Catholic" or "Jew," and if we extend this notion, why not "Black"? . . .

Many Algerian freedom fighters have written their memoirs, have provided pages of their existence, before the Revolution, within the army. They have lauded their leaders and blessed the people. Mokhtar has told us something else, much more, episode by episode, almost day by day, what that war gave and what it took away. In the end, we understand. We know what the future will be, for at no point does he avoid the facts of the experience, the role of his superiors and the wartime leaders. Rather than shy away from the darker aspects of the conduct of the war, he highlights controversy, he bares truths.

In Mokhtar's words: "I feel like that animal, half wild, half domesticated, no one ever managed to tame. I still transport on my hoofs bits of manure from that earth, that muck in which I took root."

Mokhtar would often say, "I was weaned on violence." These were the forces that shaped him: He was the last, the youngest of six brothers. The Koranic school, where all instruction was by rote and for male children only. The French primary through high schools, again for boys alone, hidebound by institutional racism. French settler society, which governed with the gun, the ruler, and hate. His father, who frequented the mosque thrice daily plus the call to prayer at dawn. His mother, who reigned inside four walls, with the power of a headmaster, over daughters-in-law confined with her. Mokhtar carried this weight, sometimes this privilege, while developing an innate desire to strike out and fly.

Mokhtar's teacher at the grammar school saw that he was meant for more than village life and tutored him for the exam to enter a lycée, the French middle school and high school. He left home, one of the few local boys admitted, to be a boarding student, in a city some distance from the society that had nurtured him. He was a good student and for eight years he learned, he accumulated knowledge from and of the Western world; he was trained to become a Frenchman. He recognized that he was in the process of leaving the womb of his birth and entering a no-man's-land of culture without his own identity. He transformed this understanding into politics, into nationalism. After independence, he would be free to be Mokhtar.

Mokhtar had a sharp critical sense. He had a strong moral sense, morality being what he judged to be right or wrong. He would always stick to his values. Once he'd made a decision, he would not be swayed. Come what may.

He was a tall, strong man, used to getting his way either by force or by logic. During the signal corps training, he had to fight to control both his tongue and his fists when he perceived heresy, faults, or the horrors of injustice. He would repeat to himself that once the training was over, he would be operating as a soldier with a radio transmission kit. He would be wearing the uniform of a freedom fighter, he would be a warrior for the independence of Algeria.

In his memoir, we are admitted into the complexities of organization, the duplicity, the brotherhood and the sisterhood, the ignorance and the intelligence. We witness the reality of the struggle. Finally, Mokhtar decided to go beyond the army and the war; he offers us entry into his family and the society.

When we met in 1972, Mokhtar had already suffered many defeats, disappointments in work and relationships, a loss of confidence in the future. When I was deported for refusing to become an informant, a mole, for the "services," the Algerian spy and intelligence apparatus, it was the final blow. He wrote at the time: "My last illusions are gone. Exile remains the ultimate solution when mediocrity and feudalism triumph and return as our judges."

After my extradition from Algeria in 1974, we lived in Paris for twenty years. Mokhtar wrote young adult books for French publishers on subjects ranging from Islam to the Maghreb. I made and sold ethnic-style jewelry and wrote young adult books in French on the Civil War and the Black neighborhoods of New York, as well as guidebooks in English on Paris and France.

Mokhtar and Elaine Mokhtefi, Algiers, 1972.

It was in Paris that my first contact with Algeria had occurred. On May Day 1952, I attended the grandiose annual parade of French workers. As it was breaking up, thousands of men appeared out of nowhere, running in formation, ten to twelve abreast, attempting to catch up with the vanishing demonstration. They were young, grim, poorly dressed. They shouted no slogans, carried no flags, no banners; however, it was evident that they bore a message. I would learn that they were Algerian laborers who had been banned from the workers' parade. Their message: freedom, independence for Algeria.

It was that event that shocked me into reality. From there to an understanding of colonialism was quick and deep. I was after all from a country that had long practiced slavery and segregation, whose effects were still very much alive, dehumanizing. I had always sided with the underdog, the castigated, the outcast. Was I not one myself, the child of a Jewish family, object of prejudice and discrimination, in a land where the color of one's skin, one's native origins, were the individual's identity to be carried into the future.

I associated those gaunt, olive-skinned men on a Parisian boulevard with my Black compatriots on the dusty roads of the South, on the tarmac of northern cities, along the railroad tracks of my small New England town. That image has never left my head; I can resurrect it today.

From there on, I saw and recognized North Africans everywhere, on the streets of Paris, in the international meetings where I found work as translator or organizer. In Ghana, at a congress of the World Assembly of Youth, they were Frantz Fanon and Mohamed Sahnoun. Fanon was there as Algeria's wartime ambassador on the African continent, Sahnoun as the Algerian student representative. We became associates and friends, the three of us. When I returned to New York following the congress, I joined and went to work for the National Liberation Front, the Provisional Government of the Algerian Republic, in their small New York offices. Our chief task was to lobby the United Nations for a resolution favorable to Algerian independence.

When Fanon was sent to the United States by the FLN for treatment—he had contracted leukemia—I visited him regularly at the hospital in Bethesda, Maryland. He sorely missed his comrades and being actively part of the struggle. One day, he sat up in bed and, looking me straight in the eyes, said with ardor: "Ce n'est pas une mauvaise chose de mourir pour son pays." (It's no bad thing to die for one's country.)

Frantz Fanon was born on the island of Martinique, in the depths of French racism. He had fought with the Free French during the Second World War, was educated in France, but became Algerian, both civilly and ideologically.

He is known as a social philosopher, a militant, a crusading revolutionary. He was also a psychiatrist who had been thrown out of Algeria, where he was head of a psychiatric clinic at the start of the war. Officially French, he was deported from the country that claimed him as a national when he defended the Algerian people's right to be independent. He left with his wife and child for Tunis, the rebel capital, and joined the fight. That was his calling.

Fanon's voice would be heard throughout the world demanding the end of racism and self-flagellation (*Black Faces, White Masks*), calling for colonial peoples to rise up and fight for their freedom (*The Wretched of the Earth*). Among those listening were the leaders of the Black Panther Party of the United States. They required that these exceptional works be studied chapter by chapter, that individual readings take place in every branch of the BPP across the United States.

Little could Fanon have imagined how essential his writings would become around the world, and for other generations. And even less that an American Black liberation organization, the Black Panther Party, would establish the first outpost of Black Americans abroad in independent Algeria.

For me, it all began one summer evening in June 1969, when Charles Chikerema, a comrade, representative in Algeria of the Zimbabwe African People's Union, called me to say that Eldridge Cleaver, the outlawed Black American exile, had arrived secretly in Algiers and was stranded and needed help. I hightailed it to the third-rate hotel he and his wife Kathleen, Emory Douglas, and Bob Scheer were holed up in and offered to contact the authority in charge of overseeing the installation and activities of freedom fighters' organizations in Algeria, Commander Slimane Hoffman. The group agreed, though I could tell from their faces that they were hesitant, unbelieving. They weren't sure to whom they were entrusting their future. Who was this American woman? But Chikerema would not let them down, they were also thinking...

*Eldridge Cleaver and Elaine Mokhtefi
at a press conference, Algiers, 1969.*

That afternoon, when I reported back to Cleaver that his group was authorized to stay in Algeria, to organize an international press conference, and that the BPP was officially invited to attend the First Pan-African Cultural Festival, scheduled to open on July 14, a few weeks hence, Eldridge, the stoic, expressed his appreciation with a solemn "You have saved my life."

To say that the Pan-African Cultural Festival was unique is the kind of understatement that makes me smile softly. Like Woodstock, it was an amazing, mesmerizing event. No one involved—organizers (of which I was one), participants, or guests—can ever forget the two weeks that transformed Algiers into the African and international music, dance, theater, art, and cinema capital of the world. Try to imagine Nina Simone, Archie Schepp, Dave Burrell, Alan Silva, Miriam Makeba, Grachan Monsur III, Sonny Murray, Cal Massey, Clifford Thornton, Marion Williams, and Oscar Peterson on the same city streets, at the same intersections, theaters, and squares, performing alongside the artists of the thirty-one newly independent African nations and six national liberation movements. I do believe that only Algeria, in all Africa, could have pulled it off.

Recently, I read on the Internet commentaries on the Pan-African Cultural Festival. One writer said: It was magic; *tout simplement magnifique*! Another message, from Alissa, declared: I was sixteen years old, in high school. Every night there were several concerts. All of Africa was there. Another said: It was only seven years after independence. These images make me cry. What have they done to our beautiful country? An American wrote: It was more than Woodstock...

The Panthers brought over a strong delegation. They were, alongside the American musicians, poets, writers, the stars. They were tall and handsome, were themselves, naturally open and inquiring. For the first time in their lives, they were face to face with their roots.

The Algerian authorities had given the Panthers the keys to a storefront on one of the main commercial thoroughfares of the city, where they displayed their wares: photos, films, brochures, newspapers, talks, interviews, conversations, day and night. They wandered the narrow, winding streets of the old city, the Casbah, the Mediterranean's shoreline, the cliffs overlooking Algiers; they found it all extravagant, an awakening, unthinkable just a few weeks back. Kathleen Cleaver gave birth to her son during the festival. The world was opening up. The BPP had found a home abroad.

Legacies are real, palpable. There isn't an American who doesn't acknowledge, at least there where innermost thoughts and feelings are lodged, that racism in the United States is tangible, blatant. Discrimination and prejudice are basic to the system. Just as in the colonial world. Mokhtar was raised in a country of inequality, social injustice, political obstruction, blackballing, incarceration, and death. When we moved to New York in 1995, he understood immediately, one might say atavistically, the lot of Black Americans.

Portrait of Mokhtar by Elaine Mokhtefi, 2000.

Time has passed. The threads of memory have given place to orthodoxy, to corruption, to the manipulation of society, to self-absorption. Ideals were placed in a box mothballed by officialdom.

After 1988, things got complicated. Political parties and organizations were at last authorized. New press organs, private and critical, came into being. Opposition showed its face. Then, in 1991, an Islamic party, the Front islamique du Salut (FIS), won an election victory that the regime refused to recognize. The elections were canceled and violence followed. A nasty, horror-ridden war, internal war, endured until the end of the century. Well over one hundred thousand died. Algeria was, once again, profoundly mutilated.

Petroleum and gas, the sole exports, dipped and soared depending on the world market. The regime used the revenue to expand its governing caste outrageously, to buy off the reticent if they weren't muzzled. And to import food. In that former agricultural preserve, Algeria, the bread basket was empty.

When I lived there in the 1960s and 1970s, there were roughly ten million people. When I went back in 2018 for the first time in forty-four years, there were more than forty million, on the way to fifty million. And almost as many cars, with no place to go. They rev motors, wade and wallow in traffic jams, park on the streets.

In 2018 I felt how empty the discourse was. Leaders were spouting the same soured, forlorn lines. People went about their business. I felt no energy, just abnegation, complaint, wishful thinking.

Mokhtar with Amara Lakhous, New York, 2015.

And then abruptly, without asking permission, thousands upon hundreds of thousands, literally millions of people descended into the streets in February 2019 crying out: *Let us live, give us back our country, give us back our past. Enough is enough.*

This movement has a name, Hirak, the Movement. Every Friday afternoon, for a year, the people mobilized, from Algiers to Constantine and Oran, to desert installations and oases, east to west, north and south. The long-ailing, absent-from-view president Abdelaziz Bouteflika, who had ruled over and molded Algeria for twenty years, was gone, castigated and routed. But the regime, assisted by the army and the virus, is still in place and still raising havoc.

Mokhtar would have cheered the Hirak. It was the outcome he had been waiting for, his type of event, grand, spontaneous, people-powered. Together, we would have mixed with the sea of faces and descended rue Didouche Mourad to the main post office, the center of Algiers. Our hearts would have echoed with the crowds . . .

One evening long ago, Mokhtar explained to our friend Amara Lakhous, the Algerian novelist, that there are bonds that can never be cast off: "Algeria lies under our feet and in our hearts until death."

A few days later, Mokhtar rummaged through an old box, where I store mementos of our militant past, for a button inscribed with the words "I am a world citizen." Every day thereafter he pinned that badge on his shirt. Mokhtar's gestures and statements were not unthinking; with his badge, he was not contradicting himself. He was making a final statement, charting the future for us all.

Memorial bench facing Riverside Park, New York City, with plaque dedicated to Mokhtar. It reads:

MOKHTAR MOKHTEFI

1935 Berrouaghia, Algeria

2015 Riverside Drive, New York

"Nous avons vécu tous les ages, tous les temps"

Elaine Mokhtefi

Mokhtar Mokhtefi wrote this book at the end of his life. He never saw it in print. He died a few days after his Algerian publisher, Selma Hellal of Éditions Barzakh, told him they would publish it as a memoir. Mokhtar descended into death's thralls, satisfied...yes, satisfied. He had accomplished his life's work.

Part One **CHILDHOOD**

"A woman's opinion is not an opinion," my father says.

His comment is directed at Imma, my mother, who's clearing the dinner table. She has just told my older brother what she thinks of the money Baba has borrowed from the bank: "All his work will go to enrich Pastor." (Pastor is the director of the bank.) She holds an empty platter in one hand and with the other wipes the tabletop, all the time shaking her head from side to side, her way of insisting how right she is.

"Have I ever told you what spices to put in the soup?" my father quips, half in jest, half serious. She shrugs her shoulders, grunts, and moves toward the kitchen. Baba is certainly right, he's one of the rare Algerians to frequent the bank, who can get credit, and my mother is no businesswoman: she's never left the house without being swathed in veils, she's never entered a store in the village, not even my father's butcher shop.

My thoughts fly to Madame Lavallée, the second-grade teacher, and I wonder if she doesn't have some opinions that are as good as a man's. She's the only female teacher at my school and she certainly holds her own with the men, the way she does with her pupils. Madame Lavallée is as pretty as a flower in springtime, her walk is a stride, she's so sure of herself. Her voice carries and with her ruler she batters kids' fingers and palms and keeps the bullies at bay, or so says my brother Mustafa, who is in her class and is my chief informant on all things.

My mother doesn't like Pastor because he put a lien on the house before granting the loan; she doesn't want to lose her home. I can understand that and I should defend her, but I don't say anything because I know that a child mustn't contradict his father, or any of his elders for that matter. My brothers keep their mouths shut too. As soon as Baba finishes telling us about his meeting with Pastor, he clears his throat and pronounces the *bismillah*, as he does every evening after dinner: "In the name of God, the Beneficent, the Merciful..." Like my brothers, I repeat the *bismillah* after him and we begin reviewing the Koran. I should say *they* begin since the recitation starts with the longest sura, one I don't know yet. I wait until my father finishes my brothers' recitation and begins the sura I've memorized. As the singsong drags on, I fight against falling asleep and think about Madame Lavallée. At school she's surrounded by men, just like my mother at home with her six boys and my father.

My mother's main preoccupation these days is to marry Ahmed, my oldest brother, who was born in January 1919. He was called up for military service at the beginning of the war, but he hated taking orders, doing military exercises, and being closed in generally, so he took to the woods, he deserted. One day, there was a knock at the stable door and I went to see who was there. What a surprise, it was Ahmed! He looked funny with his military cap askew, his leggings and heavy military shoes covered in mud. Imma was happy to see him, but she must have had some doubts because she asked right away if he was on furlough. From the way he explained things, I gathered that Marshal Pétain had declared the war over and that the food at the barracks was inedible. As he was taking off his shoes, he also mentioned that he had entered the village through the fields, so the gendarmes wouldn't see him. My brother Mustafa, who is three years older than me, doesn't believe the war is over.

Mustafa takes me to school, he's my protector and my guide in life. When I told him that Blanchette is no longer at my school, he explained why. Every morning on entering the girls' school where my classroom is located, Blanchette, wearing a nurse's uniform, holds up two long sticks and uses them to inspect the heads of us Algerians to make sure we don't have lice.

"She's been fired because she's Jewish," Mustafa explains.

Since I don't get what that means, he adds: "Hitler doesn't like Jews."

"Does Hitler like us?" I ask.

Disgusted by my stupidity, he shrugs his shoulders. "On the list of races, Hitler thinks the Arabs come after the frogs."

The gendarmes arrested Ahmed for desertion. They turned him over to Mr. Tob, the head of the municipal jail; since Tob knows the family, he puts him to work in the vegetable garden next to the jail. I drop him off a container of food at noon and after school. Imma has warned me not to tell Baba, she doesn't want to hear him reproach her for being soft on her "delinquent son." Sometimes she reminds him that when Ahmed was little, he was gaga over him.

Before Ahmed there were two little girls, Zeineb, who died within the year, and Aouisha, when she was two. Four years after Ahmed came Mohamed. My father wasn't lucky enough to go to school, but he managed to enroll his first-born, even though, for the local population, enrollments are limited. Growing up, Ahmed began to dress "modern"; he swapped the djellaba, the *sarouel*, and the skullcap for European-style clothes. Baba approved of his son's modernity, he was pleased that he was in the same class as Benyoucef Benkhedda, the *kadi*'s son, but he wasn't able to help him with his homework or control what he did at school. Left on his own, Ahmed failed the primary school final exam. He took to the streets.

Following Ahmed's arrest, Imma worked on Baba to speak to someone in authority. He finally got Ahmed out of jail so he could go back to work at the slaughterhouse... and he started to drink. Furious and anxious, Imma never stopped repeating: "If he's in trouble, it's because of the riffraff he frequents."

I think she's right. Ahmed is a very sweet guy. He likes having me around and loves it when I sing the first French song I learned in first grade: "Il faut te marier, papillon, couleur de neige." (You have to get married, butterfly, white as snow...) I adore that song, so he's started calling me Butterfly. He loves it when he sees me in the street and I come running. He gives me a coin for candy or takes me to the bar with his friends and buys me a drink I love that tastes like sweet mint. Once he gave me a wonderful gift: he took me to '*ammi* Salah's, the tailor and photographer, who set his magic box on a tripod and took our photo. I was seven, the first time in my life that I had my picture taken. Imma has put that precious souvenir away for safekeeping. On the other hand, she didn't at all appreciate it the day I arrived home smelling of perfume like a beauty parlor, my pockets filled with candy. Ahmed had taken me to the brothel to meet Arbia, his special friend there. As soon as the women saw me they knew I was Butterfly: they started screaming, pinching me, covering me with kisses and lipstick. Arbia gave me a bag of candy and a coin to buy more, then she grabbed a vaporizer and sprayed me with eau de Cologne. When my mother opened the door, she smelled me, wrinkled her nose, and asked the ritual question.

"Where have you been?"

I replied in an offhand way, "With Ahmed."

She lowered her head and sniffed my hair; then with a threatening voice and her arm raised to slap me, she repeated the question. Forgetting my promise not to say where I'd been, I told her: "With Ahmed in a kind of *hammam* [bath house] with a lot of women."

I thought she was going to lacerate her cheeks as the women criers do over a dead body. She screeched, let out a long scream and damned Ahmed over and over. Then she grabbed me by the collar and took me to the bottom of the staircase and stood me next to the water tap in the courtyard. She stripped me down, she was beside herself. In a panic, I screamed it wasn't my fault and sobbed as she filled the water pail. I shouted that I had been to the hammam the day before with my father. Nothing stopped her. She lathered me with soap and scrubbed as hard as she could, then threw the pail of water over me.

"So you saw that bitch of a woman," she said.

I raised my head, and with my eyes and mouth closed, murmured "Ahum." Then she rinsed me off and dried me. I no longer smelled of the accursed perfume and I could feel her anger fading. As though nothing was amiss, of any importance, she proceeded with the inquiry.

"What's she like?"

"She has tattoos on her face," I said, pulling away, pretending to be hurt.

The last time I heard Imma mention Arbia was when her friend Fatma Bent al Ouenes, the village talebearer, came to visit. Since she wanted to be alone with her friend, she told me to go out and play, but I hid on the staircase and listened to them talk.

"You're giving yourself heartaches over that woman," Bent al Ouenes was saying. "Forget her, let Ahmed do what he wants. That shouldn't stop you from helping Mohamed get married."

"Oooh, but I can't marry the second boy before the first. That's not done."

"You worry too much about what people say. Think of your boys. Who invented the custom that the firstborn must marry first? Men did. It's not one of God's dictates. You're not going to deprive Mohamed of founding a family because his brother has a mistress!"

My mother is always happy to see Fatma, even if after she leaves she criticizes her. "I thought she'd never go home," or "She thinks she's something because she took the boat from Morocco to Algeria with a group of French women, the wives of some French generals. What's there to be so proud of?" I think Imma's envious of her experience and of her frank way of speaking her mind. Fatma Bent al Ouenes is older than Imma, she's a widow and has no children.

She was also the first woman from the village to go to school; she speaks beautiful French. "Boys waited for me in front of the school and threw stones at me," she once told me. Among them was the man who's the village imam today...but we're both old now, so I forgive him," she added laughing. Her husband served under Lyautey in Morocco; the wife of the future marshal of France was an acquaintance of hers.

My mother must have followed her advice. She stopped criticizing Baba for "working for Pastor" and set about convincing him to let Mohamed marry first. She also talked him into selling our car, a six-cylinder Citroën. She never stopped repeating: "That car is of no use to anyone." Given the wartime restrictions, there wasn't any gas for sale anymore so it never left the garage. On the back window were letters in white: DELIVERY.

I'm mad at the war for requisitioning our livestock for the military and ruining the butcher business. The number of animals authorized for slaughter and the consumption of meat by the local population have been severely limited. The mayor is French and has issued orders for the local butchers to serve the European population first. The Muslims and the Jews get what's left. Given the lack of animals and the need to supply his customers, Baba has been slaughtering sheep secretly. His friend Nedjar, the rabbi, comes to the house and slaughters them, too. I carry around a basket and make deliveries to my father's Muslim and Jewish customers.

Baba has begun following the war news. In the evening, after we've recited the verses of the Koran and repeated the day's prayer, he turns on the radio on the nightstand next to his bed. He listens to Radio London in Arabic on shortwave. The crackling noise on the frequency bothers him so he ups the sound, provoking Imma's protests: "Turn down the noise, the kids have to get their rest." Mustafa and I sleep in the far corner of their room.

Since Berrouaghia is located in a hollow surrounded by the Titteri Mountains, Baba has my brother Basha go up on the roof and change the direction of the antenna. Later he learns that the crackling noise is due to the Germans' jamming of the frequencies.

In the summer of 1942, when an unidentified airplane crashes into the quarry at the edge of the village, rumor has it that the pilot was German. Another rumor that spreads around is that we are going to be bombed. But the rumors don't frighten the local population, on the contrary, the plane becomes an object of curiosity. I go to see it with Mustafa and some other kids from the neighborhood. It's a one-seater and didn't explode. One adult says it must have run out of gas and the pilot must have parachuted. He doesn't know whether he ran away or gave himself up, nor what his nationality was.

For my mother, the plane is a bad omen. She enumerates over and over again the calamities that will befall us: drought, famine, typhus, rationing, black market, crickets, and insists that we don't need any more invasions or bombs. She invokes God and asks him to relieve his creatures of their suffering. Baba doesn't miss an occasion to chastise the population for its lack of faith: "First of all, his creatures should think about obeying him. The mosque is empty and the cafés are full. In addition to which there are those sinners who drink, who steal, and worse."

"You want everyone to be like you," Imma comments, mocking him. "If we're all different, it's because God wanted it that way. You think that it would be better if we all resembled one another?"

Appealing to religion is standard procedure, but ever since Baba heard on Radio London in Arabic that the Americans have landed in North Africa, he talks politics more. He initiates discussions with Mohamed, who reads the French newspaper. He's so interested in politics that he's even begun cutting the time spent reciting the Koran so as to get into bed and listen to the radio. Mustafa and I are hoping that the Allied landing in Oran will make him forget the recitation of the Koran altogether. But no such luck.

"The Americans are here," my neighborhood friend tells me when I meet him after school, a school where he hasn't been admitted. "They're going to live in the village." He repeats what he's heard some adults say. Because of their equipment and their language, the villagers have taken the English for Americans, but the confusion lasts barely a day. They set up their command center in the former postal relay station next door to the gendarmes. Their troops have been quartered near the railroad station not far from the town soccer field.

Very quickly I start running behind their trucks to hear them laugh; they throw us chewing gum, cigarettes, and words that no one understands. Instead of the resin off the mistletoe, I start chewing mentholated gum. My brother Basha gets hold of cans of food but my mother refuses to touch the corned beef because it's not halal. The poor are less picky and eat it. The rumor goes around that the cans contain monkey meat, not beef.

"The English are brutes," according to Mustafa after a soccer match that ended with the local team being whipped. Heavier and more determined, the English dominated from beginning to end. The players on the SOB team (Société omnisport de Berrouaghia) are mostly Europeans and lack experience, a handful of Frenchmen with few real players. Unashamedly chauvinistic, the Algerian fans express their support for the SOB loudly and frantically.

It seems the Europeans don't like the English. They didn't attend the dance organized by the authorities at the municipal hall. Aren't these soldiers here to fight against the Germans who are occupying France? Maybe it's because most of the French here are for Vichy. The settler who lives next door to us is the leader of the French People's Party (Parti du peuple français). Someone, however, has painted a sign on a wall at the entrance to the village saying: ONE GOAL:

VICTORY. Our teacher has written the same phrase on the blackboard and we no longer sing "Maréchal, nous voilà devant toi, le sauveur de la France" (Marshall, here we are with you, France's savior!).

Given our chauvinism at the soccer matches and our unrelenting pestering of the English for chewing gum, they can't abide us anymore. They call us pickaninnies, sons of bitches, and scream at us: "Fuck you! Fuck off!" But we're not shy and we send the insults back at them in their own language with a supplement in Arabic. When they leave Berrouaghia, however, I begin to realize that their Sunday soccer matches were a nice distraction...

"Since Ahmed is still running around and doesn't want to settle down, we've decided not to wait for him," my mother tells her friends. It's her way of justifying going against tradition and not respecting her firstborn's rights. It's 1943 and Mohamed is twenty years old. He has always lived up to our parents' expectations, he's never disappointed them. He passed the primary school certificate with high marks, he can recite the entire Koran by heart. At work, he's as good as Baba on the butcher block and handles the clientele with courtesy and discretion. He doesn't hang out in the cafés playing cards or dominos. He smokes but never in front of my parents.

My mother has chosen a young woman from the Ould Cheikh family. She has seen her several times at the hammam and gets along well with her mother. Ould Cheikh, a devotee of the mosque, sells spices in a shack next to the indoor market. He's a good-looking older man, small with a large white beard, shaped with care. My father is delighted to ask him for the hand of his daughter.

Mohamed has never seen Rezkia. The day after the wedding, I slide into their room behind my mother and am the first of my brothers to get a look at her. She's light-skinned, her face is round, and she has lovely dark eyes and well-arched eyebrows. She's almost as tall as Mohamed and only speaks when spoken to, her eyes facing the floor.

According to custom, the presentation of the bride to family and friends takes place on the third day of the wedding ceremonies. The house is full of women. The patio is covered with flowers and gives off wonderful scents. I wander from one spot to another, following the trays of pastry as they move around. I share some with two of my buddies from the neighborhood, who are too shy to come forward but are as gourmand as me.

Rezkia is sitting on a sofa between two young girls. She doesn't say a word and seems indifferent to the singing, to the sounds of the *derboukas* and the women dancing. From time to time, she gets up, disappears, and comes back dressed in a new outfit. Each time she enters the room, the women squeal and *youyou* so loudly they can be heard all over Berrouaghia and beyond. While all this is going on, my mother calls me to her side. She hands me a heavy woman's belt made of silver and, pushing me in the direction of the bride, says: "Put it around her waist."

The bridesmaids get Rezkia to stand up. The noise stops. One of my aunts shows me how to put the belt around her waist and buckle it. Rezkia smiles and kisses me. The aunt gives me a piece of sugar to place in the bride's mouth. As I do all that, the *youyous* start up again and the women gather around and kiss me, covering me with lipstick.

With the arrival of Rezkia I notice a few changes in the house. She calls my parents Imma and Baba and kisses their hands every morning, like the rest of us. She never enters a room in which my father and Mohamed are alone together. According to Imma, it's a question of modesty and will last a year. I don't understand what she means by modesty.

My own life hasn't changed. I get up at dawn, eat breakfast, and try to ignore Imma's prattle. I hate to get up early, to run from one school to another. If I had the choice, I would take the blackboard and the playground of the French school over being closeted in a tiny, airless room repeating the Koran. Baba, who never attended the French school, would certainly not agree. His concern, above all, is my progress in memorizing the holy book. When I recite a new verse correctly, he gives me a coin to buy candy. Since I would never go against his will, I tell myself that he wants me to become a good Muslim to ensure my future life in Heaven.

Every day as the sun rises, Baba rushes off to the mosque to deliver the call to prayer at daybreak. He has been playing this role since last summer when he and the imam argued over the imam's decision to eliminate the muezzin's daybreak call. According to the imam, "It disturbs people who need their rest before a hard day's work."

Baba doesn't agree. In his opinion, "the prayer is more important than sleep. The early morning prayer awakens the conscience of the faithful for the rest of the day." Since the imam refused to rescind his order to the muezzin, my father took on the task, judging it his duty as a Muslim. Every day, before sunrise, he mounts the steps of the minaret and delivers the call to prayer. Imma says his voice is more melodious than the muezzin's.

With the coming of winter and the first snowfall, the imam raises the question again. "People can't do their ablutions, the water is frozen," he says, rightly so.

"I will pay for the wood and for someone to heat the water," my father replies.

My brother Mohamed is critical of the imam because he's an employee of the French administration and accepts a monthly salary, despite the fact that he's the owner of a vineyard of table grapes and of a grocery store that a paid employee manages. The imam is very urban—he's from Medea, the former capital of the *beylik* under the Turks, whom he claims are his ancestors. He's smug and treats everyone with disdain. I kiss his hand whenever I meet him in the street. He extends a white, fleshy blob and doesn't say a word. He's cold and heartless. People avoid looking at him when he passes, some turn their backs.

My father never criticizes the imam, at least not in our presence. But he is one of the few people who face up to him, especially on questions concerning the mosque. To listen to my mother and my brothers, the differences between the two men are fundamental. The imam is disdainful of country people because they're uneducated. "Put a bit in his mouth and a rein around his neck," he screams at the peasants when they don't line up right for prayers.

The imam and the handful of members of the local branch

of the Ulema Association look down on country people because they are superstitious and frequent the *zaouias*. While not opposed to the ulemas, my father is proud of his country roots. As a young man, after learning the Koran by heart, he wanted to deepen his understanding of the holy book, so he moved into the Douaiers *zaouia* to learn more of the holy writings. On his bedside table is a book by Sidi Khellil, a well-known religious scholar. He reads *El Bassaïr*, a newspaper published by the ulemas.

Disagreements at the mosque are not settled in the same way as those at the Koranic school. I found that out one Sunday afternoon when, in the middle of a full class, I was mumbling the verses on my tablet. Suddenly, my neighbor shoved his elbow into my side, twice: "Move over," he whispered abruptly.

I continued balancing my body back and forth, at the same time edging my behind away from him as much as possible. A couple of minutes later, this guy gives me another shove with his elbow. I stop the recitation, give him a dirty look, and spit out, "If God made you blind in one eye, it's because you deserve it."

He turned red as a beet and threatened to beat me up after class. He isn't bigger than me but he's two years older and always looking for a fight. As soon as the teacher lets us out, I run to Mustafa to tell him what happened. The villain is waiting for me outside, his fists ready, his face in a growl. He advances in my direction, his chin thrust forward, and he says: "Repeat what you said in class."

My brother steps between us, grabs his arm on one side and mine on the other, and leads us in the opposite direction from home. After about thirty yards, he stops, places a hand on each of our heads, and says: "Now fight!"

In a panic, I hold onto Mustafa's body and begin to snivel. "Where's your *nif*, your honor?" he chides me. "Grow up! Fight like a man!"

His tone, the vehemence of his remark, crush me, break my heart. All of a sudden I want to live up to his expectations and not be dishonored. I'm no longer conscious of the boys around us. Like a wild beast, I thrust my head into the asshole's body, pushing him back so hard he falls over. My fury unleashed, I jump on him, grab the collar of his jacket. He's struggling and trying to hit back at me with his knees, he bites my forearm. He strikes at my face with his nails; I manage to turn my head away, but he scratches my neck. My arm hurts and my rage gets the best of me. I start hitting his face, his head. He screams: "Stop! Stop!"

I can't control myself, I'm as if possessed and can't let up. Mustafa grabs me by the collar and pulls me away. My heart is throbbing, my breath is coming short and heavy like a bull after a race. My enemy is sniffling, he blows his nose on his sleeve and, head bent, turns to walk away. Mustafa takes hold of him by the arm, gives him a few taps on his back to dust off his jacket and issues a command: "Now shake hands."

All the way home, my brother keeps telling me how I should have fought, why I shouldn't have dashed forward with my head because he could have sidestepped me, caught my foot and I'd have fallen flat on my face. He complicates everything on purpose just to show, as he always does, that he's stronger, cleverer. He does recognize that I won and saved my honor. I avoid asking the question that's bothering me: in Arabic *nif* means nose, what's the relationship between that piece of flesh and bone in the middle of the face and a man's honor?

In 1944, after the passage of the British troops, the conflict that's ravaging the world sends us Italians, prisoners of war. They were dropped off at the central prison, a former *haras* of the bey of Algeria, located about a mile east of the village. They are not housed with the other prisoners but quartered in the barns and granges of a farm adjacent to the prison. They wear their army uniforms, come into town to shop, speak a mixture of Italian and French, laugh and bargain with the shopkeepers. They surprise everyone by adopting an orphaned shoeshine boy they call Balella. They make a uniform for him, place a cap on his head and shoes like theirs on his feet. My father has a contract to provide meat for the prison and learns that among the prisoners are masons, floor-tilers, and other artisans who are available for hire. He decides to take advantage of this opportunity and add a two-room upper floor to the house.

Baba left his family household on the Ouled Fergane mountain when he was twelve years old. "I knew what year it was when I heard some children argue as they were leaving the school yard," he told us. One of them said, "It's 1906."

In the town hall records, he is "presumed" to have been born in 1894. On arriving in the village, he went to live with his older brother Bachir in Drâ'a Essouk, the neighborhood the Europeans, who never set foot there, call Niggertown. He attended the Koranic school and found work doing odd jobs. During grape harvest time, he worked for the Garniers, owners of the largest estate in the area, crushing grapes in their cellar with his bare feet. "Nights, I couldn't sleep" he told us, "my feet burned so."

Once he committed the holy book to memory, he went to live at the Douaiers *zaouia*, volunteering to help out in exchange for being housed, fed, and taught theology. Then back to the village to work in the slaughterhouse and later in the Djouïa brothers' butcher shop. The brothers, who were Jewish, took a liking to him: he was honest and a hard worker; they taught him the trade, the Latin alphabet, and rudiments of arithmetic. When his brother Bachir convinced him he should get married, through his own wife's family he found a young woman from Medea, her hometown. Fatma-Zohra, my mother, is *kouloughli*, a descendant of the union of a Turk and a local woman. For Bachir and Miloud, my father, marrying a city girl constituted upward mobility, though it didn't mean they severed all links to their tribe. Neither their father nor their sister ever left the Ouled Fergane mountain.

Once Miloud had a trade, he wanted to set out on his own. On Wednesdays, market day, he would slaughter a lamb and set up a table at the weekly vegetable market: he was in business. With his savings, he bought a wagon and a horse and sold meat from farmhouse to farmhouse in the region. When he heard that a butcher shop was for sale in Sour El Ghozlane, a town with a military base, he bought it. He bid for a contract to supply the barracks with meat but lost out; it was difficult to build a clientele otherwise. That experience was disastrous and came just as my mother had to be hospitalized and miscarried.

They returned to Berrouaghia when the Djouïa brothers were leaving the village to open a butcher shop in the city of Blida. My father took over their business. With his turban and a white apron over his traditional garb, he astonished the European clientele with his expertise in preparing cutlets *à la parisienne* and the dexterity with which he dressed shoulder lamb, seasoning and tying the meat for the oven. He gave housewives advice on the time needed to roast a gigot and the choice of the proper cuts for whatever they planned to cook. He kept the shop as clean as a whistle. He rose at dawn, worked hard, and didn't call it a day until well after sundown. His business success was invigorating: he saved his money and realized his dream of buying land and building his own house. His good reputation and his lucky star were all it required to convince a settler to sell him the field he had an eye on. His dream became reality. The house he built is located at the end of a street that opens onto the boys' public school. Beyond the house is an empty field and Chauvau's vineyard. Unlike the Algerian homes in the neighborhood, our house has running water, electricity, and a drainage system. At street level, there is an entrance foyer, a two-car garage, and a storage area for forage and grain.

Since the sale of the Citroën, the garage is used to stock cement, plaster, and porcelain tiles bought on the black market. From the entryway, a staircase leads down to a courtyard bordered by three rooms in which nine people live, the family. A door on that patio opens onto a garden and beds of aromatic plants. A stable large enough for half a dozen cows and about forty sheep is also reached from the courtyard. I often hear Imma attack Baba for providing more space for his animals than for the family, and, since Mohamed has married, I have to say she's right. The beams on which the floor of the two new rooms will lie are laid over a portion of the courtyard and the stable.

I spend part of the summer of 1944 helping the Italian prisoners of war. Their overseer speaks French with a singsong accent. I serve them coffee and pastries made by Imma and my sister-in-law, who function behind sheets strung across the middle of the patio. I warn them when one of the workers wants to use the bathroom. The Italians love the couscous the women make every Saturday. Baba is pleased with their work; his house is finally finished. They complete the job just before school starts in the fall.

I enter second grade, Madame Lavallée's class. The last lesson before our winter vacation is a reading lesson about Christmas holidays. I know we never eat turkey at home, I also know that Father Christmas only visits the houses of Europeans. But my house is along his way when he goes to the Mattes' and the Lavals'. It will be nighttime and he could bump into mine or make a mistake...On December 24, on the sly, I leave my shoes in the fireplace. In the morning, I run to see what's there and, *voilà!* a package. My dream has come true. My screams of "Santa Claus! Santa Claus!" wake up Cherif, who sleeps in that room.

He calms me down and watches me as I take off the string around the package wrapped in brown paper. I open it, aflame with happiness, to find a carrot, a turnip, and a piece of wood. I throw it all on the floor in disgust. Cherif bursts out laughing. I cry my heart out. "Stupid!" he yells, "Didn't you know that Santa Claus doesn't exist?"

A week later, on January 1, 1945, Rezkia, assisted by her mother and mine, gives birth to a boy, Brahim. When Imma calls Mohamed to come see his wife and the baby, I slip into the room behind him. Smiling, Rezkia hands the boy up to him. I'm horrified by the wrinkles and grimaces of the newborn child. Mohamed takes him in his arms and gazes at him for a long moment. He's in seventh heaven holding him. Suddenly, he turns to me, extends the baby in my direction, and, laughing, says, "Go visit your uncle!"

What a marvelous gift! His words lift my heart, I'm no longer the baby of the family.

Come spring, the nightly sessions reciting the Koran are shortened, even sometimes canceled, thanks to the war. After dinner, my father is in a hurry to listen to the radio. My older brothers go out to one of the cafés and meet their pals. I don't understand why, but the adults speak less about the Americans and more about the Russians. They're excited by the advances of the Red Army toward Berlin. Anyone listening to my father would think the Russians have won the war.

I'm ten years old. On May 8, 1945, our teacher announces that we're going to march to the war memorial to celebrate the Allied victory. I jump with joy; with the other kids in the class we sing the new song we've just learned: "La Victoire en chantant, nous ouvre la barrière, la Liberté guide nos pas..." (Singing Victory opens the gates, Freedom guides our steps...) Despite the excitement, our teacher manages to calm us down before we join the other classes in the courtyard. We leave the school in rows two by two, the smaller kids in front, the higher classes behind. Rue de la Gare, near the war monument, is overflowing with people. On the sidewalk, everyone moves back to let us pass. The crowd advances slowly. I know most of the people, many of them are young and jobless and can generally be found hanging out in the cafés or wandering around the streets. There are also some workers and storekeepers. They form rows of ten to fifteen people and walk, as in a funeral procession. They say little, seem to be holding back. In front of the Café des Voyageurs, across from the town hall, some of the young guys ogle our teacher. Farther on, everything remains silent, which is surprising. However, a banner is floating over the heads of the marchers, with two words written on it that I don't quite understand: Free Messali. The first row of demonstrators has been blocked in front of the post office by three gendarmes. I see my brother Mohamed there. Over his head, another banner, that I don't understand any better: Sovereign Constituent Assembly.

After the post office, the street and sidewalks are empty but in front of the war memorial, it looks like all the Europeans have gathered together. I note among them a few blue-and-white burnouses of some *kadis*, the brightly colored uniforms of the commune's *mokaznis* and the fezes of civil servants from the *mahakma* and the town hall. When we arrive at the little square where, in the summertime, the customers of the bar of the Hôtel de la Gare play *boules*, it's quiet. The silence is broken by a bugle emitting a dismal sound. Standing too far away, I can't see the musician, only the back of the statue of the helmeted soldier wearing a long military coat, carrying a rifle slung over his shoulder, and waving an olive branch. The music stops, the crowd sings "La Marseillaise," the older classes, too. I only know a few words. Then come some long, boring speeches. Finally, we take the road back to school. Some people stay in the street, but the demonstrators have disappeared.

Two days later, I come home from school to find my mother and Rezkia crying. "Your brother Mohamed was arrested by the *Lassourtia*," my mother manages to say between two waves of tears. She means the security police, the judicial police. I have heard that word before, when they came from Medea to inquire about the assassination of an Algerian by a European who suspected him of being his wife's lover. But what crime could Mohamed have committed? I have the feeling the earth has opened up. Imma's pain, her stammering speech, affect me tremendously, I burst into tears. "Don't cry, my son," she says as she wipes her face, then mine, with her handkerchief. "They say he's a *watani*."

"What does that mean?" I ask.

"A *watani* is a *watani*. What else can I say," she answers.

She replies like that when she wants to hide something from me or when she doesn't know the answer. Mustafa arrives with fresh news. "They've taken them to Medea," he says. Then he lists the people arrested: the miller and his son, the doughnut vendor, the fruit and vegetable seller and his brother, the two barbers, the notions store owner, the peddler, the grocer, and a few unemployed men. They are the same people who were present at the luncheon following Brahim's birth. Except for the miller, no one is over twenty-five years of age.

As soon as I'm alone with Mustafa, I repeat my question. "To be a *watani* is to be for a free Algeria," he explains. "For the Europeans, *watanis* are people who don't like France, who are anti-French."

"That's not true," I cry. "It's they who don't like us."

He shrugs his shoulders, puts on his superior air, and walks out, leaving me there with my questions unanswered.

How can anyone say that Mohamed is anti-French, he who's so nice, so courteous with the clientele. Madame Lavallée can witness to that fact, she's a customer and a woman who speaks the truth. During our civics lesson, she explained the meaning of the phrase inscribed over the entrance to our school: *Liberté, Egalité, Fraternité*. I wonder what she thinks of my brother's arrest. I remember that at the war monument, she didn't applaud after the speeches. One of the older boys said it was because she didn't want to applaud men who supported the Vichy government and were collaborators. It's complicated, but my brother and my father are not collaborators, on the contrary, they reacted against the decision of the mayor to serve the European clientele first because there wasn't enough for everybody. He had the rabbi come over to slaughter sheep. I carried baskets of meat around to Baba's Jewish customers. I find it all very perplexing.

Imma has practically stopped eating, she says everything has a bitter taste or no taste at all. She says the baby's crying puts knots in her stomach. Stoical, Rezkia cries in silence. My mother presses Baba to intervene with the authorities, even though he has just told us that tens of thousands of people have been killed and arrested around the city of Constantine. "The French and their army are killing thousands of innocent people in Setif, Guelma, and throughout the region. They're just like Hitler. They'll lose just as he lost and justice will reign in this country," he predicts.

"I want them to give me back my son, I don't want them to massacre him like they are doing to others," Imma interjects.

"Keep the faith," Baba tells her. "Never forget that the only one to fear is God the Almighty."

The way she shakes her head on leaving the room, I can see that she doesn't agree. A week later, she starts again: "See, they've let the *kadi*'s son go, and the son of the *bach adel* who's at the *mahakma*, and the imam's nephew, all because their relatives intervened." Baba's silence unnerves her. She raises the tone: "You're not going to let my son wallow in prison."

He shakes his head, looks her straight in the eye, and says: "Your son is also my son. And he's not the only one in this situation."

Imma convinces Basha, the hardiest of my brothers, to go to Medea. He learns that the demonstrators in that city have all been freed and thinks that "the others will soon be, too." He's so convincing that each time I knock at the door, Imma opens it, takes a look at me, and with a tremor says: "I thought it was your brother Mohamed."

At the end of May, all the demonstrators are freed with the exception of the miller, Hassan Bey, called Cheikh al Hamidi, his son Benaceur, and my brother. When Basha goes back to Medea he learns that they have been transferred to the military prison in Bâb el Oued, a neighborhood of Algiers. He tells Imma that the transfer is a formality before they are let out. However, a little later, I hear him tell Cherif that it doesn't look good for Mohamed.

Our anxiety endures until, finally, we receive a letter in his own hand. "I'm in good health, don't worry about me," Mohamed says. He indicates that he is in prison with the miller and his son at Camp Bossuet near Oran. No one in the family knows where Bossuet is. Mohamed doesn't say how long he will be interned. In another letter, he asks for clothes. Imma multiplies the number of packages, adding coffee, sugar, pastry. Often, in the middle of a meal, she complains of not being able to send her son his favorite dishes; sometimes she stops eating and cries. She doesn't laugh anymore, her body heaves to and fro, she breaks out in tears. She doesn't invite her friends around to talk, to listen to records of Meriem Abed, Hadj Mrizek, Rachid Ksentini over coffee or tea. She no longer wears the face of a happy woman content to be alive and see her friends. She refuses invitations to weddings and circumcisions. She no longer trots out her fancy dresses, her gold coin, turquoise, or pearl necklaces. She's in mourning.

Baba, for his part, doesn't show any emotion, no sentiment, no particular trouble. He gets irritated quickly, however, when Cherif doesn't prepare a cut of meat the way he wants. He snaps at him when, between customers, Cherif disappears behind the counter and opens the book he's reading instead of rearranging the display case, cleaning the chopping block or the floor...

Since Mohamed's arrest, no one misses a meal at home. The brothers don't show it, but they are all as worried as I am. Basha and Ahmed damn the villagers who avoid them, who change sidewalks when they see them coming, or lower their heads and don't greet them. Cherif has noticed that the Europeans have started frequenting a competitor, a grocer who has opened a butcher shop near the gendarmes' head-quarters. He mentions a customer by name, however, who has come back, who admitted that the meat and the style are better at Baba's. When my mother asks why only Hassan Bey and Mohamed haven't been freed, no one can provide a sat-isfactory answer. Everyone just repeats what they have heard:

"They're accused of organizing the demonstration," says Basha.

"They're the leaders of the PPA, the Algerian People's Party," Cherif and Ahmed say.

I discover that the members of this party are *watanis*, nationalists, *el watan* meaning the nation, in other words Algeria.

I learn more troubling facts. At school we are told that Algeria is composed of three French departments or states, that the inhabitants of Brittany are called Bretons; but the Europeans never call us Algerians. For them, we are natives, Muslims, or Arabs, and our cafés, which they never enter, are Moorish cafés. When there's fight, they call us by a vari-ety of dirty names. My brothers say the French are racists. Baba raises his shoulders and quotes a hadith of the Prophet: "All men are equal like the teeth of a comb." Of course, all the French are not bad people, but at school I don't know a single Algerian who has a French friend. In the courtyard, they refuse to play with us, outside of school they ignore us. In our reading book, however, there's a story about François and Abdallah, who end up friends. I like that story. But since Mohamed's arrest, I find it hard to believe.

Madame Garnier-Grizot, the widow of the vine grower whom Baba worked for crushing grapes when he was twelve years old, has always been a customer of his. She uses *tu*, the familiar form of *vous*, when she speaks to him, and calls him by his first name: "Miloud, it's a pity that your son has gotten mixed up with the scoundrels who want to throw us out of this country. I know he's not like them. I know him, he's very nice, well brought up."

Baba lays down the chopper, turns toward her, and wipes his hands on his apron. He looks her straight in the eye, points to the floor, and states quietly but firmly: "Madam, we are here to serve the customers, not to talk politics. Outside, my son does what he wants. He's an adult, it's his right."

He turns away, picks up the chopper. Silent, her head bowed, she has only one desire: to get out of there as quickly as possible.

According to Cherif, among the Europeans who are boycotting the butcher shop are our two neighbors. Their villas are adjacent to our property. The closer neighbor has a large garden protected by a scrappy dog and a wall topped by a grille and a roll of barbed wire. In the summer, the honeysuckle covering the wall smells wonderfully sweet. I like picking the flowers and sucking the nectar. The other villa is located at the corner of our street and the one that passes in front of the gendarmes' headquarters. It opens onto an elevated terrace. After listening to Cherif, I think about how to get revenge; an idea trots around my head. I keep it to myself. The next day, I find a stone and take it to the spot in the gutter where a lead water pipe emerges and connects to the second villa. I make sure no one is watching, then with rage pound the water pipe but don't manage to flatten it. I leave my tool near the objective and every day give it a few blows. I finish by flattening it and, content with my handiwork, cover the pipe with the stone.

Days go by peacefully until one morning when, on leaving the house, I see the police chief's Algerian auxiliary at the end of the street, in the middle of the road. I wonder what he's doing in our neighborhood and continue walking toward him. When I get close by, he points his whip toward the wall where two of my buddies are standing and orders me to join them. They have no idea what's going on. The auxiliary tells us to march in front of him to the police station. The chief, an old man with a mustache and white hair, is a "Frenchman from France" who's called a *cheikh ânnia*, a naive old man. He gets up from his chair, puts on his cap, and has us line up against the wall.

"Someone broke your neighbor's water pipe," he says, leveling his eyes on each one of us. "It's one of you. Or maybe two or three of you. I want the one who did it to come forward. If any of you knows anything about this, speak up. If not, you're all going to prison."

The auxiliary translates his remarks in a menacing tone.

I can't believe what's happening. Once I'd satisfied my rage, I'd forgotten about the pipe, I only wanted to punish the neighbors who don't like Mohamed and his ideas. I never mentioned what I'd done to anyone because it only concerned them and me. I decide to keep it to myself. My buddies swear they haven't done anything, I do the same.

"Follow me," says the chief.

"Outside!" yells the auxiliary in Arabic, gesticulating as though he's herding animals.

The police station is on the ground floor of the imposing town hall building; in its cellar is the jail. Drunks and small-time delinquents are locked up there for a day or a night. Once outside, we turn left. The chief opens the sliding steel door, points his finger to the steps so we don't fall, and says sternly, "Inside, all of you!"

The jail isn't empty. Among the people hanging around at the foot of the steps, I see Mustafa and am less worried. The four buddies who are with him live on our street, a few houses away. The door closes and we are suddenly in the dark.

"They didn't even tell us the name of the neighbor," I hear a voice say.

"You can tell us, we won't repeat it!" says another.

As the time passes, my disquiet increases. Some accuse others. I must seem really innocent, no one looks my way! After the town hall clock strikes twelve noon, the kidding around ends when Mustafa calls out: "Shut up, I hear some noise in the street."

The heavy sliding door opens and the police chief appears, a club in his hand.

"Come out, one by one. You get it? I said one by one,"

the left index finger pointing upward. No one wants to lead the way.

The old man shows his impatience, the older boys push each other aside. Finally, Mustafa races forward, skips two steps, and lands on the top. Poor judgment: he receives a hit on his back with the cudgel. I'm one of the last to go, get my hit, and run toward the empty field to join the others. Everyone cracks up with laughter!

One Sunday afternoon my mother plans a trip to Sidi Djebbar with her neighbor. To obtain permission for me to skip class at the Koranic school, she gives me a coin for the teacher. "Tell him you have to take your mother to the hammam."

I look at her surprised. Then she gives me a smaller coin: "Buy yourself some candy, and don't tell your father!"

She wants to ask Sidi Djebbar to intervene on behalf of Mohamed. Sidi Djebbar is a large oak tree decorated with ribbons and multicolored candles, located behind the hospital, between the water tower and the tennis court reserved for Europeans. Women go there to implore the saintly tree for help for various causes. They burn incense and candles at the foot of the tree. Some of the women prepare coffee or tea for other visitors, a way of adding weight to their own requests.

Sidi Djebbar has competition in the village. There's Sidi Nadji, a circle of stones alongside the path that leads to Parpète Pond, the reservoir of a former farm prison. Sidi Yahia, located a few miles down the road to Aumale, organizes a yearly *rakb*, a meeting of its followers that lasts for three days and ends with a procession through the village and ritual chants and dances at the cemetery. My father says these practices are pagan, fetishes that only the ignorant practice. "The Sunna condemns such idolatry," he cries.

It's too bad, but he turns a blind eye to Imma's torments. Her son is never absent from her thoughts. She's desperate and even visits a fortune-teller who reads the future in bits of molten lead. Of course, I'm warned to keep all this to myself.

The storks that nest on top of the mosque's tower have already arrived when, in the spring of 1946, Mohamed is released from prison. My brothers and a large group of friends escort him to our house. Imma cries with joy, embraces him, and never stops repeating, "My son, my son."

Rezkia's *youyous* echo through the patio, an expression of both the long wait and her happiness on having Mohamed back home. With a gesture indicating the stairs down, Imma tells him to go see his son. Mohamed smiles, but before taking to the staircase, he asks Basha to have his friends wait for him upstairs and Cherif to go to the butcher shop and replace Baba.

When he returns, he joins his good friend Ali Baha and the others and answers their questions, sometimes serious, sometimes laughing, about his time in prison in Medea and Algiers. The interrogations he was subjected to were aimed at finding out who were the organizers of the demonstration and the names of the members of the party in the village. Both police and soldiers used physical force on the prisoners before sending them to the military prison in Algiers. He met a militant there who was condemned to death, who had been tortured as he had been. He was a noncommissioned officer in the French army who had fought in the Italian campaign and received a decoration. His name was Amar Ouamrane. Admitted to the officers training school in Cherchell, he had organized a nationalist party cell there; he was accused of planning to take over the base. Mohamed is enthusiastic about the militants in the camp, their struggles and strikes to obtain status as political prisoners, despite the racism of the administration and the personnel. He describes the literacy classes they organize as well as the lessons the more educated prisoners prepare for the others on a variety of subjects.

I was fascinated by his maturity, his eloquence, even if I didn't understand everything he said. I did learn a number of new words: *al hizb* (the party), *al zaïm* (the leader), *al istiqlal* (independence), *el watania* (nationalism), *al isti'mar* (colonialism). The conviction with which those words are pronounced intensifies their meaning. The clandestine nature of events adds an aura of mystery, of magic to them. Mohamed doesn't reveal how these ideas and the words arrived secretly in Berrouaghia. He makes his friends laugh when he tells them that Hassan Bey, the miller, has decided not to shave his beard until independence, like Messali.

His stay at the Bossuet camp has inspired Mohamed with new ideas for the butcher shop. With Baba's agreement, he has it repainted by the Kebaili brothers, one of whom is both a militant and an artist. He has the facade covered with white tiles to roughly a man's height; then, above the tiles they apply red lacquer with, in the angles, a sheep's head on one side and a calf's head on the other. A new sign is tacked on the top announcing in Arabic and in French the shop's name:

THE MODERN BUTCHER SHOP. Just below is my father's name and telephone: 042 in both Arabic and Latin script. It's the only bilingual sign in the village.

If being modern means being of one's era, Mohamed is definitely in the vanguard. He's tall, slim, and elegant, and he wears horn-rimmed glasses that give him a distinguished, serious air. He and his friends meet at the café at the corner of rue de la Smala and rue de l'École, he doesn't play cards or dominos but is there to talk and discuss. Most of the customers at that café wear European-style clothes, whereas those at the Makhkouf Café, across the way, dress according to tradition. It's Baba's favorite café. It would seem that one café is in favor of modernity and one in favor of tradition, which is not absolutely true, for my father has an open mind and other qualities of a modern man. Mohamed and his friends develop a ritual of sorts prior to the evening call to prayer: they take a walk along the street that leads to the station. Europeans do the same but stop at the war memorial. The two groups take the same walk but willfully ignore each other.

When I enter fourth grade in October 1946, Monsieur Colin, the teacher, starts off by having each French pupil share a desk with an Algerian. He sits me next to Gilbert Darmon in the middle of the class. Some time later, he seats me in the first row next to Pierre Guedj, the doctor's son. I get along better with Gilbert but neither he nor Pierre speak Arabic, even though their parents are fluent.

Charles Colin has a pinkish, smiling face with wavy light brown hair, and wears a black coverall; he speaks softly and clearly. He schedules question-and-answer periods and tries to have everyone participate. Only the roughnecks in the back row, who are taking the class for the second time, make a point of not taking part and not doing the lessons. I adore the recitations. In dictation I often have zero faults and in mental arithmetic only Mohamed Azzoug is as good as me. Every two weeks we have to hand in a paper on a subject of our choice. Monsieur Colin returns the copies corrected and graded on Saturday morning. I write a story on a visit to the barbershop, and he asks me to read my text to the class. Saturday afternoons are the best. Gathered around the heater in winter, we listen to him play a tune on the violin and learn a song. I can see his face hugging the instrument, his eyes half closed, a smile on his lips. With immense pleasure, we start singing:

> *Ma blonde, entends-tu dans la ville*
> *Siffler les fabriques et les trains*
> *Allons au-devant de la vie*
> *Allons au-devant du matin...*

> *(My blonde, can you hear in the town*
> *The whistles of the factories and the trains*
> *Let's go forward toward life*
> *Let's go forward into the morning...)*

With the coming of spring, our Saturday afternoons are devoted to amusing and instructive visits to village craftsmen. Before entering the carpenter's, the blacksmith's, the shoemaker's, or the saddler's shops, Monsieur Colin explains the utility and the dignity of that person's trade. The artisans explain the different stages in the making of their crafts. We take walks in the fields with Monsieur Colin; he tries to sharpen our sense of observation and to instill a respect for nature.

My learning is put to task one day when I meet *'Ammi* Hamouda coming out of Chauvau's, where he works. He's from the Ouled Fergane tribe, my father's tribe; he often gives me a coin "to buy candy." On his job he's the foreman, but he doesn't know how to read or write. I greet him and he invites me for a lemonade at the café near the church. Like most adults, he asks whether I like school and if I study hard: "What do they teach you?" he inquires.

Very confident, I reel off the lesson we have just had on how rain occurs and make the contrast with the pot of hot water giving off steam that condenses when it comes into contact with the pot cover. "The clouds, that's the steam," I say, smiling.

"That's what they teach you?" he asks.

"Yes, and when a cloud comes into contact with cold air, it rains."

"Does your father know that?"

"What do you mean?" I ask.

"That rain doesn't flow from the will of God, but from a kettle?"

That evening when Baba questions me, I tell him about my conversation with Uncle Hamouda. "Your uncle is ignorant," he comments, smiling. "I'll have to remind him of the hadith of the Prophet that tells us "to look for Science, be it in China." He adds, "He'd be better off taking care of his bosses' vines than worrying about your education."

When Monsieur Colin asks Ortola to make an effort so as to pass and not have to redo the class again next year, he snickers: "Why knock myself out, whatever happens I'll be a prison guard like my father." Ortola is big and heavyset. He's Corsican, like all the guards at the central prison. He's just waiting for the day he'll don the uniform and take over from his father. I wonder if, myself, I'll be a butcher like my father. Which is one reason why I'm dumbfounded the day Monsieur Colin takes me aside and says: "I want you to take the sixth-grade exam."

I'd never heard of that exam and I don't know what its purpose is. I do know, however, that Baba wants me to pass the primary school certificate (CEP) next year. When I told him that I was promoted to fourth grade, his only question was "Is that the year you pass the primary school certificate?" That certificate is the unique goal for him, for the entire family. Of my five older brothers, only Mohamed has passed it. I want to do like him and please Baba. Wary, I hedge answering Monsieur Colin's question: "I don't know, sir. My father wants me to pass the primary school exam."

"Ask him," says Monsieur Colin, "and if he doesn't say yes, I'll go see him."

As expected, Baba demands that I pass the CEP first. I have no idea what the sixth-grade exam means and can't explain it to him. I report back to Monsieur Colin and learn that if I get into sixth grade I can continue my studies until the middle school exam and even till the high school diploma and further if I wish.

That evening, my father, visibly delighted with the teacher's visit, announces: "Your teacher came to see me and I told him: 'My son will do whatever you decide.'" I learn that if I pass the exam I'll be admitted to middle school and be eligible for a scholarship, according to a new decree that no longer limits those privileges to the children of Algerians "having rendered signal service to France."

Because of its excellent reputation, Monsieur Colin signs me up for the sixth-grade exam at the Duveyrier high school in Blida, not the one in Medea which is closer, but he warns me that the school is known for being tough. Duveyrier is attended by the children of the city's Europeans as well as those from the fertile Mitidja plain nearby. There is a small minority of Algerians. Monsieur Colin also applies for a departmental scholarship for me. Proud to be taking the exam, I receive a letter confirming the date, a Thursday morning in the month of June. It means, of course, that I have to work hard and not miss any of the special classes that Monsieur Colin has organized for the candidates. I rush to tell my father. He stops work for a moment, looks surprised, and says, "What exam?"

I remind him of his commitment to Monsieur Colin; he thinks a moment and says: "If you take the train or the morning bus, you won't be on time. You'll have to leave the night before, but since it's a Wednesday, market day, your brothers will be busy at the slaughterhouse or in the butcher shop, so no one can accompany you. He turns his back to me and returns to work. Horrified, I stand there in the middle of the shop with the impression that my life has dropped into a hole. I thought my father was pleased with the idea that I was going to pass an exam that would eventually allow me to go to high school. None of my brothers has been that lucky. I was so sure that Baba would be proud to take me to Blida. I was already imagining him with the parents of the other candidates and wondering if there would be other Algerians in traditional dress. Unable to hold back the tears, I begin sniffling noisily. "Stop crying," he orders me, "we'll try to find a solution."

That evening, Basha tells me: "Don't worry, I'll take you. We'll go to the cousins' for the night." He promises to finish work earlier at the slaughterhouse and explains that we'll take the last bus for Blida at noontime on the day before the exam. It's an express bus that doesn't stop everywhere like the morning bus. I feel better because I know that Basha is clever, he's sharp. Hasn't he founded his own business in addition to his work at the slaughterhouse? He began by preparing and grilling merguez sausages and brochettes in our garage and selling them off a table next to a bar. With his savings, he bought a bicycle shop and rents and sells bikes. He has an employee who specializes in repairs. When he was younger, with his friend Brahim Baha, he invented an act to impress the kids at Drâ'a Essouk. He would walk barefoot over broken glass and Baha would spit fire. He wanted to be a bike racer but was finally discouraged by the hills near town that are at least 1200 meters high. In the summer, at Parpète Pond, he creates a sensation diving from a tree and screaming like Tarzan in the jungle. The other day, at the slaughterhouse, he literally knocked out a bull that resisted him with an uppercut to the head.

The famous Wednesday, I put on my best holiday clothes,

a white shirt, a jacket, and short checkered pants. My mother examines me and tells me to calm down, plus some other advice that I don't listen to. I do register the names of the members of my aunt Hanifa's family where I'll sleep over. At ten o'clock, I'm beside myself with anxiety; she suggests I stop fidgeting and go wait for Basha at the butcher shop.

On entering, I approach Cherif at the cash register. He smiles and congratulates me on my attire. Between two customers Baba sits down next to me and also tells me how nice I look. I ask the time, he says it's only 10:30. He puts his arm around my shoulders and questions me: "If you pass, what would you like to have?" Without a moment's hesitation, I reply, "A bicycle." He smiles, shakes my hand as if to say "it's a deal" and moves toward the customer entering the shop. It's a dream come true. Along with the *mokhazni*'s son and the commune administrator's son, I'll be only the third kid in the village to own a bike. It will be metallic beige with a mudguard, a carryall, three speeds, a headlight, and a cable brake. I'll whiz around the village ringing the bicycle bell. I'll be the envy of them all.

Suddenly, I stop dreaming and realize that Basha is not yet here. I tell Cherif that I'm going to the slaughterhouse. On market day there are so many people I have a hard time passing through the slow-moving crowds. I take a shortcut behind the town hall and come up to the front of the building. Tchatchou, our donkey, and the wagon that we use to transport meat are nowhere in sight. "They just left," I say to myself. I push the metal grille of the door to the slaughterhouse, look inside, and think I'm going to die: I can see Basha in the back grappling with a sheep's intestines and want to scream. I can hardly see his back through the fog clouding my eyes; I lean against the door, hold on to one of the bars. It seems like ages before he turns and sees me. He throws whatever is in his hands into a pail and comes running. "What's wrong? Don't you feel well?" He pushes me outside. "Don't dirty your clothes," he says, not knowing what else to do.

I gather all my force and manage to form the words: "You promised—" Just then I hear the wagon in back of me.

"Look," Basha says, "Tchatchou is here. Don't worry, I'll load the wagon, then go change my clothes. Don't wait here, go home. I'll be there in a moment."

Basha leaves me. I turn to see Mustafa sitting in the wagon. He's pulling on the rein and spitting out sounds to get the donkey to line up near the door and wait for the meat to arrive. He announces that he's just come from the bus station and has reserved two seats on the noon bus. I'm so relieved I want to kiss him. He smiles and goes inside.

An argument between the driver and a passenger doesn't stop me from hearing the town hall clock strike twelve noon. The bus door slams shut, the motor starts up, and a blast of the horn announces our departure. Happy to be leaving, to be sitting high up as if on a balcony overlooking the street, I watch the farmers and their animals departing the market. They're in no hurry to get out of the way so the bus can move forward. Basha glances toward his bicycle shop to see what his employee is doing. Surprised to be viewing things from this height, I smile at the soldier on the war monument with his olive branch.

Basha tells me he will leave me at our cousins' house, that he will take the late train back home. "The four cousins work," he explains. "One of them will take you to the school tomorrow morning."

"I'll be okay," I assure him. I've been waiting for this day, for this trip for so long that I'm exhilarated. I'm finally going to realize my dream and discover the city: Blida, the capital of the Mitidja, the mythical plain that seasonal workers drift to every summer, the El Dorado of so many laborers, the place of dreams, my life's adventure.

"May God grant them mercy," Basha whispers as we pass by the Muslim cemetery, a field dotted with tombstones, wild grass, and small trees. I imitate him and, in my heart, pray to God to help me pass the exam. I see the small vineyard on the hillside covered with *berrouagh*, the asphodels from which the village takes its name. Farther away, on the rocky hills a flock of sheep is munching grass. The driver changes gears to maneuver along a wide, steep curve. I can see the village in the distance with the slate roof of the church and the minaret of the mosque. It's a wonderful vista. Monsieur Colin's geography lesson comes to mind: he told us that "Berrouaghia is located in a hollow..." The memory leaves me feeling nostalgic.

We've reached the cork oak forest of Fernel. Lower down there's an imposing metal bridge and a tunnel through which a single railroad track passes. After the forest, the land is covered with vineyards on both sides of the road. Basha smiles and tells me how he traveled this road from Berrouaghia to Medea on his bike, twice, back and forth. "The first time, I finished the slope up to the Ben Chicao pass on foot." His story reminds me that if I pass the exam, next week I'll have the bicycle of my dreams. I don't tell him that it won't be a racing bike.

"There's the Assistance," he says, pointing to a two-story building that belongs to the public assistance department of the city of Paris. It's a sanatorium for orphans. As we head over the pass, I see the sign for Loverdo, a one-street town with houses on either side, and I wonder if all the inhabitants are Europeans. As we mount the next hillside, I notice the pine trees in the middle of the vineyards and feel my eyes starting to close.

Basha pokes me with his elbow and wakes me up just as we enter Medea. We are in a tree-lined street with shops. People watch the bus go by without seeming to see it, though some kids put down their water buckets, smile, and wave to us. I don't wave back. I see apartment buildings on my right; Basha points to the stadium on the left. The bus turns a corner and stops in a parking lot. We've covered the thirty-two kilometers from our village to Medea in one hour. An agent yells instructions and bus information and opens the back door of the bus. I watch people move around, Basha gets up, and with the driver leaves to buy sandwiches. The bus is surrounded by noisy vendors and beggars, among them an elderly woman with a soiled veil. A half-blind vendor is selling chickpeas seasoned with cumin, another chortles a song praising his mint candies, yet another is selling salted almonds and peanuts. I'm tempted but I prefer keeping the money that both my mother and my father have given me for tomorrow. Basha returns, his arms loaded, and points to behind the gas pumps where the toilets are located. When I get back I devour the galette filled with grilled sheep's liver. Basha calls the orangeade vendor over. I down his drink in one large gulp. "Taste the world's best red grapes," he shouts as he opens a package wrapped in newspaper. The grapes are enormous and sweet as syrup.

After a half-hour halt, the bus takes off slowly, passes through a business street lined with fancy shops. We cross a large, paved square, the European center of the little city, then turn right. A big church faces us. Basha points with his finger to a monumental portal in a rampart and tells me: "That's the road to Lodi where one of our aunts lives."

On leaving Medea the road twists and turns through the mountains. Through a slit I can make out the sea. The view is majestic and I'm in awe. Then the road descends and runs between the Chiffa gorges. When a red bus from the other direction comes into view, our driver blows his horn to signal that we are moving off to the safe side of the road against a parapet so it can pass. Not long after, in a curve in the road, I see the Ruisseau des Singes Restaurant (Monkey Restaurant); several European families are having lunch outside. All of a sudden, a monkey appears, scratching and cleaning her baby's skin. The passengers laugh. I manage a smile. "They look like human beings," Basha comments.

Once out of the gorges, I feel less oppressed. On each side of the straight road there are orange groves, vineyards, and other crops, a sure indication that we are now passing through the Mitidja plain. The light, the air are different. The horizon is off in the distance. The width of the road, the sound of the motor, the breeze through the open windows, the rays of the sun on the plain trees, all is enchantment.

"*Bab essebt*, the Saturday gateway," Basha whispers to me as the bus plows through an intersection. As we glide along an avenue, I try to locate the school. The driver turns into another avenue, then a small street and stops behind another red bus. "We've arrived," says Basha getting up. He hands me my jacket, takes hold of my little suitcase, and we get off the bus. It's three o'clock. We cross a traffic circle that indicates the direction for Algiers and take the road to Dalmatie. Basha starts walking fast. I ask whether we'll pass the school on the way. "I can't say, but don't worry, the cousins will know where it is."

I'm in a hurry to get to our aunt's place. The road, the sidewalks are silent, villas with gardens and rose bushes in blossom line the way. I don't remember Aunt Hanifa living in such an elegant neighborhood. After a turn in the road it narrows, the houses are less fancy, the pavement and the sidewalk disappear. Basha is ahead of me, walking with a determined step without regard for the heat; I'm perspiring, my jacket is wet. The shoes my father had the best shoemaker in the village make for me are killing me. I imagine stopping, screaming "enough," I can't take another step. But I don't want Basha to think I'm a weakling. We cross a bridge over a small stream and leave the road for a dirt path.

"Is it far?" I ask, my throat parched. My brother turns, looks at me, and slows down. "No, just after the cemeteries. You don't remember? You've been here before. With Imma we spent several days at Aunt Hanifa's. You played with her daughter Zohra who's just a little older than you."

That's true, but it's a long time ago and we came by car. But speaking of Zohra brings back memories. We played in the fruit orchard on the hill, I climbed the trees and picked fruit for her. It's there that I saw a prickly pomegranate tree for the first time. I remember Zohra's smile and can hear her slow, sweet voice describing the details of the engagement parties and weddings of family members. She was proud of her abilities to weave, to knit, to embroider. To impress her, I remember inventing stories of escapades with Mustafa, I exaggerated everything. I was more at ease talking about school. One day, I recited "The Crow and the Fox" by La Fontaine and asked her if she knew any fables. She lowered her eyes and murmured with sadness in her voice, "I've never gone to school."

Instinctively, I press forward, try to forget my aching feet. Along the path there's a stream on one side and the wall of the Christian cemetery on the other. We exchange greetings with the rare people coming from the other direction: "*Essalam aleïkoum.*" I see the entrance to the Jewish cemetery surrounded by a wall and think of the ghosts that haunt cemeteries at night and wonder if they hate each other as much as people on earth do. Thankfully, the walls are no longer close by and my macabre thoughts fade. The path narrows and we arrive at the Muslim cemetery, a wide, sloping field of headstones and a few trees. We leave the path for a goat track up a hill. A little farther on I see the well and its pulley, I recognize the almond tree, the walnut tree, and the jujube tree in the orchard where I played with Zohra. A dog barks and comes running toward us, the woman who's taking clothes off the line on the terrace calms it down and takes it inside the house with her. She reappears with a scarf on her head, takes a good look at us, and calls to someone.

"It's Antar's wife," Basha says in a low voice.

Another woman comes out on the terrace and looks at us. "Aunt Hanifa, I'm Basha, my brother Mokhtar is with me." The two women raise their arms to the heavens and yell *Marhaba*. Three little boys come running toward us, the two silhouettes leave the doorway and come closer. Abdelaziz's wife, heavily pregnant, advances slowly, her hands on her stomach. Smiling, Zohra follows her, she has a small child in her arms. Our aunt welcomes us, compliments me on the big, beautiful boy I've become.

I take off my shoes and sit down next to Basha, who gives them news of our family and inquires about the health of each member of theirs. Delighted to be inside where it's cool, I observe Zohra's body as she prepares the low, round table for dinner. "No doubt about it, she's a woman," I say to myself. Antar's wife serves us coffee, adds a splash of *mazhar* and hands the cups around. When she smiles I notice the many gaps between her teeth. Basha drinks up quickly, takes the package of Imma's pastry from the little suitcase and hands it to Aunt Hanifa. He's in a hurry to leave. Aunt Hanifa insists that he spend the night but he comes up with a series of reasons why it's impossible. He puts on his sandals and gives me instructions on how to take the bus home the day after tomorrow. I reassure him and, watching him go, am sorry he won't be alongside me at the school tomorrow.

Ahmed, the youngest of the four boys, arrives with a basket of groceries, tells us he met Basha on his way up and tried to bring him back with him. Turning toward me, he says,

"For tomorrow, don't worry. I get up early to go to work and I'll take you to the school." I feel reassured.

Suddenly, the sun disappears behind the Atlas Mountains. A kerosene lamp brightens the room. On the terrace an acetylene lamp, *al karboul*, draws a circle of light. After Abdelaziz, who's a mason and tiler, Bouziane arrives with a sports bag. He works in a butcher shop at the European market and spends time at a boxing center after work. During dinner, Abdelaziz explains why Antar is not with us: "He can never come home until he's spent some time with his friends at a bar." Antar is a mason too.

Bouziane and Ahmed discuss next Sunday's soccer match between two local teams, the Union sportive musulmane de Blida, USMB, which they pronounce "Loucembi," and the Football Club de Blida, FCB. They go over the lineup that was announced during the day. They're convinced that Loucembi will win and they try to imagine the score. Suddenly Abdelaziz asks: "This exam that you're taking, what's it for?" The brothers stop talking and look at me. Surprised, I don't know what to say. He insists: "What's it good for?"

Actually, I don't know, I've hardly thought about it. I improvise and explain that if I succeed tomorrow I will be admitted to middle school and will prepare for the middle school exam, then the high school diploma, to become a *midicoul*, a school teacher. They all nod their heads. Abdelaziz says softly, "*Inchâallah*."

The clock says six o'clock when Ahmed and I leave the house. The sky is a soft blue, the air is cool, there's an odor of jasmine mixed with roses that tickles my nostrils. I've hung the bag that Rezkia made for me over my shoulder and feel light, ready to trot, even to sing. When Ahmed interrupts my reverie to say that we will stop first at his place of work to tell the boss he'll be late, I realize that we are close to the square with the road to Algiers.

The city is just waking up. A strange silence hovers over the little streets. The few people we meet are in a hurry. The pastry shop where Ahmed works is at the corner of a street across from the European market. The sign on the front of the building is painted in gold. He says it's the finest pastry shop in the region. Ahmed goes in through a side door and comes back a few minutes later. We go down a wide slanting street with a sidewalk lined with orange trees, Boulevard Trumelet, which leads to the Place d'Armes, an immense paved esplanade, lined and shaded by a double row of trees. In the middle is a music stand in the neo-Moorish style with a palm tree in the center. I'm startled and can't take my eyes off it. Imposing stone buildings line the square on all sides. Horses and buggies are stationed in front of the arcades that shade a number of cafés. I absorb the opulence and imagine that I'm in the heart of El Dorado.

Ahmed walks ahead, indifferent to the surroundings. He seems at ease but it's obvious that he is as much a foreigner here as I am. We cross a square, take the rue Bizot. There are no people around. We pass in front of a few handsome buildings but no stores. At the end of the street are the Bizot Gardens. The high school, a large dark stone building, is the last one: its thick walls and its high, narrow windows with grillwork accentuate its mournful air. In the middle is an archway over a monumental doorway with a sculpted-wood entrance door that's closed. Over the doorway is an arched name plate: COLLÈGE DUVEYRIER. We both smile. I notice that across the way there's an officers' mess hall. The rest of the block is occupied by army barracks. Blida, a bastion of colonization, is also a military town.

Since I'm early, Ahmed proposes that we have coffee across the square in the rue d'Alger. He orders black coffee for himself and one with milk for me plus a chocolate Danish. He drinks his coffee quickly, sticks a banknote in my pocket, and says, "For your lunch."

He reminds me that he'll be waiting for me there at six o'clock. Then he pays the waiter and parts. I keep my eyes on the clock behind the counter and leave at ten after seven. From the middle of the square I can see people in front of the school and begin to run. On rue Bizot, some boys accompanied by their parents are walking in the same direction as me but not hurrying. I slow down and notice that they are carrying leather briefcases by the handle or under their arm. I take my bag off my shoulder and hold it close to my body. Only one side of the door is open. A mother kisses her son goodbye and pushes him in its direction.

"Only candidates may enter," says a man standing in the entryway. He checks my name on a list.

I climb the large white marble staircase and follow another candidate who seems to know the way. I measure the importance of the exam when I enter the schoolroom. Instead of tables with a bench for two boys, each candidate has his own desk and chair. There are four rows well spaced. The blackboard is not standing on a tripod, as in my classroom, but is attached to the wall and extends the entire width of the room. An attendant points to a place for me to sit. When I hear the chairs scrape the floor, I'm drawn out of my state of wonderment. I get up, too. A tall, white-haired man has just entered with sheets of paper in his hand. He stops in the middle of the low stage, looks around the room, and says, "Be seated."

From the talk around the room, I understand that his name is Leblond and he's the administrator. He asks for silence and calls the roll. After ensuring that he hasn't forgotten anyone, he announces that the exam will start with dictation and will be followed by a composition. After a fifteen-minute break, there will a math test. The results will be announced at four p.m. this afternoon, and the list of candidates admitted will be posted at the entrance to the school. He gestures toward two assistants, who take a sheaf of papers off the desk and distribute them.

The dictation is easy: only the accent mark in the word *amène* troubles me; I'm not sure that it's an *accent grave*. I manage to recopy my draft before the order to stop writing is announced and the papers are collected. In the recreation hall, I'm happy to find three boys from the village, though they're not really friends of mine. Mohamed Benturki, son of one of the commune's *mokhazni*, was in my class until his father was transferred to Boghari / Ksar El Boukhari, some forty kilometers south of Berrouaghia. Abderrahmane Megateli is the son of the *mouderes*, the local Arabic teacher. In order to ensure his son's success, his father enrolled him in a final primary school class in Blida the year before. Saïdi Larbi was in the same school. As for the *accent grave*, there's a difference of opinion among us. There are two boys from my own class, but they don't associate with Arab students: Pierre Guedj, the doctor's son; and Cherif Farès, known as Mimi, the notary's son. His father was the first Algerian to occupy that post, and rumor has it that since only "real" Frenchmen may occupy such a post, Farès had to renounce his religion. "He's a *mtourni*, a renegade," everyone says.

For the math test, I remembered Monsieur Colin's advice: "Take time to reread the problem and think about it before you begin."

Outside, several candidates are arguing about the solution to the problem. They're Europeans. One of them has found the same result as me but, since no one asks my opinion, I leave them to go eat. I'm starved.

On the Place d'Armes, the terraces of the cafés have now filled up, with mostly Europeans. I look for a place to eat and take the rue d'Alger, then another street to the right. As I walk along, I notice that the sidewalks have narrowed. I no longer see any Europeans, there are more turbans around. All of a sudden I find myself in the middle of a busy square. The crowd, the cafés, the stores, the market are exclusively Arab. I follow the familiar cooking odors and enter an eating place. It's a wide corridor without windows, filled with wooden tables and benches. The customers look morose, are not very talkative; they are mostly seasonal workers from the High Plateau region here to make a little money on the fertile El Dorado plain. On entering I exhibit my banknote under the mustached nose of the man behind a small counter, and say, "I want to eat."

He points to a chair at an occupied table and watches me

sit down. Immediately, a young man runs over and deposits a small straw basket containing a galette and a piece of brown paper intended to serve as a napkin. He stands there without moving a muscle, stares at the ceiling, and, in a monotone voice, reels off the menu: "We have *douara*, *lham koucha*, *dolma*, *bouzellouf*" (roast meat and potatoes, meat-filled pastry shells, dolmas, sheep's head). I make my choice, the waiter turns his head toward the kitchen and yells, "One *bouzellouf*." He comes back with my order almost immediately. I devour the dish with my eyes first and quickly forget Duveyrier and the exam.

Having eaten my fill, I wander around the neighborhood, then go window-shopping along the rue d'Alger and take a walk around the Place d'Armes before finding a bench in the shade. Drowsy, I hear the chimes of a clock nearby. Suddenly, I'm submerged in doubt, imagining I'll get a low mark on my composition and that I made some dictation errors. My anxiety is at its maximum when I leave the square for the rue Bizot. It's empty, the garden also. My heart throbbing, I observe a crowd at the school entrance. Guedj and Farès are accompanied by their mothers. The women are wearing perfume like none that I've ever smelled. I've never been in a crowd of Europeans before.

The window of a small balcony to the left of the door opens and a man with a crew cut of white hair appears. It's the administrator. The crowd reacts noisily. Leblond, looking severe, raises a hand holding some sheets of paper. The crowd calms down, is silent. I feel a chill down my back. He speaks loudly and announces that he will read the last, then the first names, in alphabetical order, of those admitted to sixth grade. He pauses and begins reciting. Cries of joy, a few claps of hands interrupt the procedure.

"Benturki Mohamed," the *mokhazni*'s son. He doesn't pronounce Farès and Guedj's names. My throat hardens, my cheeks are aflame, I tighten my fists and hear: "Megateli Abderrahmane." Then comes my last name followed by my first name. I stop listening, repress my desire to cry out and jump up and down. I start immediately at a run toward the Place d'Armes, where, under the arcades, I'd noticed a post office. I go up to the young woman seated at a desk perched well above floor level and say: "Madame, I would like number forty-two in Berrouaghia, please." She records the request and says, "A ten-minute wait."

I sit down on a bench thinking of what to say to my father: that I passed and that the doctor's and the notary's sons didn't.

"Berrouaghia, booth number two," the telephone operator announces. I enter the booth and pick up the phone. A woman's voice says, "Berrouaghia on the line."

"Hello, Baba? It's me."

"Hello, where are you?"

"Baba, I'm in Blida. I passed. I passed the entrance exam for junior high school!"

"That's fine, my son. When are you coming home?"

It's the first time I hear my father's voice on the telephone. It's pitched lower than usual. "Tomorrow I'll take the bus, the regular line. Baba, will you buy me the bicycle?"

"Come back and we'll see later."

"You'll buy it for me, Baba, won't you?"

"I said we'll see later."

"I'll be home tomorrow. Goodbye, Baba."

Disappointed, I regret that my father wasn't there for the reading of the results. He would have seen the crowd of French people and heard my name pronounced by the supervisor. I'm sure he would have been proud of me and wouldn't hesitate to buy the bicycle. I forgot to tell him about the doctor's and the notary's sons.

Rue d'Alger is crowded with people. Car horns are honking to gain passage through the large number of horses and buggies that jam the square. I almost get run over crossing the sidewalk. Here comes Ahmed from the rue du Bey. "I passed," I say calmly.

"*Mabrouk*, congratulations!" he cries and hugs me tight with both arms. His show of affection makes me happy. "You looked so anxious this morning."

Along the way, I answer his questions about my future, the follow-up to the exam. "I'll be living at the school and will have my middle school degree in four years, the high school diploma in three more."

"Middle school is fine, but the other is too long."

I say to myself that he doesn't know what the high school diploma represents. Actually I don't either, having heard it mentioned for the first time when Monsieur Colin talked to me about going to school in Blida.

"Praise be to God, may he continue to guide your path," declares Aunt Hanifa.

After dinner, Ahmed explains how to go to the station the next day to catch the bus for Berrouaghia. I'm a half hour early. The driver recognizes me, is surprised to see me alone. I tell him about my trip with Basha and, with pride, that I passed the exam to go to school in Blida. He congratulates me and, as a reward, gives me a front row seat.

Imma is happy to have me back and that I succeeded in passing the exam, but what really interests her is my stay at Aunt Hanifa's. She asks all sorts of questions about what my aunt said, about what her daughters-in-law are like, what they are doing, their husbands, the number of children, the food served at meals. I'm obviously incapable of satisfying her curiosity. And she's incapable of understanding that I was more preoccupied with the exam and discovering the school than with Aunt Hanifa and her family. I leave her to go to the butcher shop. I'm drawing up the arguments that can induce Baba to buy me the bicycle of my dreams. I surprise him when he learns that the overwhelming majority of the candidates are French, that the children of the *mokhazni* and the *mouderes* and his friend who owns the dry goods store also passed the exam. He raises his head, squints his eyes. I'm convinced my success means something to him. I take advantage of the moment to give him the reason that will decide him: "The sons of the notary and the doctor were there and took the exam, but they didn't pass."

He smiles and says: "Go tell the waiter at the café to bring us a coffee for me and mint tea for you."

When I return he's scrubbing the floor getting ready to close. "Baba, when will you get me the bicycle?"

"We'll see later, my son."

I refuse to admit that we have honored my success with just a coffee and a glass of mint tea. I put the question to Baba again during the weeks that follow and obtain the same reply each time. I stop asking for the bike the day a letter arrives from Duveyrier. It confirms my admission to the school and to the dormitory and lists the clothes and other articles to bring. I'm given a number, 94, that has to be sewn onto anything made of cloth. The list includes clothes and underclothes that I have never worn. I'm shaken and hesitate but finally read the list to my father. Without turning away from the task at hand, cutting up a side of meat, he listens to the enumeration: twelve handkerchiefs, twelve pairs of socks, six undershirts, six underpants, six napkins...

"You going to open a restaurant or what?" he comments with irony.

I continue, try to explain and justify the need for two clothing bags. "What's that, a pajama?" he asks irritated. My reply doesn't satisfy him. He repeats what I said, barely opening his mouth: "'an outfit to sleep in...'"

I continue: "a clothes brush, a shoe brush, a toothbrush..."

Slowly, he puts the knife down, takes the sheet of paper from me, and tells me to follow him. He tells Mohamed, who is standing outside the shop talking to a friend, that he'll be across the street. *'Ammi* Rabah, who owns the dry goods store, puts down the newspaper and takes hold of the sheet of paper my father hands him. He tells us, with his strong Kabyle accent, that he's received the same list. He confirms my definition of a pajama, of underpants. Seeing the state we're in, he suggests: "Miloud, you don't have to buy pajamas and underpants. You can replace them with *gandouras* and cotton shorts. I have the cloth you need and your wife must know a dressmaker."

"Can you tell me why this child needs twelve handkerchiefs and six pairs of sheets for his bed?"

Rabah bursts out laughing and comes up with another idea: "Ask the women to cut some sheets in two and from another sheet cut out some little handkerchiefs."

"And why a coat when this kid has always worn a *kachabia*?"

"I'm sure they won't accept a *kachabia*," Rabah says sternly.

Baba turns to me, smiles, and puts his hand on my shoulder: "I'll have my tailor make you a camel hair coat."

I stiffen and reply: "Camel hair is good for a burnous, not for a coat."

"You'll see," he says, "it will keep you warm and will be more beautiful than a store-bought coat."

'Ammi Rabah offers to buy the black coverall and the number 94 tabs to be sewn on all the clothes next time he goes to Algiers. Relieved, my father tells me to go order two coffees.

When I read the list to my mother, she raises her arms to the heavens and lets out a series of screams: "All this expense, for what? This is not for us."

"I want to continue my studies," I repeat for the umpteenth time.

"I don't see the relation between studies and all these clothes and stuff," she growls.

"So you think that Benturki, Megateli, and Saïdi have the right to go to school and not me?"

"If the others agree to imitate the French and eat pork, you're not going to do like them. Anyway, I forbid you to do so."

A few days later, I learn that my parents are preparing for my older brother Ahmed's wedding. He doesn't drink anymore, he helps Basha at the slaughterhouse, he comes home for meals. However, Imma's efforts to find a village family that will agree to give their daughter to him hit a dead end. My father decides to give it a try. He turns the problem over to his sister's husband, a landless peasant, and asks him to see if, among his relatives, there might be a young woman who would do. My paternal aunt once came to visit us after Mohamed was let out of prison. She was very thin, her skin well tanned. She had an angelic smile and spoke little, but her sharp eyes took in everything. She dressed and wore her hair as peasant women do and didn't wear a veil. Very affectionate and welcoming, she invited me to go home with her. I agreed with joy. For my mother's approval, however, I had to wage battle. I spent three marvelous days at my aunt's.

She and her husband have no children. They live in an adobe house with a thatched roof, without running water or electricity, in a hamlet close to a large grain farm. My uncle only gets seasonal work. My mother doesn't like them and calls my uncle a parasite because he comes down to the village on Wednesdays, market day, and stops by for a visit with Baba, who often invites him home for lunch. She gripes, reproaches my father for not letting her know in advance, and accuses her brother-in-law of coming by the butcher shop at lunchtime on purpose.

I spent three days playing with their neighbors' children, who are goat-herders. My aunt spoiled me, made me galettes with rancid butter, semolina-and-date desserts (*rfiss*), egg dishes, and she killed a laying hen. On my return home, my mother washed my hair and changed all my clothes because, according to her, I must have picked up lice.

With her mandate from Baba, my aunt picked the adopted daughter of the head of the tribe and informed my parents. Everything went very fast. Imma visited the hamlet and was shown "a young, light-skinned girl, in good health, tall and pretty." The men gave their agreement. A ceremony took place and she and Ahmed are now married. Her name is El Garmia but Imma finds this peasant-type of name distasteful. "It's a name that doesn't jibe with our habits and customs," she tells the young bride as soon as she arrives. "In the future, you'll be Rokia." No sooner said than done!

Three days after the wedding, my mother goes looking for her dressmaker friend. "For your trousseau," she tells Rokia.

My father, on the other hand, takes me to his tailor. "Mokhtar passed an exam and will be going to school in Blida. You have to dress him up like a gentleman. He needs six shirts, a suit, and a coat."

"You're going to have the best clothes in the village," the tailor tells me, smiling.

I believe it, until the day Basha and I arrive in Blida weighed down by two large suitcases. The concierge directs us to the laundry, above the dining room. I think we're in a clinic when I see the woman in a white uniform parceling out laundry on the shelves. She looks at us but doesn't answer our "Good morning, Madame." Dark hair, fine features with lots of makeup, she has a sour look.

"You could have knocked," she says dryly.

"Madame, I knocked," says Basha.

"I didn't hear you. Put the suitcases over there." She points to a counter behind her and adds, "Open them."

She takes my things out, counts everything, and verifies that there is a number on everything. "I presume these are for sleeping," she says, as she refolds the *gandouras*. I say yes and watch her pick up each piece of underwear with two fingers, murmuring under her breath.

She unfolds a napkin and cries: "What's this? Are you sure it's been washed?"

"Madame, everything is clean," Basha replies in a firm voice.

I have the feeling he's ready to rage at her. She must have felt it, too, because she stops talking. When she leaves the counter to put everything on a shelf, I see that she limps. Outside, happy that the suitcases are empty, I turn to my brother: "Do you think she's nasty like that because of her infirmity?"

"It has nothing to do with her infirmity, she's racist, that's all."

The day school begins. I am totally disoriented. In my school, there was only one courtyard, in which teachers and pupils mingled during recreation periods, and classes took place in the same room throughout the year. At Duveyrier, there are six courtyards, three of which are for recreation. In my school, the principal designated a student to pull the cord that activated the school bell, whereas here an electric buzzer signals the beginning and end of classes. Every hour, pupils change rooms, while the teachers remain in the same classroom year after year.

I arrive in the courtyard for sixth-grade pupils just as Leblond, the administrator, claps his hands for silence and announces: "I'm going to call your names and ask you to line up two by two in front of me, those studying the classics to my left and those doing modern studies to the right."

I have no idea what is meant by classic and modern studies and can't ask my neighbors because no talking is allowed. Luckily, the first name on the list is an Arab name, Selim Abdelwahab. He goes to the left, to the classics side. I feel relieved, I'll be classic, too. But later I realize that the other Algerians are all in the modern line, so I change lines. Leblond interrupts the roll call, stares at me fixedly, and yells: "You ass, don't you know what you want?" Confused because of my error and devastated by the ugly remark, I bear down hard on my teeth to stop myself from expressing my desire to ram into the French boys who think it's funny and are laughing. I haven't come all this way to be treated like an ass and humiliated. I repress my anger and later learn that those taking Greek and/or Latin are in the classics section.

I go from discovery to discovery. For the first time I use what's called a urinal. In the toilets there's no pail or bucket. It's true I haven't always done as my father taught me: to piss crouched so as not to wet myself, but for the rest, I wash myself ever since I learned how. Baba taught me to pour water in my right hand and use the left to clean myself.

In addition, students call each other by their last names. I'll have to get used to that. In the school in the village, only the teachers use the family name. Village people call each other by their first names. If two people have the same name, it suffices to add the father's first name or his profession.

In the dining hall there are twelve tables, each accommodating ten boys. Since the Muslims don't eat pork or drink wine, they have three tables to themselves. The napkin holders are all alike, made from red-and-white-checkered material, each with a different number. Mine is 94. The few day-pupils have lunch in another room near the kitchen. The administrator and a student monitor are on hand to see that entry to the dining hall goes smoothly.

I take a seat in the back of the hall between Larbi Saïdi, the son of *'Ammi* Rabah, and Silhadi Mohand, who speaks a hesitant Arabic with a strong Kabyle accent, and has a tic: when he laughs, he puts his hand in front of his mouth. Across from me is Mahieddine Titteri; this is his third year as a boarding student; he's the table captain. He has a happy nature, serves everybody, notices that several of us don't know how to cut our steak, laughs and says that before coming here he'd never eaten with a knife and fork either and tells us to watch how it's done. His friendly tone and the demonstration help me overcome my hesitation. Titteri, a redhead with rosy cheeks, is from the town of Boghari, down the road from Berrouaghia.

In the study hall, I share a table with Cazeaux, a French kid from Mouzaïaville who's chosen the classics. Pleased to have established contact with him, I tell him that my maternal aunt lives in Mouzaïaville and that her husband works for Germain, the largest settler estate there. I avoid telling him that my mother's sister and her family live in a hamlet of adobe houses with other employees of the landowner.

Cazeaux's father is a mechanic whose garage is on the main street of the town. To my question "Why did you choose the classics?" he replies: "It was the local priest who told my mother I should."

After the last buzzer of the day, we all gather at the bottom of the staircase to the second-floor dormitory. We go up two by two in silence. I'm curious to see the place where I'm going to spend my first night with the French. It's a large room with two rows of iron beds separated by a central aisle. About forty beds in all, with the same pink bedcover and a nameplate attached to the foot of the bed with our number. My bed is between two French boys: one in sixth grade doing classics, the other in seventh grade.

The monitor points out that on each bed there's a pair of sheets and orders us to make our beds. I don't know how to start. At home, my mother or Rezkia lays out our mattresses every evening with pillows and blankets. You don't get a sheet until you're married. I observe my neighbors and imitate them. I realize that Imma and the dressmaker were short-sighted, my sheets don't fully cover the mattress. After going to the shoe storeroom, the dressing room, and the bathroom, I realize that all the Algerians are wearing pajamas, I'm the only one not. When I put on my *gandoura*, the terrified look of a neighbor, the disdainful look of another, are chilling. All of a sudden I feel like an outsider, an intruder. Mortified, I get under the covers and let the tears flow. I hold it against those boys but also against my father, who refused to buy me pajamas, the article of clothing that would have helped me integrate in this environment. I know that pajamas are worn by people who have "evolved," that they signal modernity. In the Egyptian films I've seen, the men go out with their families to the parks and in the streets of Cairo in their pajamas. Baba, of course, has never been to the movies.

From morning till night, the electric buzzer punctuates our activities. Everywhere, before entering, we have to line up, await orders, in silence. I imitate my comrades going from one courtyard or class to another. Barely seated, you have to jump up when your name is called and answer "Present." The advantage is that by the end of the first day, I know everyone's name.

The French teacher, from mainland France, looks severe and has the reputation of being tough. After his first dictation, on which I made one small error, he seats me in the first row, next to a European who made the same little error. The math teacher is young, easygoing. He motions us to come in and sit down and doesn't demand silence first. Because of his elegance and his goo-flattened hair, we call him Zazou. I like the way he passes from arithmetic to algebra and geometry.

Strict and dry, the history teacher pleasantly surprises me when he announces that the day's lesson will be on Egypt. "It's in Egypt that one of the greatest civilizations in the world was born," he states. I take notes, not wanting to miss anything. He cites the dynasties, the pharaohs, the temples and pyramids, as well as the gods, represented by animals: dogs, cats, birds. Instinctively, I stop taking notes or I leave out words, parts of sentences. I no longer believe what he's telling us. For my twelve-year-old child's brain, fashioned by religion and fifteen memorized chapters of the Koran, the

Egyptians have always been Muslims. I conclude that the teacher is lying, like the one who had us recite "Our ancestors, the Gauls." It's true that there are pictures in the history book, but in the one in my school there were portraits of the different "races" living on our planet. "The white race," says the caption, "is the superior race." For the first time since I've arrived, before falling asleep that night, I recite the *chahada*, the testimony to my faith: "There is no god but God. Mohamed is the messenger of God."

Saturday, at four o'clock, many of the boarding students go home for the weekend. Sunday morning, those who have a correspondent can leave after breakfast, and the others at two o'clock. The administrator refuses to let me go out because he hasn't received written authorization from my parents. "The form was sent to your family with the list of supplies," he says, referring to the trousseau that caused me so much trouble that I paid no attention to that authorization form.

I pretend that I never received it and obtain a new form. Instead of sending it by mail, I wait until the following Saturday and, tears rolling, manage to see the principal, who is willing to call Baba so that I can go home for the weekend. The shouts and threats of Leblond, the administrator, no longer intimidate me. The good humor of the principal, Monsieur Aimé Périller, who addresses me with the formal *vous* and calls me "my child," moderates my feelings of revolt, my desire to flee. I leave the school with a sense of freedom such that I run all the way to the station on the outskirts of the city. The train will be leaving at seven in the evening; I'm taking it alone for the first time. A steam engine, it links Blida and Djelfa along a single, narrow track. I buy a third-class ticket and observe that there are no Europeans occupying the car's stiff, wooden benches.

As the crow flies, Blida is only fifty kilometers from Berrouaghia, but the trip, with its interminable stops, takes three hours. To overcome my anxiety, I count the number of tunnels, fifteen, and think of the extraordinary stories I will tell the family about my new life. Mustafa and Cherif are waiting for me at the station; we're happy to see each other. Almost immediately, Mustafa tells me that Mohamed is running for municipal office, that he spoke in front of a packed house at the town meeting hall. I realize that the results of tomorrow's elections are of more interest to them than my life at school.

Imma, however, is moved and keeps repeating, "I missed you, my son." She takes me aside, asks if I've eaten, and lays out the part of dinner she's saved for me. The rest of the family goes to bed. She watches me eat, asks about the food at school, how long I'll be home. When I tell her, she gasps: "You've made this long trip just to go back tomorrow?"

"I have to be at school at eight on Monday morning at the latest. If I take the train or the bus, I'll be late."

"Eat and we'll see tomorrow," she orders.

I sleep like a log and wake up after all the men have gone out. "Your brother Basha has reserved a seat for you on Monday morning in a collective taxi. You'll be at school before eight o'clock," Imma informs me.

Seated across from me, while Rezkia serves me breakfast, she continues yesterday's questionnaire, wants to know if I have enough blankets and, above all, if I remember to recite the *chahada* every night. Her other preoccupation is the food; she's relieved to learn that in the dining hall the Muslims sit at separate tables where neither pork nor wine is served. To get away from her insatiable curiosity, I pretext the need to go to the butcher shop to have my weekend authorization signed. She tries to stop me. "Your father will sign the paper at lunchtime. Sunday morning, there are a lot of customers, you'll only be in the way."

I kid with her: "But if you come with me, I'm sure he won't feel bothered." She laughs and stops insisting.

I rush behind the counter where Baba is sitting, embrace him, and kiss his hand. "The air in Blida must be good for you, you've grown," he comments.

I take the crumpled form out of my pocket and point: "You have to sign here. I'll fill in the rest."

With great care he writes his name: family name and given name beginning with small letters. "There, are you happy?"

"Yes, but you know, Baba, in French proper names begin with a capital letter."

"And you, did you know that in Arabic there are several types of script: *maghrebi*, *naski*, *koufi*, and more?" He illustrates the differences on a page of the notebook that is always in his pocket and where he keeps track of his purchases at the animal market and on the farms.

The atmosphere in the village has changed and seems odd to me. Near the town hall, where a lot of people have congregated, I meet Mustafa and some friends. I embrace Mohamed, who has just finished speaking to the group. There are two lists, the "first list," with the majority of seats to be filled, for which only the French vote; and the "second list," with just three posts, for which the Algerians are authorized to vote. The mayor, of course, is always a European. On the second list, voters have to choose between those representing the Movement for the Triumph of Democratic Freedoms (MTLD), successor to the Algerian People's Party (PPA); and the Democratic Union for the Algerian Manifesto (UDMA) and the Independents. The Algerian Communist Party (PCA) has only a handful of members, so no candidates. My brother Mohamed is head of the PPA–MTLD slate, which includes Hadj Hamdi Lakhdar, a vegetable grocer, and Nabi Miliani, a shopkeeper. All three have primary school certificates, the CEP. They denounce the colonial system, the statutes that govern us, the repression, and demand the election of a sovereign constituent assembly and freedom for all political prisoners. They reprove the other Algerian organizations and their leader, Ferhat Abbas, for wanting to remain tied to France and for not advocating total independence for Algeria.

The candidates on the UDMA–Independents slate are prominent men, well-heeled, middle-aged merchants, close to the ulemas. Their leading personalities are the imam and the *mouderes*. To the MTLD radical platform, they oppose an action program of apprenticeship, literacy, housing, improved health service, sports facilities. With little support among the village population, they denigrate their adversaries, calling Mohamed's slate "enraged young men who want to chase the French army out of Algeria with slingshots."

Mohamed is only twenty-four years old and most of the MTLD militants are under thirty, though they include some older men like Hassen Bey, the miller. The nationalists chide their adversaries by broadcasting the famous statement of their leader, Ferhat Abbas, that "the Algerian nation doesn't exist." The virulence of the campaign widens the gap between the more prominent members of society and the village people who support the PPA–MTLD and its leaders.

The next day, at six in the morning, I leave the house with my father to get the taxi. The idea of seeing the supervisor, who refused to let me out, the memory of my tears when I asked to be received by the principal, leave me with little desire to go back. On the other hand, my visit was revealing of the fact that, other than Imma, my new life doesn't interest anyone in the family.

Baba stops a few yards from the taxi, takes out his thick wallet, and hands me several bills: "Here's for your books and pocket money." I kiss his hand. He pulls me over, embraces me, and says: "I know it isn't easy to live away from your family, but remember the hadith 'Look for Science, be it in China.' Take care of yourself." He goes over to the driver, pays him, and leaves for the mosque.

Science isn't in China anymore, as in the Prophet's time. Now, to find it, you have to frequent the colonial high school in Blida. In the movies, Shanghai is a center of vice, of prostitution, of opium dens: the streets are overrun by coolies and starving beggars in rags. In the grade school textbook, the Chinese and the yellow "race" are, with the Blacks, the Indians, and the Arabs, one of the inferior races.

I take the seat next to the driver. Three other passengers

are sitting in the back. They're wearing traditional clothes, are probably from the countryside. They know my father. The oldest says that Baba is a pillar of the mosque and mentions that, every year, on the Achoura, he invites the needy to his home after prayers to receive the *zâkât*, alms. The previous year, the line was impressive.

The tires of the car screech in the gorges. I hold on to my seat to steady myself. When we hit the straight road, one of the passengers breaks the silence and we learn that he goes to the Mitidja plain at different seasons to trim vines, work in the orchards, or take part in the harvesting. The older man admires the orange groves and the vineyards along the road: "I wonder why God gave all this wealth to foreigners," he comments. "God knows what he's doing," the driver says, and reminds the older man "that nothing is eternal in this world."

I fill in the form Baba signed and grant myself permission to leave school on weekends and holidays. Since for the Saturday night–to–Sunday authorization the name of a correspondent is required, I write in my cousin Ahmed's name and his address as Dalmatie Road. When I hand the paper to the administrator, he notes that it's creased and throws it on the counter without even looking at it. "A rag," he says, and points to the door. "Get out of my sight," he growls, his voice full of hate.

November 1, All Saints Day, falls on a Saturday. I could leave on Friday afternoon and go home, but the desire to see the family and the nostalgia for the village that had me in tears in bed at night no longer seem so urgent. I decide to stay and study, visit the city. Jacques Caseaux, my tablemate, left at four on Friday. The study hall is half empty and discipline is less strict. Mohand Silhadi, a classmate, sits down at my table. He's from Michelet (Aïn El Hammam) in Kabylia. The first time he ever left his village was when he came to pass the sixth-grade entry exam, so he doesn't know anyone here. Since I don't want to spend the holidays at my aunt Hanifa's on the mountain, with no running water or electricity, we go out together, walk around Blida, come back at five o'clock, and go to the study hall. Monday, with Cazeaux's return, we go our separate ways, but we meet again for recreation and classes, except for the foreign language courses. I've chosen Arabic in order to perfect my knowledge of my mother tongue...and to get a good mark on the exams. Silhadi is taking English. When I ask him why, he says, "Because England is more powerful than France."

I don't regret my choice, even though I find the Arabic class disappointing. I thought I would learn about the wealth of literary and scientific works of our civilization, but, because of the presence of three Europeans and because the Algerians in the class never went to Koranic school, the lessons begin with the Arabic script and the alphabet. I do learn, however, that my own name is open to question. When the Arabic teacher called the roll the first time, he asked me, "How do you pronounce your name?" "Mok-te-fi," I replied. "So why is there an *h* after the *k*? It changes the meaning." I explained that all our names in the family are spelled differently on our official papers: my older brother Ahmed is Moktafi, Mohamed is Moketefi, Baba and I are Mokhtefi. I didn't tell him what I really think: that the French treat us with total disdain. They never bothered to check the spelling of our father's name when they registered our births.

Over three-quarters of the students at Duveyrier are of European origin. The Algerians, in the minority, are of differing social backgrounds. A few day students come from well-to-do bourgeois Blidean families. The best known are owners of a tobacco company; the others are the sons of businessmen, government employees, teachers, lawyers, doctors, pharmacists. As for myself, uprooted and marginal, even within this minority, I'm forever ill at ease sharing the lifestyle of Europeans. I'm afraid of doing things wrong, of seeming backward. I'm ridiculed because I arrive in French class with my dictionary under my arm. Whatever the case, the day the composition results for first semester are posted, I'm second and proud to learn that only the guy who was first and myself have passing grades. In addition, I get the highest mark in Arabic. Despite all, I can't seem to shed my inferiority complex. The day before Christmas vacation, the supervisor arrives suddenly in class, opens a large register, and announces the list of honor students. My name is among them. Although it wasn't his intention, he rids me of the unreasonable and painful feelings that were constantly dogging me.

A line of demarcation, a subtle nuance exists between the Algerians who, like me, roll their *r*'s and those whose *r*'s are soft like the Europeans. In primary school, the Algerians roll their *r*'s, adults in the village who speak French do, too; it's probably a manifestation, conscious or not, of our otherness. Softening the *r*'s comes to mean a desire to assimilate. The boys from Blida's bourgeoisie and those from Kabylia who have attended the priests' schools in their region have the same accents as the French. Sometimes, we oscillate according to the people around us: among Algerians we roll the *r*'s and with others we soften them.

"Those who don't like shrimp can pass them this way," Titteri announces, advancing his plate. On Fridays, we've always had fish, but I've never seen these little pink beasts with their wild mustaches before. I empty my plate into the table captain's and watch him lick his fingers, covered with sauce, lovingly. The day before vacation, we're served a Christmas cake with icing like nothing I've ever eaten.

In the winter, our village disappears under the snow and the road through the Benchicao pass is closed to traffic, sometimes for days. Mohamed, who has been elected assistant mayor, says the mayor is arrogant and racist. He holds against him his refusal to connect Drâ-Essouk and the other Algerian neighborhoods to the conduits for running water, and his not installing drainage systems or electricity in those quarters either. In an exchange with the elected officials of the second list, the mayor snarled at the three Algerians: "Don't forget that we shed our blood to conquer this country and we're ready to begin all over again to remain here."

The nationalists' electoral success drives the French crazy. The new governor-general of Algeria, Edmond Naegelen, does everything possible to destroy the MTLD. He doesn't declare it illegal, because this would tarnish France's image abroad and because he knows it will just reappear under another name. His technique is to multiply the number of arrests of militants under false pretexts and to refuse authorizations for public meetings; and he promotes so-called independent candidates. He delays elections for delegates to the Algerian Assembly for several months in a vain attempt to show who's boss.

The first round of elections finally takes place on April 4, 1948, during my Easter vacation. The MTLD candidates win hands down. Naegelen, his back against the wall, makes his own arrangements for the second round. At the polling station in Champlain, a commune within Berrouaghia's jurisdiction, the nationalist poll watchers realize that the urns have been stuffed with votes for the administration candidate prior to the opening of the polls. They protest. The authorities expel them from the polling station and close the doors at eleven a.m. A fight breaks out. The gendarmes and the security police, backed by a large number of settlers, attack. The result: four dead and dozens of wounded among the Algerian population. When Mohamed is informed, he leaves immediately for Champlain, only to be arrested on arrival.

I go back to school. My mother is in tears.

I begin the third semester deathly afraid that Leblond and the school administration will learn what has happened to my brother. I don't tell anyone about it, not even Silhadi. According to the *Echo d'Alger*, Mohamed belongs to "an obstructive force hostile to everything French." I know that's not true, and I don't want to be expelled from school. My anxiety lasts until the day class prizes are distributed. I receive first prize in Arabic and honorable mention in French. I pass to the next grade without having to take an exam.

On returning home for the summer, I'm happy to find Mohamed there. At the end of the first week of vacation, I try to argue Baba out of sending me back to the Koranic school. "You've had enough fun for the time being," he says. The next day Mustafa and I pick up our wooden slates, sit down on the straw mat, our legs crossed under us, and suffer the hubbub and ungodly heat in the room that serves as a school. When Ramadan begins, however, after breaking the fast, my father goes to the mosque and I can spend my evenings outside with my buddies.

One afternoon, Mohamed is at the barber shop across from the town hall getting a shave, when someone runs in to warn him that Piera, the police chief, has just stopped Nabi Miliani, one of the three Algerian town councilors, and taken him to the police station. Piera has recently taken over from the kind Frenchman known for maintaining calm in the village. Formerly the rural warden, Piera was named chief by Pergaud, the mayor. His father was a wagon carrier and, according to rumor, his mother was the owner of the brothel next to which he resides. He speaks fluent Arabic. Mohamed has known him since grade school. The general opinion is that Piera is a dunce.

Mohamed jumps up from the barber's chair, wipes his face, and runs out. He catches up with Miliani and Piera a few steps from the police station and places himself between the two men. Furious, he upbraids Piera and reminds him that Miliani is a town official elected by the people.

"Elected or not, I don't give a damn! I follow orders. There's only one man who commands here and to whom I owe respect, it's Monsieur Pergaud." Piera's audacity, his cocksure air, only intensify Mohamed's rage. He raises his hand, slaps Piera across the face, and points to the mayor's office. "Now tell your master to come get us," he says. His hand on his cheek, Piera mounts the steps of the town hall. Mohamed turns to Miliani and assails him for "blindly following that good-for-nothing." Patient and nonviolent in his habits, Miliani justifies his conduct: "I didn't want to have a fight with him in public in front of my stall. I felt it was better to go to his office."

Mohamed calms down and returns to the barber's chair and Miliani to work in the indoor market. As Mohamed leaves the barber shop, two gendarmes encircle him and lead him to the judge's offices. The news spreads around town like wildfire. The militants all come out and stand on the esplanade across from the judge's building. Other village men join them as soon as they hear what's happening. The square is packed with people, men of all ages but especially the youth, many of whom sit on the ground. Like everyone else, they remain silent.

The sound of the sliding door of the market closing means that the time to break the Ramadan fast is coming, increasing the tension in the crowd. "They're keeping us here because of a slap on the face of a dirty bum," says a man near me, alluding to the police chief's reputation as a pimp. A guy who plays on the local soccer team says: "And what if we go get Piera and give him a beating he'll remember for the rest of his life?" A militant quickly intervenes: "Take it easy, stay calm."

The crowd quiets down, silence reigns, only to be broken by the muezzin's call: "*Allahou Akbar*," God is the greatest! A murmur runs through the crowd; the siren blasts announcing the end of the fast for the day. A few people walk through the crowd and leave. With sundown the bats come out and speed across the sky. What is the tenor of their message, I wonder? Inside the building, Mohamed is with Judge Antoine, a man who does his best to stay away from the underhanded ploys of the settler population. He is reputed to be honest and upright.

"It's a provocation, sir," Mohamed explains. "By arresting Miliani, the mayor hopes to humiliate us. He wants to show the voters that their elected officials represent nothing. Piera got my dander up when he said that he only respects and obeys Monsieur Pergaud. He may owe his job to the mayor but he forgets that he's paid with the taxes of all the citizens and has to respect their elected officials."

"Is that a reason to slap him? You've gone beyond your mandate and you've put me in an embarrassing position. You should have controlled yourself and settled the problem with the mayor. I don't want any trouble, I want this village to live in peace."

"Sir, the troublemaker in the village is Pergaud. He's arrogant. He refuses any proposals we make, he threatens us with bloodshed if we question his right to rule over us."

An understanding man, close to retirement, the judge wonders what he should do. After the siren stops, he raises a corner of the window curtain to see what's happening in the street. His face turns somber. "Mohamed, go tell the demonstrators to go home."

"I'm sorry, sir, but it's not for me to do that."

"It's my job to maintain peace in the village and I don't

want to get involved in your political quarrels." He sighs, looks out the window again, and says: "Mohamed, I'll say it once more, I don't want any trouble. I beg of you: tell the people outside that."

Satisfied, Mohamed leaves the office, passes by the two gendarmes in the corridor, and opens the front door. When he appears on the steps, the crowd applauds. I jump with joy, the militants scream in Arabic and in French: "Long live Messali!" "Long live free Algeria!"

Mohamed gestures to the crowd for silence. When everyone calms down, he begins: "Thank you, thank you very much. I'm very moved!"

The cries, the clapping, start up again, more intense. Mohamed lowers his eyes, his face hardens. He raises his arms to obtain silence, clears his throat, and speaks again: "Your presence here is the proof of your solidarity, of a sense of fellowship that I shall never forget. You have just proven that together we are strong. You have shown the mayor, the colonialists of his ilk, and their masters that we are not impressed by them and that in the future they must respect us." Interrupted by shouts and applause, he raises his arms again for silence. He concludes: "Once again, thank you. I don't want to keep you any longer. Hearty appetite and leave in peace."

He remains at the door of the courthouse where the other council members, Nabi Miliani and Lakhdar Hadj Hamdi, as well as Mohamed's close friend Ali Baha, have joined him. They are smiling, satisfied, and watch the crowd disperse. I run home with the news. Seated on a cushion at the low dining table, Baba is waiting. I see that he has broken the fast with a few dates. He straightens up, listens to me, but makes no comment. A few minutes later, my other brothers arrive with Mohamed, who, embarrassed, apologizes for being late.

"Your father refused to eat," Imma says as she places the *chorba* on the table.

As usual, we are silent during dinner. Mohamed waits until the end of the meal before telling us what happened inside Judge Antoine's office. Then, in a hurry to smoke a cigarette, he gets up from the table and goes out.

Mohamed and his colleagues are organizing an evening of theater. The mayor has refused to turn over anything to do with the budget or social affairs to the MTLD representatives on the municipal council. In an effort to neutralize and diminish them in people's eyes, he puts them in charge of sports activities—activities limited to the local soccer club headed by a rich settler—and cultural activities, of which there are none.

This is the first time that a play in Arabic will have been produced in the village. The event, and the rumors that circulate about the presence of a woman in the troupe, are at the center of every conversation. The men speak in low tones about Zarga, the eighteen-year-old woman who will be acting in it. Zarga is veiled, but everyone, young and old, knows she's beautiful. It seems she goes to the rehearsals veiled and unveils for her role. Zarga is also known for having stood up to her father, a porter, when he tried to force her to marry a rich old widower. Her decision to appear in the play without the veil scandalizes everyone in the village. One night during Ramadan, I remember hearing Imma say that "Zarga is going to ruin her life"; someone else claimed that "Zarga will end up debauched." The women gossip about her at the hammam.

The third day of the Eid holiday, at eight in the evening, I'm in seventh heaven, sitting in the first row of the balcony at the theater, thanks to Basha, who convinced Imma to serve us dinner before Baba's return from the mosque. Basha was able to get tickets without asking Mohamed. With his highly developed sense of justice, Mohamed, always a stickler, would have refused and demanded that we stand in line at the box office like everyone else.

I have climbed the white marble staircase to the balcony, the place usually reserved for Europeans who arrive with their wives in long, formal gowns. They have priority at the ticket counter, thanks to the Algerian police auxiliary, who pushes the Algerians aside. They mount the staircase like nobles in their castles or princes in their palaces. Hanging onto the wooden ramp, I overlook the packed orchestra and see where my brothers are sitting. Suddenly a long, dull sound like an earthquake puts an end to the noise. Two distinct, drumlike sounds echo through the house, silencing everyone. On the third stroke, the velvet curtain opens, the movie screen has disappeared. I'm amazed to see a desolate rural scene with a hut in the back from which an old woman, a peasant in rags, appears. It's Zarga, I recognize her. Doubled over, she sweeps in front of the hut with a broom made from palm fronds and sings a sad ballad about poverty, about the son who enrolled in the French army and died in a war between Christians, far from his people, from his country.

An old man, her husband probably, wearing a torn burnous, enters and speaks with the accent, intonations, and
gestures of a peasant. The theater bursts out laughing. My
neighbors whisper the name of the actor, Hassan Bencheikh,
the barber. Later on, he'll take the stage name of Hassan El
Hassani and will be inspired by his role that night to create a
character he'll call Bou Bagra (the Man with the Cow), who
will make millions of spectators laugh.

The play tells the story of this peasant family whose
ancestors were expropriated by French settlers. The author
and director of the play is from Baba's Ouled Fergane tribe.
This is Mohamed Ferrah, who will become Mohamed Errazi
when the party and the officials on the Algiers municipal
council charge him to write plays for the Algiers opera house.
The play ends with a patriotic song sung by Zarga wearing
a long dress and surrounded by all the actors, who join in
the refrain. The personalities seated in the first row of the
orchestra, among whom I see Mohamed, applaud, standing.
The rest of the spectators follow suit. I stand up and applaud
and yell. I'm over the moon. The organizers want to schedule
the play for another evening, but the mayor refuses to give
them the hall.

The MTLD councilors create the ESMB (Berrouaghia
Muslim Sports Star), a soccer team. A few players abandon
the blue-and-white jersey of the SOB (Berrouaghia All-
Sports Association) for the green-and-white jerseys of the
new team. During training sessions, I get a kick out of seeing Mohamed wearing shin guards. Most of them have never
worn athletic shoes with spikes. The coach, Ahmed-Cherif
Slimani, left the SOB, where he was the star striker, to join

the new team. He takes his role to heart, obliges the players to run around the stadium and do gymnastic exercises before touching the ball. Watching them make these efforts, sweating it out, I think that one day they'll supplant the SOB. While awaiting the agreement of the soccer federation to be officially accredited, they organize a friendly match with a team from Boghari. There's a big crowd, the atmosphere is electric, but no incidents mar the game. The following week, however, the mayor refuses to grant the subsidy requested by the soccer association. A local grain farmer, the European president of the SOB, intervenes and gets the soccer federation to reject the request for membership of the ESMB in the third national division.

A member of a well-to-do family, a party militant, wants to open a movie house in the rue de la Gare. Only after the work on the building has been completed does the subprefecture in Medea refuse authorization for him to open, pretexting the lack of a safety exit. The owner's intention was to specialize in Egyptian films.

That summer I stop going to Koranic school; the evening recitations of the Koran stop as well. Mohamed can no longer be present because he is devoting more and more time to party meetings and activities. One evening, when I arrive at the door of the house, a man standing nearby comes up to me, says hello, and asks if I know Mohamed. He gives me his name, no doubt a pseudonym. In secret, the party has selected tried-and-true militants to be trained to form a special unit in preparation for armed struggle. That was my deduction, on learning sometime later that Mohamed had joined the OS, the Special Organization.

At school I have problems in math with algebra, whereas in all the other subjects my grades are above average. At the end of the year, the math teacher doesn't pass me, "to incite me to work on math over the summer," he says with a smile. I'm really upset but two weeks before going back to Blida, I open my math book and dig in. This time the exam goes smoothly and I pass to eighth grade. That was a warning call, however, that inspires me to study more. I apply myself, learn the lessons, and do my homework. At the end of the quarter I make the honor roll.

Home for Christmas vacation, my father shows me a bill he's received from the school's accounting office and says: "Son, business isn't good. I'll pay the money they're asking for but I won't be able to do it another time." The bill is for my boarding fees for the quarter. I'm so terrified, I choke up, I can't speak. Has my scholarship been canceled without my knowledge? Or is it an administration error? Obviously, Baba doesn't know. Maybe *'Ammi* Rabah, Larbi Saïdi's father, has received the same bill. I cross the street, find him alone, seated next to the *kânoun*. No, Rabah hasn't received a bill. He looks at my face, advises me to calm down and listen to him.

"I'm sure Pergaud, the mayor, is behind this. He detests your brother Mohamed and your family. Your father won't do what I'm going to suggest, but you have to do it because it's your future that's in question. Go see the *bachagha* of our district at the council-general's office in Algiers. He's a yesman but he has pull and would be delighted to show that he's got more influence than Pergaud. Your family would never ask him for anything, so don't tell anyone. I repeat: it's your future that's in the balance. Go see him."

Rabah tells me how to find the *bachagha*'s offices. I leave him not sure what to do, though I'm convinced he's right. Baba and Mohamed wouldn't want to owe the *bachagha* anything, for them he's a collaborator, he's sold out. Would they admit that I've suffered collateral damage because of the mayor's hatred of the nationalists? I know they wouldn't. The idea that I'll have to stop school this year, just before the exams for the middle school diploma, overwhelms me. I decide to follow '*Ammi* Rabah's advice.

At the prefecture in Algiers, seat of the council-general's office, the doorman indicates an office on the second floor. I give my name to the secretary and add "from Berrouaghia." I wait in the hall a few minutes before a man dressed like a European comes toward me smiling. In the village, the *bachagha* wears a *gandoura* and a burnous. "I'm Miloud's son, the butcher's son," I say. "I can see that." he replies. "You look like Miloud. How is your father, Basha, Mohamed?" he asks. He barely listens to my reply, asks why I've come to see him.

"I have a departmental scholarship that's just been canceled." I explain what's happened and conclude: "In my opinion, it's the mayor who's behind this."

He nods his head, gives me a steady look, at ease. "Don't worry, my son. I'll take care of it. Give my regards to your father and your brothers." He accompanies me to the end of the hall, shakes my hand, and repeats, "Don't worry, my son." Reassured by the welcome and the *bachagha*'s promise, I say to myself that "'*Ammi* Rabah is right. I shouldn't tell anyone about this."

When I arrive home for Easter, I learn the terrible news that Mohamed has been arrested. He's not alone, a large number of militants have been, too. The newspapers announce arrests throughout the country; they speak of the "nationalist conspiracy," of "a secret paramilitary organization" with, in the colonialist dailies, photos of the arms seized. *Alger Républicain*, the communist daily, calls it a conspiracy organized by Governor Naegelen and his administration to justify the repression inflicted upon the Muslim population. They call him a terrorist and I agree with them. Radical newspapers in France denounce the torture practiced systematically by the police, whom they label "the Gestapo." Those arrested are beaten and subjected to waterboarding, electrodes on their genitals, bottles in the anus, etc. The country is terror-stricken.

"Let my son sleep, he's only a child!" screams my mother.

I open my eyes and see her in the light between two men in civilian clothes, who are punching the mattress on which I'm sleeping. It's early morning. The family has been rounded up and held in my room by some gendarmes and policemen while others are searching the house. Mohamed and the vegetable grocer on the municipal council have been brought from prison and are being detained in the courtyard. Imma follows the inspectors around, shouts in Arabic at the Algerian who accompanies them, harasses the others in a kind of jargon explaining that her son hasn't done anything wrong. They take Mohamed and his companion into the garden. I don't see what they leave with.

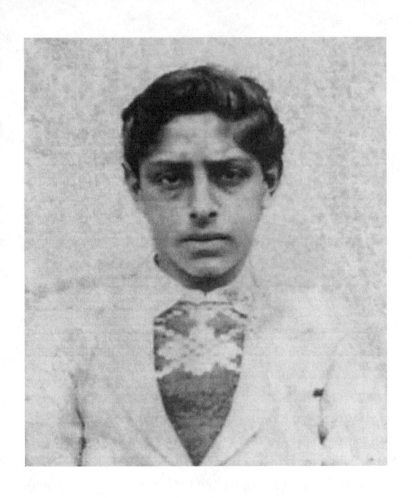

Mokhtar, fourteen years old,
at school in Blida, Algeria, 1949.

After the grocer is freed, Basha maintains he heard him, before the search, whisper, "Mohamed, tell them where it is."

Was he afraid of being tortured again? Was he more compliant with the party's rules? Because the party had issued orders to its leaders to take total responsibility for any actions in order to save and free the largest number possible of members of the Special Organization. I am sure that Mohamed's reticence was due to the oath he had sworn on the Koran to never reveal his activities within the OS. His faith forbids him to betray his oath.

I leave for school, my family in disarray not knowing where my brother has been imprisoned. The only person I tell about Mohamed's arrest is my close school friend Mohand Silhadi.

I begin to wonder what France's "civilizing mission" is really about. It deprived my parents of an education. We're six brothers and I'm the only one going to secondary school. It destroyed our culture in order to replace it with theirs. While it's undoubtedly a privilege to be in school, but lacking a bilingual education, I have the feeling that I've been amputated of part of myself. My Arabic is weak, I can't hold a conversation on my favorite subjects, the books I read, the poetry I love, my inner thoughts and turmoil, my gradual discovery of who I am...I feel mutilated, bouncing back and forth between the traditional family, the village, and my life at the school and in the city. I'm discovering how complex the question of modernity versus tradition is. I know it's not about the clothes you wear, your appearance. Evolution concerns the very essence of oneself. At school, I develop and assume a variety of personalities. I see that the habits, the beliefs, the way of thinking and acting acquired in my original environment are eroding. I'm "Frenchicizing," one might say. I have to sort out what represents progress and what tends to depersonalize me, what in fact negates centuries of history.

History, after all, is written by the victors and contains a multitude of lies and distortions. Since I started school I've been learning the names of monarchs, emperors, generals, and valorous French heroes. My head is full of dates, battles, and great achievements. Have I ever heard mention of the fact that the Europe of Charlemagne survived in darkness at a time when a brilliant civilization was resplendent in Spain and the Arab-Muslim world? The power, the grandeur, the beauty, the superiority of France is what is being inculcated, the supremacy of the conqueror.

On the other hand, I appreciate the values I'm taught: *liberté, égalité, fraternité*, universal suffrage, human rights. In mathematics, natural science, physics, chemistry, I want to learn and progress. I love the French language, the great poets and novelists, I want to be a writer. I've abandoned my adolescent dream of becoming a teacher in a French provincial village where I'd be respected like Monsieur Colin. There is an entry in my personal journal now that declaims: "I want to be Victor Hugo."

Alongside this tendency to become more French, there is the battle being waged by my brother. The injustice of his situation is monumental. In my relations with others, I filter my behavior. I have become flexible, judging each situation on its own. I don't talk about Mohamed; I've adopted self-censorship. I avoid political discussions with my European friends. When I bring up the question of nationalism with Algerians, I run up against their desire to remain apolitical, to escape, to condemn my positions or remain indifferent. Like me, they are the products of their education, of the ideas received within their families and their social environment. Most of them come from families dependent on the French administration. The generation of their elders has long sought assimilation, has proclaimed its attachment to France and vaunted the advantages of colonization.

Just before Easter vacation, Baba comes to see me at school. My parents are going to visit Mohamed, who's been incarcerated in Blida.

At the end of the school year, I pass the *brevet*, the middle school exam. My father smiles and says solemnly: "That's good, my son." When one of his customers reads my name in the *Journal d'Alger* in an article entitled "Successful Laureates" and congratulates Baba, he says: "I hear your name was in the paper. What's this exam?" "It's a diploma that gives me the right to work in the administration or to enter teacher training school." My explanation seems to please him. To celebrate the event, he has me order a cup of coffee and a glass of mint tea at the café. After the first sip, he admits, "I hadn't realized your exam was so important."

The next time my parents go to see Mohamed in Blida, I accompany them. While waiting outside the prison door, Imma goes over to a woman she met on the previous visit who is accompanied by the prisoner's uncle. When the door opens and a guard calls our name, he also yells out "Ben Bella," the prisoner the others have come to visit. The guard takes us into a tiny room separated by two long metal grilles, in between which is a space about a yard wide. The wait is endless. Finally, Mohamed and Ahmed Ben Bella are brought in.

Well dressed, clean shaven, my brother is smiling, happy to see us. His hands on the grille, his arms wide open as though to embrace us, he asks how everyone is, he congratulates me on the middle school diploma. "Imma," he says, "I want you to give my watch and my signet ring to Mokhtar. They're my gift to him." He asks Baba how business is. "The boys take care of the shop. I go to the markets in Boghari and Laghouat and buy sheep that I sell in Boufarik and Algiers."

When Mohamed inquires about his sons, Brahim and Khaled, Imma breaks out in tears, and choked up says: "They're well. They miss you." Embarrassed, Mohamed begs Imma not to cry, adding: "Don't forget, I'm here for a noble cause." My father says nothing, he knows she's inconsolable. Suddenly, Ben Bella moves in front of us and displaying intense irritation, says in a strident tone: "Mother, stop crying. You've come here to encourage us to resist, not to deflate us." Mohamed pokes him in the ribs, he moves away. Imma stops sniffling but gets in the last word: "You can't know how much your mothers and wives suffer knowing you're here." Mohamed shakes his head, lowers his eyes. He gestures toward me and reminds Imma: "Don't forget the ring and the watch for Mokhtar."

The guard announces: "Time is up. The visit is over."

One day, while talking to my friend Abdelkader Boukhari on his doorstep, the new priest in the village approaches us. The parsonage is just across the street. The man in the long priest's robe introduces himself: Father Delahaye. We exchange a few words and he invites us over for tea.

Father Delahaye is from Brittany, is friendly, happy to be in Algeria. He lends us two books: *Cry, the Beloved Country*, by Alan Paton, about Blacks in South Africa; and *The Mother*, by Pearl Buck, about China. These are the point of departure of our relationship. He tells us that the parish clubhouse is not reserved for Europeans: "You can meet other young people there, establish more open relationships. I believe that new ties are possible among the youth."

The enthusiasm with which he develops his idea is contagious. Our arrival in their midst surprises everyone, including two boys playing Ping-Pong, who stop briefly and stare. I keep a smile on my face and greet some former primary school classmates. I've played a little Ping-Pong in Blida at the café Tabarin, so I watch the game and congratulate the winner. "Want to play?" he asks. "Here's a racket." "I don't play well," I answer. "It doesn't matter, practice makes perfect." I lose, which seems to delight Abdelkader. I enjoy the visit and think I'll go back another time.

In midsummer Father Delahaye organizes an excursion to Tikjda, a mountain resort in Kabylia. Abdelkader and I are invited; we'll leave from the parsonage at six in the morning. As soon as we board the bus, I realize that our presence is embarrassing, a number of heads look down or turn away. I greet those who look my way, some nod in reply, some not. I sit down next to Abdelkader. The bus takes the road through the grain fields and sheep pastures of the Beni Slimane plain. After Bouira, the road rises and serpentines up to Tikjda at 1500 meters in the middle of a forest of majestic cedars. The view from here over the Djudjura Mountains is splendid. We picnic, the atmosphere is gay. Father Delahaye circulates among the little groups, he spends time with Abdelkader and me. On the way back, we are again seated alone, while the others are bursting with energy and excitement. Songs break out, among them one notably racist, about an Algerian scrub woman, and one a patriotic song about the French conquest of Algeria...

When we see Father Delahaye the following week, I understand, from the way he lowers his eyes and crosses and uncrosses his fingers, how sorry he is, how much our experience pains him. "But I'm not pessimistic," he tells us. "In my part of France, we are known for being patient and stubborn."

Father Delahaye comes up with another scheme a few days later. It concerns the Garnier family, whose wheat fields and vineyards extend as far as the eye can see to the south and east of the village. The stadium, the hospital, the municipal jail, the Christian and Jewish cemeteries are all located on land that was theirs.

I listen to the priest speak of their generosity and smile. I don't mention the scene I once witnessed at the butcher shop. One day Baba prepared a rack of lamb *à la parisienne*, as Madame Garnier requested. He weighed the meat and announced the price. Dressed all in black, her face gaunt, she snapped, "It's too expensive." Slowly, my father withdrew the meat from the scale and, pointing to the door, said: "Go somewhere else, somewhere where it costs less." Speechless and petrified, Madame Garnier remained planted in the same spot. Baba turned his back to her and placed the meat on a porcelain tray that held some cutlets. When she realized that he was putting the meat away, she came to and said: "Now, Miloud, I didn't want to make you angry. Give me the cutlets." In response my father ignored her and began cutting a shoulder of veal. She left without her rack of lamb, and came back several days later as though nothing had occurred.

Father Delahaye tells us that this same lady has invited us to meet for coffee with her grandchildren, who live in Algiers and are here on vacation. They were not present on the excursion to Tikjda, even though they attend church. There is a line of demarcation among the parishioners, and Father Delahaye probably feels that it will be easier to establish relationships between us and the families of those considered "real" Frenchmen, those originally from France, the local elite. He feels they are more open-minded. We accept the invitation.

Located at the edge of the village, the house and the farm are surrounded by a never-ending stone wall. Two gates protect the entrances. At five in the afternoon, Abdelkader and I enter through the gate for farm vehicles and deliveries. We have been announced, and Madame Garnier is waiting for us on the veranda. "I know you," she says, extending her hand to me, "but not your first name." The grandchildren appear. The young man, wearing riding boots and jodhpurs, doesn't come inside with us. The two sisters, dressed in pretty flowery dresses, provide a happy note to the dreary atmosphere in the living room. Full of antique furniture, paintings, and objects of all sorts, the scene reminds me of films set in aristocratic homes. The way the young girls sort of curtsy before extending their hands also reminds me of stilted manners from old movies.

I've often seen the girls in town, even in the butcher shop when they accompany their grandmother, but we've never exchanged a word, not that I wouldn't have wanted to. Abdelkader and I have often watched them go by. Both of us find the younger the prettier. She's sixteen, has a curvy body and a sexy way of swinging her hips, and seems less stuck-up than her sister. Her face is round, her eyes are big and bright, her hair dark and curly. She smiles naturally. The older sister is eighteen and almost as tall as me. She has an angular face, squints, and lacks the spontaneity of her sister. She greets me as though she's never seen me before, whereas the younger girl seems happy to finally be able to talk to me. The grandmother asks us about our studies, our pastimes.

"I like to read," I say. "Father Delahaye lent us two fascinating books, *Cry, the Beloved Country*, and *The Mother*, by Pearl Buck, which takes place in China."

She wrinkles her nose and nods her head: "That doesn't surprise me. He's such a dreamer. But he's also a music lover. Have you listened to music with him?" When I say no, she seems surprised and says: "Do you like classical music?"

"I've rarely had a chance to listen to it," I reply.

Her grandson having just entered, without his riding boots, she asks him to put on a record of classical music. It's a pleasant revelation for me and I tell her so, adding that my favorite instruments are the lute and the cithara.

"I admit I've never listened to Arab music except in passing in front of a Moorish café," the grandmother comments. I offer to bring some records of Farid Al Atrache, the Egyptian singer, the next time we meet.

On the third visit, Madame Garnier begins the conversation by asking if we are practicing Muslims. "You know," she says, "the mosque was built by France." I don't mention the rumor in the village that the architects didn't respect the rules concerning the direction of the mihrab toward Mecca.

"And your opinion on the relationship between men and women?" she asks.

"I'm not counting on my mother to select a wife for me. I don't care where she comes from or the religion of my future wife, what matters is that we love each other."

Abdelkader says something similar, after which she turns to her granddaughters and says: "What a success! These young men are the personification of the success of France's civilizing mission." I nearly fall off my chair, Abdelkader too. We look at each other. The girls smile.

Satisfied with her observation, Madame Garnier looks straight at me and states: "I don't see what you can hold against France."

I smile, shrug my shoulders, and reply: "Nothing, except that you've taught us your motto *liberté, égalité, fraternité*, but have made sure that neither of us can ever hope to be mayor of this village."

Her face hardens. "I haven't invited you here to talk politics."

"It wasn't my intention," I reply. A few minutes later, we say goodbye and leave.

When I tell Father Delahaye about our experience, he closes his eyes and shakes his head. I assure him that neither the excursion nor this incident affects our relationship.

"I'm grateful to you," he says. "Often, in my prayers I thank the Lord for directing me toward the two of you. I've learned, I've discovered so much from our contact."

"The same is true for us," I say.

A number of changes take place the following year, in tenth grade. In study hall, each student has his own desk with a rack for books and papers on the side. Our courtyard is larger, we can play soccer, can even smoke in the corner near the toilets. New Algerian faces arrive from another primary school. They are day students, sons of grocers, bakers, tailors, barbers, even the son of the imam, and are less snobbish than those I've been seeing for the last four years. However, they have some of the same prejudices: for them, southerners are gross, brutal, lack refinement. And like the others, they are for assimilation, are not ready to contest the established order.

The lack of interest they display when I mention anything political has one advantage, I can avoid talking about the trial that's taking place in a courtroom in Blida. Starting in January 1952, there are daily headlines about "the trial of the Blida fifty-six," which include my brother Mohamed and other members of the Special Organization. Six well-known lawyers from Paris are defending them. According to the press, letters, telegrams, and petitions addressed to the court are arriving from all over Algeria, from France, even from

Egypt, calling for justice for the accused. Albert Camus has written to the head of the tribunal: "France's cause in this country, if it wants to make sense and have a future here, can only be that of absolute justice..." A number of well-known men and women from France appear in court on the defendants' behalf. Claude Bourdet, a famous resistant and the director of the weekly *France Observateur*, begins his article on the trial: "Is there a Gestapo in Algeria?"

The defendants are accused of "aggression against the State and being members of a criminal association" as well as "breaching State security." They plead not guilty and announce that their confessions were extracted under torture. They denounce the barbarity of police methods and use the trial as a public tribunal to proclaim their determination to fight for the independence of their country. To stifle their voices, the court orders that the trial take place behind closed doors. It lasts two months. Mohamed is sentenced to four years in prison, five years of village confinement, and ten years of loss of civil rights. Ben Bella, sentenced to seven years, escapes from prison a few days later with another prisoner. He had defied the court by stating during the trial that he would not finish his sentence behind bars!

The escape is thrilling. Silhadi and I share our excitement with Mahieddine Titteri, our eternal table captain in the dining hall. Titteri began by telling me that his uncle was in the party, the MTLD, in Boghari, and then slipped me a copy of the clandestine party newspaper *l'Algérie libre*. Silhadi and I read it closeted in the dorm toilet.

Mokhtar (standing, third from left) with his philosophy class at the Lycée Duveyrier, Blida, Algeria, 1953.

Monsieur Thiers, the French professor, has instilled me with the desire to read. He devotes recreation periods to distributing and collecting books stored in a locked glass cabinet. As I never know what to choose, he advises me and I'm rarely disappointed. I discover Montesquieu, Voltaire, Rousseau, and others. I find it difficult to say which philosopher I prefer. I'm attracted by their attitudes on the obscurantism and absolutism of religion, their denunciation of injustice and lack of freedom. I admire Rousseau's thoughts developed in *The Social Contract* and adhere immediately to the idea that we are born free and equal, that we are naturally good but are transformed by society. His demonstration of man's evolution from a primitive state to a society of citizens, after passing through periods of slavery and bondage, I find convincing. Rousseau keeps me company on Sunday afternoons in the Bizot Gardens. I read *Reveries of a Solitary Walker* instead of going to the movies or the soccer match or visiting the women in the reserved quarter. I'm drowning in romanticism, even melancholy. I drift toward the poets: Baudelaire, Verlaine, Alfred de Vigny. I go through a phase of questioning life and my inner self and, more painful, I find myself at sea between the traditions of the society from which I hail and the one I'm called to join.

And I keep growing, my pants are always too short and the kidding I get from my classmates is annoying. My height, though, is not only a source of mockery. In boxing, I have a long reach that I use to keep my opponent at a distance and execute repeated jabs. I'm good at long jumps and high-jumping; I run fast. I play soccer and basketball in the courtyard. And I take part in a new sport, handball, joining the school team.

I've had a series of female correspondents: first Josette from France, then Annie, also French, and Christina from Vienna. This year I've been corresponding with Adelaide, she's Tahitian from Papeete. In the photo she sent me, a large, white flower is entwined in her dark hair. I find the machine photo I took too somber, not flattering enough, so I send her the picture of a friend who resembles me somewhat. As with my former correspondents, I tell Adelaide that I like classical music, Arab music, and the theater. She writes often and talks about herself easily, about what she's doing. Her spontaneity in describing her feelings is both naive and wonderful. I love reading her letters but am incapable of communicating with the same freedom and trust. I try to be interesting but I'm well aware that my letters are a laborious exercise of imagination and style. I invent facts and situations that I try to make dramatic or funny, states of mind that are the pretext for quoting the titles, the authors, and the poems I like. When she writes to say that sailors from New Caledonia stop in Papeete every two weeks and want to date her, I become insanely jealous, send her a spiteful letter, and break off.

At the end of April 1952, we learn that Messali Hadj, the nationalist leader, will visit Blida on a Sunday. Titteri, Silhadi, and I decide to welcome him on behalf of high school students. We run the risk of being arrested or thrown out of school, but that seems minor compared to the honor of approaching the *zaïm*. I remember when he visited Berrouaghia, the enthusiasm of the crowd was incredible. His speech was interrupted by fervent cries of "Long live Messali!" The frenzy was such that my brother Basha jumped from the balcony screaming "Messali!" Our main concern is how to address him and if we should kiss his hand, his forehead, or his shoulder, since he wears a fez. We decide that Titteri should leave school at eight in the morning and go see the organizers to find out what the protocol is. Silhadi and I will leave at 11:30 and meet him at the Place d'Armes.

"We have to buy a bouquet of flowers," Titteri reports.

Silhadi and I break out laughing. "You're kidding, no?" Titteri insists.

"A bouquet of flowers, for what?" I say.

"They say if we want to see the *zaïm*, it's a must. It's the tradition."

We realize that he's not kidding. I say nothing for a moment, wonder what it means. "Who are 'they'?" I ask. "I thought you offer a bouquet to women, not to men." I'm getting annoyed. I can't believe that Messali demands that we offer him flowers. "Did they give you the money to pay for them?" I ask.

Silhadi laughs with approval, since we both know that Titteri is always broke. I refuse to spend money on flowers, to admit that the party has introduced a practice that has nothing to do with our traditions. If someone wants to pay for the flowers, I'm not against taking part in the delegation. Titteri says he's flat broke. I get the feeling that our enthusiasm is waning and suggest: "We give up the idea?" They both nod yes. Since we can't go back to school for lunch, Silhadi and I invite Titteri to a restaurant in the "native" quarter.

On May 24, Messali Hadj speaks in Orléansville in central Algeria. The police fire into the crowd, leaving two dead and several wounded. Many arrests are made. The authorities impose martial law, arrest Messali, and take him to France, where he's placed under house detention. I don't regret not having bought him a bouquet of flowers, but I'm nonetheless sad. I admire his determination in fighting for an ideal for his people. He's of a different breed from the leaders of the other parties and organizations.

I pass my exams and enter my junior year. And best yet, Smaïn Bendifallah invites me to go camping at the seaside during summer vacation. Smaïn, who's two years older than me, arrived at Duveyrier last year; he's a boarding student, a very nice guy, good-looking with large dark eyes, light skin, and a mop of thick hair. His back teeth are capped with silver. He's as tall as me but seems more adult, more sure of himself. He jokes about his father, a Muslim judge who's raised eleven children, has a waxed mustache, and travels around town on a bike. Everyone calls him "Uncle."

Smaïn has a series of brothers; the oldest is a lawyer and the one we're going camping with is in the police. Smaïn meets me at the bus stop and the next day, as in a dream, I discover the beach at Fort-de-l'Eau with Ahcene, his brother, and Laguel, a soccer player friend. The beach is wonderful: just a few umbrellas along the extended sandy expanse between a row of villas and the sea. I'm the last one to put on my bathing suit and finish by admitting that I don't swim well.

"The way to learn to swim is to throw yourself into the water," says Ahcene with his slight Berber accent. "Don't worry, you have three strong swimmers around you." I watch them and want to do the same. I swim out to a rock where Laguel has caught a baby octopus, something I've never seen before. He holds it up to show us and then bangs its tentacles against the rock. Smaïn gathers mussels underwater. Ahcene joins me on the rock. I ask him where Verte-Rive is located. "It's a crowded beach, not as clean as here but not far." I ask because my friend Roger Fernandez lives there. Two years ago, he invited me to his house during the summer. His parents own a bar and have a place on the beach. If I didn't go it's because my mother was absolutely opposed to it and said: "You don't go to people's houses if you don't know their parents." I showed her the postcard Roger had sent me confirming his parents' invitation and translate it for her. She then spits out her obsession: "They're going to make you eat pork!" I say to myself that before leaving the seaside, I'll stop and see Roger. He'll be surprised.

I watch Smaïn and Laguel dive in and out of the water. Cautious, I make my way to solid ground and simply enjoy being there. Little by little, the parasols disappear, the color of the water darkens, and the bright red sun fades behind the horizon. Smaïn and Laguel suggest we run along the beach. I take in the sights, the architecture of the fancy houses, the exotic plants. Then I help set up the tent, lay out a carpet and the utensils, while the others light the little gas-cooker to heat the stew their mother has prepared for us. I'm amazed by the relationship between Smaïn and his brother, they're so much more familiar with each other than I am with my brothers. I laugh outright when they tell stories about their hometown in Kabylia.

When I wake in the morning and come out of the tent, I'm overwhelmed by the beauty of it all. Like a sleepwalker, I advance toward the water and contemplate the day breaking, measure the immensity of the horizon as it meets the sky. Seagulls break the silence with their screams. Ahcene is coming toward me with a fishing rod in his hand. "I got up early," he says. "but the fish are avoiding me for now."

Ahcene is twice my age, thirty-five, but his sunken cheeks and wrinkled forehead make him look older. He looks toward the tent and sees Smaïn and Laguel straightening the carpet. He runs over to tell them to take the tent down. "We don't want anything to be seen during the day!" he yells at them. Laughing, Laguel says: "You're afraid we'll be taken for Arabs?"

Ahcene begins dismantling the tent and we make everything look as it did when we arrived. The good humor returns, we drink the coffee Smaïn has prepared with croissants that Laguel has bought. The morning air, the blue sky, are soothing. I walk along the sand, dangle my feet in the water, watch my companions wading in the calm, flat sea. Suddenly Smaïn's calls interrupt my reverie; he gestures to Ahcene to look toward the beach. I turn around and see two cops tapping our baggage with their feet. Laguel comes up to me, sees that I'm concerned: "It's nothing. Ahcene will talk to them and we'll be okay. He's a colleague of theirs, after all. He's on vacation, if not he'd be in uniform."

Ahcene rummages through our stuff and takes out some papers that he displays. It seems they're not impressed because we can see him insisting; he walks a few steps with them. They leave. As soon as they turn their backs on us, he gestures with the papers as though to throw them away and comes toward us, his face crestfallen. Furious, he swears in Berber and says softly: "We have to go."

I can't believe my ears. Laguel and Smaïn say they don't understand. Ahcene tells us that his colleagues had come to take us to the police station and charge us. When they heard of his job, they said just get out of here, because if we stay we're breaking the law. They said they'd be back in an hour and if they find us here, they'll take us in and seize the tent and the rest. They'll accuse us of noise and drunkenness.

And so ends our escapade!

On the way back to Berrouaghia, an idea awakens in my head: to open a class for school kids to improve their math and language skills. Abdelkader Boukhari and I will use our garage in which Basha, since he's opened the bicycle shop, no longer prepares snacks to sell outside one of the cafés. We borrow some tables and benches from Abdelkader's father and begin our courses for kids from our respective neighborhoods. The waiter at the café, from the same tribe as the Boukharis, the Beni 'Affou, is delighted. During the school year, his son and the youngsters from their tribe come to school on foot from miles away. A week later, we have a dozen boys including the waiter's son and two others from Beni 'Affou. We give each one a notebook with the multiplication table printed on the inside cover, a pencil, and an eraser. Abdelkader teaches them math; I'm in charge of the language lessons. The experience is an education for us. We agree to speak only French in class. Some of the kids address me with the same words of respect as those used in Koranic school. I make an effort to enunciate clearly.

On the junior handball team, I play right wing. The local newspaper *Le Tell* publishes a photo of the spectacular goal I make during the qualification match for the North African School and University Games. We beat the team from Algiers. Our junior soccer team is also qualified. A winning basketball team from the local girls' high school will also take part in the trip to Rabat (Morocco), where the games are to take place.

As part of our physical and psychological preparation, the gym teachers organize an outing for the two boys' teams in the Mahelma forest. After a morning running through the woods and doing exercises in a clearing, we join the soccer players for a giant picnic on the grass. Two *méchouis* are on the menu. The lambs, the personnel, and the instruments for roasting them on spits are the gift of a *caïd* from the High Plateau region, father of a member of the soccer team. A settler has a container of wine and crates of oranges and tangerines delivered. Cold cuts, various local products, and cheeses complete the meal. When the men roasting the sheep have finished and withdraw, the European comrades smile and raise their eyebrows as if to ask how to get meat onto their plates. The teachers improvise a procedure with their knives, cutting strips off the gigots. Instinctively the five Algerian players and I dig in with our fingers. Little by little the others do likewise.

After the feast and a lot of laughter and singing, some lie down for a nap. I join my four Algerian teammates and go for a ride in Algiers in the *caïd*'s car.

Because of gigantic demonstrations taking place in the major Moroccan cities, the games are canceled. The protests have been organized by Istiqlal, the nationalist party, in support of Sultan Sidi Mohamed Ben Youcef, who is demanding that the protectorate treaty imposed by the French government in 1912 be revised. Demonstrations also break out in Tunisia, where, in December, the French secret police assassinated Ferhat Hached, a leading trade unionist.

Finally, the games take place during Easter vacation in Sidi Bel Abbes, a small Algerian city near Oran and headquarters to the French Foreign Legion. Our handball team manages to qualify for the final against the team from Meknes (Morocco), and we play in front of an appreciable crowd. Meknes leads at halftime, 6–0. The final score: 11 to 1. A disaster!

The last night, in the courtyard of the school where we're housed, a comrade and I meet a group of Tunisians in their red-and-white training outfits, their national colors. I ask what sport they practice and then try to find out what's happening politically in their country. They clam up. In an attempt to cool it, I raise my fist and yell in Arabic "Long live independent Tunisia!" They laugh and go their way. The comrade thinks I'm crazy.

After the games and Easter vacation, I delve into my books and study math for the final. I skip a number of chapters and select a few questions that I learn by heart. They do not come up on the exam and the problem is a tough one. I fail, but have enough points otherwise to pass in October.

The family doesn't comment on my failure; not that they're indifferent, they just don't know what to do to help. They're proud of me, I remain for them the little brother they love and whom they admire for his high level of education. My brother Mustafa stopped school after a year at the Zitouna in Tunis. He's working in the butcher shop and is a dedicated member of the local soccer team, along with my friend Abdelkader Boukhari, who works at the town hall. At the end of July, I open my math books and start studying. The only good writing table in the house is in my parents' room, but because of the noise, the comings and goings, and the torrid heat, I go out on the patio after dinner to study. Thanks to Smaïn Bendifallah, I've discovered Maxiton, a stimulant that I dope myself with and that leaves me with a feeling of deep lassitude.

For my last year I choose to major in philosophy, because I have a new dream: I'll become a lawyer and defend the nationalists undergoing repression and, of course, widows and orphans. With the professor's help, I discover the Greeks: Plato, Aristotle, Socrates. I delve into ancient Greek history, the gods and the myths. Descartes's *Discourse on Method*, recommended by the professor, is not easy. I'm disoriented and my dissertation on "I think, therefore I am" is a fiasco.

Philosophical dissertations have always been difficult for me. Already in primary school, I conceived of essay writing as an exercise in imagining situations and objects to talk about and describe. The unforgettable example was the subject "Describe Your Christmas Eve." The teacher knew we were Muslim, so we had to invent and lie and take inspiration from the class reader. I was especially proud of my good essay. At Duveyrier I adapted when writing essays by inventing and seemingly implicating myself. It's more difficult, however, with literary and philosophical subject matter.

I'm enchanted with the easy atmosphere Professor Charlety creates. He arrives in the morning with *Alger Républicain* under his arm. A redhead with a fair complexion, he's very relaxed, tells some amusing anecdotes. He grades severely, however, rarely going above 12 on a scale of 20. I hit the median. I love listening to him: with simple words he explains concepts, theories, and the most complex currents of thought. I appreciate the way he brushes aside with humor supernationalism and other extreme views. His manner of pinpointing an action, the basic reasoning of a trend of thought, is fascinating. I read as I've never read, with a tremendous desire to make up for my ignorance.

On Sundays, I go to soccer matches or to the movies and meet my buddies in a café near the "native" market. We play cards to see who'll pay for the drinks. When I have enough money I go around to the red-light district. As exams approach I realize that I haven't opened a natural science textbook. The professor is decidedly racist and the manual gives me indigestion. I choose a few questions to study in the hope they'll come up on the exam; they don't and I fail.

Back home for vacation, I find my brother Mohamed. His four years in prison have aged him. He's thirty-one but looks fifty. I find him silent, disturbed. Perhaps it's because of the confusion in the party. Messali wants to be elected president for life with full powers, but the central committee doesn't agree. The members occupy the party headquarters and take over the newspaper *l'Algérie libre*.

Part Two   AWAKENING

Cherif and Mustafa have been running the butcher shop for the last four years. When Mohamed is offered a business partnership in a butcher shop with an apartment in Boufarik, he jumps at the chance. Rezkia and their two boys join him after Basha's wedding in August.

Cherif surprises me with pocket money for a trip to Algiers: "Have some fun," he says. When he was my age, he dreamed of moving out, of doing something different, not working in the butcher shop. Baba had him apprentice with the local barber but what he really wanted was to take off. He found on-the-job training as a mason near Algiers, then moved to Casablanca. A few months later he was back. He missed the family.

In Algiers I find a hotel in the rue de Malte between the Casbah and the European city. Walking around the business streets of the European quarter, I see few Algerians, the rare veiled women look like cleaning women. Farther on, I feel too much out of my element. I take the trolley to the upper neighborhoods and out toward the sea. The passengers are a mixed crowd and the atmosphere is more congenial. Just below the Casbah, around Government Square, known as Horse Square because of the statue of the Duke of Orléans on horseback, the crowd looks more like me. There are vendors and people going back and forth to the three mosques that surround it.

I like the square, especially at sundown, and buy myself meat on skewers and lamb sausage snacks. I have lunch in the lower Casbah in a restaurant where the cooking resembles home with a menu that changes daily and often includes my favorite dishes. For the first time, I succeed in entering a brothel reserved for Europeans, La Lune. The women circulate in panties and bras, approach the men in a central patio. I agree to follow the first one who speaks to me. She washes me and asks, "Are you Jewish?" I laugh and deflect the question by asking where she's from. "I'm from Brittany," she says.

I move to a cheaper hotel in the lower Casbah and realize that the Casbah is not the cutthroat quarter that people who have never been there think. I walk through the market and the surrounding streets. I see some militants distributing tracts and learn that there's been a party congress and that the central committee has dethroned Messali. However, his supporters have held a congress of their own in Belgium and have elected him president for life and excluded the members of the central committee. They are referred to as Messalists and centralists.

Back in Berrouaghia, I find the militants in a state of incomprehension. The chickpea vendor and the perfumer, aware that I've been in Algiers, question me. They are illiterate and are impressed when I tell them that tracts are distributed in full daylight near the party headquarters. They count on me to inform them about a conflict that I don't understand that well myself. "It's normal that Messali retain the position of president," says the perfumer. "He founded the party, he was the first nationalist, and is persecuted by the colonialists because of that."

I reply that "becoming president, with full powers for life, equals dictatorship. The party will no longer be a movement for the triumph of democratic freedoms. A central committee freely elected by the militants is a must."

"That's the kind of thinking of people who have too much education and whose parents work in the administration or who are rich," the perfumer comments.

"But the party needs people who have knowledge and can think," I counter. "Excluding the centralists, who are for the most part educated men, risks pushing people to join Ferhat Abbas's organization or the Communist Party."

The house resembles a beehive. The women are preparing for Basha's wedding. Imma has obtained the hand of a young woman from Medea, thus satisfying her bourgeois prejudices, according to which city girls are more refined than the young women from the village. Medea, her hometown, and Halfadji, her Turkish-sounding family name, are the backbone on which Imma's preconceived ideas rest. A long procession of cars filled with women brings the bride into town. It advances slowly through the village, calling attention to the event with horns blowing and the women's ululations and chants. In the evening, it seems like every young person in the village is at our house. The Korteby brothers' orchestra and Basha's friends create an extraordinary atmosphere throughout the evening and again at the luncheon the next day.

The festive atmosphere seems even to have marked our next-door European neighbors. The Algerian house attendant of the wealthy settler asks if the settler's two girls may attend the celebrations on the third day reserved for women. Surprised, I appreciate the initiative of their parents; I imagine that Father Jean-Claude Barthez, who is replacing Father Delahaye for the month of August, has something to do with their coming. Father Barthez, a worker priest who belongs to the French Mission, is about thirty years old and speaks with the charming singsong accent of the South of France. He's athletic and plays tennis with a settler's wife. He lives in the suburbs of Algiers and is a member of a social action association that brings together people from different origins, including Scouts and students. According to Father Barthez, when young Christians, Muslims, and Jews come together and get to know each other they will eliminate prejudice, the objective being to show that cohabitation in a spirit of friendship is possible, that new relationships can be established among the younger generations for a more harmonious future life. I attribute the initiative of the neighbors to the young priest's influence, for I often see the members of that family in the street but have never exchanged a word with any of them.

Monique and Danièle are fifteen and thirteen years old. Happy to welcome them, my mother compliments them on their good looks. She takes advantage of the event to employ the few French expressions she knows. Their eyes wide open but totally silent, the girls are decidedly intimidated; this is the first time they've entered an Algerian home. They look awestruck on seeing the richly dressed guests. They, too, are objects of curiosity of the women present. I take a photo of them with the bride, they smile but show no reaction, say nothing, ask no questions. I only understand their stiffness and relative indifference when the Algerian attendant tells me that it was his wife's idea to induce them to come.

I see Father Barthez around and introduce him to Mohamed Nabi, a high school student from Algiers who spends his summer vacations in Berrouaghia. His family lives in the village but he's grown up in Algiers at his grandfather's, a former docker. Mohamed is a child of the Casbah and if he wasn't forced to come spend time with his father, he would certainly pass the summer at the old harbor in Algiers diving from the high concrete blocks into the water and gathering mussels. His father lives in the passage across from our neighbor's wine cellar. One of his uncles was elected to the municipal council at the same time as my brother Mohamed, he's the man who was provoked by the police chief Piera.

On September 9, an earthquake whose epicenter is in Orléansville devastates the village of Sidi Rached and leaves 1,450 dead. People in our village claim they felt the aftereffects. The centralists have created a new newspaper, *La Nation algérienne*, but I haven't seen it in the village. I hear that they have organized a new grouping, the Revolutionary

Committee for Unity and Action (CRUA), with a view to reconciling Messalists and centralists before taking action. They've published a bulletin called *Le Patriote*, but it, too, has not been distributed in the village.

For the first time since I've been at Duveyrier I have to retake a class and, surprisingly, it doesn't particularly affect me, maybe because this is my eighth and last year here. I have a seat in a study hall with no surveillance, frequented by a few junior and senior boarding students, for the most part Algerians. They're majoring in science or mathematics, their intention being to go on to college and become pharmacists, dentists, or engineers. In the courtyard I discuss and debate with the Algerian comrades about the emancipation of women and about religion, subjects that fascinate us. I read *Vocation de l'islam* by Malek Bennabi, and reject the opinion of the comrade who lent me the book as to the concept of colonizability. "If we are colonial subjects," he maintains, "it's because we're 'colonizable.'"

"I accept Bennabi's description of the causes of our society's backwardness but not that notion, it's self-deprecating. Look at the fight the Tunisian and Moroccan patriots are waging."

He replies: "Personally I'm against the recourse to violence."

"You're what I call a soft nationalist," I say, disgusted.

Monday, November 1, All Saints' Day, is a holiday. Many of the boarding students take the long weekend off and go home. After lunch, I go out with Ahmed Saoula, who is in the same study hall as me. I like his spontaneity, his frankness and gaiety, and his accent from the High Plateau region. We take a walk around town and then meet some friends at a café near the "native" market. Saoula doesn't like to play cards, so we join in a game of dominos and listen to Arab music.

The following morning, on taking my seat in the philosophy class, I see, just before Charlety folds the newspaper, the headline all across the front of *Alger Républicain*: "Armed attacks throughout Algeria." I can't believe it. I'm thunderstruck, I'm incapable of following what Charlety is saying. I spend the hour staring at the briefcase in which he's hidden the paper. So many questions cross my mind: Who's behind the armed attacks? Algerians? From which organization? I figure that attacks all across the country can only be the work of Messalists, of Messali. Few of the day students have heard the news and those who have don't know any more than I do.

After lunch I see Aït Zaouch, a surveillant I was talking to a few days earlier in the courtyard, who was reading a book called *Kaputt*. I asked him whether he read German. "It's translated from Italian," he replied. "The author is a man named Malaparte, who was a member of the Fascist Party and then spent several years in prison for criticizing Mussolini, and has since become a communist."

Aït Zaouch has read *Alger Républicain*. "The police station in Khenchela, my hometown, was attacked," he tells me.

"I think some other places were hit," I add.

"There were three bombs at Radio Algeria, fires broke out in a cork storage plant in Azazga, at the paper warehouses in Baba Ali and the citrus fruit cooperative in Boufarik. In all, seven people were killed."

"Who's behind all that?" I ask. The newspaper says they're some provocateurs, adventurers. "Do you think it's Messali's people?"

"I have no idea, but I've always known that groups of guerrillas roam the Aurès and Nemenchas Mountains," he admits.

In the days that follow, the main news is the death of a teacher from France who was on his way to Annaba to take up his post. He was killed and his wife was wounded when the bus they were on was attacked. I find that news horrifying. To attack a young couple who agree to go to the ends of the earth to dispense knowledge to children, Algerian children, is a cowardly act, not to anyone's honor.

The rumors spread by the press are of no help in discovering who's behind the action. *L'Echo d'Alger*, *La Dépêche quotidienne*, and *Le Journal d'Alger* say they're bandits or outlaws manipulated by a foreign power. For them it's incidental news; no one pays particular attention since the city is calm, as is the rest of the country.

The comrades with whom I speak about these events refuse to believe the people behind them are Algerian. Some say they must be Tunisian bandits or Arabs from the Middle East. "No party or organization in this country is capable of taking up arms against France," others reason. Even Saoula counters me: "The nationalists are too intelligent to try to attack the French army with shotguns and tin cans filled with powder like they were real bombs."

For me, it's Messali who's behind what's happening. I suspect him of wanting to resolve the crisis in the party and rally elements in Tunisia and Morocco behind him.

Happily, I am less disoriented in class. The philosophy class is astounding. I discover whatever it was that escaped me the year before. Socrates' method for discovering the truth is amazing. The use of Bergson's tool of immediate experience and intuition makes a deep impression on me. On the first quarter's composition exercise, I get the highest mark in the class.

When I arrive home for Christmas vacation, I learn that Mohamed has been arrested again; Miliani, my friend Nabi's uncle, and other village militants as well. The MTLD has been banned. Mohamed was picked up in Boufarik and jailed in Algiers. My brother Cherif has gone to Boufarik to run the butcher shop and Mustafa is replacing Cherif in Berrouaghia alongside Baba. My mother is in her depths, never stops crying, complaining that her boys are all dispersed. She includes me in the displacement of her brood. I spend two mournful weeks in the winter-enclosed village and return to school.

Boarding students from Kabylia, Miliana, and Orléansville whisper news gleaned at home during vacation. In low voices they provide accounts of attacks and aggressions in their regions. They mention a mysterious National Liberation Front and Army. Like me, they presume that Messali is the instigator and don't know the origins of the participants and the names of their leaders.

At the end of January, Nabi writes to tell me that high school students in Algiers are creating a student association and encourages me to attend the founding meeting. I meet him on a Sunday morning at a café in the lower Casbah. He's with a comrade by the name of Mohamed Amara Rachid, also in his senior year at a school in Algiers. Like Nabi and me, he's tall and thin, wears glasses set on a strong nose. His way of looking people straight in the eye, his laugh, his easy and often amusing way of speaking are engaging. He wastes no time in informing me that the new group will be called the Algiers Muslim Students Association (UGEMA), and its activities will include cultural, sports, and social events, that they will organize lectures, a theater group, a newspaper, excursions, and sports competitions. He quickly adds, in a more confidential tone: "Nabi says you were at school in your village and in Blida with Cherif Fares, the son of the president of the Algerian Assembly. He's joining our association and will be at the constituent assembly. Try to convince him to become a member of the executive committee, that would be helpful in getting the authorities to approve the organization."

I understand that Fares will serve as a cover but I wonder why a youth association aimed at sports, theater, and other cultural activities needs a cover in a town where MTLD–elected officials are members of the city council. I don't feel it's the moment to ask why, and instead reassure him: "Cherif and I are both on the school handball team. I know him well."

As soon as other comrades arrive, we leave the café and the Casbah for the European sector of the city, where the meeting will take place on rue Mogador. Amara and I walk ahead of the others. "Would you be willing to set up a similar association in Blida?" he asks.

I'm taken by surprise and tell him that the students there aren't interested in politics, "only in soccer and girls."

"It's the same in Algiers, but that has to change."

"I agree," I say, "but I don't see how. The boarding students have no access to a radio or newspapers. It's the day students who keep us informed about Tino Rossi or Annie Cordy's latest hits! We know all about the who-done-its and Eddie Constantine's role as Lemmy Caution, special FBI agent. How can we change all that?"

"By creating students' associations in the cities that have secondary schools, we can encourage a change in attitude." I smile, shake my head, not convinced. "After almost one hundred twenty-five years of colonial domination," he says, "our people have been reduced to a shadow of themselves, they are resigned. Our comrades have no sense of their responsibility toward the Algerian people. They're concerned with graduating from high school—that's one of our objectives, too, for you, for me, and the friends who think like us. What can't be tolerated is their indifference to the plight of the immense majority of the population. Our associations can become the springboards of their awakening."

"I'm less optimistic than you," I say, "but I'm willing to try to set up an association."

Amara unbuttons his raincoat and dips his hand into an inside pocket. He pulls out a sheaf of folded papers. "Here's a copy of the bylaws. Take them. For your association, all you have to do is replace 'Algiers' with 'Blida' and add the minutes of the constituent assembly and the names of the executive committee members."

He finishes talking just as we arrive at the meeting hall. Among the people he questions, no one has seen Cherif Fares. I'm struck by the number of students there, over a hundred, including some young Algerian women. I wander among the little groups, Nabi too, but no one has seen Cherif, better known as Mimi. The speeches are well applauded, the bylaws are read out, and questions taken and answered. The assembly elects its executive committee. It includes one young woman.

The bylaws specify that only students having reached their sophomore year may join the organization. Other than the president, the members of the executive committee are the secretary general and the assistant secretary general, the treasurer, and the assistant treasurer. The fact that their names will figure in the minutes of the meeting that will be deposited at city hall constitutes a real obstacle for me. I realize how difficult it's going to be to find people who will join me on the committee. The events that follow and the conversation I have with Amara Rachid convince me of the necessity to establish a similar association in Blida.

Amara enlightens me as to the political situation. I get the impression he's an insider. When I mention Messali's probable role in the launching of the armed attacks, he smiles and states unequivocally: "Messali has nothing to do with the first of November uprising. The personality cult and his taste for power have turned his head. He's had his supporters name him president for life; he wants to be considered the supreme guide."

I abstain from telling him the story of the bouquet of flowers when he came to Blida. "Do you think it's the centralists?" I ask. "They're collaborators," he comments. "They work hand in hand with Jacques Chevalier, the mayor of Algiers, and the French secretary of state for defense." "So who's behind these events?" I ask. "Just ordinary Algerians," he says.

Aware of the cloud that has descended on me, he explains: "They're the leaders of the former Special Organization, the OS. When they failed to reconcile the two factions, they set up the CRUA, the Revolutionary Committee for Unity and Action, which they have now transformed into the National Liberation Front for the launching of an armed struggle. The FLN aims at bringing together the various tendencies but also the more moderate nationalists and the Communist Party."

"But the public is unaware of all that. We don't even know the name of their leader," I complain.

Amara shrugs his shoulders. "After Messali, Algeria doesn't need another *zaïm*. The personality cult has been abolished once and for all and is being replaced by a collegial leadership committee. If their names have not been revealed, it's because of the need to remain clandestine, it's a necessity in this struggle."

Back at school I tell the comrades in the upper classes about my trip to Algiers and the extraordinary student meeting I attended. I avoid the political side of it all. On the contrary, I insist it's apolitical. I talk about the goals and advance the projects of organizing lectures on Arab literature, publishing a journal to discuss our ideas on the emancipation of women and other social problems, and creating a theater group. After three weeks of talking it up, I count about ten supporters for the creation of an association, though most of them are afraid of getting into trouble or of being thrown out of school. Out of conviction or friendship, whichever, three comrades agree to join, but when I ask them to become members of the executive committee, one, the son of a *caïd*, and another, the son of an imam, refuse. They fear for their fathers' positions.

Disgusted, even sickened by the cowardice and the egotism of my comrades, I drop Nabi a note and tell him how down I feel. The following Sunday, Amara and Nabi come to see me; they want to meet the comrades. If they had warned me, I would have reserved a meeting room and invited some day students. I improvise, however, and tell them I'll meet them in the Bizot Gardens at two p.m. During the recreation period I announce the news to those who might be interested; I insist that my friends have come from Algiers especially to tell them more about the need to organize and about the possible activities of an association. I announce the meeting in the study hall and again at lunch. Someone at the other end of the table pops up and says: "This association you're trying to impose on us is only going to get us in trouble. Rather than listen to your crap, I prefer to go see the ladies or play dominos."

I stop him short, threaten to smash his head in. The sound of my voice and the expression on my face frighten him, his sneer disappears, he lowers his head, doesn't look up from his plate. All around the table, silence reigns. My appetite is gone; I stop talking. After lunch, Bouabida, a junior who was present in the dining hall, comes up to me and says he'll join me in the gardens at two.

Amara and Nabi have brought two other people with them: a young woman, Chafika Meslem, and Abdelkader Belarbi. From Duveyrier we are finally about a dozen boarding students. We head for the most isolated spot in the gardens. Amara describes the Algiers association, announces that the first issue of their newspaper, *L'Action estudiantine*, will be out in a few days. He also announces the creation of similar student associations in Constantine, Philippeville, Mostaganem, and Tizi Ouzou. As he explains it, these associations will enable the individual participant to come out of isolation, to contribute to the group in order to progress both personally and collectively. "We need these associations," he says. "They are a stepping-stone for the expression of ourselves as Algerians, to maintain our heritage as part of the Arab and Muslim worlds. The schooling we have received has given us the privilege of modernization, of progress, but we must remain who we are, conserve virtues forged through centuries of history, founded on principles that are our own."

Belarbi, speaking softly, evokes the relationship between various student associations in Algiers and their decision to inform Governor-General Jacques Soustelle of the problems faced by Algerian students. Chafika Meslem is more strident: "Our identity has disintegrated; it's been crushed and vilified; even our language is considered a foreign tongue in our own country. In my opinion, we have to face our societal problems, for example the status of women and their emancipation. It's our duty, a duty that requires courage."

Hanane, a math student, asks, "Why is the organization called the Muslim Students Association and not simply the Students Association?"

"Because," says Amara, "on my official ID where it states my nationality, I'm called 'French Muslim.' Neither you nor I asked to be classified in that way. It's just another sign of discrimination."

"Won't we, in turn, be accused of discrimination?" Hanane asks.

"I don't think so, since other organizations exist like the JEC (Christian Student Youth), the UEFJ (Union of Jewish Students of France), the SMA (Algerian Muslim Scouts)."

Few of my comrades intervene. Amara insists on the need to take oneself in hand. At the end we split up into small, separate groups to cross and leave the gardens. Attracted by the charm and beauty of Chafika Meslem, Hanane strikes up a conversation with her, which also contributes to his support for the association. Mohamed Bouabida from Affreville also joins me and accepts membership on the executive committee and lets his name be on the list presented to the regional authorities. He even offers the address of his mother's house in Blida as the seat of the association. I have trouble finding a fifth member for the executive committee. Fear is the culprit.

I hold off telling Nabi and Amara of my failure to find a fifth student with enough guts to advance his name. As we near the end of the school year and exams are on everyone's mind, it's going to be even more difficult. I leave for home for Easter vacation. In the train I meet the usual crowd of students, including those from the towns of Boufarik and Laghouat, beyond Berrouaghia. I know them all and am friends with a few of them, especially with Abdallah Douro, with whom I talk politics. After discussing the state of emergency and the censorship decreed by the French government, we evoke the Bandung conference in Indonesia, attended by Nasser, Chou En-lai, and Nehru. A resolution condemning France for its political aggression in North Africa was passed there.

When I tell Douro that I was at the founding assembly of the Algiers students association and that I'm trying to set one up in Blida, he suggests that I widen the base of the organization to include the other high schools in the region and call the organization the Mitidja Muslim Students Association. In that way, he would be able to join and become a member of the executive committee. "As for me," he says, "giving my name to the authorities doesn't frighten me."

On arriving home, I learn that Mohamed has been let out of prison and is back at the butcher shop in Boufarik. The following Sunday, another surprise: he arrives on a scooter, a new Vespa. During lunch, he describes his trip to Berrouaghia: "There was a military checkpoint in the Chiffa Gorges, the soldiers were probably from France. When I showed them the ID I carry since I was arrested and deprived of my civil rights, they didn't recognize it. They showed it to their chief, who didn't understand it either. He shook his head and waived me on."

After lunch, Basha asks Mohamed if he can take a turn on the scooter. Mohamed shows him how to drive it and gives him the keys. Basha motions to me to get on behind him and we take off. After a drive around the village and a halt at Basha's bicycle shop, we take the road to Medea. Cautious, Basha tests the scooter's staying power on the sinuous mountain road. We pause for a while in the town, then begin our way back down the mountain. We round a bend and hear a horn bellowing behind us. A large truck with an empty trailer passes us, raising a cloud of dust. The driver slams on the brakes—heaven knows why—and the truck swings to the right, overturns us, and lands in a ditch off the road. Two Frenchmen in a car trailing the truck pull me out from under the monster. "I thought we were going to find you smashed to smithereens," says one of them, who, as luck would have it, is a doctor.

He checks Basha, who doesn't have a scratch, but seeing my injuries, he insists on taking me back to Medea in his Renault. "We need to clean those cuts and I want to give you an anti-tetanus shot for safety's sake. It won't take long."

I sit down on the back seat of the Renault. Basha gets on the scooter and follows us. The two men couldn't be nicer. "We were going to have a drink in Loverdo and then go up to Benchicao," they explain. I listen and look out the window but the scenery no longer offers the same enchantment as earlier in the day. The man beside the driver opens the glove compartment and I see it contains a revolver. My blood chills.

A week after Easter vacation, on a Sunday afternoon, we hold the constituent assembly of the Mitidja Muslim Students Association (AJEMM). There are twelve of us on the sunlit patio of Bouabida's mother's place. I explain our objectives; Saoula reads the bylaws. We discuss the association's goals and draw up a list of potential activities. I move to elect the members of the executive committee and try to get someone to accept the chairmanship. Since no one moves, I'm forced to take it on myself. By unanimous vote, we elect Saoula and Bouabida as secretary and assistant secretary, Hanane and Douro as treasurers. I send the documents to the county authorities and write to Nabi and Amara to announce the good news.

Proud of myself, I go to see them in Algiers and attend a lecture organized by a group of Catholic priests. Amara insists I come back the following weekend for another group get-together, the quarterly forum of Youth for Social Action (AJAAS), an association that brings together Europeans, Jews, and Muslims of various organizations. I take advantage of time alone with Amara to question him on the situation in the nationalist movement.

"The origins of the crisis and the split in the party began in 1950," he says, "when the police discovered the existence of the OS, the Special Organization. Those who were not arrested countered the centralists, who were essentially reformers. They opposed Messali's organization, even though they had once worshipped him, because he's become so megalomaniac, only interested in personal power."

"But who are these new leaders you're talking about?" I ask.

"They are men who have been in the maquis for years and men who are underground, revolutionaries, intellectuals, strategists who have a plan. Their names are best kept quiet for the moment."

The meeting with the AJAAS takes place in the middle of a forest. Young men and women of different communities have come together. The atmosphere is friendly, they seem to know each other. The discussions center on the country's problems: the talk is political, the many injustices are evoked, repression, the lack of freedom. Amara seems to know everyone. He introduces me to the head of the Muslim

Scouts Association. I see my former history and geography teacher, who's also a head Scout. He points out a member of the central committee of the new nationalist organization, the National Liberation Front (FLN). I ask Amara if other nationalist leaders have joined the FLN. "Not all of them," he replies. "But they will, very soon, I'm sure."

Amara introduces me to Pierre Chaulet, a member of a Catholic organization. Pierre says, "You're at Duveyrier, my sister is at the girls' high school in Blida. She didn't come today but if you're interested, I can have her drop you off an issue of our review, *Consciences maghribines*." He notes my name on a piece of paper.

As we leave the outing, I ask Amara his opinion on the place of Europeans in an independent Algeria. He replies with the frankness that characterizes him: "They will have to choose between Algerian nationality and their original nationality. If they want to remain French, they will be treated like foreigners, according to the laws of the new country. France will have to recognize Algeria's sovereignty and negotiate with the National Liberation Front on an equal footing, with mutual respect, in order to define the relationship between the two nations.

A few days later, I'm called to the visitors' parlor. It's a small reception room, the walls lined with wine- and gold-colored velvet. I see a young girl, about my age, European. Her skin is milk and honey, her hair curly and reddish, her eyes green. She looks at my worn cotton work shirt of an undefinable color and smiles. I wonder if there hasn't been some mistake.

"I'm Anne-Marie, Pierre Chaulet's sister," she says, still smiling. She hands me a package, lowers her voice: "Two issues of *Consciences maghribines*."

I thank her and mention meeting her brother. "The outing was great, but I've never read your review."

"There'll be a new issue soon, I'll bring it around for you," she adds.

She uses the informal *tu* when addressing me; her spontaneity and her promise to come back again, the fact that she didn't simply leave the package at the door with the attendant, intrigue me. I invite her to have a seat. The chair she chooses is covered with the same fabric as the walls. She asks what class I'm in. I answer, avoiding *tu*. I ask her if she's a boarding student at her school.

"No," she replies, "I have a grandmother who lives alone. My parents have forced me to keep her company and pass my high school diploma in Blida." She speaks naturally, without affectation. How different from the Europeans in the village. She expresses her opinions with ease, about the school, the town, the mentality of the inhabitants, and remarks that she doesn't appreciate that of her schoolmates.

"You must really love your grandmother," I advance.

"Yes, she's special, a real character. In the family, we call her Granny Chaulet." She recounts her granny's background, that of her grand uncle Leo, Granny's brother, and the house. She has no idea of the amazing effect she has on me, a divine surprise: a fairy tale of a beautiful young French girl in a stylish parlor tête-à-tête with a young Arab. I listen to her; I can't stop glancing from her lovely green eyes to her fleshy rose-colored lips. She continues her tale.

"My grandmother is supposed to watch out for me and the people I frequent. When I said I was coming to see you, I said it was Pierre who told me to look you up—Pierre is her favorite grandchild. She asked for your name and screamed, 'You're going to see an Arab!' I thought she was going to faint. I had to repeat that you're a friend of Pierre's and that I was only going to meet you in the school visitors' parlor." She laughs wholeheartedly. I smile politely. The racism of her grandmother doesn't astonish me; I'm more surprised by the attitudes of the granddaughter.

"She's going to want to make sure I'm telling the truth and will probably invite you to the house to give you a look-over and be reassured. So don't be surprised if I come back in a few days. I'll make sure the invitation is for a Sunday afternoon."

Her decision to invite me without consulting me leaves me confused. Her insistent look and equivocal way of smiling at me are troubling. I let my imagination take a fling and dream of love at first sight. My fantasy world takes a beating that very night, however, on reading the article signed by Pierre Chaulet in *Consciences maghribines*. He denounces the ill-treatment of the nationalists by the police, cites the testimony of Algerians who have been tortured, and provides the names of policemen guilty of such acts. I reason with myself that this man's sister is not seeking a sentimental relationship. The young woman comes back the next day and asks at what time I can leave school on Sunday to have tea at her grandmother's. So as not to disappoint her, I wear a suit, knot my tie with extra care, and part my hair. Lovely in a flowered skirt and a white blouse, Anne-Marie is waiting for me on the sidewalk across the street from the school entrance. Smiling, balancing from one foot to the other, she watches me cross the street. My heart is throbbing.

"Your buddies have been looking at me strangely," she comments as she shakes my hand. "Why?"

"Because you're in front of the officers' mess hall and, maybe, because you're waiting for an Arab."

"For how long are you going to use *vous* when you talk to me?" she barks.

We walk toward the Bizot Gardens, then take the Avenue de la Marne. "It's the Sacred Wood Trail loved by André Gide," I comment. "Does your grandmother like it as much as he did?" I ask.

"No," she answers. "I'm not even sure she's ever read Gide but I'm sure she likes neither marabouts nor Arabs. Be ready to hear her make racist remarks. She was and remains a Pétainist. Until recently, a portrait of the Marshall hung in a choice spot on her living room wall. The family had a hard time getting her to take it down and relegate it to the cellar."

The grandmother's villa resembles those along the Avenue de la Marne and is surrounded by an immense flower garden. She's an alert little old lady, austere-looking. I try to keep smiling, reply to her questions as to my village, my family, the high school, my studies. After the interrogation and tea, she suggests that her granddaughter and I sit in the shade in the garden while she rests. Anne-Marie sighs with relief and smiles at me. The setting is romantic. I ask her questions about the association, the AJAAS, and *Consciences maghribines*. I observe that she, like her brother, advances pronationalist opinions and cites the names of Algerian militants, members of the MTLD. Her remarks about the repression, the injustices, and recognition of the Algerian nation have me wondering. She is expressing the same ideas as her brother, but hearing them from the mouth of this young French high school student shakes me up. Fearful that I won't be able to control the desire that mounts in me, I change the subject.

"Do you go to surprise parties?" I ask. She rounds her shoulders and displays the disgust my question inspires.

"My school friends adore them, are always talking about them as if life is only about dancing and boyfriends."

The conversation turns to themes associated with our philosophy classes. I evoke my favorite authors: Gide, Sartre, etc. She mentions François Mauriac and Bernanos. When the grandmother reappears, I leave the two women, pleased with my afternoon but still asking questions. My intuition tells me that the enthusiasm and the laughter that Anne-Marie indulges in mask a real sadness. When she mentions her parents, I sense resentment. According to her, they are not in agreement with her ideas, but is that sufficient reason to exile their daughter to a grandmother whose ideas are of another age?

"Hey," she announces a few days later, "my grandmother was really taken with you." She hands me an old issue of *Consciences maghribines* and says she hopes we'll see each other at the next AJAAS outing.

I receive the bulletin of legal announcements, the equivalent of recognition of the association by the authorities, just as studying for final exams is most intense. The end of the school year is too close to begin organizing activities, but the association now exists legally. I feel sure my successors will have an easier time with less fear expressed, less indifference. The route has been drawn, they have only to follow it. I work hard. In the dormitory, after lights-out, I sit in the toilets and study under the feeble night-light until very late. Happily, my efforts are not in vain. I receive my diploma in June and am immensely relieved. I have the feeling that, at long last, I am master of my destiny. I apply for law school and also file a request for a job as supervisor in a secondary school in order to ensure my financial future.

After eight years as a boarder in a school and a town that I've never loved, I am overcome by a feeling of infinite freedom. I have lived here through times of sadness. In my early years, I had a hard time accepting being transposed from my family surroundings to a foreign environment. At school, I lived with Europeans, discovered their way of life without understanding their indifference to everything that concerned their Algerian comrades. They don't want to know us, are content with the prejudice inculcated by their parents and can't seem to realize that ignoring others engenders fear and fear engenders arrogance and racism among the victors.

Living in this community, receiving the same teaching, has transformed me; it has been an enriching experience. What saddens me is the gap that has been created between me and mine. Without seeking it, I am conscious of being mentally estranged from them. My parents have never undergone French schooling. I am the youngest of six children but none of my brothers has been to secondary school. In an insidious way, the raising of my intellectual level has become an obstacle. I can no longer dialogue with them, profit from their advice and assistance. They have no awareness of my difficulties or of my successes. They have no idea of the content of my classes. They always ask the same question: "Are you studying hard?" and make the same recommendation: "Above all, work hard and don't play too much." There is no exchange among us. I would have loved sharing with my parents the wealth of knowledge my classes have brought me, talk to them about my favorite authors, the subjects and ideas that I am passionate about. I can do it only in French, a language they barely understand. Their Arabic and mine are too simple, too poor. I can't translate from French the culture that I've acquired; it's impossible. They are pleased to hear I have graduated but that does not heal what I see as my mutilation.

Whatever the case, I shall always retain from these years the incalculable knowledge gained. The teaching I have received at Duveyrier represents a tremendous opening to the modern world. The memory of my reaction during the history lesson on ancient Egypt and its gods when I was in my first year makes me laugh. I do remain critical of the history program concerning Algeria and the French empire, although this has not stopped me from appreciating Monsieur Demichelis, the history and geography teacher. I take with me the highest esteem for the math teacher and will never forget those who taught natural science and philosophy. I will always remember tall Monsieur Gauthier in his white work apron explaining the reproduction of amoebas against a background of well-defined drawings on the blackboard. I can still hear his strong voice, during one of our last classes, hammering out his truth: "the human brain is constituted by millions and millions of neurons attached to each other by synapses," a phrase that he accompanied with gestures and mimicry. The previous year, I'd failed natural science. I hadn't done well because I wasn't interested in a field taught by an openly racist professor. One proof among many: he never gave a high grade to an Algerian without giving the same grade to a Frenchman whose name he would announce first. But, since I paid closer attention the second year, I really enjoyed the classes on the physiology and anatomy of the human body.

As paradoxical as it may be, I was happy to have taken the philosophy class twice. I adored Monsieur Charlety's course, a teacher who constantly renewed his material. Thanks to him, I acquired and consolidated knowledge, a way of thinking that opened my mind. These were basic notions, of course, but they dealt with ideas, the way of thinking that's at the base of Europe's power.

To celebrate my success, my father offers me... a glass of mint tea! When he tells me to order it at the café, Cherif laughs and says: "You know, Baba, the high school diploma is worth more than that. Mokhtar merits a vacation, a trip to Algiers." "And why not?" Baba replies. "But that shouldn't stop us from having coffee and mint tea together." When Cherif asks when I would like to go to Algiers, I tell him that I really want to go to France. I don't add that my dream is to visit Paris, the City of Lights. He tells me to find out how much the crossing by boat costs.

Nabi has also finished high school and filed for a job as surveillant. He informs me that Amara Rachid wants me to send
a telegram supporting the creation of the General Union of
Algerian Muslim Students (UGEMA) to take place from July
8 to 14, 1955. I send the telegram to the Algerian student
headquarters in Paris, 115 Boulevard Saint-Michel, in the
fifth arrondissement.

In France the Algerian students are opposed to including "Muslim" in the title of the organization. They want it
to be called the General Union of Algerian Students. Amara
says that the Marxists among them are members of the Communist Party, who hope, in creating a secular organization,
to control it, as well as eventually the National Liberation
Front. I also learn from Nabi that the new governor-general
of Algeria, Jacques Soustelle, has been in contact, through
members of his cabinet—Vincent Monteil and Germaine
Tillon, the well-known ethnologist—with the FLN. European members of AJAAS served as intermediaries. Amara
thinks that both sides are testing the waters and that negotiations are in the offing.

I receive notice to appear for my army physical at the
town hall, along with about thirty Europeans from the village, twenty years of age, and three other Algerians, two
high school students in Medea and the *mouderes*'s son. The
examination takes place on the ground floor of the building,
in the assembly hall where the Europeans vote. Undressed,
we wait in our underpants and in alphabetical order. When
my name is called I undergo the examination and am told to
wait. An officer informs me that I'm exempt. Mustafa thinks
it's because "our name is underlined in red since Mohamed's

arrest in May 1945." He points out that, with the exception of Ahmed, who deserted, none of the other four brothers has been declared "apt" for service.

I am rather of the opinion that it's because of my eyes. During the test, I was only able to make out the largest letters with my left eye, whereas with my right eye I could read almost every line. Before this examination, I had never felt the need to consult an eye doctor, even though when I was studying in the toilets after hours my eyes would constantly tear. Mohamed recommends a specialist in Algiers, one of the rare Algerian ophthalmologists, who observes that my left eye is essentially useless and my right eye is myopic. He prescribes glasses that correct the vision of the right eye.

While in Algiers I inquire about the price of the Algiers–Marseille crossing by boat. Cherif gives me fifteen thousand francs to cover my living expenses. Baba pays the ticket. Nabi decides to come with me. The money his father and his uncle give him just covers the crossing, plus a small amount for pocket money. I promise to pay for the tickets from Marseille to Paris. He's convinced we can hitchhike to Paris and save our money.

We stop to see Father Barthez, who has just arrived to replace Father Delahaye for the month of August. When I tell him we're going to Paris, he offers to have us stay with the working priests in Saint-Ouen, on the outskirts of the city. He gives us the address of the priests at the French Mission in Marseille and urges us strongly to visit his parents in Béziers, also in the South of France.

We are so happy to be off that we barely notice the heat and humidity of Algiers. We join the group of Algerian workers boarding the boat for Marseille. The wait is long. The Europeans are let on board first. By the time our turn arrives, impatience reigns and everyone pushes and shoves to get on board. The name of the boat is *Le Kairouan*. We are placed in steerage alongside our compatriots. There are no chairs, no benches, no amenities. Disappointed and silent, Nabi and

I watch the workers call out to each other, look for a spot to drop their bags. Poor and unemployed, they are embarking for France to work in the mines, in the iron and steel industry, in construction. At the beginning of the century they were taken on board with a sign around their necks with the name of their employer, something on the order of the tag around the neck of a dog with the name and address of its master.

The priests of the French Mission live in a large apartment near the harbor. The welcome is warm. They are four in all, they wear civilian clothes and have jobs. They point out the places to visit and how to get to them. We have dinner together in the evening. They question us about life in Algeria, about religion and Muslim traditions. The group leader displays an interest in the political situation in our country. I take advantage of the discussion to give them a brief history of the nationalist movement, the reasons for the uprising, and the aims of the National Liberation Front. I think they would have liked us to stay longer but Nabi and I are in a hurry to see Paris. However, we do decide to take a side trip to Béziers first. The welcome we receive from Jean-Claude Barthez's parents is unforgettable. They are delighted to meet their son's friends and do everything possible to show it.

The attitude of Catholics like those of the French Mission is so different from that of the immense majority of the clergy in Algeria. Contrary to Father Foucault, who preached for the evangelization of the Algerian people, the priests at the mission interpret maps and geography in a much different way. For them, the Strait of Gibraltar that separates Morocco from Spain and Portugal is only thirteen kilometers wide. The distance from Sicily to the African shore is but 183 kilometers, and the movement of the tectonic plates is forever narrowing the distance between the two continents, just as the members of the mission are working in their particular way to bring people closer, to incite us all to live in harmony and with mutual respect.

The Barthez family home is a pleasant two-story house with a garden. They have four children, three boys and a girl. The oldest is in the military, the youngest has just finished high school. He's two years younger than Nabi and me and leaves for a Scout camp the day of our arrival. Françoise, the only girl, is nine; she resembles her mother and gratifies both of us with a slight bow and an angelic smile. Of medium height and thin, Madame Barthez is charming, has graying hair, a soft voice, and the same large brown eyes as her daughter. She's a magnificent cook and is happy to feed us the traditional cuisine of southern France. The young woman who works in the house prepares the table and serves the meals in the garden. During dinner, the conversation immediately turns to the situation in Algeria. Our hosts are surprised when I tell them that after 125 years of French colonial rule, less than

15 percent of school-age Algerians are in school and that less than 14 percent of the adults know how to read and write. Françoise, in a low voice, asks her mother a question; I hear her reply, "It's too complicated, I'll explain it to you later."

As soon as she's finished her dessert, Françoise leans over to her mother and whispers something in her ear. Madame Barthez smiles and announces: "Françoise has a joke to tell us before she goes to bed."

Happy to be the center of attention, she wriggles from side to side on her chair, lowers her eyelids, and tells us a cat-and-mouse story. I burst out laughing and congratulate her. Delighted with the effect she's produced, she kisses us all good night and goes to bed. After each meal at the house, she tells us a joke or little story with the same grace. We return to the conversation about Algeria after her departure. Monsieur Barthez, engineer with a subdivision of the Bridges and Roads Authority, has no end of questions. Moved by what he learns, he proposes having us meet friends of the family who are especially interested in Algeria. Madame Barthez points out the tourist attractions in Béziers.

The next afternoon we meet Monsieur Barthez at his office and accompany him on a visit to a work site in the region. We arrive at the site just before quitting time. After a short discussion with the overseer, he offers to give him a ride home so as to show us the man's village. The hamlet, located on a mountainside, has one straight street, too narrow for a car to pass. The village dates from the Middle Ages. We walk up the street as women, dressed in black and wearing head scarves, get up hurriedly from chairs in front of the houses and rush inside. I find it difficult to understand the worker because of his accent and the local dialect. He invites us to have a drink at his house, a low-ceilinged building, poorly lit. It is composed of a large room with an immense fireplace darkened by soot. A table and hand-hewed benches occupy the center of the room. I wonder if there are other rooms and other people in the house. Our host opens a bottle of fruit brandy he has made himself. Shocked by our refusal to drink, he listens to Monsieur Barthez explain that we are Muslims and that Islam condemns alcohol. It seems he has never heard the words "Muslim" or "Islam" before. Monsieur Barthez whispers a word to him and he jumps up and cries, with the singsong accent of the South: "Mohammedans!" I laugh but don't manage to convince him that we only drink water with our meals. Against his better judgment, he serves us a glass of mint-flavored syrup and water.

As we descend the narrow street to leave the hamlet, we are followed by a band of kids, out of I don't know where, who point at us and scream, "Mohammedans, Mohammedans!" Monsieur Barthez lowers his head and increases his step. He most certainly hadn't envisaged that in these medieval surroundings the voices of children would reveal the persistence of a legacy from the Crusades!

The Barthezes organize a reception for us, and friends of theirs organize three evenings for us to meet members of the Catholic Workers movement, the People's Freedom Movement, and Christian Witnesses. From the outset I realize that they all believe that the uprising on November 1 was Messali's doing. Some of the people present know Algerian workers who are members of Messali's organization, the Algerian National Movement (MNA). Without contesting our position in favor of the FLN, they remain skeptical. They believe their comrades and do not doubt their good faith. One evening, after a passionate discussion that lasts until two in the morning with members of the People's Freedom Movement, while we don't get them to change their minds, we certainly shake them up and leave them with doubts and a better understanding of the FLN's goals. A truck driver present at the last meeting offers to drive us to the outskirts of Montpellier and leave us at a spot where we are most likely to pick up a ride north.

Here we are at eight in the morning near an intersection on the north side of Montpellier. The plane trees that line the road remind me of my village; the vineyards and crops resemble those of the Mitidja. Nabi extends his arm, wags his thumb, and smiles like someone who has hitchhiked all his life. I place his bag and my suitcase next to a tree, stand behind him, and make the same gestures. Cars pass but no one stops.

"I told you I didn't believe in hitchhiking, in traveling without paying the price," I shout at him. "That's because you have no patience," he argues. An hour later, I lower my arm and sit down near the bags. When I get up and offer to replace him, Nabi refuses, convinced that a driver will judge his face more amenable than mine and will stop for us. Two hours later, his irritation is on display: "Thousands of cars have gone by, none have even stopped to ask where we're going."

At about two in the afternoon, dying of hunger and thirst, I see a bus coming. I jump up, plant myself in the middle of the road, and wave my arms for the driver to stop. He's headed for Nîmes. We jump on the bus, no more hitchhiking. In Nîmes, however, we have a hard time finding anyone who knows where the youth hostel is located. Most people don't even stop to listen to our question, and, if they do, they shake their heads no. The rare individuals who try to help us send us in the wrong direction. Exhausted, sweating, we finally arrive at the youth hostel as the sun goes down and spend the night. At the railroad station the following morning, when I hear the price of tickets to Paris, I realize that our money is barely enough to pay for them. We're faced with a dilemma. Fulfill our dream, see Paris, and die of hunger, or change our plans. I refuse Nabi's suggestion that we try hitchhiking again. We spend a good deal of time in the station waiting room smoking cigarette after cigarette, in silence.

I suddenly remember how excited Smaïn Bendifallah was when he came back from his vacation on the French Riviera, just after our attempt to camp at Fort-de-l'Eau was thwarted. He had discovered an international camp at La Bocca, near Cannes, a camp frequented by foreigners, both men and women, near the sea. Smaïn said that for very little money he had a bed, breakfast, and one meal a day. Attracted by the idea of the seaside, Nabi is once again in a good mood and remarks that with his Scout bag he's more likely to pass for a camper than me. Arriving at the camp with a suitcase is not what bothers me, I'm just hoping that Smaïn wasn't exaggerating. The cost of the train ticket to Cannes is within our means, so off we go.

La Bocca, of course, doesn't replace Paris, but Cannes and its famous Croisette are only about a mile away and the

camp is not what I had feared. It in no way resembles the
military camp in the middle of an open field that I had imagined. It is located in a wonderful verdant area; the tents are
not lined up like an army encampment but are large, comfortable, and scattered among the many umbrella pines. The
beds are not one on top of the other as at Duveyrier. Tables,
chairs, and parasols placed here and there are an invitation
to relax, to hang out. The beach is on the other side of a narrow, local road. Nabi is in a hurry to get in the water; we
go to the nearest store and buy swimming trunks. I'm not
much of a swimmer, whereas he swims fast, with style, and
dives down and under the waves. He shakes his head like an
animal when he comes up for air, flattens his dark straight
hair. I'm in admiration, somewhat envious. I content myself
with the breaststroke and stay near the shore so as not to lose
my footing.

At lunchtime, we line up with everyone else. We sit down
on the terrace at a table with a parasol. Nabi manages fairly
well in English and strikes up a conversation with a young
couple who sit down at our table. I'm surprised how easy it
is to join others in conversation. Many of the campers are
from northern Europe and barely speak French. It's the case
with three ravishing young Dutch women with whom we
lunch the second day. They are between eighteen and twenty
years old, understand French, and manage to reply, picking
out their words with care. I laugh my heart out when we
talk about food and the blonde with blue eyes asks how to
make "couche-couche," meaning couscous. I meet two other
Dutch women and am fascinated by one of them: she's about
thirty, mother of a three-year-old. Blond with a great figure

and a gorgeous suntan, she never stops staring at me. I manage a few compliments, she replies in English or Dutch. I understand that her husband has left the camp and manage to make a date for that evening.

The older woman with her speaks good French. I learn that she was born in Indonesia. "It's a splendid country and exudes extraordinary spirituality," she says. She registers my surprise and continues: "You're from a Muslim country, you know what djinns are. Well, in Indonesia, there are a multitude of spirits in the air." She lived there for many years and is very critical of the Dutch and their materialistic behavior, their obsession with money and profit. She lives in Amsterdam and invites me to visit her. "My real country," she insists with a defiant look in her eyes, "is Indonesia."

When I refuse the pork sausage that the waiter is about to drop on my plate, he asks in proper French but with a heavy accent what country I'm from. He realizes I'm Muslim and offers to make me an omelet, then does the same for Nabi. He has the stance and face of my brother Basha: heavyset, full cheeks, and a thin mustache. That evening, as Nabi and I are walking along the Croisette, he comes up to us and cheerfully invites us for coffee in a nearby café. He's Muslim and from Yugoslavia, Bosnia-Herzegovina to be exact. His name is Hadzi Selim Selimovitch. Back home he was a surgeon. A member of a soccer team, he took advantage of a game in Nice to "choose freedom" and remain in France. Selim is abreast of what's happening in Algeria. He tells us that he interpreted for a French delegation during an official visit to Yugoslavia.

He remembers the Muslim member of the Algerian Assembly who was on the delegation and who insisted that he was French. We discuss Algerian nationalism with him and describe local elections and the way they are "fixed." Suddenly I wonder if he's not an informer for the French police. He keeps asking questions about the Liberation Army, about their numbers, where it is most active. I become evasive and reply, "I don't really know" or shrug my shoulders. I see that Nabi is also wary. Selim has understood our sudden reticence. He looks me straight in the eyes and says: "I want to join the Liberation Army and save my Muslim brothers' lives."

His statement doesn't dissipate my mistrust. A rapid look toward Nabi confirms that he has similar doubts. "Why did you leave Yugoslavia?" I ask. Without hesitation he replies: "Because of the persecution of Muslims by the communist regime." His father, a well-known personality and fervent Muslim, died under torture. Selim tells us that protests by Muslims are repressed forcibly. He swears that soldiers have raped women hiding in mosques before exterminating everyone inside the building. "Do you understand now why I want to use my capacity as a doctor to treat Muslims and hopefully save lives?" I nod my head but remain cautious. Nabi, too, is perplexed. After that evening, Selim really takes care of us. He doubles our portions of food, insists on inviting us out for coffee. We remain vigilant, however, even after accepting his good faith.

"Read *Paris-presse l'intransigeant*: 428 people killed in Algeria," the newspaper vendor calls out as he runs along the beach. The headline announces an uprising on August 20, 1955, in the North Constantine region. When I tell Selim that we've decided to leave and go home, he says he absolutely wants to see us alone once more. When we meet, he exhibits his identity papers, which state his profession as a surgeon, and repeats that he wants to save lives. Nabi and I promise to do our best to help him join the Algerian struggle. As soon as we return, Amara Rachid has the FLN's branch in France contact him and arranges for him to join the Liberation Army. I will learn, much later, that Hadzi Selim Selimovitch did "save his Muslim brothers' lives." He died when the French army bombarded the hamlet in which he set up his field hospital.

At the harbor and in the streets of Algiers, I see no sign of the state of war we had imagined. In Berrouaghia, however, people speak in low tones of the exploits of the Liberation Army, albeit no one has met or seen one of its soldiers. Rumors circulate that combine irrational reasoning with divine intervention. One of the stories that travels around is that of a covered truck transporting freedom fighters that is stopped by French gendarmes who, on raising the cover on the back of the truck, find just a few sheep.

At the Café des Sports, where I spend most of my time, the foosball table, the latest innovation, attracts a lot of young men including high school students old enough to frequent the place without fear of their parents' sanctions. Among them is Ahmed-Cherif Bousmaha, who has been a boarding student at Duveyrier for the last six years and who considers me his elder and mentor. The August 20 uprising and the ferocious repression that followed are the main topics of conversation. The guys no longer talk sports and films so much. They don't avoid local gossip entirely, but the guerrilla attacks and ambushes are now high on their agenda. I tell them what I know about the national movement, the crisis within the MTLD, the CRUA, and the creation of the National Liberation Front and Army. I take Ahmed-Cherif aside to talk about the Mitidja Muslim Students Association and ask him if he's willing to take over the leadership. He accepts, I give him a copy of the bylaws and describe the projects I had envisaged: a bulletin, lectures, excursions, a theater group. Far from hesitant, he is enthusiastic.

At the end of September, Nabi is notified that he has been appointed resident monitor at the French-Arabic high school in Tlemcen. When I receive notice to report to the Aumale lycée in Constantine, the school year has already begun. The trip by train seems endless, though I do get to see other landscapes and scan the mountains in the naive hope of detecting some freedom fighters.

On leaving the station I know immediately that the city and the country are at war. The building is surrounded by armored cars and soldiers in combat dress. The nearby bridge I cross in a taxi is guarded by armed soldiers. The driver tells me that the bridge is called the Al Kantara and that it crosses the deep-set gorges of the Rhummel River. In the rue Georges Clémenceau I observe a number of patrols and military vehicles of all sorts. The women in the streets are dressed in black from head to foot. On the death of Ahmed Bey, who heroically defended the city against the French invasion in the nineteenth century, the women of Constantine adopted the black veil as a sign of mourning.

"I've been waiting for you like for the Messiah," says Monsieur Horst, the school administrator, with a smile and strong handshake. He's tall, robust, is wearing a light brown suit, and plods like a peasant. He offers to carry one of my two suitcases and leads me to a room on the third floor. As we proceed, he explains that without sufficient personnel, he's had to overtax his staff. The pink bedcover reminds me of the dormitory at Duveyrier.

"You can't see the Rhummel Gorges from your window but the main courtyard and the rue de France are not unpleasant," he says. I don't know what to reply but appreciate his kind welcome. He asks me to meet him in his office where he will introduce me to Monsieur Martin, the supervisor, and Monsieur Daumas, the principal.

The reputation of a study hall monitor, as far as the students are concerned, is made on day one. That's something I learned during my eight years as a boarding student. As soon as I enter the study hall, I demand silence and remind everyone present that study hall time is for work and not for gossip, that to leave the hall, permission is required, that consideration of others is essential. There are always a few black sheep, smart guys ready to show off, who will be observing my conduct. To discourage them, instead of reading or working, I spend the first sessions watching the hall. If a student whispers to a neighbor, I intervene with a strong *psst* and a nod and, if necessary, I leave my desk and give him a warning. Students in the lower classes are the most difficult to discipline.

There are fewer students here than in Blida, but the proportion of Algerians is higher. They are mainly the sons of notable personalities from the region. The day students are mostly Europeans, with a large percentage of Jews. The Constantine region is the most heavily populated and Constantine itself is the second largest city in the country. There's even a high school in which Algerians are in the majority.

I'm surprised to run into Saïd Benkhaled, who began secondary school in Blida, living at his brother's. Heavyset, light-skinned with wavy hair, he is in his last year and is happy to see me again. When I'm on duty monitoring the courtyard, we get together and recall memories of school in Blida and exchange information on current events. I'm horrified by what he tells me about the massacres, the destruction and fires lit by the French army after the August 20 uprising. The ferociousness of the repression has traumatized his comrades.

This news, however, doesn't stop *'Ammi* Mokrane from believing that foreigners are responsible for what's happening in the country. *'Ammi* Mokrane, who cleans my room, is about seventy but refuses to retire. "Retirement, what's that for?" he asks, "to spend my money in the cafés and listen to the stupid stories people churn out?" He's a little man, originally from Kabylia, worn down by time and work. He slowly sweeps the room and stops for a bit of conversation. He has a strong native accent, speaks Arabic with hesitation and French barely. He tells me about his vacation back in Kabylia, where some of his family lives. Suddenly, he asks: "Do you know where these *fellaghas* who are causing so much trouble come from?" Wary, I remain silent. "They're from Tunisia, Egypt, and some other countries," he spouts with confidence.

I smile and say to myself that the colonialist propaganda machine has done its job. The National Liberation Front distributed a proclamation on November 1 that few people have read. Six months later, a tract was distributed calling upon the Algerian people to support the FLN, but again it hasn't been read nor its message distributed.

Saïd tells me that the head of the Constantine Muslim Students Association is a resident monitor at the Franco-Muslim High School, Ali Abdellaoui. Of medium height and dark skin, Ali's eyes shine with intelligence. He has an open smile and immediately gains my confidence; a slight lisp adds to his charm. "You've arrived right on time," Ali says when I tell him about the Mitidja association. The activities of his organization have been frozen because of the repression. "I have a scholarship and am leaving for Paris," he tells me. "You could replace me at the head of the association." I try to refuse, telling him that I don't know the students in the city well enough. "It would be better to have someone local head it up," I suggest. The student he had intended to pass the chairmanship to has a brother who left school to join the Liberation Army and might find himself in trouble with the authorities, he informs me.

The night before Ali leaves for Paris, we meet at the Café Excelsior, a spot popular with the local elite. As we leave the café, I bump head-on into Anne-Marie Chaulet with a girl-friend. I can't believe it. Her eyes pop out, her faces reddens. She raises her arms and advances her cheek for a kiss. "I'm monitoring at Laverand, the girls' high school," she tells me.

"And I'm doing the same at Aumale down the street from here," I inform her.

The surprise is heaven-sent, as awesome as the first time I saw Anne-Marie in the visitors' parlor at Duveyrier. And as on that first meeting, my heart skips some beats. In my fantasy, Anne-Marie is the ideal woman, the wife of my dreams. We did see each other again after that first encounter and nothing happened, I mean no flirting or anything sexual between us. Anne-Marie had her convictions and I had mine, which included friendship between men and women. Since I last saw her, I have been in France and have certainly lost some of my inhibitions. I still believe in friendship between men and women, but I say to myself that "luck should be given its chance." If it crosses our path, it might well be in the interest of a common destiny, no?

Anne-Marie comes to see me the next day and over time we become fast friends. We find a café in the rue Rouhault de Fleury, halfway between the European center of the city and her high school and in which I've never seen another Algerian seated at a table with a French woman. In the weeks that follow, at the café and during our walks, we talk about ourselves and, little by little, Anne-Marie's story reveals itself. I learn that she was sent to her grandmother's in Blida after telling her parents that she was in love with one of the leaders of the Algerian Scout movement whom she met at an AJAAS outing. "An Arab in the family? Papa isn't ready to swallow that," she says with resignation.

Anne-Marie's father is head of the Christian trade unions in Algeria. He is neither a democrat nor a radical. He was scandalized when his son Pierre signed a resolution that was published in *Alger Républicain* — the newspaper backed by the Communist Party — entitled "Repression will not solve the Algerian problem." Pierre had to hide out at his maternal grandmother's in order to prepare for the oral exam for an internship. His mother finally intervened and he was allowed back home. Pierre is the eldest of seven children: four girls and three boys. He was educated at a school run by Jesuits. Anne-Marie, who adores him, is second in line. The family is close to priests who are more open-minded than the usual run of priests in Algeria. Anne-Marie failed her senior exams and has to repeat the year. She's twenty-one and refuses to be chaperoned by her granny any longer. The job at the girls' high school ensures her financial independence. Her love's name is Salah Louanchi, who was a member of the central committee of the MTLD and has now joined the FLN. He escaped arrest in December and is living underground.

"Pierre got married in September. His wife's father is a gendarme," she says, her tone ironic.

"Are we responsible for our parents' professions?" I ask. "Might you not be jealous of the woman who now stands between you and your favorite brother?"

"But the rest of the family also feels Pierre could have done better," she insists.

I finish by learning that Pierre's wife is not religious and imagine how that thunderbolt must have wreaked havoc in this very Catholic family.

I've been invited to attend the General Assembly of the Constantine Union of Youth for Social Action (UJCAS), of which the students' association I have come to chair is a member. Like the AJAAS, this organization brings together members of various community organizations. Before leaving Constantine, Ali Abdelaoui introduced me to the chairman, the gynecologist Jean Le Bail, a very pleasant man. On opening the meeting, Le Bail introduces me to everyone. Meriem Saadane, a twenty-three-year-old nurse, and I are the only "natives" in attendance. When Le Bail mentions that I'm a resident monitor at Aumale high school, a very distinguished lady, Madame Thierry, tells me that her two boys are students there.

Madame Thierry outlines the program of activities for the coming year: "We have to set up extensions in the poorer neighborhoods and one at the town hall in order to help people deal with the administration, hospital visits, schools, etc. We might also instruct local women in the rudiments of hygiene, childcare, and so on."

Louis Vandevelde, who works at the regional interprofessional council, adds a comment: "In my opinion, in addition to our social programs, the assembly should address itself to the causes of the turmoil the country is experiencing."

Dr. Le Bail adds, "Some fundamental political issues have been raised. I feel we have to deal with them."

Their remarks are reassuring. In these times, the association should not be content with simply acting as good Samaritans. During the discussion that follows, there's mention of "rebels," *fellaghas*, "outlaws," qualifiers used throughout the administration and the press by the Europeans but also by Algerians. For many of the latter, the National Liberation Front and its structures and leaders remain a mystery. Deeply disturbed MTLD militants haven't accepted the fact that the insurrection has not been led by their idol, the father of Algerian nationalism, Messali Hadj. In this assembly of Europeans, who know nothing about the Algerian nationalist movement and the crisis, I find myself in a strange position. It is neither the moment nor the place to attempt to enlighten these people of goodwill. However, I don't want to use the same terms when speaking of the front and the Liberation Army. For the moment, obviously, I can't call them *maquisards*, partisans, resistance or freedom fighters, so I come up with the expression "those facing us."

Louis Vandevelde asks for the floor: "I propose that we prepare a statement on the association's position and make it public. I suggest it include an appeal for negotiations with 'those facing us.'" At that point, a businessman who has not yet spoken intervenes to say: "May I point out that the bylaws of our association state clearly that we are apolitical. I oppose putting the resolution to a vote."

The last item on the agenda is the renewal of the executive committee. The chairman says: "I'm overwhelmed with work and won't be able to head up the association any longer. However, my office can continue to serve as its headquarters. If I may suggest someone to replace me, it would be Mokhtar. He has attended meetings of the AJAAS and will bring fresh ideas to our group."

I react quickly: "No, no, I've just arrived here and am still not familiar with the city or its people." Vandevelde and Madame Thierry support Jean Le Bail's proposal. I'm unanimously elected chairman of the Constantine Union of Youth for Social Action. Dr. Le Bail tells me I can use a desk in his office and the services of his secretary.

Anne-Marie, who wasn't able to attend the UJCAS meeting, tells me that Louis Vandevelde is head of the Constantine branch of Vie Nouvelle, an organization in favor of independence for "native peoples," words she pronounces with a sarcastic twist. It's a pejorative and paternalistic expression that I'm pleased to see she also finds objectionable. I feel sufficiently confident with her to mention that I've not been able to make contact with an FLN representative in the city. "Imagine," she recounts, "that last night I danced with a young Algerian lawyer, who has a very European look about him, at the Hotel Cirta. The civil and military elite of the city were all there with their wives but no one realized that in their midst was a leader of the city's outlaws!"

Two days later, Anne-Marie leads me to a building on rue Clémenceau to meet Mohammed Ameziane Aït Ahcene, an apprentice in the Hadj Said law office. With his light brown hair, his long light-skinned face and tinted glasses, he easily passes for a European. During our conversation, he mentions the measures the French administration has just adopted with respect to the sale of antibiotics. In the future, not only will Muslim customers need a prescription at pharmacies, but they will have to present an ID for any purchases. Aït Ahcene denounces the discriminatory, inhuman nature of the measure and feels it will most certainly have an effect on obtaining medical supplies for the Liberation Army.

When we leave his office, I remember Dr. Le Bail and wonder if I can't ask him for prescriptions for myself and for friends of mine. But would I not be throwing myself to the wolves and risk coming to the attention of the police? Also, I barely know the doctor. However, when I went by his office, in between two patients, he came out to ask if I wouldn't wait for him to finish so that we could have a talk. He's the only gynecologist in Constantine who practices the new technique of painless childbirth. He teaches at the hospital and tells me that among his patients is the wife of a French general, and comments, "I couldn't refuse her." I pay close attention to what he says, looking to see how far his ideas go and what he thinks of the FLN and the National Liberation Army (ALN). A good talker, he passes from one subject to another, jokes easily. He tells me that during the Second World War, after the Americans landed in North Africa, he crossed Franco's Spain to join the Free French Forces. General de Gaulle and the National Council of the Resistance had set up their head-quarters in Algiers. There he met a young European woman, whom he married. He's in his late thirties, has light hair slightly balding, is of medium height, and wears very thick glasses. When he stops to reflect, he smiles in a dreamy way. I like our conversations and am aware that I intrigue him. He seems to want to situate me in relation to what's going on but I remain evasive. Nothing he's said yet gives me the impression that he favors Algerian independence or that he knows how to hold his tongue.

Among the samples I see on the shelves of the office are antibiotics. I could just take off with them but then think better of it, given the general air of suspicion that reigns in the city. Now that we've entered a state of war, the army and the police are everywhere; Algerian stool pigeons, too. However, MTLD militants still linked to Messali are more rare than in Algiers. A few days later, I decide to take my chances and stop at Le Bail's office almost every day after the secretary has gone to lunch. I pick out the boxes of penicillin and other antibiotics and shove them into my book bag; I hide them in a box in the closet of my room. The secretary, a young Algerian who learned typing at her primary school, has no idea of what I'm doing. Her centers of interest are elsewhere, more frivolous.

The political situation is evolving. Less than a month after the creation of a Maghreb liberation army in Morocco, the puppet sultan, Ben Arafa, resigns. The French government is forced to reinstall Mohamed Ben Youssef on the throne and negotiate. On November 6, 1955, the negotiations, held in France, end with a statement recognizing Moroccan independence "freely consented." Another amazing piece of news occurs on November 11, when nineteen men condemned to death escape from prison, among them Mostefa Ben Boulaïd, head of the Algerian Liberation Army in the Aurès Mountains. He had been arrested in February at the Tunisian border as he was heading for Libya to buy arms. His arrest served to inform the public of the name of one of the leaders of the Revolution of November 1, 1954.

Constantine resembles a city under siege. The shock is unbelievable. The military and the police multiply the number of house searches in the Arab neighborhoods and the number of controls in the streets and on the highways. European fear is manifest. Algerians, resigned and mistrustful, rarely advance an opinion. According to rumor the prisoners who escaped hid in the Rhummel Gorges and have now joined the Liberation Army. One tale I hear claims that a winged horse whisked them to the mountains in the dark of night.

At the high school, the Algerians speak in half-tones about the evasion but don't let on what they think. According to Saïd Benkhaled, the students from the mountain areas are enthusiastic about Ben Boulaïd and his companions. The four European colleagues say nothing, at least not in front of me. The same is true of the three professors from metropolitan France who eat with us in our special dining room. Of the four other monitors, only one is from Algeria. One day after lunch, one of them shows us his revolver and compares it to that of a colleague who did a stint in the air force. Pierre Gagneux, who is preparing a doctorate in history, demands that they put their "toys" away. Pierre reads *France Observateur* and never hesitates to let the table know his opinion of what's happening. The French colleagues are embarrassed and don't want to associate with him. A big guy with a round face, glasses, and a goatee, Gagneux tells me that he is "for the emancipation of Algeria."

"Arlette has really fallen for you. You're the only one who doesn't seem to realize it," Anne-Marie says with a laugh. Arlette Gil is a friend of hers and also a resident monitor at the girls' high school. She's tall and stocky. She laughs a lot, talks loudly, and starts singing the minute anyone mentions the title of a song by Tino Rossi, Edith Piaf, or Luis Mariano. I appreciate her spontaneity and sensuality. She's very natural in her ways and easily displays her soul in song. One day, she gives me a picture of herself and adds on the back the words of a song by Dario Moreno:

> *Jusqu'au bout du monde*
> *Tant que tu vivras*
> *Tu verras mon ombre*
> *Se pencher sur toi…*

> *(To the ends of the earth*
> *As long as you live*
> *You'll see my shadow*
> *Alongside you…)*

When the box of antibiotics is full and I'm ready to take it to Aït Ahcene's office, rue Clémenceau, I think of Arlette. The soldiers and cops are adept at racial profiling. Luckily, the day I was stopped and frisked by a patrol, I had nothing on me. Arlette picks me up at the school, but before going to our favorite café, we leave off the package, which I tell her is filled with toys that I'm giving to a friend who's leaving for Berrouaghia the next day.

Aït Ahcene, furious, tells me that the Jewish consistory has replied negatively to the FLN's request for support. "We are French and want to remain French," they insist. In the old city, the Jewish and Arab quarters are adjacent. Here, as in the rest of the country, Jews and Muslims blend together with their looks as well as their customs, cuisine, and music.

Before Christmas vacation, Aït Ahcene, who is leaving Constantine and whom I suspect had something to do with Ben Boulaïd's escape from prison, introduces me to Salah

Kedid, who will replace him. The new FLN representative is about twenty-five years old, is short and thin. His head sinks into his shoulders, he speaks with a low voice and swallows his words. The first time I meet him, I find it difficult to understand him. With his brother, he runs the Scheherazade Café on the upper level of the Arab neighborhood, near the Place de la Laine.

As usual, I leave Constantine for two weeks with the family, but on the way stop off in Boufarik to see my brother Mohamed. I spend the night and, for the first time, dare talk politics with him. Like my parents, he wanted me to concentrate on my studies and not get involved. I tell him what I know about the crisis between Messali and the central committee after the discovery of the OS, about the creation of the CRUA and the National Liberation Front. I presume he was not able to follow events while he was in prison. Fearing that he still supports Messali, I have held him in my thoughts for months. He listens to me, gives no indication of what he thinks. Has he been shocked by my audacity? I go further and say: "As far as I'm concerned, I've made my choice. The people behind the uprising and the members of the FLN are former members of the Special Organization who denounced the personality cult and are in favor of collective leadership."

Mohamed raises his head, seemingly satisfied, and comments on the deviations that destroyed the party. He knows that Ben Boulaïd was a member of the OS and thinks he knows the names of other former members. Relieved that we are in the same camp, I describe the situation in Constantine and the overwhelming presence of French soldiers, and note: "Here, as in Algiers, I haven't seen anything that would indicate the country is at war." "In Algiers, in the Casbah, nationalists are killing nationalists," he says with a sad voice. The struggle between members of the FLN and Messali's followers now plays out with guns and knives.

In Berrouaghia, it's cold. The streets are empty but the cafés are packed. I hang out with my student friends at the Café des Sports. Ahmed-Cherif Bousmaha is proud of the Mitidja association's new executive committee. I'm surprised to learn that my friend Ali Baghdadi is now the chairman; just a few months ago he had refused to be on the executive committee. His father is a *caïd* and he feared damaging his career. But since then, a certain number of supporters of the French administration have joined together in a resolution known as the "Motion of the 61" representing the views of elected officials, members of the French National Assembly, the Senate, the French Union Council, and the Algerian Assembly. It calls for recognition of our "national reality." They are finally shedding the myths of assimilation and integration. Bousmaha plans to launch a journal with the title *Student Awakening*.

The "events," as they are called, are grounds for questions concerning Messali's role and the identity of the FLN leaders. "The people heading the struggle have to keep their names secret. We don't want leaders who take themselves for *zaïms* or guides. The personality cult is a dead issue," I tell them.

My explanations satisfy the young people at the Café des Sports. However, the MTLD militants with whom I talk at the Café des Voyageurs find it inconceivable that a revolution is

taking place without the father of Algerian nationalism. They
have never forgotten Messali's visit to the town, the delirious
welcome the villagers gave him. He is their liberator. Without
him, there is no guiding light. The perfume salesman, known
for his desire to be in theater and emulate the Egyptian actor
Youssef Wahbi, leaves me in a state of wonder. After listening
to me talk, he subjects me to a series of questions intended to
amuse three of his friends who are present.

"Do you remember the last earthquake in Algeria and the
city that was most affected by it?"

I smile, not knowing where this is leading: "I don't see
what that has to do with the subject of our conversation. But
of course, I do: it took place in Orléansville in September
1954." The earthquake devastated the town itself and the
hamlets along the Chelif Valley. It left hundreds of people
dead, thousands wounded, and tens of thousands homeless.

"Do you know the cause of that earthquake?" he asks.

"I give up," I answer.

The perfumer adopts a serious, mysterious look: "The
Orléansville earthquake was a sign from God the Almighty.
He was announcing the November first events. Our Lord
chose Orléansville to remind us that in that city Messali was
stopped from holding a rally. He was arrested and deported
to France."

These militants, for the most part illiterate, discovered
nationalism with Messali in 1941. The regime had condemned
Messali and his nephew, Mohammed Memchaoui, to sixteen
years of hard labor. Messali was sent to the penal institution at
Lambese, whereas Mohammed Memchaoui was placed under
house arrest in Berrouaghia. Residing in a studio across from

the war monument, Memchaoui would meet and talk with the young people of the village. It was he who encouraged my brother Mohamed, Ali Baha, and Ahmed-Cherif Slimani to create the first cell of the clandestine Algerian People's Party (PPA). The authorities later transferred Memchaoui to western Algeria. They only discovered the impact of his stay in the village at the time of the May 1945 demonstrations at the end of the Second World War.

I stop to see Father Delahaye and learn he has tuberculosis and is leaving the village for a sanatorium. I'm losing a friend and the village a priest who tried to change the attitudes of his parishioners from total disdain to one of understanding. I hope that failure has had no effect on his illness and wish him well.

According to rumor, combatants have been seen in the outlying regions of the village. Yahia Ferhat, whose brother was a member of the Special Organization and one of the many held in prison in Blida, tells me he is in contact with some guerrillas and through a contact with a local merchant has been able to obtain sixty pairs of army walking shoes but doesn't have enough money to pay for them. I give him what I can.

In January I return to Constantine and the climate of war. The sight of uniforms and weapons on the city's streets reinforces the feeling that I'm slowly stifling. I'm thankful for the friends and acquaintances I've made. The students and the staff at the high school are engaging. And, of course, there's the incontrovertible 'Ammi Mokrane.

"I spent my vacation in Kabylia," he tells me. "Everyone is freezing to death. The poverty and the snow are horrible." I see from the insistent look on his face that he has something to tell me. He drags his broom to the half-open door, closes it, and with an inspired air plants himself in the middle of the room. He places his weight on the broomstick and, with a proud look in his eyes, announces: "You know that the men fighting in the mountains are like us." I say nothing, I especially don't want to remind him that not long ago he was convinced they were Egyptians or Tunisians or other foreigners. He smiles his toothless smile, shakes his head, not understanding how I can be so ignorant, and continues: "I saw them with my own eyes, like me here in front of you. They were wearing uniforms, they were carrying weapons and are from the region."

"Were they from your family or your tribe?" I ask.

"No, but I know they're from Kabylia."

On January 2, 1956, the French elect a new National Assembly in which the Republican Front dominates. "Peace in Algeria" was at the heart of its electoral program. On February 1 Guy Mollet, the secretary general of the French section of the Workers International, is named prime minister. General Catroux is named governor-general of Algeria. The next day, an immense crowd acclaims Jacques Soustelle before his departure from Algiers. A year earlier, the same crowd had taxed him as a Semite sent by the Jewish prime minister, Pierre Mendes-France. When on February 6 the head of the French government arrives in Algiers, he's greeted with cries of "Mollet to the Gallows." When he lays a bouquet on the war monument, the demonstrators throw tomatoes, rotten eggs, and buckets of dirt at him. He replaces General Catroux with Robert Lacoste and, ten days later, states that "France must and will remain in Algeria." He obtains the support of the French Communist Party for exceptional security measures. Those in favor of French Algeria are jubilant. The University Action Committee for French Algeria decides to stop Professor Mandouze, director of *Consciences maghribines*, from teaching his courses. When they arrive with a rope to hang him, they face a barrage of UGEMA students. A fight breaks out, but the Algerian students succeed in protecting the professor.

At the UGEMA congress in Paris from March 24 to 30, the sixty delegates vote unanimously for the independence of Algeria, the liberation of all imprisoned patriots, and negotiations with the National Liberation Front. I read in the *Le Monde* of April 3 the speech by Mohammed Khemisti, who chaired the UGEMA congress: "How can we study when our feet are bound with the chains of colonialist slavery? Depersonalized, uprooted, exiled from their language and their past, the Muslim students of Algeria demand the right to be themselves, to study their language, to explore their cultural roots. Their cause is first and foremost that of the freedom and sovereignty that command the rest."

Salah Kedid, who replaced Aït Ahcene, is not as timid as I first thought. I realize that he's simply more at ease in Arabic than French. "The brothers need a way of printing their tracts," he tells me. "It's difficult to get a duplicating machine without becoming suspect, but we have the money to pay for it." And I know it's impossible for an Algerian to buy a mimeograph without being reported to the police.

"I'll try," I say. I exclude the idea of making the purchase on behalf of the Constantine students' association or the local Muslim youth association. I consider talking to Pierre Gagneux about it. He regularly lends me *France Observateur*. I know he's for "the emancipation of Algeria." But will he prove it?

"The students' association needs a mimeograph, which I can't buy without being reported to the police. Can you do it for me?" I ask. "No problem," he replies.

The first store he enters doesn't have a mimeograph in stock. The storekeeper says he can order it and then asks for his name. In the second store, the salesman tells him he has to show his ID, explain the use the machine will be put to, and understand that he may be called in by the police for questioning. "It's to print my doctorate," he explains. The salesmen finally talks him into buying a duplicator that is not subject to the same regulations. Convinced he will be saving money for the association, Gagneux goes for it. The machine contains a gelatin plaque that can reproduce one page at a time by hand. I thank him, reimburse him, and think about who I can contact for the purchase of a real automatic duplicator.

"The house is always open," Father Chanut told me the day Anne-Marie introduced me to this Jesuit priest who lives in the Arab sector of the city, at the edge of the Jewish quarter. When we visited him, I saw several Algerian children come and go. Aged about fifty, with a smiling, round face, Father Chanut adores the area and his neighbors. Anne-Marie insisted that he is extremely open-minded.

I find him in his office, behind a desk cluttered with papers, books, and newspapers. I waste no time: "We need a printer, a duplicator," I tell him, "and we can pay for it. Can you get one for us?" Still smiling, he stares at me and nods his head. He doesn't seem surprised. He says to come back in two days and tells me about how much he thinks it will cost. I come back with Salah Kedid, who gives him the money. They decide which day he will pick up the machine.

When I first met Amara Rachid at the Café du Hammam in Algiers, I was immediately struck by his intelligence, but I hadn't yet realized he was a genius. He's managed to find my trace and comes to see me at the high school. He's on a mission for Algiers. I accompany him to the mosque in the rue Clémenceau, where he has an appointment with Cheikh Kheireddine, a leading figure in the Ulemas Association that is in the process of joining the FLN. In the afternoon I meet him with Djamel Amrani, president of the Philippeville Muslim Students Association. Heavy, though not exactly fat, Amrani has the looks of an actor. He's on the point of leaving Philippeville to join Mostefa Ben Boulaïd in the mountains.

Amara comes to Constantine on three occasions. I'll never forget the day we're crossing the Valée Square: he suddenly stops, asks me to look at him straight on, and proudly announces, "I've seen the Algerian flag floating over free territory. These army boots I'm wearing carry traces of freedom's soil." Moved, I nonetheless react: "They're typical partisan boots and could get you in trouble." Amara couldn't care less. With his usual verve, he says: "you can't imagine how happy I am since I've experienced life as a free man with the National Liberation Army. I've realized my dream and can die in peace."

I understand him. I've read Amara's poems, I recognize him as someone who is seeking love and freedom, who is haunted by injustice. I love his romantic side, plus his intelligence and courage. "The landless peasants and farm workers support the Liberation Army without question," he tells me. "They form its indestructible base. The officers are militants from rural regions, some of whom did their military service in the French army. Others were merchants or craftsmen. To achieve its goals, the Revolution must include every layer of the population. And I can assure you that our leaders are doing everything they can to that end."

Amara has not told me why he's been visiting the region. However, he has talked about the extraordinary men who are leading the Revolution, without revealing their names. I have since discovered that the two main personalities he has worked with are Larbi Ben M'Hidi and Abane Ramdane. In addition, I know he was stopped by the police when accompanying Ferhat Abbas to a meeting with Cheikh Kheireddine and that he played a role in the decision of the organizations of those two men to join the FLN. I am led to believe today, a posteriori, that as a close collaborator of Abane Ramdane and Larbi Ben M'hidi, his trips to the region were involved with the organization of the Soummam Congress.

The spectacular execution, on March 29, of Jean Sammarcelli, the police commissioner of Constantine, shocks the city. The Algerians whom he terrorized dubbed him "the hangman." His funeral gives vent to a "hunt" to kill Arabs. It seems that Sammarcelli's son, a student at Aumale, was the first to scream for vengeance and start shooting. The civil and military authorities make no arrests. The tension among the Algerian students and personnel is at its maximum. The students talk about joining the Liberation Army. I set up a cell to collect money for the FLN. Two members of the cleaning staff donate part of their salaries. A student at another high school meets with students from Aumale and claims he is in touch with some combatants. Maybe he is, but if so, he talks and brags too much and I'm mistrustful. It's difficult to verify all the talk: Constantine falls between two military zones, the Aurès Mountains and North Constantine.

The Mouloud, the Prophet Mohamed's birthday celebration, like the other Muslim holidays, is not a legal holiday. After lunch, I invite my colleague Benyoussef Baba Ali for coffee at the Excelsior. In the courtyard of the high school we hear gunshots and think they might be fireworks for the Mouloud. A few yards farther on, however, in the rue de France, we see men with guns shooting at others who dash into nearby alleyways. We run back to the school courtyard. At the sound of the shots, Monsieur Horst, the administrator, and Monsieur Delmas, the supervisor, come outside; we all line up at the iron grille along the street and witness the horror. Three young Jews from the neighborhood, revolvers in hand, are running after the man in a *gandoura* and traditional skullcap who was on guard at the site of some street repairs. They kill him point-blank. Horrified, we agitate our arms and howl. The assassins begin shooting blindly, jump, scream, dance something resembling an Indian war dance. A military truck arrives and slows down to make the turn into the avenue leading to the bridge over the Rhummel Gorges. The criminals shout "Long live France" and try to get a hold on the truck and hoist themselves onto it, but the soldiers stop them, stamping on their hands and feet with the butts of their rifles. In the distance we hear more gunshots.

The murderous attacks go on for hours. They began with a grenade in the bar of a police informer in the Jewish quarter, then extended to a section of the Arab quarter and continued until nightfall. Fear takes over throughout the city. Two days later, I meet Salah Kedid. He tells me 425 people were killed. When he sees the look of surprise on my face, he adds: "Whole families were assassinated, their neighbors, even their cleaning women."

The way Salah confronts the army and the police is amazing. He has very little formal education but a million ideas. He tells me that since the rampage he's decided to mark every Saturday with an attack in the center of the city. And for the day he runs out of explosives and weapons, he is training militants (*fidayin*) in the use of bows and arrows. "Bows and arrows?" I ask. "Yes, real bows and arrows." "I don't see our guys circulating in town with bows and arrows and not getting picked up by the police," I comment. "They won't be in the street. They'll be behind curtains or in doorways and using poisoned arrows." If anything, Salah certainly doesn't lack imagination!

For Easter, I decide to go to Morocco to see my friend Abdelkader Boukhari. Morocco became independent on

March 2. The Moroccan flag is everywhere, at the stations, on public buildings, on the houses and shanties I see from the train. Abdelkader lives in Oued Zem, the very city that revolted the year before, leading to the return of Sultan Mohamed V. Abdelkader works at the courthouse, has a villa and a car. His friends are from wealthy families. The contrast between the luxury of some and the poverty of others hits me square in the face. He shows me the traces of burned bodies visible on the tar of certain streets. The August 20 uprising began when a European dietician opened fire on some demonstrators. Every Moroccan I meet, on learning I've come from Algeria, says: "Soon, Algeria will be independent, too!"

On my return, Mohamed Drareni, the head of the General Union of Algerian Workers (UGTA), asks me to organize a teachers' trade union. Wherever they teach, at Aumale or the modern high school or the Arabic high school, the teachers are reticent; they're afraid of the police, since the head of the Algerian hospital union was assassinated, and they're afraid of losing their jobs. The only people willing to join the union work in the sanitation services or the dining halls.

At the high school, since some of the European students took part in the slaughter of Arabs after the death of police chief Sammarcelli and on the Mouloud holiday, the Algerians want to join the freedom fighters. One Sunday evening, four boarding students are missing: Hamza Benamrane, Abdelmadjid Hihi, Abdelaziz Kara, and Abdelaziz Zerdani. A fifth, Abderrazak Bouhara, catches up with them a few days later.

In rue de France and rue Caraman, there are patrols every few yards. One Saturday morning, I drop by Dr. Le Bail's office; a violent explosion in a nearby street stops our conversation dead. Le Bail leaves immediately to see if he can be of help. When he returns he says: "Nasty all that, it was a horrible sight."

"I agree with you, Jean, it's absurd," I comment. "But what can a defenseless people do against the wholesale murder of Arabs, napalm dropped on their villages, shoot-outs in the stadiums? These are people who have been abandoned by French public opinion and the powers that be."

Le Bail lowers his eyes, is silent for a moment, then looks at me fixedly: "All I can say is that if a wounded combatant is brought in here, I will take care of him and definitely not inform the police." I congratulate him on doing his duty as a member of the medical profession. "It's not just that," he says, "it's a commitment. As you know, I'm from France but my wife and my children were born here. It's their country that I've decided to live in. I've chosen the side that wants a new Algeria, one that is just and democratic. But don't ask me to take up arms against my own country."

We are both caught up in the emotion of the moment.

In early May, I receive notice of a student congress to take place in Algiers; the Constantine Muslim Students Association is asked to send two delegates. The association has no money, I pay what I can for the train tickets and their stay but come up short. I decide to let two colleagues, Benyoussef Baba Ali and Pierre Gagneux, in on the plans and request a contribution: they gladly chip in.

On Saturday, May 19, before the delegates return, the news breaks that Algerian university and high school students have voted for a general unlimited strike of classes and exams. Benkhaled and Maouch come back on Sunday evening with the tract announcing the decision: "...Will a degree make us better corpses?...Duty demands that we fight day in and day out alongside those who are dying as free men combatting the enemy...We have to leave the university's halls and join the struggle..."

Sunday morning, the Algerian students come down from the dormitory with their baggage. The attendant refuses to open the gate and informs Monsieur Horst. He and the supervisor beg them to go back upstairs. The principal arrives and explains that he can't allow them to leave the grounds without their parents' permission. The students hesitate but finally decide to return to the dormitory.

I learn that at Duveyrier, the European students arrive in class with pistols in their pockets and belts. How can anyone study or take exams in such conditions? The following week two students running from the police, Tayeb Ferhat and Mohamed Tahar Ben M'hidi, the brother of one of the leaders of the Revolution, arrive in Constantine in the hope of joining the Liberation Army. I inform Salah Kedid. A few days later, they are on their way. Another student arrives, Lamine Khene, a member of the UGEMA executive committee. The police are on his trail; he needs a secure hideout while waiting to leave for the mountains. Dr. Le Bail agrees to put him up.

Anne-Marie tells me that several girls in their senior year at Laverand high school want to join the maquis. Salah reminds me that the army doesn't lack men for the moment and that these women would only be useful if they were nurses. "And if we provided the training for them?" I propose. "Great idea!" he replies.

I inform Dr. Le Bail that the army needs nurses and ask what he can suggest. He is willing to begin training at his office and will try to find a way for practical training in a clinic or hospital as well. He gasps and says "Wow" when he opens the door to my office the next morning and finds me there with three candidates: Fadhela Saadane, eighteen years old; Malika Boudoukha, the same age with two long braids; and Zina Mahdi, twenty years old. "I want to serve my country, my people," Zina announces.

A few days after the training begins, Meriem Saadane, whom I know from the Union of Youth for Social Action, arrives at Le Bail's with her sister: "I'm a trained nurse and I want to join the maquis, too," she says. I introduce Meriem to Salah Kedid.

My colleague, Benyoussef Baba Ali, also wants to join the Liberation Army. Salah warns me: "There are too many people at the moment who want to leave for the mountains. If he's running from the police or has had military or hospital training, okay. Otherwise, he'll have to commit an attack in the city."

Madame Thierry of the Union of Youth for Social Action invites me for lunch. Her husband wants to meet me. Their two boys accompany us at the table, then Monsieur Thierry and I have coffee alone in his study. He's a member of the executive council of the Ouenza mines and knows politicians in Algeria and in France. "My friends Pierre Pflimlin and

Maurice Schumann are coming to Algeria on an information tour and will visit Constantine with René Mayer, the former representative of our city in the French National Assembly. Their hope is to establish contact with "those who are facing us," he tells me solemnly.

"Their political leaders can no doubt be found in Algiers," I reply.

He continues: "My friends have a concrete proposal to make to resolve the Algerian problem. They want to know what 'those who are fighting' think."

I answer: "The three-step proposal being put forward— 'cease-fire, elections, negotiations'—is certainly unacceptable."

"I totally agree with you."

I continue: "Algeria must go forward, like Morocco and Tunisia, with negotiations that recognize our right to independence."

"The problem is more complex," he notes. "Neither Morocco nor Tunisia have nine hundred thousand Frenchmen on their land. Given the diversity of the population, we could envisage an independent Algeria in association with France."

"Ferhat Abbas suggested that formula ten years ago," I point out, "and as you know, he just joined the FLN in Cairo."

Monsieur Thierry becomes more specific: "An independent Algeria would have a constitution similar to Lebanon's. The national assembly would include representatives of the various communities: French, Arab, Berber, Mozabite. The head of state would be French, the head of government Arab, and the head of the national assembly Berber."

Unimpressed, I make no comment. When he asks for my opinion, I simply say, "I'll transmit."

I report the conversation and the proposal to Salah.

Pflimlin, a Christian democrat, is a member of the MRP, the Popular Republican Movement, and René Mayer is a member of the Radical Party. The constitution France has imposed on Lebanon is based on religion. It ensures that the Christians maintain power. Even if the intention is to come between the Algerian people in accordance with the principle of divide and conquer, I feel that the proposal should be transmitted to our leaders. I never receive a response.

One day Salah knocks at my door. He sits down, takes off his shoe, and lifts the inner sole to take out a piece of paper that he hands to me. "The guys in the mountains need this stuff," he says. I look at it and see a list of surgical instruments and, on the last line, 120 reams of paper. An Algerian who's not a doctor or a pharmacist can't buy such tools without running the risk of being arrested. Ditto for the 120 reams of paper. "Okay," I say. "I'll let you know."

When he's finished putting his shoe back on, I announce: "You know, at the end of this month the school year is over. I mention it because I want to join the maquis then."

"Our brothers need arms not men," he replies. "They don't need you there. You're more useful here."

"But I can't continue living at the high school, and I'm not from Constantine."

"Let me think about it," Salah says, ending the conversation.

When I show the list to Dr. Le Bail, he frowns and says, "If they need such instruments, that means they have a hospital. I'll buy them." For the reams of paper, I remember Father Chanut, who got me the duplicator, and also think of Louis Vandevelde, who works for the Social Security Administration. It would be a way of testing Louis. I've become friendly with him and his wife Hélène. They often invite me for dinner and Louis is giving me driving lessons in his little Renault. I'm sure they're for an independent Algeria but I've never tested their commitment.

"Louis, can you buy some copy paper for me?" I ask. He smiles, looks at me with wonder. I insist: "Maybe you don't know it, but in today's world buying a ream of paper is risky business for an Algerian."

"I can give you what I have here at home right away," he says, "and if you need more, let me know."

"I need one hundred twenty reams."

"I presume it's not for your personal use." He thinks a minute and then adds, "I'll arrange for them to be delivered to the house."

The administrator of the high school comes up to me in the courtyard and warns me not to let any strangers in while I'm on duty.

"Of course, but why?"

"Yesterday, I surprised someone looking at the courtyard bulletin board and I feel sure he wasn't there to read the grades that are posted but for something else. I had the feeling it was a cop. I asked him to leave and he turned and left."

I don't tell him that a few days earlier, *'Ammi* Mokrane, the sweeper, surprised probably the same person outside my room. Then Anne-Marie reports that Arlette Gil heard the daughter of a colonel tell her girlfriends in the dining hall: "It seems that Mademoiselle Chaulet is dating a *fellagha*." She exclaims: "Arlette's the one who's flirting with that guy and I'm the one they're accusing of dating an outlaw!"

The father of the student in question is a colonel in the CRS, the state security forces. I become more wary and once again ask Salah to arrange for me to join the army. "If you can't stay here you can certainly be useful in Algiers," he replies. I'm not so sure, but in any event I can't live in Algiers without a job or a room. My work stops on the last day of June. Once the school administration gives me my written notice of summer release, I can go. It's only a formality but it ensures a salary during the summer months. Since the state of emergency has been instituted, if I want to leave the country it's a piece of paper I'll need.

On June 19, Ahmed Zabana and Abdelkader Ferradj, two Algerian patriots, are executed by guillotine in the courtyard of the Barberousse prison in Algiers. I ask Anne-Marie, who is leaving for home, to reserve a hotel room for me in Algiers beginning July 2. Rumor has it that the FLN will be calling a general strike as of July 5, the date French troops occupied Sidi Ferruch in 1830. I want to use my stay in Algiers to make contact with *Ennidham*, the Organization.

I'm happy to learn that the training program for our army's future nurses is going well. According to Jean the hospital personnel are delighted with such studious and serious women. Vandevelde and Le Bail have bought the surgical instruments and the reams of paper. On Saturday, June 30, I take Salah to meet Dr. Le Bail. He reimburses him for the equipment and makes arrangements to pick it up. Then we take a bus to Avenue Bienfait, where the Vandeveldes live. We get off at the last stop, Place de la Brèche, and decide to continue on foot. Salah looks at his watch and becomes agitated: "Quick, walk fast, faster!" "We're not far," I say, "we don't want to attract the attention of a patrol." "At five o'clock there'll be an attack," he confides. "Where?" I ask. "Right here, in front of the Casino."

I speed up but the sidewalk is full of people. A few yards from the Casino, the explosion hits. The gust of air raises the glasses off my nose. People scream, run in every direction. Salah heads for the taxi stand, I follow him. He jumps into a car that takes off without giving me time to get in. Salah yells: "Take the one over there!" But the driver of that taxi refuses and drives off. There are no more taxis, they've all disappeared. I walk fast, try not to run. I avoid rue Caraman, take a parallel street to the left. The explosion must have been heard here too, everyone seems to be on the lookout. Near the Ahmed Bey palace, I turn right, heading for the rue de France. Out of a bar, a soldier with a revolver in his hand is yelling something. He stops me and points his gun: "You're the one who did it," he snaps, raising the revolver toward my nose. He's obviously been drinking and wants to impress the people who come out of the bar as well as the neighborhood people who stop to watch. He repeats: "You're the bastard."

I raise my hands and say: "No, Monsieur, you can search

me, I'm a monitor at the high school just down the street." A Jewish woman wearing a scarf like my mother's, crazy with anger, stands behind the soldier and screams: "It's him! It's him!" She draws closer and spits in my face. I wipe my face but she continues spitting and yelling insults. The soldier turns his weapon away and with it indicates the direction of the school. "Get outa here, you bastard!" he says, dismissing me.

For the people watching, the show is over. I walk slowly down the street, perspiring profusely, not sure that's the end of it. I wipe my face again. In my room, I wash up and lie down on the bed exhausted. I want to cry. All the soldier had to do was pull the trigger. I was no doubt afraid, but I can't say I saw death close up. I've seen animals die at the slaughterhouse; the idea of touching a dead person doesn't frighten me. The thought that it could have been me back there enrages me.

According to *La Dépêche de Constantine* the attack left three people dead and forty-five wounded. When you learn that a hand grenade contains forty-eight pellets, that means that each piece of steel hit a victim. In other words if the terrace of the Casino hadn't been packed, Salah and I could have received one. The newspaper article mentions that among the dead was a shoeshine boy, a kid. When I take Salah to the Vandeveldes the next day, he tells me that he has sent some money to the child's parents.

Monday, July 2, 1956, I leave Constantine for Algiers. From the train I see sawed-off telephone poles near the railway. The train slows down for a series of freight cars overturned along the tracks. Near Bibans, the landscape is wild, spectacular. Dark cliffs dominate and set me dreaming. I imagine walking on those crests in the uniform of the Liberation Army with a rifle slung over my shoulder.

The trip seems endless. At the station in Algiers, a smiling Anne-Marie is waiting for me. I'm happy to see her. She gives me a peck on the cheek and in her singsong voice exclaims, "You're still tall and gorgeous." The compliment is exaggerated; it's true I'm six feet two but definitely not "gorgeous." I'm used to Anne-Marie's tendency to overstate everything. When we leave the station, she announces, "You know that the UGTA headquarters was bombed."

"Yes," I reply, "I heard it on the radio."

"The police were able to get their hands on a lot of documents. Your name figures among them. A number of trade unionists and activists have been arrested already. Next week's strike is going to provoke them, there'll be a lot of shakedowns everywhere and you're on their lists. So there's no question of going to a hotel. You'll stay with us."

I can't believe what's happening. I put my suitcases down, the time to absorb the news and start asking questions. She tells me it was Mohamed Drareni, the trade union leader, who warned her. "In that case," I reason, "I want to leave for the mountains."

"There are so many men trying to join the Liberation Army. You can be more useful elsewhere."

"I've heard that song before."

"Don't worry," she says, "tomorrow I'll have more information and tomorrow night we'll have dinner at Pierre and Claudine's."

When we arrive at the Chaulets' apartment, on the second floor, 3 rue Monge, her mother welcomes me warmly. I see that Pierre resembles her. Except for Pierre, all the other children are on hand: four girls and two boys. They watch me put my suitcases in the hall. The living-dining room where I'll be sleeping has a window that opens onto a balcony and the street. The table is set for dinner. Madame Chaulet asks whether I would like some lemonade, tells Marguerite to serve it, and disappears into the kitchen. Each time she appears, a quick look from her keeps the children calm. She reminds me of my father, whose presence alone would keep us all quiet. Her way of doing things is that of a woman sure of herself and capable of great affection for her family and others.

Pierre and Anne-Marie resemble their mother, whereas Marguerite, nineteen, and Yves, nine, resemble each other. Tall, with an oval face and blue eyes, Marguerite has reddish hair worn in a long braid down her back. I can see she admires Anne-Marie and wants to share the friendship that links her sister and me. She reddens when I look at her. Jean-François is fourteen, Suzette twelve, and Christiane ten. When their father arrives, I realize that Marguerite and most of the others resemble him. His hair is graying, his mustache is straight and full, his eyes piercing. He is not intimidating, as I had feared. He smiles, gives me a strong handshake, and thanks me for helping his daughter. At dinner he says: "The November first events have opened my eyes and made me aware of how enormous the Algerian problem is." On the way from the station, Anne-Marie had told me that her parents have become less reticent concerning her relationship with Salah Louanchi.

I spend the next morning at the apartment while Anne-Marie goes to get "fresh orders." She comes back at lunchtime with her father and takes me aside: "You're to go to Paris and work with the FLN's French Federation. They need you there. Since it's difficult to reserve a seat on a plane right now, I've spoken to Papa and he'll be able to do it for you."

I'm completely disoriented. "But I have no desire to land in a city where I don't know anyone. I want to join the army," I repeat.

"Whatever you decide, you'll be safer in Paris than here."

Monsieur Chaulet asks when I want to leave and offers to make the reservation. I thank him and tell him I want to go home and see my family first.

"You're right," interjects Madame Chaulet, "go see your mother. I'm sure she's waiting impatiently for you."

That evening Marguerite, Anne-Marie, and I have dinner at Pierre and Claudine's. For the girls, the couple is Pierre. They adore him. Despite Anne-Marie's description of Claudine as the daughter of a gendarme, I find her tall and lovely. Her brown hair is long, she has a well-shaped mouth that makes different movements as she describes her experience of painless childbirth. She's proud of having practiced the new method with Luc, their newborn. The two sisters are in ecstasy with their first nephew, a two-week-old baby who swings his arms and legs about and cries. He's lying in a soft, pillowed cradle. At his age my body, my arms and legs were bound tightly and I slept in a wooden box. The girls make silly faces at the baby and make me laugh. Claudine and Pierre are happy and very affectionate. When Pierre offers to drive us back downtown, the girls refuse. We leave the heights and descend the slopes through small deserted streets, singing and laughing. Marguerite and I start running; I'm first to get to the telephone pole we selected as a goal. Marguerite, overcome with excitement, grabs my arm and says she's going to retain me with a judo hold. "I'll show you what I can do to you," she brags. "I warn you," I flash back, "I took boxing lessons for three years. I don't want to break your nose. Let go of me." She calms down for a moment, then suddenly jumps on my back and tells me to trot. Anne-Marie yells at her to stop it. I don't know what to think, Marguerite is nineteen years old.

The next day, Wednesday, July 4, I go to the central post office and call 042 in Berrouaghia to announce my arrival. I leave the Chaulet family, my emotions in havoc.

In the village, soldiers are everywhere, as during the Second World War. But they're not Englishmen stationed here before going into battle against Nazi imperialism. They're French conscripts here to bolster a racist, unjust, freedom-smashing system. Thursday, July 5, the day of the strike, my parents are up before dawn, as usual. After drinking his coffee, my father goes to the mosque for the early morning prayer, then comes back home. He sits down to read Sidi Khellil, his religious mentor. Two hours later, there are heavy, loud knocks at the door. My mother lets out a few words of malediction and goes to answer the knock. Mustafa and I follow her. From behind the door, she cries, "Who's there?" A voice with authority replies: "Tell Miloud to come open the butcher shop." From her limited vocabulary, she finds the right French phrase:

"He's sick." The voice continues: "Tell his son to come supply the army."

Mustafa and I move away from the door. He tells me that
my father has a contract to supply the army with meat and
that if he refuses to obey, there'll be consequences. I suggest that he tell them he'll serve them and will close up again
afterward. And so it is. "The stores are all closed," Baba says,
"and in the streets all I saw were soldiers."

The atmosphere in the village is nothing like the last time
I was home. Withdrawn, mistrustful, nobody knows who's a
Messalist and who's a Frontist. According to Mustafa, Yahia
Ferhat was captured and killed. He was supplying a Messalist
group of soldiers. At Christmastime I had given him money
to pay for army boots the combatants had ordered. Frontists
from the Liberation Army arrived in the village and executed
him. I'd known Yahia all my life and don't doubt his patriotism, his good faith. The maquisards with whom he was in
contact were fighting against the French army in order to
free the country. They sold him on their way of thinking.
Like others in the village, he was part of Messali's cult.

Part Three

SOLDIER OF THE ALN SIGNAL CORPS

I've made up my mind. I won't go to France but to Morocco. Abdelkader Boukhari had told me he was in contact with FLN leaders there. Also, if I tell my mother and the family that I'm going to visit my childhood friend they'll be reassured. I'm sure I won't be in Morocco for any length of time and just pack a few underclothes and shirts. My mother notices and questions me: "Is that all you're taking? And your other suit, your other shoes?" "I won't be gone long," I answer.

Awake before dawn, she's already served my father breakfast and he's left for the mosque. When I'm ready to leave to catch the 6:30 train, the rest of the family is still asleep. She accompanies me to the door and, as when I would leave for school in Blida, she slips a bill into my pocket. I protest. She says, "Just in case you need it." I give her a kiss. Her face tightens, she starts to cry. I hug her firmly and murmur, "I'll be back in a few days." She sniffles and wipes her eyes with her scarf. "You promise you'll be back in a few days?" Her maternal instinct must be at work, she feels something's up, that I'm keeping something back. Does she have a sixth sense that's telling her I'm leaving for six long years, that she won't see me again until the war is over? I nod, say nothing, pick up the close-to-empty suitcase, and hurry down the street. When I look back, I see her head in the doorway, she's watching me. I hold back, so as not to run.

Now that my name figures on a list of suspects, I know that on crossing into Morocco I run the risk of being arrested. In Blida I buy a second-class ticket for the express train between Tunis, Algiers, and Casablanca. I'm the only Algerian in the compartment I enter. I greet the two men already seated, place my suitcase on the baggage rack, and sit down near the doorway. The younger of the two passengers is about my age. Like me, he's wearing a suit and tie. The other man is wearing a short-sleeve shirt, must be about twenty-five. He opens the conversation. "Are you from Blida?" he asks.

"No," I reply, "but I was a boarding student at the high school there for eight years. So I had time to get to know the city. It's a lovely place. It's called the 'city of roses' and is known for its yearly flower festival. After I graduated I was a resident monitor in a high school in Constantine."

"I'm from Meknes, in Morocco," he tells me. "I've just finished twenty-eight months of military service. I'm a lieutenant now. The only part of Algeria I got to know is Kabylia and the High Plateau region south of Setif. That's where I took the train. I'm glad to be out of the army alive and in good health. But I can't help wondering what life in an independent Morocco will be like. How did you like Constantine?"

"It's an old city," I say.

"I was there for forty-eight hours. It's sinister and the girls are stuck-up."

More at ease, I take off my jacket, unbutton my shirt, and loosen my tie. I listen to the other passenger, who's from France. "I've been living in Algiers," he says, "in training for my degree at the National School of Administration. I'm working in the Algiers regional director's office. I have a few days off for the July 14 holidays and I'm going to visit a friend in Rabat and see something of the country." We ask him questions about his program, his university, the degrees, his future. When we arrive in Oran, the train stops in the station for ten minutes; the student trainee offers to buy us sandwiches. They accompany theirs with a beer, I stick to lemonade. After eating, the student takes a pack of cards from his briefcase and begins shuffling them. He asks whether we play, then deals. We keep playing until an officer appears at the door of the compartment. "Passports," he calls out.

This is the moment I've been fearing since getting on the train. "Don't panic," I say to myself as I search my pockets and give the officer time to look at the other two passports. I show him mine, my military deferment, and the document from the school authorities in Constantine. He looks them over briefly, returns them, says thank you, and closes the door of the compartment. The customs inspector who follows him opens it, puts his head inside, and asks, "Anything to declare?" then shuts the door. No one seems aware of my immense relief.

Tired of playing cards, we talk awhile, then as night falls the soldier stretches out on one of the benches. I return to my seat next to the door. The student presses his head against the window. When we stop in Meknes, I hear the lieutenant take his bag off the rack and quietly open the door. I look up and murmur: "Have a good trip home!" He smiles. I lie down on the bench he's vacated but can't sleep. At daybreak, I sit up and look out the window: Moroccan flags are everywhere, even in the shantytowns along the tracks. My heart quickens as I imagine Algeria covered with the national flag. The train slows to a stop, the Frenchman extends his hand. We wish each other a pleasant stay in Morocco.

An hour later, I get off the train in Casablanca and arrive in Oued Zem in time to have lunch with Abdelkader. I describe Berrouaghia and the July 5 strike. "I've been trying to join the army and then remembered that you said you were in touch with the FLN in Morocco. I want to make contact with the people in charge," I tell him.

"In fact," he answers, "I have an appointment with two militants here tomorrow."

The next day I meet Ahmed Chaoui and Habib Djafari. "You're right on time," says Djafari from behind his dark glasses. "You can help our brother Abdelkader mobilize the Algerians in Oued Zem." They've come from Casablanca so I presume they're part of the FLN hierarchy.

I discover that the Algerians living in Morocco don't necessarily have the best reputation; Moroccans refer to them as "second-category Frenchmen," a rancorous term. It dates from the arrival of Algerian translators and interpreters accompanying the French army when it occupied Morocco in 1912. The movement of the two populations in both directions, however, has been constant over time. Several childhood friends of mine belong to families from Morocco but have never set foot in the country of their ancestors. The villagers still call them Moroccans, a number of whom are FLN militants.

In Oued Zem there are about a hundred people from various parts of Algeria, of very different social origins. Among the merchants is the man who runs the grocery store in the European quarter of the town: he wears a beret and sells pork sausage and wine.

The first FLN cell meeting I attend in Oued Zem takes place in the home of a landowner. He wears the traditional Algerian costume and a fez and travels into town on a bicycle. We are five men in attendance, the two others are small shopkeepers in the medina. The meeting takes place over a copious dinner and consists of an exchange of information gleaned from the radio and newspapers. Abdelkader reports on the dues-paying Algerians. "It's difficult to get some of them to pay dues regularly," he complains. "Is it because the battlefield is too far away and the links with the home country too sparse?" I ask. "Their involvement is slowly being consolidated," our host explains.

The day we receive copies of *Résistance algérienne*, the FLN newpaper, I offer to distribute it. With the papers under my arm, I saunter up and down the main street yelling in a loud voice: "Revolution by the people and for the people," the newspaper's motto. Astonished, people smile, a few put their hands in their pockets and come up with some change. In the medina, the crowd is more compact. I wave a copy and yell out the name of the paper in Arabic: *Al Mouqâwama al djazaïria*. Passersby and shopkeepers buy copies, thank me with a smile and words of encouragement. A few hold the paper upside down: they're illiterate but it's their way of aiding their Algerian brothers.

When I announce, at the following cell meeting, that I sold all the copies, the landowner says: "It's not for someone like you to be selling the newspaper. I prefer paying a kid to do that."

"It's an honor for me to distribute the voice of those who are fighting, it's a militant act," I reply.

"I understand," he reacts, "but honestly I don't see myself selling newspapers on the street."

I bring along a friend of Abdelkader's and mine, Thami Sekkal, an assistant surveyor, to join the cell. I also become friends with an Algerian student in Casablanca who knows one of the sultan's sons and often spends the night at Abdelkader's, Cherif Belkacem. He's fun to be with, something of a bohemian, and is always joking and making fun of himself. His guttural laugh is contagious but I also glimpse a sadder side. Is it because his father, an Algerian, died young, and his Moroccan mother finds it difficult to make ends meet? His friends are from wealthy families, drive flashy American cars, own lavish homes. Cherif tells me about another Algerian he's met, Ben Boulaïd's nephew, who comes to Morocco to buy fruits and vegetables for resale in Batna (Algeria). His business serves as a cover; in his truck is a hidden compartment in which he stocks arms for the combatants in the Aurès Mountains.

I decide to stay in Morocco and look for work in Oued Zem. I find a job in the accounting department of Esso, the American oil company, managing the stock in their warehouse. Rumors spread about secret contacts between the FLN and emissaries of the French government in Belgrade and Rome. The sultan of Morocco receives four leaders of the Revolution: Ben Bella, Boudiaf, Aït Ahmed, and Khider, to be followed by a meeting in Tunis of the three North African countries' leaders. I have the feeling that the Maghreb is a living reality at last. Has the French government understood that they cannot divide the Maghreb indefinitely, that the unending conscription and their four hundred thousand soldiers blanketing Algeria make no sense?

On October 22, 1956, disaster strikes with the French government's act of international civil aviation piracy, the first in the world: the Moroccan plane transporting the Algerian delegation to the conference in Tunis is ordered to land in Algiers by the French air force. The photos of the four leaders of the Revolution in handcuffs on the tarmac is aired around the world. The leaders, who just yesterday were received by the sultan of Morocco, are presented as common criminals. The FLN calls for demonstrations.

In Oued Zem, the byword is to avoid violence. An enormous crowd marches through the town to cries of "Long live independent Algeria" in Arabic and "Lacoste to the gallows" in French. At the edge of the medina, I listen to Djafari and Ahmed Chaoui address the demonstration; the latter has the oratorical power of *Saout el 'Arab* (Voice of the Arabs), a radio broadcast from Cairo. The crowd reacts strongly; I have the feeling that the slightest spark can ignite a renewal of violence. Luckily, nothing occurs. We move on to Beni Mellal for another enormous rally. The Moroccans are furious, extremely sensitive to the affront to their sultan.

At the end of October, Cherif Belkacem calls to say there's an opening at the Moulay Abdallah high school in Casablanca if I'm interested. I take off immediately and am recruited. The school is run by two Frenchmen, Monsieur Conil, the supervisor, about forty years old with carrot-colored hair, and Monsieur Violet, the administrator, a young skinny guy with a voice that's barely audible. I'm to take over administrative tasks previously handled by Violet. Since I'm single, I get to share an apartment on the grounds with two compatriots of mine: Sid Ahmed Daheur and El Hadi Rahal from Nedroma, who are teaching math. They were both students in France until the strike launched by UGEMA. The apartment is brand new and furnished. It's located near the entrance to the school and has three bedrooms, a living room, kitchen, and bath.

The following Saturday, I have an appointment with Djafari in a café on Suez Boulevard owned by an Algerian. The Organization has asked Algerians to contribute 10 percent of their salaries to the FLN. I give Djafari what I earned in Oued Zem. "We're only asking for 10 percent," he remarks. "I've got enough to keep me going next month and I won't die of hunger," I tell him. "Others are dying to liberate Algeria."

Djafari introduces me to Si Omar, the head of the FLN in Casablanca. Short, dark-skinned, unsmiling, he's a grade school teacher. He says he's trying to set up a political commission and asks me to join. I'm delighted, I'm all for brainstorming and look forward to working with others. The idea is to exchange information on the situation inside Algeria, to write articles for *Résistance algérienne* published in Tetouan, to come up with studies on Algeria's economic and social situation. The members of the commission have to chair meetings of militants and give lectures regularly on the second floor of the Suez Boulevard café.

At my first meeting there, the main topic under discussion is the Franco-Israeli-British attack against Egypt. After others have spoken, I begin by mentioning the ship delivering weapons for the ALN that was captured by the French navy on October 16. I talk about the plane that was pirated by the French and, given the negative impact of that event, try to attenuate its importance and remind everyone that the ALN began the struggle with hunting rifles and that, two years later, we learn that the ALN is receiving boatloads of arms by sea. As to the leaders arrested, I assure the group that when one brother falls, ten come out of the shadows to replace him. The failed triple-backed invasion of Egypt has revealed Nasser's triumph, the triumph of the Arab world and of Algeria. "It marks the beginning of the end of France in the third world and as a major power."

I'm also involved in meetings of student groups separately. I meet young people, students on strike, others from cities on the border between Algeria and Morocco, in particular Nedroma and Tlemcen, who have fled conscription into the French army. I describe the structures of the FLN: the CCE, the executive power, the National Council of the Algerian Revolution (CNRA), the equivalent of a national assembly or parliament. I tell them about the judiciary that's in its embryonic stage with courts, judges, and lawyers. In addition to which the structures of the national army (ALN) have been modernized and Arabized; the army comes under civilian power and the decisions of those fighting in the interior have precedence over those outside the country.

I try to interest my two roommates in joining the FLN cell. Rahal starts by excluding anything political but as he witnesses Daheur and my activism, he finally joins us. He's bought a Vespa and pays a daily visit to his brother, a pharmacist. Daheur, whose father is a high school administrator, is, on the contrary, very political. Like me, he dreams of joining the Liberation Army. I introduce him to Cherif Belkacem and Benchehida, the two leaders of UGEMA in Morocco. We decide to hold the yearly general assembly immediately. Daheur convinces colleagues at the high school to attend. I do the same with the students I've been meeting at my lectures. Cherif and Benchehida have never seen so many students in one room. Criticism of the current leadership is rife and they are both on their best behavior. The students want to know why the treasurer has resigned and why they haven't received a report on the Paris congress that Cherif attended back in March. When elections for the executive committee come up, someone nominates me. I nominate Daheur and Rahal. The three of us are elected by secret ballot. Daheur chairs the committee, Rahal is the treasurer, and I'm named secretary.

When I report the results of the assembly to the FLN head official, I ask him what the procedure is for those who wish to enlist in the Liberation Army. He sends me a pile of forms. Both Daheur and I fill ours out and return them, though Daheur, who knows the leadership better than I do, is not optimistic. I conclude that the surest way to join the army is to get possession of a weapon. Daheur agrees.

I figure that at the harbor in Casablanca, there must be a lot of illicit activity and it should be possible to buy two guns. We need to find a docker. One evening as I mount the stairs to Thami Sekkal's parents' apartment, I bump into their neighbor, an Algerian married to a Moroccan woman, to whom Thami once introduced me. I know he doesn't work, drinks, smokes hashish, and beats his wife. He has a large scar on his cheek, gold on his teeth, and walks with a swagger. As he puts the key in his door, I stop him: "Say, Boumediene, do you happen to know anyone who works on the docks?" Surprised, he avoids a direct reply. I start over and in a low voice say: "Between you and me, I have a friend who wants to buy a gun. He thinks that maybe someone who works at the harbor..."

He pretends to think about it and then says: "Perhaps, but it'll be expensive."

"How much do you think?"

"About seventy thousand francs, probably." That's the equivalent of the advance I received when I started working at the high school, but I decide not to bargain with him.

I add: "I may have another friend who wants to buy one, too." He doesn't inspire confidence and Daheur isn't optimistic. We keep our scheme to ourselves, mention it to no one.

"The neighbor wants to see you," Sekkal's mother tells me months later. At long last, the neighbor's come up with something. Scarface exhibits his gold-covered smile and directs me to his bedroom, where he lifts a corner of the mattress and takes out a gun and some bullets. He shifts the weapon from one hand to the other to display its weight and I don't know what else. I tell him I'll be back the next day with the money, except that so much time has gone by that I don't have much left in my account. I've bought a motor bicycle and some clothes. Daheur has bought a scooter and can't come up with enough for a second gun. Finally, we each put in thirty-five thousand francs.

The following day behind the closed door of my room, we examine the P38 like two kids exulting over a Christmas present. Daheur, a born tinkerer, starts to take it apart. I stop him and suggest we go into the woods one day and "try out our artillery." We decide to order a second gun for March.

On February 20, 1957, I'm twenty-two years old. A week later, after the eleven o'clock recreation period, Violet, the administrator, comes in from the courtyard and says, "There's a man looking for you. He's waiting near the entrance to your building." The person I come upon is wearing a dark blue suit, a white shirt, and a dark tie. He extends his hand and says solemnly: "I'm Mohamed Kellou from the UGEMA Executive Committee. I've come from Paris." He frowns, then continues: "Not long ago, you asked to join the ranks of the National Liberation Army. Do you still want to enlist?"

"Of course," I reply.

He relaxes, smiles, and continues, using the familiar *tu*: "Do you know where I can find Sid Ahmed Daheur? Do you think he's still ready to go along?"

"Wait here for me, I'll get him," I say.

I climb up to the second floor, where Sid Ahmed has a

class. I'm flying. I call him out to the hallway, he turns the class over to one of the students. "The day of glory has arrived!" I announce.

Kellou asks him the same question and obtains the same reply. "Okay," he says, "you have to be at the frontier tonight."

I presume that he doesn't realize that the border is six hundred kilometers away and suggest: "Since we agree, we need a few hours to get ready. We can leave tomorrow."

"The orders are precise: tonight, not another day."

"How can we get to the border tonight?" I ask.

"Go to Rabat, Temara Avenue. There, you'll be told how to get to the border." He gives us the address and a password, shakes hands, and leaves.

There's a bus to Rabat every hour. We decide to take the three o'clock and meet at the station fifteen minutes before. Sid Ahmed returns to his class and me to my office. At noon, as soon as the bell rings, I hear clapping coming from the second floor and imagine that Daheur has informed his students that he's leaving for the good cause. The administrator comes out and asks where the noise is coming from, so I announce that I won't be coming back to work in the afternoon. He rolls his eyes, he's stunned. I knock at the supervisor's office, extend my hand, and say: "Monsieur Conil, I'm sorry I have to resign from my job on such short notice but I'm leaving the establishment."

Surprised, he gets up, his face somber: "But what's happened that requires such a precipitous departure?"

I tell the two men: "I want to thank you for your kindness and the cordial atmosphere you've created here."

"We're very happy with your work but we don't understand what's going on," Violet says.

"Duty calls," I explain with a smile. They look at each other, embarrassed.

As I walk out, the supervisor says: "I need a letter of resignation."

"Of course," I say, "I'll put it in the mail."

Sid Ahmed is already in the apartment. He wants to take his possessions and his scooter to his cousin's. I'll give mine and the motor bicycle to the Sekkal family. We decide to split the "artillery" between us: he'll carry the revolver and I'll take the bullets.

Rahal arrives and can't believe the disorder he sees: "What's going on?" he asks.

"It's over, we're leaving you the entire apartment."

Daheur and Rahal are always chiding each other. I suspect that their conduct is a reflection of the history of Nedroma, their hometown. Rahal looks in my direction, I laugh and confirm that we're leaving. "Duty calls," I tell him.

That stops him dead in his tracks, he starts tapping his foot on the floor, then jumps from one foot to the other: "You bastards," he screams, "you're not going to leave me here alone! You can't do that! I'm coming with you!"

Sid Ahmed yells back at him: "If you think you can join the army like you go home to mother, whenever you like..."

Rahal grabs my arm: "Tell me what I have to do, I want to go with you."

I try to reason with him: "You can't make a decision that important on the spur of the moment, without taking time to think about it. If you really want to come with us, speak to the people we'll be meeting later and maybe you can join us in a few days." He insists, and won't let go of my arm. I give in: "Listen, we have to be at the frontier tonight. We're taking the three o'clock bus to Rabat. If you still want to come, be at the bus station at 2:45."

He jumps with joy and says, "I'm going to the pharmacy to tell my brother."

"Don't forget to ask for Papa's permission," Sid Ahmed taunts him. He turns, swears at us, and runs off.

I jump on my motor bike and head for Suez Boulevard to say goodbye to Si Omar, and then to the Sekkal family. Si Omar is not happy, tries to pull rank to stop me. "You can't leave without my authorization. That's an order," he says. "Remember, I'm a free man," I reply. "A militant must adhere to the discipline of the Organization," he argues. "I'm a militant who is abandoning Suez Boulevard for the field of honor." He doesn't know what to say, he watches me go, his sad-looking face more mournful than ever.

Daheur and I arrive on time in Rabat. Mohamed Kellou's name is an open sesame. Rahal is given the same train ticket for Oujda (a Moroccan frontier city) and the same address there. Outside a café on the main street I see Missoum Ferrah from Berrouaghia on the terrace with a group of students. We're all going to the same place. "Up until the student strike, I was in a drama school in Strasbourg, that's where Laurence Olivier studied," he tells me. Lamine Allouane recognizes our accent from the High Plateau region and interrupts to ask where we're from. He's from eastern Algeria but he worked in Medea at the law courts as a stenographer.

In Oujda we're taken to a house with an indoor patio and quartered in a large living room facing it: the floor is covered with carpets; benches with mattresses and pillows line the walls; low tables are scattered around. The owner of the house, an Algerian, welcomes us and says his teenage son will take care of us. Neither he nor his son, who becomes our sole contact with the outside world, knows how long we'll be staying here. We end up sprawling out on the mattresses and pillows and falling asleep. Breakfast and lunch are delicious and copious. Crossing the courtyard to go to the toilet has become our only chance to see the sky. Our bedroom–dining room without windows forces conversation and we get to know each other.

Abdelhamid Hellal, who was born in Meknes (Morocco) in 1933, was a teacher at the Mohamed V high school in Rabat before the strike. He has dark skin and eyes and straight hair, and has a carefree way about him that I like. He's surprised to learn that there is a family in Berrouaghia with the same name. Khelladi, short with bushy eyebrows, is more distant. Abdelaziz Maoui, even taller than me, has a pleasant smile, says little. He began law studies but found them uninteresting. He gets excited when talk turns to American cars and nightlife in Rabat. We are still waiting around when dinner is served. Nothing happens in the evening.

The following day, I ask the young man to buy me cigarettes again. The laughter and discussions are less frequent. Ferrah, Allouane, and I have run out of jokes. Boredom makes the time seem longer and more tiring. After lunch, I try to sleep but can't. About six o'clock, the door bursts open. Two men enter and immediately throw off their *kachabias*. One of them is wearing a uniform. He yells: "*Istaâd!*"

No one understands what he's said, nor why he has such a severe look about him. I sit up, slowly. While the other man folds the *kachabias*, the soldier repeats his order. Missoum, who studied at the Arabic-language *zitouna* in Tunis, murmurs: "Attention!"

The man in civilian clothes looks us over from behind dark glasses and says, "*Istrah!*" He sees that we don't understand and translates: "At ease."

The two men do not introduce themselves. We learn later that the name of the man in civilian clothes is Abdelhafid Boussouf, alias Si Mabrouk. The other man is Mohamed Boukharouba, alias Boumediene. The first is the commanding colonel of Wilaya 5, covering Oran, its surroundings, and the southern territories. The second is a commander and the first man's assistant. Boussouf draws a piece of paper out of the pocket of his brown jacket. We're standing in a half circle. He looks us over and says: "Tonight you will cross the border. Three-quarters of you will die, either from stepping on a mine or hitting the electrified barbed-wire fence. If you are not ready to make this sacrifice or if you have any health problems that prohibit you from coming with us, speak up. Later, it will be too late."

He stops talking but keeps looking around at our faces. He advances toward me because I'm standing at the head of the line of men. I see that his glasses are extremely thick. His short hair and small mustache have a reddish tint. He asks my name, raises the sheet of paper to within inches of his eyes, then looks at me fixedly. With an accent that is obviously from the Constantine region, he smiles and asks: "How are the brothers?" I imagine he means the OS militants from the village and reply instinctively: "Fine." "Do you see well?" he asks. "Yes," I reply. "Do you hear well?" "Yes." "No health problems?" he inquires. "No, none."

I haven't told him the whole truth because, despite the eyeglasses, I only see out of one eye and my left leg is slightly shorter than the other leg so I totter a bit. Boussouf goes to the next person, asks the same questions. One man asks if he can have a lung X-ray, another asks to see an ophthalmologist. Obviously disconcerted, the colonel tells them to step out of line and stand in the corner. As soon as Boussouf finishes questioning everyone, I nod to Daheur, who exhibits the P38 and hands it to Boumediene. I take the box of bullets from my coat pocket and hand it to him as well. The commander stands in the doorway and verifies that there are no bullets in the chamber of the gun. The two men glance at each other and, suddenly, Boumediene strikes the floor with his foot and yells: "*Istaâd!*" He stands at attention and salutes. We try to imitate him but are clearly sad sacks. Boussouf tells us to be patient and says, "At ease." The two men put on their *kachabias* and leave with the two students. I feel for them and can't understand why they were taken out of the group because they requested a medical exam. Maybe they thought there would be a physical, as in a regular army. No one in the group seems to give it any thought.

The contact with two of the top authorities in the Liberation Army gives rise to renewed enthusiasm and comments. I express my admiration for the simple uniform the colonel was wearing, point out that while his accent is from eastern Algeria, he is a commander in the western region, another proof of the indestructible unity of the Algerian people. Everyone jokes about the military orders delivered in Arabic. I blame the colonialists for our ignorance of our own language and am happy to observe that the Revolution has introduced the recovery of our homeland and our dignity into the armed struggle.

After a final dinner, we leave the smoke-filled building in single file and pile into two cars stationed out front. The driver, to be sure he is not followed, makes several detours in the town before taking to the road. I have the feeling we are skirting the border, aiming for a spot where the crossing is not too risky. Suddenly the car turns to the left, slows down; the driver turns off the headlights but leaves the parking lights on. I look in vain through the window and see nothing: we are in total darkness. The car begins to bump up and down, we've turned onto a dirt road. How far are we from the electrified barrier? Will an ALN unit accompany us? Will we receive weapons and uniforms before crossing the border? The driver turns off the parking lights, advances in total darkness. I can see the outline of a building ahead. He stops in front and says: "Don't get out till I tell you."

The silhouette of a *kachabia* comes toward us, looks into the car, returns to the building. A door opens. "Get out quickly," the driver urges.

We run toward the light of a door guarded by three *kachabia*-clothed men carrying machine guns. Six other men in uniform are standing in the middle of a concrete-covered courtyard barely lit. They are not armed, seem relaxed and happy to see us. Our surprised looks, no doubt disconcerting to the point of seeming stupid, make a few of them laugh. The chief, wearing a white scarf around his neck that's shoved into his perfect battle dress, is the only one who speaks. One of the attendants shows us the toilets and the dormitory, a long room with two rows of bunk beds. I choose the upper bed at the end of the room. I realize that no one has slept in that bed before. A half hour later, lights out.

So instead of crossing the border into Algeria with the risk of being electrocuted or ripped apart by a mine, here I am in a dormitory in a secret place, I don't know where. The only thing I'm sure of, we're still in Morocco. The wait, while we were confined in the house in Oujda, was, I suppose, intended to keep us quiet while they checked on us. The colonel's bluff, verifying our spirit of sacrifice without revealing our destination and the training we would be receiving, seems strange but exciting. I am finally in the National Liberation Army. I am a happy man.

Early the next morning, I discover the rest of the building. Other than the green swinging door we entered through, there is no opening to the outside world. Over the entrance door to the various rooms are neatly drawn signs: TRANSMISSION CENTER, DINING ROOM, RADIO STATION, DORMITORY, OFFICERS' QUARTERS, TRAINING CENTER, BATHROOMS. The locale has a name: Signal Corps Technical

Instruction Center (CITT). Wow! The Algerian army has a signal corps school!

Daheur recognizes one of the center's staff, Abderrahmane Berrouane, an old friend. They were students together in Toulouse. He's the master sergeant and has changed his name; he's Saphar now. Daheur is shocked to hear the tone the captain uses when he speaks to Berrouane and feels he's on his guard. When he asks him, discreetly, what's going on, Berrouane warns him: "Call me Saphar, forget the past and your ideas. Be careful!" Daheur tells me: "I know his politics. He's as patriotic as you and me. I knew he wanted to join the Liberation Army. I don't understand what's happened to him, nor what he meant."

In the morning, we change our civilian clothes for uniforms; there's a lot of joking around. The uniforms are not khaki-colored or olive green like most soldiers' uniforms. They're made of beige cotton, uniforms of the Spanish army. The shoes are made from the same thick cotton with soles of alfalfa and make no noise, are meant to be silent. The pants are not long enough for me, nor for Rahal, whereas Ferrah swims in his uniform.

Shortly afterward, Saphar has us move into the transmission center, where the officers are waiting for us. It's a long room filled with a dozen tables composed of boards on trestles or benches. On each board there are four transmitters and four earphone sets. The captain and his lieutenants inform us that we shall receive training in Morse code and become radio-telegraph operators. Each of them, in his own way, tells us how exalting the training is and how much the leaders of the Revolution have placed their confidence in us. Captain Telidji insists on the need for absolute secrecy and informs us that all messages are transmitted in code to the Liberation Army receivers and that noncoded messages are not allowed.

"For reasons of security, you all have to adopt new names," he says. "You have five minutes to choose an alias. It's not only a way to disconcert the enemy, it's also a way of protecting your families," Saddar adds.

"In the future, you should forget your previous identity and never question anyone as to his," says Hassani.

The name that comes to my mind is Amara. Last summer in Casablanca, by chance, I learned of the death of Mohamed Amara Rachid. I was walking in the medina when I looked down and saw the magazine *Paris Match* on the ground. It was open to a photo of two armed *moudjahidine* with three young women in nurses' uniforms. Amara was one of them; he was wearing a soldier's cap and a military uniform and carrying a submachine gun. I adopt his name with the feeling that he's passing the freedom flame on to me. The companions choose new first names: Sid Ahmed Daheur becomes Mustafa; El Hadi Rahal, Salah; Abdelhamid Hellal, Amine; Missoum Ferrah, Hamma; Lamine Allouane, Abdelillah. In the evening, after dinner, another group of young men arrive, among them is my friend from high school Ali Baghdadi, who replaced me at the head of the student organization of the Mitidja. He adopts his father's first name, Abdesslam.

At about the same time, the next day, a group of young volunteers lands in the courtyard. Every evening, others arrive. What a surprise to see Abdelkader Boukhari, my childhood friend, and two colleagues from Moulay Abdallah high school: Lahbib Naas and Brahmi Ghaouti. They hold it against us that we left without telling them. They must have made the decision to come from off the top of their heads, which can seem insane given the possible consequences of their action, but it is nonetheless revealing. These college and high school students are not from poor families, they are not the sons of workers, of landless peasants; they haven't come out of shantytowns, of poor neighborhoods; they are the children of interpreters and translators, of merchants, landlords, gendarmes, and civil servants who have served the regime of the Moroccan protectorate and now are in the administration of independent Morocco. They are renouncing their relative comfort. It's all to their honor.

When I visited the country a few weeks after the return of the sultan and the declaration of independence, I noticed that some Moroccans still called those Algerians "second-class Frenchmen." The protectorate had granted them a status that was superior to that of Moroccans. They were French-Muslim Algerians and came under the authority of the resident general; in other words, they were not recognized as subjects of the sultan. Today, the National Liberation Front benefits from the support of the Moroccan people and the Moroccan authorities who want to include the Algerians in their ranks. They are at a crossroads: they have to choose to become Moroccan subjects and descend on the social scale, or take this occasion to become full-fledged citizens of an independent Algeria by joining the Liberation Front. At Oued Zem and in Casablanca, I saw that very few of them had known Algeria. For these students, the strike and making a commitment give real meaning to their lives. They become actors, heroes of a movement which, soon, will bring about independence. By joining us, they will rid themselves of the status of French Muslims to which they were reduced. To put an end to that humiliation and age-old injustice, I know of nothing more heartwarming.

We are forty-two trainees who have changed our names. The pseudonym becomes a new identity. I try to remember the names of each one of us; it's a way of getting to know each other. I soon realize that many of them know each other. Twenty of them were born in Morocco, mostly in Oujda. Sixteen are from the Oran region, of which eight are from Nedroma. We are six from the center of Algeria, of which three are from Kabylia. Only my four friends from the Moulay Abdallah high school and myself were enrolled at the university. Hadjerès Hanafi, who chose the name Nasser, was born in 1930 in Larba'a Nath Irathen; he is the oldest. Hanafi is the brother of Sadek Hadjerès, an MTLD militant—later of the Algerian Communist Party, which has signed an agreement with the FLN to integrate the communists in our struggle. I tell Hanafi that my family remembers his when they lived in Berrouaghia. He confirms it but reminds me that we have to abstain from talking about the past.

I see a blondish youngster with very white skin who gives off the impression that if we squeezed him, milk would spout from his nose. His name is Sifaoui, he's timid but seems happy to be wearing the uniform.

(left to right) Mohamed Amara Rachid, Meriem Belmihoub, Fadila Mesli, Safia Bazi, and Abane Ramdane in a war zone, Algeria, 1956.

"It's not against the rules to ask your age," I say, repeating his name.

"In a few days I'll be seventeen."

His real name is Mohamed Berri. He was born in 1940 in Taourit. Five other recruits are not quite eighteen years old. I am impressed by their desire to look and act older and by their willpower.

In the narrow courtyard of what was a small farm before serving as a home for some fifty men, groups form, reform, and walk together, talking, smoking. Ahmed Belbey, who chose the name Khaled, is surrounded by young recruits from Oujda, where he was born in December 1932. Since he is older, and a former scoutmaster, he likes telling stories that he mixes with the history of the national movement. He realizes that the patriotism that follows from the unlimited strike of classes and exams and that has brought about this arrival of high school and college students does not come from real political awareness. These young men born or brought up in Morocco are no more politically aware than their counterparts from the Duveyrier and Aumale high schools. Their enthusiasm is marvelous. I admire their ardor, their generosity, and their abnegation. I am overwhelmed when Mohamed Moudjebeur, alias Haroun, tells me that he can't wait to discover Algeria, where he has never set foot. He was born in 1934 in Marrakech. His father is a merchant.

On the fourth day, endowed with uniforms and new names, we are called into the training center.

"In rows of three with the tallest men in front!" Sergeant Berrouane shouts.

Rahal, his cousin Zoheir, whom we now call Abdessamad, and myself are at the front of the squad, facing the bathrooms, our backs to the dormitory.

"*Ljtami'ou* means to stand at attention," the sergeant announces before translating the orders for turning to the right, to the left, about face, and at ease.

In the French army and in the gym classes at high school, the order to turn left is "Left, left!" In Arabic it's "Left, turn!" Some of us hear these terms for the first time, confuse them, and turn the wrong way. Berrouane tries but cannot stop the laughter in the ranks. By the end of the morning, however, he manages to transform us into a company. We assemble again in the afternoon and enter the training center in good order. The officers, including Telidji, follow us and position themselves in front of the new blackboard. In his elegant battle dress, his eyes squinted, the captain examines us with a look that is not particularly friendly. He waits until the noise stops. Then with a loud and assertive voice, he announces: "Discipline is the principal strength of an army."

Telidji, head of the officers in charge of our training, had been a career soldier, a sergeant in the French army. Twelve years of service in the signal corps of the enemy's army have given him time to acquire the technical skill and experience that few Algerians possess. Much later I will learn from one of the people who claims he was present at the scene that he was kidnapped by the National Liberation Front in Rabat, where he was sent, in furtherance of a Franco-Moroccan agreement, to train the first telegraph operators of the Royal

Armed Forces (FAR). Instead, he would be training the first round of operators for the Algerian army. The training took place in a house in Oujda from August 7 to September 10, 1956. There were twenty-seven trainees. A second trainer was a German deserter from the French Foreign Legion, Edwing Reinhold, who was born in 1916 in Tianjin, China (his pseudonym was Zidane). At the end of the first training period, Telidji was named captain and head of this new center, where this second group will be trained. He's an astonishing individual. His uniform is brand new, his hair is plastered with brilliantine, he emits a strong odor of toilet water. He uses his uniform, his loud voice, and the language of a former French army sergeant to impress. I say to myself that the Revolution has to use competence where it finds it. Like a strong current, it captures everything along its way.

Captain Telidji turns the floor over to Lieutenant Senoussi Saddar, called Moussa. A nationalist since he was a member of the Algerian Muslim Scouts, he is the only official who has actually served in the war. His talk is aimed at providing us with the spirit of abnegation and brotherhood reigning among the soldiers of the Liberation Army inside the country. He talks of his time in the Oran mountains and describes briefly the difficult conditions in which our predecessors were trained. He had been in charge of their thirty-two-day training course. Boussouf chose him because he had done his military service in the signal corps equipment center of the French army. When he was demobilized, he opened a shop in Oran where he sold and repaired radios. Also, he was the only one of the group who had been inside with the

Liberation Army. At the end of the course, Telidji was named captain and Saddar lieutenant. However, he no longer has a room to himself and is especially aware of the fact that his educational level is insufficient. He has trouble speaking in public and is charged with providing technical classes, in particular for radio repair work.

Lieutenant Abdelkrim Hassani has been designated to provide our theoretical training. He was a first-year student at the Algiers faculty and arrived in Oujda just as Boussouf was planning the center for telegraphy transmissions training. A childhood friend of Mohamed Tahar Ben Mhidi, brother of the head of the army in the Oran region, Hassani was a member of the first training class. However, he couldn't transcribe Morse, so he would not be able to man a transmissions center. For that reason, and because he was a math, physics, and chemistry student and a friend of Ben M'hidi's brother—for whom I organized the trip from Constantine into the interior in May 1956—he has been called upon to give us our theoretical training.

Lieutenant Abdelkader Bouzid, on the contrary, is a brilliant operator. A schoolteacher and musician, he loves the *gembri*, a primitive lute which contributes—along with hashish at times—to pleasurable evening programs. Bouzid is in charge of teaching us Morse. Sergeant Berrouane wasn't lucky; despite studying law at Toulouse University, he wasn't able to read Morse at an acceptable speed. A big smoker, deprived of cigarettes because of the decision of our higher-ups, he suffers from instantaneous withdrawal symptoms. He even faints. I could see that the role of sergeant weighs on him.

Corporal Loucif Boughara looks even less the soldier. Ill at ease in uniform, heavyset, he doesn't speak French. The letter *v* doesn't exist in Arabic, so he distributes *corfées chi-ott* to the trainees. Even though the lowest of the teaching squad, he is a telegraph operator. When the war started, he was studying at the University of Al Azhar in Cairo, and when the FLN obtained three receivers from the Egyptian authorities to be used for training, he was recruited, along with four

other students, and taught to use the equipment. Those posts were intended for the three departments of Algiers, Oran, and Constantine. Capable of decoding in Arabic, Boughara and the other students, as well as the equipment, were sent to Morocco. However, the posts are over six feet in height and three feet wide and only function when hooked up to an electric outlet. Their size and the need to use them with electric current make them useless in the maquis. The operators being solely Arabic-speaking, they were sent to army units inside the country, with the exception of Boughara. He does the best he can, joins us speaking Arabic in little groups, learns Morse, and studies French.

After Saddar, Hassani, the "intellectual" among the officers, speaks. He outlines the responsibilities of a militant and illustrates his remarks with anecdotes from the student movement at the University of Algiers. He follows up with a long list of slogans from National Liberation Front documents. He leaves me feeling uncomfortable; I can't stop myself from finding his talk pompous. He probably wants to impress us and show his colleagues that his educational level is superior to theirs.

With a sardonic look on his face, Captain Telidji intervenes: "The training session will begin tomorrow and will last about two months. Your predecessors were trained in a month and are capable of taking Morse at a level that Frenchmen reach after twelve to eighteen months. As Lieutenant Saddar has told you, the first training session took place in extremely difficult conditions. With the equipment and the time at your disposal, no one should fail. Your success depends on your determination. For the Revolution, failure is a sign of intolerable ill will. So consider yourselves forewarned." The warning seems strange to me. The captain then details the program we are to follow. He insists on the importance of learning to understand Morse, to write in Morse, the procedures and the coding which will be taught by him and by Lieutenant Bouzid. Saddar will deal with the technical side and Hassani will teach math and electricity.

The next day, Thursday, March 7, we are awake at six and line up, in silence, in front of the bathroom, which has three sinks and three toilets. At 6:45 we do calisthenics with the sergeant. At 7:15, in the dining room, low talking is permitted. At 7:55, we assemble for inspection under the eye of Lieutenant Hassani. He comes out of the officers' room, exchanges a salute with the sergeant, passes among us, and distributes the tasks that the corporal, who follows him, jots down in a notebook. At eight a.m. we enter the classroom.

As much as I was delighted to discover, the morning of my arrival, that the center resembled a small military barracks, this caricature of an exercise taken from the enemy army is grotesque. In order to appear soldierly, Hassani expands his torso, salutes with rapid-fire gestures, and speaks forcefully. Somewhere between the phony tough guy and the corporal who walks and acts embarrassed, the sergeant looks ill at ease. The call to assemble reminds me of my time as a high school monitor, the bell that rings, the distribution of duties, the reprimands, the officials and the underlings. That all may be necessary, and since "discipline is the principal strength of an army," I am accepting it all. The main thing is to leave for the interior with telegraph equipment and to concentrate on that objective.

In the classroom, under each set of earphones are paper and a pencil. With his Clark Gable mustache and his ready smile, Lieutenant Bouzid is well liked by the guys from Oujda. Very calm, he announces: "Before initiating you into understanding Morse, I have to tell you that to spell phonically, each letter has a name which is different according to the country. Our army has its own names for the letters. They are denominations to be copied and learned by heart." He rises and writes on the blackboard:

A = Alpha
B = Bravo
C = Charlie
D = Delta
E = Echo
F = Foxtrot, etc.

He holds back a laugh and continues:

M = Mike

. . .

W = Whiskey

X = X-ray

Y = Yankee

Z = Zulu

"These words are employed when using a post with a micro- phone, like in a telephone conversation." Then Bouzid explains that the teaching of Morse consists in transcribing a mixture of long and short sounds heard on the earphones. The lieutenant gets up, erases the list of letters, and says, "Those among you who were in the Scout movement know how to transcribe Morse." He writes the letter *A*, a dot followed by a dash, then the letter *B*, a dash and three dots, and then the rest of the alphabet. Bouzid returns to his desk and turns on his key device, then announces: "I am the sender and you are the receivers."

He sends us our first signals: *ti-ta*, a dot and a dash, i.e., the letter *A*; then *ta-tititi*, the letter *B*. After fifty-five minutes, we are allowed five minutes' rest in the courtyard, just the time for a cigarette. Some of the guys are super-excited, to such a point that Boughara calls for order, to stop the screaming and wild laughter. "*Ijtami'ou!*" and calm returns. Bouzid continues his demonstration, manipulates the letters with patience. I try to keep up, write down what I can get. Both annoyed and stimulated, I keep trying. From time to time someone shows his irritation and groans. After explaining that a coded message is composed of several letters and numbers, the instructor taps out distinct groups of letters or numbers.

Freshly shaved, perfumed, his hair covered with brilliantine, Captain Telidji takes over at eleven o'clock. He taps out a series of V's rapidly, which provokes a number of cries, complaints. His purpose is to test the apparatus but also to provide a sample of his superior skill and speed. Delighted with the effect he obtains, he announces that the lesson will begin. I feel the difference; his transmission is definitely firmer. The letters are clearer, better separated. From time to time he asks a question of someone and little by little increases the speed. There are some reactions of despair. At noon, incapable of taking down all the letters, I realize that most of my companions are at the same point.

At two in the afternoon, Lieutenant Hassani gives us a lesson in electricity. The class level is far from equal. The majority of the trainees were in the last year of high school. The others find it hard to keep up and the teacher doesn't appreciate their questions and reactions. He simply repeats the explanation without changing the terms or the demonstration. He shows his irritation, makes some nasty remarks, ridicules those who don't understand.

From three to six p.m., Bouzid and Telidji come back one after the other to teach the use of the sound keys. The rest of the week we spend seven hours a day learning Morse and alternate the classes given by Lieutenants Hassani and Saddar. The drilling begins to show some results. I remember Pavlov's dog and its conditioned reflexes. I am beginning to write letters automatically when I hear the signals. However, the conditioning is not learned at the same speed by everyone. The pharmacy student Naas Lahbib, who has chosen to be called Hamza, is in despair. He can't stop hitting his head with the palm of his hand each time he reflects on what he's doing. I listen to him, am amused by his reflections: "Damn it! My God! If the captain says the French army manages to train Senegalese fighters who have no more than a grammar school certificate, I should be able to do this. If I can't it means that I'm a real idiot, an asshole!"

"Of course, we'll get there," I say. "In the meantime, I'd say that our captain is racist."

Lahbib acquiesces and lays his hand on his thick growth of black hair.

Sunday is our day off. After morning gymnastics and breakfast, we line up for showers. In the afternoon we wash our clothes. Behind the radio station is an old animal drinking trough, which now serves as a washbasin for our underwear. This free time is used by our leaders to find out our reactions by visiting the little groups that form in the courtyard. Telidji, Saddar, and Hassani approach the one I'm in with Daheur, El Hadi Rahal, and Brahmi. The captain starts the conversation.

"What do you think of the classes, the way the sessions are organized? I want to hear what you really think, not some hypocritical remarks."

My friends hesitate, so I reply: "We're happy..."

"First of all, you have to say 'I.' In the army, there is no 'we.' And secondly, I don't know what 'happy' means. It's hypocritical."

Furious, I stare at him. He turns to El Hadi Rahal, questions him with a movement of his chin. El Hadi expresses his satisfaction, then adds: "I must say that I am surprised to find myself in the Liberation Army, receiving three meals a day with knife and fork!"

The lieutenants nod their heads with approval, but Captain Telidji lets out a caustic laugh: "The worst is yet to come, my friend!"

After questioning Daheur and Brahmi, he turns to me again.

"I have the same reaction as my friends. But our schedule doesn't include any political training."

He grimaces, then looks toward his lieutenants, who remain silent.

"You're here to learn and send Morse. For the rest, we'll see later."

At the end of the second week, we have our first test in Morse. It consists of receiving and transcribing a given number of letters in a given length of time. The results? After fifteen days of training, the majority of the trainees can take Morse at a speed of 300. This represents the first level; 600, 900, and more will follow. In general an operator should read at the minimum speed of 900. It seems our instructors are satisfied. They stop treating the brother who finds it difficult to follow as a faker. "I can only hear a buzz sound and that gives me a headache," he complains, not understanding. I realized when we started our training that he barely knows how to read and write.

The results at the end of the third week, on the other hand, are not brilliant. Only a minority reaches the 600 level. I feel that is due to the deterioration of the brotherly relationships that stimulated us. Two of the trainees are at swords' points. They are placed in quarantine, as in primary school. The claustration, the nervous tension, modify the carefree attitudes that were natural. The officers increase the humiliating sanctions inflicted. They no longer meet with the little groups relaxing, talking, and laughing. They are more distant.

During the following week, the captain requires the petulant Naas Lahbib to have his hair cut off because he swore out loud on missing a group of letters during a lesson. The naked head of Lahbib amuses some among us but doesn't lessen the unjust aspect of the sanction. Gestures and words of solidarity help Lahbib smile again. But he still lays his hand on his head when he reflects.

One morning, during the dress review, Lieutenant Hassani reproaches us because he finds us insufficiently dynamic. "Think of the Hitler Youth, who did their gymnastics with their chests bare in the snow," he cries with irritation.

When he hears that I criticized his reference to the Nazis, the captain repeats in an insidious manner that the walls have ears!

The subjects of our conversations seem to intrigue him. And, for no apparent reason, he evokes the serious sanctions which contesters are subjected to in the army. A climate of suspicion enfolds us. Some among us imagine that others have become spies for the officers. Because he is seen talking regularly with one of the sergeants, one of the trainees is suspected of reporting our conversations. This is ridiculous, but I find it difficult to convince some of the others. Another is actually accused of being a traitor. On leaving the classroom he made a ball out of his copy papers and threw it over the wall of the compound. The guardian runs to tell the sergeant. The

trainee apologizes as best he can. The captain, before authorizing someone to go outside and pick up the object of his
crime, screams at him: "You wanted to inform the enemy, traitor!" He is charged with cleaning the toilets for two weeks.

Emulation helping, at the end of the fourth week, I reach the
900 level, with about a dozen comrades. Most of the others
are at the 600 level but there are still a few who can't get past
300, despite their goodwill. A few are very unhappy. I don't
manage to persuade Mohamed Moudjebeur, alias Haroun,
who laments that he is only at 600, that he'll make it. I discover that he admires the knowledge, the dynamism of Lieutenant Hassani. Moudjebeur has probably taken to heart the
officer who discouraged him by saying, "For me, anyone who
doesn't transcribe at 1200 is no more than a bit of dust, he
doesn't exist." The demagogic language, the martial attitudes
of Lieutenant Hassani are perhaps impactful, but he himself
is incapable of taking Morse at 1200, has never been in the
maquis. However, in the eyes of Moudjebeur, who has never
been inside Algeria, Hassani is a hero, a kind of Algerian
John Wayne.

One day as we assemble to enter the classroom, the captain reminds us that, according to the rules, certain infrac-
tions are punishable by death. Then he gives us to understand
that two trainees tried to have a sexual relationship in the
dormitory. I am not the only one who finds his remarks grotesque. Certainly such activity cannot take place without the
entire dormitory being aware of it. Thanks to the confidences
of intimate friends, everyone knows who has masturbated or

had a wet dream. The speech by Telidji is probably intended as preventive, because an ill-intentioned trainee from Oujda pretends that a trainee from that city is homosexual. Maybe the captain wants to justify the heavy dosage of bromide that gives our coffee a strange taste and seems to be working. I don't feel the slightest sexual pulsation. Is it because of the bromide or my capacity to hold myself in check? Perhaps a little of both.

The word gets around that during the first class, three recruits deserted from the French army by leaving their unit stationed in Marrakech and came to Oujda in the hope of being sent into the Algerian interior. When the leader said that he had been trained in hand-to-hand fighting, Boussouf wanted him to prove himself in a trap set for Si Mokhtar, a section head who had come to Oujda to contest the leadership in his Wilaya. The leader carried out orders and executed him. The three deserters, including the leader, were then included in the training program for the signal corps. Boussouf gave the leader a pistol and the responsibility of keeping watch on instructor Ali Telidji. "Don't hesitate to off him if he attempts to escape." After the training course began, the two other deserters couldn't stand being deprived of their freedom. They told Telidji: "We've received training in barracks and in the fields as infantry men and don't need more training. We want to fight with a gun." He replied: "For me, you're here and I've received orders to turn you into radio operators. Orders are orders."

That night the two men fled. Two days later, they were

captured, tied up, and brought back, then strangled to death with the trainees present. The trainees received orders never to talk about what had taken place or they would be subjected to the same end. Terrorized, they kept the traumatizing event they had witnessed to themselves.

This event was confirmed to me by a trainee from the first class who was present, which is why I risk the hypothesis that with the threats of death and the climate of terror that was fostered by our instructors, they are attempting to terrify us, just as they were terrified during the summer of 1956 and have remained so.

As soon as the majority of trainees is able to register transmissions at 900 symbols a minute, the classes in procedure begin.

Radio operators communicate with each other by using either the Q code or the Z code. In our networks, we use the Q code. It is a code that replaces clear, everyday language. Therefore, to tell my correspondent that I have three messages to transmit, it is enough to say QTC3. If I don't have mail for him, I say QRU. To indicate reception of a message it's QSL. Some of these groups of three letters beginning with Q are used to convey the quality of reception, provide one's position, authenticate, etc. The procedural class teaches us how to redact the preamble of a message: number, degree of urgency (flash, extremely urgent, very urgent, urgent, routine), date and time, code of origin preceded by FM (from) plus TO (to), the code in usage, the number of groups used in the text. The Base Order of Transmissions (OBT) covers the frequencies, the station addresses, and the list of authorities' addresses.

The learning process is all very exciting. At long last, it isn't forbidden to touch the key in front of each one of us. Finally, I am going to use the key with three fingers to emit the signals we have been learning for the past three weeks. When pressed down it sends electric waves into the circuit. Each hit produces a dot or a dash. The art of transmission consists of composing letters with these dots and dashes or numbers.

Learning the technique is amusing, even spectacular. Outside the classroom, the trainees tap the signals on their thighs as they walk around. Some, in the dining hall, train with their forks and spoons. One guy claims that he saw his neighbor in the dormitory practice on his nose. One astounding observation is that the sonority of the taps of each operator is different and even leads to everyone being identified. One joker says that my taps evoke the music of Mohamed Abdelwahab!

From confused and boring, the classes given by Lieutenant Saddar become interesting, because, finally, we are going to become familiar with the transmitters. These have either been recovered from the enemy or are contraband instruments from the American military base in Morocco. Sometimes they are incomplete. The walkie-talkies (ANPRC6) function but the SCR300 (Signal Corps Radio) doesn't contain the wire to connect it to an electric outlet and we don't have a generator. With this infantry equipment we are studying ART13 (Aerial Transmitter Radio), a post used by the US Air Force. The receiver can be either a BC348 or an SP600. Even though its signals are far-reaching, it is heavy, unwieldy, and difficult to use in the interior. It serves for training at the instruction center and for transmissions to Rabat, Tunis, or Cairo.

After a reminder of the different equipment used in the infantry and in aviation, we go on to that used in the navy, in particular the RCA equipment used on pleasure boats. This equipment, the size of a nightstand, resembles a fancy chrome radio, and is sold in the Tangiers international zone. It gives out sound, has eight preregulated frequencies, and doesn't require any training. Since we don't have anything better and since it's readily available, Boussouf has ordered ten of them and our technicians have added the keys and earphones so it can be used for Morse. A twelve-volt battery turns it on. The operators from the first class went into the interior with these posts; a wooden case was fashioned as a carryall. Other cases contained the batteries and the generator, accessories and fuel, two wooden masts for the antenna. It required two mules to carry. In the interior, the equipment and the transmissions were to remain secret. Even buried when charging the batteries, the noise of the generator is as loud as a helicopter and sends out false alerts. The range is insignificant. The command post of the network (PCR) set up in Oujda can only hear them intermittently and poorly. Despite the talent of the operators in hearing and sending messages, the experience is far from successful.

The best adapted post in this situation is the ANGRC9. Of American origin, it is licensed for manufacture in France,

Germany, and other Western countries. The one that is used for training was recovered during an attack on the estate of a collaborator, a *caïd*, near Tlemcen last October. It can both receive and transmit and is housed in a solid rectangular box. It can be carried in a cloth backpack. The tripod, the generator, the handles, and other accessories (the key, the outside antenna, batteries, mike, etc.) are carried in another backpack. An over-the-shoulder contraption made of the same dark green material contains the outdoor antenna, a set of connecting metal tubes. The supposed range of this equipment is about 150 kilometers. The signal can be obtained at this distance if the outdoor antenna is held between two masts on a terrace or in a high unencumbered spot. Knowing that such conditions will not always be found in the maquis, we are to use the best possible relay station to pass our messages. But no one mentions that for the moment; the only post that the transmissions unit has at its disposal is the one that is used for our instruction.

Commander Boumediene gives us military training. It begins the sixth week. I remember our first encounter in Oujda and his orders: "*Istaâd*" and "*Istrah*," which none of us had understood. He hadn't spoken any other word. Now I see that he only speaks Arabic. His real name is Mohamed Boukharouba. He took the pseudonym of Boumediene after his arrival in Morocco on the ship *Dhina* in March 1955. He will later become Houari Boumediene. In the boat were arms, the transmitters offered by Egypt, and the operators. Like the latter, Boumediene was a student at the University of Al

Azhar in Cairo. Recruited by members of the Algerian delegation there, he received military training in an Egyptian academy. Contrary to the French-speaking radio operators, his mastery of technical terms in Arabic is an asset, as he is one of the rare Algerians to master the art of the military and its techniques in our national language.

In addition to his face, sad and cold, he is a rigorous disciplinarian. From the outset, he demands that we line up in formation, that our stances be perfect. The courtyard being too narrow and small for us to march in time, we march standing in place. His criticism is devastating. When my friend at the head of the line is not standing straight enough, he declares that he wouldn't frighten a jackal; one must stare straight into the enemy's eyes. He doesn't consider that the friend's posture has been distorted because he studied like crazy to pass competitive exams for the top French schools. When a trainee whispers in the back of the formation, he holds it against him that "he isn't any taller than a cigarette butt." Because our group isn't up to standard, he says we are no better "than Yemen's army." Aware of the fact that many of us are more at ease in French, he gestures a lot as he speaks. He is as supple as a cat and moves as fast as a serpent. To crawl through a minefield, he shows us how to snake across, advancing on one's hands and kneecaps, a technique which is both comical and painful on a concrete floor. The best among us only manage a yard or so.

Learning how to use a weapon is more motivating. Taking apart and putting together guns, cleaning them, are essential for a soldier. The lesson on hand grenades confirms for me that a grenade contains forty-eight pellets. In the attack in front of the Constantine casino all forty-eight metal pieces had found a victim. Boumediene shows us how to unpin one, throw it, and drop to the ground. He stresses the time between taking out the pin and the explosion. The explanation over, he unpins the grenade and throws it, but no one drops to the floor. Disgusted with us, he shows us the pin and says disdainfully, "At the front, you'd all be dead." He had cleverly withdrawn the detonator from the grenade.

In fact, his demonstration failed because we didn't understand his technical language in Arabic. The lack of understanding was especially hard for Naas Lahbib, alias Hamza, who was from Ksar Essouk in Morocco. During one of our exercises, Boumediene found him distracted. He pointed a finger at him and asked, "Where are you?" Lahbib understood "From where do you come?" and replied, "Casablanca." Given our outburst of laughter, Boumediene couldn't help but smile. It wouldn't happen again during our training period.

Spring has arrived. Two months have passed. We are thirty-five out of forty-two trainees to transcribe Morse at the speed of 900 and beyond. I'm one of a small group that has reached the mythical 1200. To transcribe Morse doesn't require a high level of education. Among the five failing trainees, one has graduated from high school. The captain is incapable of understanding that one can have a high school or university degree and not be able to transcribe fast. He accuses the high school graduate of hypocrisy, of fakery, and unleashes his sarcasm. To humiliate him, he orders him to clean the batteries and equipment we use in class. I can't stand hearing him treat this honest, sincere friend as a "dirty Jew," and so I step in and say: "Captain, we've suffered too much from racism to tolerate it among ourselves. Among *djounoud* [soldiers], we should command respect and our superiors should give an example."

"And what business is it of yours?"

His brown face is drained of color.

"I'm just saying what I think, Captain. We're not an army of mercenaries. We are *moudjahidine* who have volunteered to defend a noble cause."

"First of all, shut up! It's not for you to give us lessons in morality. It's in your interest to keep quiet or you'll be hearing from me."

I feel like hitting him and he knows it. He turns away, goes to his office. I'm faced with a dilemma: anyone who rebels is a traitor, and "discipline is the principal strength of an army." What can be done about that kind of mentality? Be patient until the training is over and then go back into the country, the people, and the real Liberation Army.

In his class on batteries, Lieutenant Saddar refers to Joule's law and writes the formula on the blackboard. Naas Lahbib, a pharmaceutical student, points out an error in the formula he's written.

"Get out!" screams the officer. Lahbib goes out, his hand on his head as though to protect himself from a flying object. Saddar follows him, has him take off his shirt and lie down on his stomach on the concrete with his arms and legs spread out. Saddar orders the guard on duty: "If he moves, don't hesitate to strike him!" The nastiness and injustice of the sanction are flagrant.

A few days before the exams for the end of the training period, we learn that two top leaders of the Revolution are coming to visit us. Accompanied by Boussouf, they surprise us in class. No one tells us their names, nor their ranks, none of them speaks to us. The instructor exchanges a few words with them. We will learn later on that they were Abane Ramdane and Saad Dahlab, members of the top echelon of the Revolution, the CCP. They had left Algiers after the eight-day strike and the arrest of Larbi Ben M'hidi.

After the final exam I see that I'm in the top group. Only three trainees were unable to learn Morse. The number one trainee is Rahal Zoheir. He's seventeen and a half. He was born in Sidi Kacem, Morocco, and is the son of a civil servant in the Moroccan administration. Tall and blond, he looks Scandinavian, and with his cousin Hadi and me, he's in the front of the formation when we assemble. A brilliant student, he can't be topped when it comes to literature and any of the subjects he took in class. Both discreet and calm, he often questions me on the history of the national movement. He listens and speaks softly.

With the exceptional results on the tests, calm reigns and relations with the officers are as they once were; they again mix with the trainees in the courtyard. However, they maintain a mysterious air because they don't want to say that they have no news of the equipment we are all waiting for. They refuse to answer our questions as to the date of our departure.

I ask the captain what criteria will determine our assignments. "The results have been sent to the Wilaya command post," he says. Then, keeping the tone of his voice low and serious, he adds: "They determine the deployments." Does he not know that the "command" is one person, Boussouf, alias Si Mabrouk? So as not to disavow his own role, he smiles a superior smile, looks at me straight on, and says: "It's not just the grades and the exam level that count..."

"Well, what else?"

"There's the 'love quotient.'"

I laugh and shrug my shoulders. The expression comes from the French military; he means the special appreciation accorded to favored trainees.

He insists: "The 'love quotient' can be decisive."

The tone, his insistence, sound phony, like him.

Those who have reached 1200 or more, that is, the best among us, receive the rank of first sergeant, whereas those from the first training class had been designated lieutenants. For similar ranks, the French schools name them officer cadets. Those at the 900 level are named sergeants, others are named corporals second class. The designations are absurd and only reflect poorly on those who have made them. As I see them, I am sure that my colleagues are pleased with their training and their preparations to serve their country. Like me, they are in a hurry to leave the center and go into the interior. The officers, sworn to secrecy, are not willing to tell us that there are no other posts available except for those that were used for training and those used for the stations in Tetouan, Rabat, Tunis, and Cairo. So as to keep us busy, they pretext our need for additional training, and a professional receiver is set up in the classroom, regulated to receive the broadcasts in French of Tass, the press agency of the Soviet Union. We can listen to it in our earphones.

The agency broadcasts, with a powerful signal at a speed of 1200, texts that are not in code. For the first time in three months, I hear news of what's happening in the world. Much of it is about Nikita Khrushchev, the Supreme Soviet, the decentralization of the economy. Alongside the training in the classroom, we simulate, in the courtyard, activity with the ANGRC9, the RCA, and the ART13.

When, all of a sudden during practice, we are interrupted, called into the classroom, and locked in, I imagine an alert. Often such alerts are provoked by airplanes from a nearby airfield. In addition, twice now, we have been the objects, at night, of a practice alert. The silence in the classroom makes it possible to hear people talking sotto voce, and to imagine activity. When the door opens, the courtyard is full of boxes that resemble wooden coffins. Lieutenant Saddar is opening one. Very excited, he pulls out an ANGRC9 and shouts, "It's a jewel!" The other officers approve. We share their joy and take part willingly in opening the boxes and bringing the posts and accessories into the officers' room. These ANGRC9s, made in Germany, are all new. They were purchased by Changriha, an Algerian from Morocco with an order form in the name of the Moroccan Royal Army. The achievement of Changriha is double: he bought the posts and was able to have the embargo on them lifted, since only member countries of NATO (the North Atlantic Treaty Organization) were authorized to order them. Taking infinite precautions, a group leaves the center, sets up in an orchard next to a cornfield, simulates a station, and liaises in Morse with the post in the courtyard. Boussouf comes around in order to see with his own eyes that the "jewels" have arrived. We put on a demonstration for him. Two days later our assignments arrive.

I forget what I hold against some of the officers, the unfortunate incidents. The long weeks of waiting are past. I once again am pleased to talk and laugh. I'm in a hurry to put into practice my new knowledge, without having to simulate the techniques. I'm enthusiastic.

All at once I realize that in this month of June 1957, the Revolution has made immeasurable progress. Thanks to these high school and college students, all the Wilayas of Algeria are going to receive a post that will allow them to communicate, with the speed of sound, among themselves and with the delegations abroad. This advance is prodigious. And to be participating fills me with joy. What a chance to be able to go into the interior with a radio post instead of a P38 or a rifle. What luck to be able to send and receive messages in Morse and in code! What success to be able to use a sophisticated weapon adapted to conditions in the interior. To possess an ANGRC9 is an enormous victory over the enemy. The signal corps itself, and the extent of this victory, owe so much to the student strike of May 19, 1956.

The leaders of each team for each Wilaya are chosen among the top students. The best are assigned to Wilaya 2 (North Constantine). This is probably because Boussouf is especially attentive to that Wilaya, where Mila, his hometown, is located. Two cousins are off to Wilaya 1 (Aurès-Nemenchas), the part of the country where Mostefa Ben Boulaïd and Larbi Ben Mehidi, Boussouf's former chief and head of the Oran region, are from. The Wilaya that extends from Berrouaghia, my home village, in the north, to Ghardaia, in the south, will have a mobile unit that I am in charge of. The operator will be Arif.

The operators going to the first four Wilayas, called the Eastern Group, will join their posts from Tunisia rather than Morocco. I note that out of fourteen comrades going east, eight were born in Morocco and three in Nedroma. The Revolution has managed to mix us up and assimilate the various sectors of the Algerian population. They leave the center first.

Their departure takes place in a supernatural atmosphere. Friends that I love are leaving. Not for a second do I imagine that I may be seeing them for the last time. Is it because I have integrated or repressed the idea of death so fully? What about the dream of falling on the field of honor that I've been having recently? I have no memory of any discussion of that subject during our training. The concept of the *chahid*, the martyr, is a new one in military language. Its religious connotation reassures, ennobles the supreme moment: the soul of the *chahid* will leave immediately for paradise and eternal rest. This abstract representation is present in the mind of each one of us, even if no one ever prays. Religion has never been a subject of conversation among us, but no one doubts our faith. We are proud to be *moudjahids*! To disappear with a pseudonym, inform the family, friends, provide a box for the body? The Revolution will take care of all that!

Mokhtar (standing, third from left) with members of the ALN Signal Corps, Nador, Morocco, 1957.

I leave with the operators for Zone 8, the southern zone, and those for Zone 7, Aïssa Maakel and El Hadi Moughlam. They will cross the border with us and go to Tiaret. Like all of the sector heads, I receive a holder with the codes, the Orders of the Transmissions Unit (OPT) that contain the stations' initials as well as those of the authorities, the keys used for transmitting, for authentication; and a bottle of petrol with a box of matches in order to burn the documents in case of extreme danger.

Captain Telidji asks whether we need anything in particular. I ask for an extra pair of glasses. He replies: "You already cost the Revolution enough. We're not going to spend money on something extra." I don't dare reply that it doesn't stop him from soaking himself in toilet water and spraying it all over the floor of his room.

I leave the center at night, just as I arrived four months ago. With nine comrades, I climb into the back of a covered truck that is also transporting equipment. As the truck takes off, I spot the lights of Nador. I know that town is in the Spanish zone but I don't know whether it's near the sea or near Ouazzane, where I've been. I spent a few days there with Thami Sekkal at his grandmother's. It's there that I smoked hashish in a *cebsi*, a little pipe, with Thami's neighbor and childhood friend.

The little lights disappear. After four months of claustration, to feel the movement of the truck along the road, and see, above the edge of the cloth cover, constellations flying across the dark sky, fills me with a feeling of well-being. I estimate the price of freedom. We drive for hours with only a stop along the road to pee, before we come to Figuig, seat of Zone 8's headquarters. The electrified and mined barrier that is under construction all along the border has not yet reached here.

While a group of *djounoud* unloads the bags of equipment, a small man tells us to follow him. He lights the ground with his flashlight and walks with a hurried step through the maze of little streets. Suddenly he stops in front of the scruffy door of an adobe house, pushes it, and has us enter. He lights two storm lamps on the beams. Behind a little wall to our left is a hole dug in the dirt floor that serves as a toilet. A goatskin bag filled with water hangs from the wall. The man points to a pile of *kachabias*. "Each of you should choose one. It will be useful for sleeping and will serve as camouflage during the day." Then he leaves us.

The man comes back in the morning with coffee and galettes. I can see his face with its slanted eyes; he looks Asian. While we're having breakfast, he goes out and comes back several times, each time with a few large bags. They contain uniforms and caps that are probably from American stocks, and sandals made locally from strips of orange leather and tires. For an instant I am disappointed, I was hoping to wear Pataugas.

Laughing our hearts out, we try on the undershirts, the shirts, the pants, vests, and sandals. Each of us receives a bag with extra underwear, toiletries, and a Legros kit with a syringe and several vials of an antivenom serum. "Vipers and scorpions are our second enemy," the man warns. He explains where and how to make the injection, gives each of us a badge with our rank, and recommends that we sew it on the sleeve of our vests. He has a Tlemcen accent; he must be a student on strike and has the rank of lieutenant. He takes Daheur to the headquarters of the zone; he will be relieving Noureddine Benmiloud (Bensouda), an operator from the first training class. The station is equipped with a backup ART13 that we have brought with us. That night, Hassan Fethy Boukli and his assistant, who have been assigned to the headquarters in the Aïn Sefra region, leave us.

The lieutenant refuses to supply me with cigarettes, pretexting that the tobacco boycott is still on. Boussouf had allowed smoking during our training. When Daheur comes to see us, I mention my state of need. He returns the next day with two packs that I share with Ferrah, the other smoker.

Drama! The house, which smells awful, is the home of swarms of starving, aggressive flies. They descend in droves and attack our faces and hands and bite our bodies through our clothing. At mealtimes, to swallow a mouthful of food without any flies becomes a prodigious feat. Clandestinity and discipline are mandatory and either the lieutenant doesn't know or won't say how many days we'll be waiting here. Without a radio, without anything to read, time weighs on us. Happily there's the energetic and joyful El Hadi Moughlam!

Moughlam, who has chosen the name of Fethi, is the youngest of the group. He was born in 1939 in Meknes. He is eighteen years old and looks even younger. He has cut off all his hair in order to appear older. The lieutenant gives us each a belt with a holster attached, in which there is a revolver, and hands us a bag of about one hundred bullets, plus a metal drinking canteen, a dagger, and a chrome machete. Mough-lam puts everything around his waist and stands solidly in front of me, rolls his eyeballs, and, alluding to Commander Boumediene's remark to one of the trainees, says, "Would I make a Legionnaire flee?" We all fall out laughing.

The fifth day, Daheur informs us that Hassan Boukli has arrived at his destination. The link has been established with him in very good conditions. Boukli could hear him perfectly and he could hear Boukli almost perfectly. The command post in Oujda received him at about 60 percent. This news stimulates us: it's the first interior-exterior communication using the ANGRC9.

At breakfast, the lieutenant announces that the captain who is commander of Zone 8 is coming to visit us in the after-noon. Preceded by the lieutenant, the officer Ahmed Kaid, known as Slimane, rushes into the room like an actor making his entry onstage, holding a swagger stick that he hands to a subordinate while he takes off his *kachabia*. Heavy, his head shaven and covered with a cap, with almond-shaped eyes, he is surprised by the "*Istaâd*" that I yell out and the salute with which I address him. He begins by congratulating us for the welcome on arrival and follows with a long speech about the Revolution that is based on his own experience as former political commissar of the zone. With respect to the length of the war and the future, he goes over the main points while tapping the point of his stick on the soft wall of the room. He has maintained the reflexes of the teacher he once was. "Your mission is capital, which is why I will give it my special atten-tion." He stops for a moment, then points to the belt I am wearing and adds: "The machete's purpose is to fracture the head of the enemy in any hand-to-hand fighting." Satisfied with the effect he has produced, he continues with tirades on the art of guerrilla warfare. Just as he is leaving, he notices the gold-plated watch I'm wearing: "You aren't going inside with that. Give it to me. We'll give you another one." The tone doesn't allow for any discussion or objection. Deeply hurt, I obey the order. I don't dare say how much it means to me, that it was a gift from my brother when I passed an exam while he was in prison in Blida. As soon as he leaves, Missoum Ferrah declares: "There's a real chief. He resembles Mao Tse-tung." I know Missoum likes to present things dramatically or comically. I listen to him enumerate the qualities of this "real chief." When we are alone, I let him have it: "Mao Tse-tung would have explained why I should not go into the interior with a watch that means so much to me." An hour later, the captain sends me a watch and a large pair of binoculars in a black case.

That same evening, without warning, the lieutenant arrives with Daheur to tell us to put our *kachabias* on and follow him. We are leaving! Daheur waits at the door to say goodbye. I go out last and he gives me a hug. I join the formation, follow the flashlight that leads us through the uneven streets. Dogs are barking. All of a sudden we reach an open field. I hear the captain's voice, he's calling my name. In the darkness, I realize from what direction it's coming and feel the presence of people moving around. He calls my name again, just as I bump into him. I begin to distinguish faces and observe that in the distance men with *gandouras* are loading camels on the ground. Near me are two *djounoud* wearing bullet belts, rifles over their shoulders, and a second *kachabia* over the first. "This is Si Ahmed, your guide," says the captain, tapping the shoulder of the small man next to him. "I have absolute confidence in him," he adds. Then he points me out and announces: "Amara is responsible for the convoy. The equipment will be carried on the backs of the camels. Since it is difficult to send weapons into the interior, you will have to carry a rifle and a bullet belt until you reach the Third Region (El Bayadh)." He whispers to me that we will be following a very safe itinerary.

I take off the *kachabia* and attach the belt of 250 bullets, the revolver, the dagger, and the machete. I readjust the water canteen, the two containers that I carry on my shoulder, and the binoculars to make space for the rifle. I put the *kachabia* back on the other shoulder and then review the comrades. Moughlam pulls me toward him, puffs up his chest, and declares: "With all this, I would make an entire battalion of Legionnaires flee!"

The four camels are loaded and bark as they get up, setting off a concert of cries from other camels nearby. I salute the captain and join the guide who is almost done giving instructions. We begin marching, in single file, in silence. I count how many we are: seventeen. Two *djounoud* are going back on duty, one has been off, the other has been convalescing. There are eight *moussebiline*, civil auxiliaries of the ALN, of which one is Si Ahmed, the guide. There are seven radio operators. The column takes off. The animals' noise finally stops. The silence of the moonless night creates a weird atmosphere that affects me. Weren't we kept waiting for so much time because of the full moon? Crossing the frontier on a moonless night is a precaution so as not to be seen by the enemy. I imagine the mountains are not far off, but I can't see them. The guide is not big but he walks fast.

The idea of crossing the border soon is energizing. A year ago, almost to the day, I was crossing it in the other direction, from Algeria to Morocco, wearing a suit and tie, in a second-class train compartment. I was nervous about crossing because the police were on my trail. Tonight, my dream of returning to my country with the National Liberation Army will come true. I am going to walk on our national soil as a free man, armed to the teeth, with the privilege of my training as a radio operator. I wonder how, given the darkness, I will know when I reach the border. In the train, as we approached Oujda, a cop followed by a customs agent had entered the compartment. But here...

It comes to mind that, in order to test the commitment of myself and my comrades, Boussouf had warned that in crossing the border, three-quarters of us would perish, electrocuted by the high-tension barbed wire or torn to pieces by the mines planted in the fields surrounding the fence.

About an hour after leaving Figuig, Si Ahmed, the guide, slows down and asks me to warn everyone that we are stopping. I advise the person in back of me, who transmits the message to the person behind him and so on down the line to the last man. During the pause, everyone keeps his distance from those before and behind him and we remain silent. Si Ahmed tells me that we will shortly cross the train tracks and the road. "Tell your men that we should spread out and run." Then he warns me that "after we've crossed the road and the tracks, we have to march for a long time before we can stop. The Beni Ounif military camp is close by and there are frequent patrols near the road." I am almost left behind when he takes off like a bolt to cross the two routes. Carrying two bags, the binoculars, a rifle, the belt with 250 bullets, a belt with a revolver, and a sack with one hundred bullets, a dagger, a machete, a water canteen, and a *kachabia* stops me from attaining my high school speed. But the guide doesn't seem to be very young. He's got white hair and could well be in his fifties. Being at last in Algeria is perhaps the best energizer.

The second halt is welcome and the dangerous zone is well behind us. For the first time since we've left, I observe the sky of this moonless night, a fairylike show with millions of bright stars. I recognize the Milky Way. I admire the splendor of the Poet, the hair of his beloved. I see the Big Dipper, then the Little Dipper, but not the North Star, because two other stars are at least as shiny. I try to remember our lessons of cosmography in sixth grade and regret to have paid so little attention. It was a class that took place once a week, on Mondays, from eleven till noon, when we couldn't wait to have lunch.

Si Ahmed gets up, the march takes off again. He advances quickly, speaks little, his self-assurance gives me confidence. In fact, he is the compass, the map, the real leader of the convoy. He suggests that I drink less. The water in the canteen should last until the end of the night march and, if possible, a good part of the day. I begin to find the rhythm of the march too fast when the person following me asks that we stop because those behind him are finding it difficult to keep up. They risk lagging behind and getting lost. The pause is short. We reduce the marching time between halts, but Si Ahmed maintains the same rhythm. It is becoming light. A short while after a halt, the person behind me says we have to stop. Moughlam can't take another step. He's fallen, is white as a sheet, his eyes can't focus, he is unrecognizable. The white foam in the corners of his mouth worries me. I wonder if he isn't dying. On my knees beside him I try to reassure him, to encourage him. He is suffering, his face is gnarled in pain. "My legs don't hold me up anymore," he manages to say, shaking his head. I feel his calves, his thighs, his muscles are stiff. I massage them but don't manage to get him to bend his knees. Is it because he isn't fully grown? I continue to massage and try to find the right words to comfort him, and remember the bright young man who amused us with his childishness during those long days of waiting in the dusty, smelly house in Figuig. He suddenly looks old, his lips are dry and swollen, his teeth suddenly visible. It frightens me. My massage, my incantations, finally produce an effect. I help him up. Spontaneously, a *moussebel* grabs his rifle and the bullet belt. I see his face; he's about twenty years old, wearing a cap, a jacket, and a *gandoura*. Another man, also young, comes up to Ferrah, who is staggering too under the weight, and takes his 250-bullet belt and puts it on the back of the camel he's leading. Moughlam reassures me with a movement of his head that he is ready to go.

Si Ahmed is determined to arrive at the shelter before sunrise and keeps walking fast. Out in the open during daytime is dangerous in this flat region surveyed by reconnaissance planes. I order him to slow down, demand to know how far we are from the shelter.

"I wouldn't be able to tell you precisely," he says, embarrassed, "but God will help me not to lie, I would say about a kilometer or a kilometer and a half, maybe two kilometers."

I feel somewhat better. Moughlam will be able to do it. But a half hour later, Si Ahmed speeds up. I protest: "We've walked more than two kilometers."

"We have to hurry. Look, day is breaking, this is open terrain. There is no place for us to hide from the French."

Does he realize that I'm exhausted? For hours I have been trying to stick to his rhythm; to put one foot in front of the other has become a superhuman task. I do my best not to wobble like a drunk, my eyes are closing. I don't want to get mad at Si Ahmed; it's not his fault. Maybe he realizes my pain, but he certainly doesn't realize that after four months of claustration, anyone faced with such a trial would fall by the way. I want to scream, to rant against the authors of this disaster. Telidji, his officers, Boussouf, Boumediene haven't done anything to prepare us for this trial. Did they really need to load us down like animals? Men who were less handicapped would be happy to carry the arms into the interior. Indignant, I refuse to let myself believe that those leaders have precipitated us into a trap because they themselves are unfamiliar with the terrain, because in our present state, the enemy would be able to overtake us like rabbits.

I urge Si Ahmed, despite his reluctance, to make a halt. He points out that the first rays of the sun can be observed. By the light of the coming day, I see neither mountain nor hill nor any brush as I had imagined in the darkness on our departure. Looking in every direction, I see no point higher than another, no tree, no vegetation. Hungry, thirsty, the pain in my stiff legs, what can we do? I don't want to be on bad terms with a man as old as my father, who is guiding us in this rocky expanse in which I see no trace of human life past or present and nothing on the horizon. He is doing his best, but I am certain that he feels my anger when I order him "to find a resting place within the next half hour." He panics an instant, looks rapidly at the sun coming up, shakes his head to signify that he agrees. We start to march again and, a little while later, I notice that we turn slightly to the right. An hour later, we discover the dried bed of a stream surrounded by low bushes. Si Ahmed suggests that everyone find a small bush under which to hide and not budge. The observation planes can not only observe movement but also the traces of footsteps in the sand of the riverbed. I transmit his suggestion to the comrades, who all resemble zombies.

The *moussebiline* help each other, distribute water from the water bags, discharge the camels. The latter are taken far from the camp and tied down. I take my *kachabia*, try to look alert next to Si Ahmed as he gives instructions. Then I put some distance between us, lie down under the first bush I find, and fall immediately to sleep.

The guide wakes me in the middle of the afternoon and, smiling, hands me half a galette and a tin of sardines in tomato sauce. While he's bending down next to me, I finally see his bright, dark eyes, the deep lines of his weathered face. He watches me devour the first meal since leaving Figuig and says he is sorry he can't offer me a glass of tea to accompany it. "To light a fire runs the risk of signaling our presence." I feel I owe him some explanation for our difficulty in marching: our secret mission required long preparation and confinement, without exercise, for months. We remained locked in and had practically no physical exercise. I am sure that in two or three days we will be in better form. Once we are far from the border, we will be able to take a day off. Planes are few near sundown. I propose that we break camp then. It will be possible to reach the next campsite before daybreak.

Three radio operators are around Moughlam, our young man. His voice is now normal and his color has returned, though he's unsmiling. Ferrah reports that Baza, the bigger of the two *djounoud*, has said to Moughlam: "I hope your mother didn't tell you that the ALN has half-tracks at its disposal." "What a bastard," says Baghdadi, who proposes punishing Baza, breaking his jaw. He figures that it is an attack on our dignity, an insult that concerns all of us. The others approve. Physically, Baza is tall and strong. I have just seen his face in daylight: he must be nearly forty and Moughlam could well be his son. His lack of tact is indicative of his disdain for us. Since he heard us speak Arabic and French, he has relegated us to a social category that has no place in his heart. He's from the country, he disdains city folk, whom he thinks are weak and unmanly. Evoking half-tracks shows that he probably doesn't speak French but has frequented the French army.

"Baza is tough," I say. It is obvious that his remarks can be taken as provocation or an attack on our self-confidence. However, an argument, even less than a fight, is not the solution. He is pleased to see these "spoiled brats" from the city in difficulty. He has attacked our mothers to bring us down a notch or two.

We decide to react as a group, united. Baza is illiterate and certainly from a poor environment and is envious of our comfort and education. We are fighting together, it's true, but for him independence means first of all overcoming poverty and daily misery. How to explain to him that we have renounced our comfort through solidarity, so that injustice ends and universal values triumph? We decide to ignore him and, especially, to support and respect each other, to avoid incidents. To that end, I propose that we discuss any questions or problems in the future, that we meet at the end of each day. We must not forget that our road is long.

As soon as I hear a camel moo, I leave the bush and the dry little tree supposed to shelter me. The *moussebiline* have brought the animals around and are getting ready to load them. It is cooler, the sun is going down. Less uniform, the sky is a pleasant blue. Until the sun disappears, we fan out. After a few hours, I feel my legs get heavy and the line of men lengthen. A little after midnight I see that Moughlam has slowed down, is suffering. Si Ahmed consents to put him on a camel. The comrades are complaining about the speed, the long hauls between halts. I try to negotiate with the guide without admitting my own fatigue, the pain I feel.

"Are we far from the *merkez*, the center?"

"If God will keep me from lying, I would say that we still have a kilo or a kilo and a half to go."

A little later I want to know precisely when we will arrive.

"If God will keep me from lying, I would say that we will be there in an hour or an hour and a half."

I gather what strength is left, put one foot in front of the other, and try to forget the pain. I can't forget the image that I have had since the beginning of our march: an infinite landscape without landmarks. The black night increases the nervous tension. Not having a compass or map worries me. I don't know whether the Liberation Army has any maps and whether I would know how to read them. But our higher-ups could have taught us to read them. In this hostile universe, so dangerous, I have no way to help the guide should he be lacking. Especially since in the forbidden zone that we are crossing, the French pilots shoot at anything that budges.

After a welcome halt, we set out to march again. Si Ahmed has an unbelievable way of estimating distances and time. He must do it the way seamen did before the invention of the compass. The nomads and their caravans have been roaming the Sahara for centuries. Si Ahmed and the *moussebiline* belong to a large tribe, the Reguibet, that nomadizes between the Spanish Sahara, Algeria, and Mauritania. I'm discovering the existence of this tribe. In none of my history classes have I heard of it; nor have I seen it mentioned in any of the nationalist literature. They are not what are called "bluemen" or Touaregs, who also roam the Sahara freely. They don't pay any attention to the borders invented by the colonialists. The space they cover belongs to them. I have the net impression that Si Ahmed and the Reguibet are well aware of the link between their history and the destiny of the Maghreb.

The final part of the march takes place without incident. But about two hours before reaching the shelter, Si Ahmed suddenly changes his opinion. "There are people not far from here, we have to move on." How can he see people and where are they? "They're that way," he insists, pointing to the right. "Listen carefully, dogs are barking. They have smelled us." I listen and finish by hearing a faint sound of barking. Do seamen have such senses too?

At the bivouac, Si Ahmed wakes me up to introduce a visitor named Latrache, which in Arabic means the deaf one. He's in charge of the relay station and maintains and guards a store of food. He and the guide agree on the provisions necessary for the next few days. He has brought some dry dates, balls of *rfiss*, and recently cooked galettes. The young *moussibiline* continually prepare and deliver tea around.

At the end of the afternoon, Latrache comes back carrying a large *guessiaa*, a big round wooden dish with upturned edges, on his head and a water container in his hands. It's a dish of couscous covered with an onion sauce. Then he goes away and comes back with a second such dish. What a treat! We eat in silence. Baza, the *djoundi* who attacked Moughlam verbally during the first run, calls out to me: "And if we only left tomorrow night?" In other words, he is suggesting that we take a day off and rest. His face is round, tan, his eyes black, his lips thick. He has no teeth and reminds me of a peasant known in my village for his drinking, his feet callused from the many marches, someone known in the village for having taken part in the war in Indochina.

"Si Baza, I'm sure that we all need rest. The brothers and myself know that the road is long and we are in a hurry to arrive. I think we have to march on. It's a shame that the Liberation Army doesn't have any half-tracks." My comrades break up laughing. At the meeting we hold at the end of the day, they express their satisfaction and joke about it. The happiest of all is Moughlam, whom I am pleased to see smiling again.

Relaxed, we start off again on the next march, spread out fanlike before the sun goes down. Then we line up, maintaining enough distance between one another to avoid being decimated by a machine gun. Out of necessity, I stay near the guide.

During a halt, I ask him, "How do you know where we are in all this darkness?"

He points to the star shining above us. I get him to point out which one, and when he is sure that I've identified it, he places his index finger in the middle of his forehead and says: "Put this star between your two eyes and advance."

Scarcely understanding, I laugh. "And when should I change direction?"

According to his explanations, I deduce that Si Ahmed evaluates the time and the distances on the basis of a cosmos that totally eludes me. Both of us, however, are aware of the Infinite, of the beauty of the universe.

Toward four o'clock in the morning, I call for a halt. Missoum has difficulty in keeping up. To help him, the *moussebiline* have taken his rifle and munitions. His eyes are bulging; his plaintive voice worries me. I tell the guide to begin marching again but I decide to accompany my friend at the end of the caravan.

"Missoum, you know that I don't see well at night. So don't lose sight of the guy in front of us."

Careful, I listen intently, aware of the noise of the footsteps. All of a sudden I realize that I don't hear the crush of feet.

"Missoum, do you still see them?"

He reassures me. But when the first light of day appears, I don't see anyone. I stop, look for something to latch on to, an idea. Livid, Missoum takes the cap off his water canteen. His face is scrunched up, he shouts: "We're lost. Can you imagine we're lost in the middle of the desert!"

"When did you last see the guy in front of us?

"Not long ago, five minutes ago, maybe ten. They musn't be far."

His approximations remind me of Si Ahmed, who calculates distances in "kilos" and time in "hours and a half."

"In what direction were they going?"

Sure of himself, Missoum points to the horizon and says, "That way!"

I suggest we advance slowly to find traces of their steps, but other than in the riverbeds, there is not much sand in our desert. We are marching on stony land with occasional sharp-edged stones. It is impossible to see the slightest print of sandals with tire soles. After an hour, I stop. The sun has come up and the flies awaken. Hungry, they attack us, it's time for their breakfast. Missoum seems to have found some life again. He moves one way and inspects the horizon. I feel a sense of panic and stop him.

"I think we should go back, find the water hole where we made a halt at about three in the morning. If we find the spot, at least we'll be sure not to die of thirst. Of course, we run the risk of being discovered by an enemy patrol. In that case, we will fight until death. But we can also meet up with a caravan looking for water. We could force them to lead us to Figuig. Our arms will certainly impress them."

"I don't have any weapons anymore," Missoum yells, obviously not inclined to adopt my plan.

"Take my rifle, even if the bullet belt is on a camel's back. There's no one to tell them we don't have any munitions. In any event, I have my revolver and a hundred bullets that I count on using."

My reasoning doesn't seem to meet with Missoum's approval. I am not even sure he's listening to me. He is agitated again, moves in every direction, first one way and then another. He speaks of Shakespeare, of Greek tragedy. Missoum has two brothers who are in the theater. He chose the Strasbourg school to do the same. He interrupted his studies because of the strike but he hasn't lost the vocation. He would certainly have been a good actor, but the present situation is too serious. I refuse to give in to discouragement, to despair. Missoum is losing it. I have to react.

I stand firmly in front of him, look him straight in the eye, and yell, "*Istaâd*!"

He looks at me horrified, thinks I'm crazy. I show him the rank sewn on my sleeve.

"I'm the chief! I order you to stand at attention and salute."

He grimaces, raises his eyebrows and refuses to look at me. "You can't talk to me like that. What about our friendship?"

I take out my revolver, point it at him, and repeat, "Attention!"

He follows the order.

"Listen to me. We have to find a solution if we're not going to die of thirst or be hunted down like rabbits by the

French. The situation requires someone to be in charge. We are going to try to find the water hole. I don't know how long that will take us. And from now on, we have to drink as little as possible. At ease!"

He looks sick but obeys. I put the pistol back in its case. We turn back and, after one hour of walking in silence, under the hot sun, I decide that we should rest. Missoum takes a drink of water, sees that his can is almost empty. I know that mine is three-quarters full but I say nothing. I will ration it. A little before noon, we distinguish the traces of soles made of tires. I see clearly that they are going in the other direction. I brush away a fly on my temple and hit my glasses, which fall off. I swear and pick up the frames, which have hit the only big stone near my feet, breaking one lens into pieces. It's the glass of the only eye with which I see well. Missoum swears at the sky, the earth, and worries about how I'm going to manage. I control my anger, look into the tube containing the codes for sending and receiving messages, the bottle of petrol, the sheets of white paper, and the pens and pencils. I find a roll of transparent Scotch tape. I fit the two pieces of glass together, tape them, put the glasses back on, and, so as not to hear Missoum's despair, tell him that I see well. Obviously I don't. But we start marching again. I tell my friend to shut up and listen to whether he hears a plane. A little while later, Missoum believes he sees a palm tree. I speed up until he is sure. I see it too. It's our water hole. No doubt about it.

I slow down, give the rifle to Missoum, and take out my revolver. Someone might see us and hide.

"Keep your distance! Walk around back. If there's anyone there, we need to surprise him."

Ready to get down on the ground, my pistol in my hand, I advance swiftly like a wolf. I feel my heart beating faster, my legs weakening. Sweat is drenching my back, I find it difficult to spit. I try to neutralize the slight trembling of my hand. Nothing is moving, there is not the slightest noise. I gather all my force, my courage, and jump toward the palm tree. No one's there! I put the revolver back in its case.

Missoum bends down near the water and drinks. I explore the spot. The shadows that I saw last night don't bother me anymore. With majesty, the solitary palm tree dominates the little patches of greenery happy to keep it company. How do they manage to survive with the animals that can stop here? Or does it mean that wild animals have been exterminated in this forbidden zone?

Missoum and I lie down next to a bush. So that we are not surprised while sleeping, I encourage him to sleep while I remain awake and on guard. Worried, he moans, wriggles like a child; he finishes by lying down on his elbow and looking into the distance. He refuses to sleep and begs me to let him stay on guard. I accept, turn my back, and try to sleep.

"I see someone, there's someone!" he cries and shakes me as I am falling asleep.

I look in the direction he indicates and see nothing. Is it because of the Scotch tape on my glasses? "Describe him. Is he coming our way?"

Excited, Missoum waves his arms. I do the same.

"Is it a passerby? Why doesn't he reply?" cries Missoum desperately. He concludes that he is seeing no one. "It's just a mirage."

He's tired, so I replace him. The tape on my glasses affects my sight but at a certain angle, I manage to see things. The flies are infernal; the strains of life in the desert make them unbearable.

Now I see something, someone on the horizon, maybe two people, nomads who are coming toward us. I wait until they are closer before waking Missoum. I stare fixedly at them. There are two people wearing white caps. They are walking slowly or they are very far away. I don't want to get up until I am sure that they are from our caravan. Still on the ground, I wave my arm. I am sure they see better than I do. But there's no reaction. I wait, see them better. They are walking faster. I get up, I wave both arms. They've disappeared, I finally have to believe in mirages.

Awake, Missoum continues his litany, his words are defeatist, and he is wary of me. He sees nothing but I think I see two individuals who, like the former ones, are coming in our direction. They are also wearing turbans. They are walking firmly, approaching hurriedly.

"Look, Missoum, look right. Do you see something?"

He looks, takes hold of my arm, looks at me with his eyes wide open. For a moment he can't speak.

"Don't move. Try to see if they are from our group."

"Yes, yes, I recognize them!"

Lying on one arm, I wave the other. The two silhouettes persist, they reply. We exchange several signals. Suddenly, they look like they are arriving. They walk faster. Missoum and I get up and hug each other.

"We are saved," he repeats, jumping up and down.

The two *moussebiline* are very near. I recognize the older one. Smiling, they seem as happy as we are.

"Thanks be to God who allowed us to find you alive," says the older one as he hands me a water canteen.

They have been looking for us since six o'clock in the morning. Before taking off, they asked all the operators if anyone could give them an idea of what marks there were on the soles of our sandals. Several times they thought they had found traces of them but it's only an hour earlier that they were sure they had identified them. They feared finding us dead from thirst. They had abstained from drinking since six in the morning and it's now two in the afternoon.

We walk without stopping to the shelter, a gorge in the plateau alongside a riverbed with only sand. I realize that we weren't far from there when we got lost. Happy to see us, the comrades take us in their arms. Moughlam holds me tight. "We will only take to the road tomorrow night," Si Ahmed announces.

I am washed out and sleep as if dead until the next morning. I wake up feeling well, happy to see the light of day, the soft light, the tender blue of the sky. In putting on my glasses, my heart sinks. The Scotch tape, the crack between the two pieces of glass, is a handicap. I decide to send a message asking for a new pair. Not having the means to deploy the antenna at enough height, I decide to try out the whip antenna. This flexible metal rod used by military vehicles has a theoretical range of sixty kilometers. The idea pleases my comrades. I write out what is called an SVC or service message, addressed to the captain commander of the signal corps. Alongside the data concerning the glasses, I also point out that we crossed the border five days ago.

While Derdek, my assistant, encodes the message, I look

up the addresses in the transmission order, the hours and the frequencies. Si Ahmed knows that our mission is secret. I warn him that we have to leave the camp and take one of the bags containing the equipment with us. During our absence, I ask him to be sure that no one follows us. As soon as we're out of sight, we come out of the ravine and reach the plateau. We take the equipment out and, carefully watched by the other operators, Derdek assembles the pieces, the base and the handles of the generator. I connect the receiver, the antenna, the key, the battery for reception, the earphones, and the loudspeaker, so the comrades can follow the connection.

At the precise time, the key attached to my thigh, the earphones on, I move the reception key slowly, find the call data and address of the Figuig station. I adjust the microphone to the same frequency and, as soon as the network chief stops addressing us, I cry out, "Turn!" And Derdek starts up the generator. I send a series of *V*'s, my address, and "QRK5/5. QRK? QTC," meaning, "I hear you very well, do you hear me? I have a message for you." Scared stiff, I'm afraid I've regulated it badly, that I've made a mistake. I am also worried about the opinion of the comrades who are watching me. The command post replies: "QRK5/5, QSA5/5" (I hear you very well, your signals are very clear). My comrades jump with joy. I signal to Derdek to prime the handles so as to transmit my message.

Then I distinguish the sound of a powerful post that is coming onto the frequency. It enters the network, its address is PCR Oujda, and the transmission is that of Lieutenant Bouzid, the instructor of reading and procedure. He receives me 4/5, determines that I hear him, and wants to know my geographic position (QTA). He seems more excited than we are. Happy to know we are alive, he wants to locate us. I ask him to be patient, how can we give him a position when we don't have a map or a road, nor the name of a nearby village or agglomeration? I consult my astonished companions. No one can whisper the Q code, if it exists. We don't know where we are. Since it's forbidden to transmit in "clear," I have to encode another service message. "Stop. Message sent with

whip antenna Stop and End." As soon as he acknowledges reception, I announce that the station is closing down. If I transmit for more than seven minutes, I run the risk of being recognized by an enemy station.

It's done. Boussouf, the Wilaya officers, and the transmissions officers now know that we are alive somewhere in the South Oran region and that the equipment functions. I wonder if they are aware that communication with Oujda, several hundred kilometers away, is an extraordinary technical performance. Even the manufacturer of the ANGRC9 would have found it difficult to believe.

To celebrate our success, I propose sacrificing a can of water for us to shave and to brush our teeth. The tireless *moussebiline* offer us three glasses of the ritual tea. Since our departure they have been at our service, multiplying gestures of solidarity. Our conversations in French intrigue them. Our accents from the High Plateau region and from Morocco also intrigue them, but don't persuade them to approach us. I don't know how they perceive us, but they seem to have adopted us. However, I am not sure that our individualistic behavior is how we should reply to their kindness and helpfulness. After all, despite our uniforms, nothing distinguishes us. I speak of them during our meeting at the end of the afternoon and suggest to my companions to be more attentive to our relations with the other members of the caravan.

As the sun disappears on the horizon, I see the *moussebiline* kneeling behind Si Ahmed for the prayer. I join them and, quickly, the other operators do the same. Si Ahmed leaves his post as imam, takes my arm, and brings me to his spot.

"Si Amara, do us the pleasure and honor of leading the prayer."

"Si Ahmed, I have the same respect for you that I have for my father. I always prayed at his side or behind him. You are our elder, take your place again."

He insists. I suggest that I back him up and stand behind him.

"*Allahou Akbar.*" God is the greatest!

We repeat the sentence, all of us. He recites the *fatiha* out loud. Everyone prays to himself except Arif, whose light voice repeats the verses at the same time as the imam and sets off unfortunate laughter. Imperturbable, Si Ahmed continues, while Arif, wound up, insists on exhibiting his Koranic knowledge. When the prayer is over, I organize a group meeting. Baghdadi blames Arif for the laughter. Without any apology, Arif tries to defend himself, provoking the reprobation of the others. Once again, I feel that the operators who are from Oujda tend to stay clear of him.

Si Ahmed must have understood the sense of my gesture, since he invites me to join the circle formed by the *moussebiline*. He wants me to talk to them about anything I choose. I refuse, saying that I have to think about it. He insists, speaks of the ignorance of the young men who accompany him, and wants me to talk to them right away. I improvise a talk about the arrival of the French army at Sidi Ferruch on May 27, 1830, and the capture of Algiers on July 5 of the same year. I evoke the resistance of Emir Abdelkader, I insist on the ferocity of the repression, the expropriation of the land by the settlers who have arrived from elsewhere. I mention the uprisings of Mokrani, of the Ouled Sidi Cheikh, before going into the history of the North African Star of Messali, of the PPA, of the MTLD. I see that the listeners are lost, no longer following me. I try to capture their attention again by asking the question "How were the front and the national army born?" It's difficult to answer that question without mentioning the OS, the Revolutionary Committee for Unity and Action. I end with the motto "Revolution by the people for the people."

Despite the thanks from Si Ahmed, I hold it against myself for being so boring. Certainly the audience has heard of Emir Abdelkader, the Ouled Sidi Cheikh, and perhaps Mokrani. I am not sure what the name of Messali means to them. But I am certain that the ENA, the PPA, the MTLD, the OS, the crisis, and the CRUA and its founders evoke nothing for them. Moreover, I realize that the French arrival and the taking of Algiers on May 27 and July 5, 1830, make no sense to them. These men have no knowledge of the Hijri calendar. I presume that they have never seen a settler, a policeman, a gendarme. Their only contact with France is with its army. Naturally, I try to find out how the Reguibet have joined the Liberation Army. Out of curiosity, I put the question to Si Ahmed. He smiles, replies with a saying: "I can argue with my brother but if our cousins attack one of us, we forget the subject of our quarrel. And if foreigners attack our cousins, we will ally against the foreigners."

Someone points out that our belt buckles reflect the rays of the moon and can be seen from a distance. We were given these belts for close combat without thinking that they would signal our presence and make us targets for the enemy. We take them off and put them in our laundry bags.

Another evening Si Ahmed asks me to speak again. I choose to talk about what I know of the solar system. In Berrouaghia, many villagers believe that the earth is flat as a plate and rests on the horn of a bull. When the bull is tired and changes horns, an earthquake occurs. I heard this explanation following the earthquake in Orléansville. I begin my talk with a line from the Koran, the sura about Noah: "Have you not seen how God created seven skies, one on top of the other? He placed the moon as a light, he placed the sun like a lamp." I then try to recall what I learned in the cosmography class when I was in sixth grade and point out that the moon is a satellite of the earth that rotates around the sun. To illustrate the roundness of the earth, I give as an example the camel whose legs disappear first on the horizon, then little by little the load he is carrying disappears. I ask them to look at the sky, to find the Big Dipper, then the Little Dipper and the North Star. Since I don't know how to say Milky Way in Arabic, nor the word for galaxy, I point out that the universe contains thousands of stars. I try to explain what a light-year is without getting it across. My knowledge and my Arabic vocabulary are too poor. My cultural mutilation is painful. Finally, I give up and ask if there are any questions. There is no reaction. Si Ahmed thanks me.

I will never know the impact of those talks, but I see that the *moussebiline* mix with us more, talk and joke with us. They are pleased to respond to my questions about the bread (*mella*) that they make on top of empty jute bags. The loaf is round and weighs at least ten kilos. One of them kneads the dough, others ignite a load of dead wood. When the flames stop, they separate the coals and cinders, place the loaf in the center, and cover it with the cinders. It's a prehistoric oven. When the coals have cooled, the bread is ready. It is rough against our teeth because of the sand it contains, but it fills our stomachs.

One evening, we fan out to cross a trail. All of a sudden the night silence is broken by a cry and we all fall to the ground.

"What's happened?" I tell my neighbor to pass the question along.

A few minutes later the reply comes back: "A snake."

I go toward the *moussebel* who has been bitten and recognize Arif's voice among those around the victim: "I have what we need. Let me through."

With the syringe from the Legros kit in his hand, he tries to break the end of the vial with the antivenom vaccine. We can't give him light because of the risk of being seen. He breaks the vial, the liquid spills on the ground. Using my own supply, I make the injections, one near his foot, one in his calf. The *moussebel* finishes the march on the back of a camel. The next day, he can walk, he joins us on foot, is active and smiles when asked if he feels anything.

After so many days without meeting a single member of the Liberation Army, we reach Oued En-Namous (Mosquito River), a camp for recruits. The sandy riverbed is covered with wild tamarind. The operators and I are housed in a tent hidden among some low trees.

Someone wakes me up just as, in full daylight, a copious couscous with meat is being served. Si Ahmed introduces me to Lieutenant Brahim Moulay, alias Abdelwahab, and Lieutenant Bachir, called Tchrak. They are the assistant officers of the chief of the Third Region (near Gerryville–el Bayadh.) They are pleased to take possession of the guns and munitions we have transported from headquarters for them. I introduce them to Ali Baghdadı, alıas Abdeslam, and Missoum Ferrat, called Hamma, the operators assigned to their region.

Oued En-Namous is the base that stocks the arms and military equipment coming from Morocco. Caravans leave here for the Ksour Mountains and for Wilaya 4. Aïssa Maakel and El Hadi Moughlam leave the next day for Tiaret with a group of bomb experts who have come from Figuig; their leader is Miloudi, a sharpshooter who deserted from the French army with arms and baggage! Draped in his uniform and shod with Pataugas, Lieutenant Miloudi seems particularly sharp. Tall, very vocal and strong, he grips a whip in one hand and doesn't hesitate to use it on his men. There were some fifteen of them looking on. The few words I had with one of them as they were leaving made me think they were Moroccan. I hope that Moughlam, who was just eighteen in April and is lighthearted, will relax them. But I will never know how he got along with them. El Hadi never came back.

The mission is over for Si Ahmed, our guide, and the *moussebiline*. He is returning to Figuig with a company from the Ouarsenis region needing munitions. There are five of us, signal corps operators, with three radio kits to follow the route east. Si Abdelwahab, Si Bachir, and a patrol of foot soldiers (*djounoud*) accompany us. We are going to rendezvous with Si Moussa, the head of the region, at his headquarters somewhere near Gerryville.

Si Bachir, who is in charge of military affairs, is about thirty. He can't stand still and talks a lot. The only one with an American rifle, he insists that I handle it and states proudly that "it's like a feather." He wants me to test its accuracy and the next day takes me out of range and tries it on a pile of stones that he misses. I miss, too. I don't tell him that it's the first time I've ever shot a gun.

Moulay Bram, called Abdelwahab, political chief, is also from the region. He is an old-time nationalist. He warns me that I will hear talk of a problem that has recently shaken the region: the Boucherit affair. Boucherit was a heavyweight in the region who had put his fortune and himself at the service of the struggle as early as 1955. Having done this, and considering himself a warlord, he refused to recognize the authority of Mohamed Benbahmed (Si Moussa) because he wasn't from the region. Moulay Brahim also tells me that the *pères blancs* (French priests) are informants for the French special psychological services (SAS) who torture and terrorize the population. Two priests, despite multiple warnings, continued to frequent the offices of the SAS, and have been executed.

I think of Abbey Jean-Claude Barthes, Father Chanut, the priests of the French Mission, all the Christian friends who supported us.

We pass through the area south of Boussemghoun, then through El Abiodh Sidi Cheikh, and meet the head of the region not far from Brezina. Second Lieutenant Mohamed Benbahmed, Si Moussa, is over thirty. He's from Oran, where he represented JOB cigarettes. He was first a member of UDMA, then joined the MTLD and then the ALN.

The headquarters is neither a house, nor a tent, nor a hut. It's a dried-up riverbed surrounded by rocks. It's mobile, but in my imagination the headquarters of Wilaya 6, to which I am attached, is something else. It must be located somewhere in the southern Algiers region, maybe in a building, a house, a hut. The command post of the signal corps has named me head of the permanent station and Wali is in charge of the mobile equipment. At any rate, that's what those who designed the networks made us understand. But were they aware of the actual situation in the interior? Have they been inside the maquis?

After introductions are made and we are fed and rested, my companions and I decide to carry out our first trial run with the full antenna. We manage to dig up two wood sticks that normally serve to cook *méchouis* and leave the camp discreetly with our equipment in a jute bag. Baghdadi and Ferrah take out the radio and generator. Derdek, Arif, and I set up the antenna between the two sticks, and share the job of holding them up during the broadcast. Abdeslam connects the loudspeaker so we can follow the communication. Figuig hears us 5/5, Oujda 3/5, and Ain-Sefra hears us pretty well. We're jubilant! Despite the distances and our rudimentary work conditions, the stations in the southern Wilaya are in place! The radio command post in Figuig receives us perfectly. In theory the maximum range of the ANGRC9, according to the accompanying notice, is 150 kilometers with the main antenna, but Figuig must be 250 kilometers distant and Oujda at least 300. There is no doubt, this southern network has worked a miracle!

Given his style, I can feel Daheur's enthusiasm at the base. I feel sure our long silence was worrying him. According to the rules, we're not supposed to exchange any personal information or to communicate in open language. He dares an "all is well" and Abdeslam replies positively. He announces that he has three messages for the head of the region. We decode them together after closing down. "It's kind of a miracle," says Si Moussa when he opens the messages in his envelope. "I don't know if you realize it but until this day, it took a month to deliver a message." He picks up a bag near him and takes out a package of cookies and two packs of cigarettes and gives them to us. For Ferrah and me, the two smokers in the group, our dream has become reality.

Si Moussa doesn't impose the no-smoking rule since he's seen the soldiers smoking secretly. But instead of tobacco, they were using *dar'ar*, red juniper. Several cases of tuberculosis have resulted from this habit. I didn't tell him that Ferrah and I had smoked it before arriving here. On the other hand, I do tell him about an article I read in *Le Monde* last year about a battle that took place near Afflou. The journalist pointed out the accuracy of the shots of the so-called rebels. Several Legionnaires were killed with a shot to the head. He was also impressed by the qualities of the commander, a certain Si Mourad.

"Is he still alive?"

"He's in front of you but has changed his name...," he replies smiling.

Since I tell him that our signals can be picked up by the enemy if the transmission lasts too long, Si Moussa, when he hands me his first message for transmission, seems embarrassed and excuses himself: "It's too serious, our leaders must inform international public opinion."

A company from Wilaya 4, equipped and armed by the En-Namous base, has just been decimated in the Ksour Mountains when heading for the Algiers region. According to civilians, they were observed by the French army at Djebel Bou Nokta. The soldiers posted themselves on the cliffs as they were instructed to do. There was no fighting, but they were attacked by French planes. According to the *moussebiline*, "the soldiers were found in firing position, their rifles in hand, like they were alive." There is no doubt, the French planes used chemical or bacteriological weapons, weapons forbidden by international conventions. The bodies of the soldiers were exposed at the animal market in Gerryville, they had no wounds on them. Thus, following up on the smoking out of caves filled with people after the French conquest of Algeria, they are experimenting with new ways of exterminating us. This crime, a genocide, must not go unpunished. I hope that our leaders will move heaven and earth for the UN to intervene. The least they can do is send a committee of inquiry. Witnesses and the bodies exist; men, women, and children have seen them laid out in the market. Experts will be able to determine what kind of chemical or biological agents were used. Yes, may this message alert French and international opinion.

In the beginning the French army used napalm in the Aurès Mountains, far from zones inhabited by the European population. The same in the Ksour Mountains and the southern territories administered by the army since the beginning of the occupation. The use of chemical or biological weapons can therefore be kept secret. According to international conventions, the use of such weapons constitutes a war crime and a crime against humanity. Hundreds of thousands of soldiers, artillery, the navy, aviation are no longer enough. Those who head up the top brass of the French military machine now have recourse to weapons of mass destruction! What is the French population waiting for to react? Their children are carrying out these crimes. Those called to duty see well enough that Algeria is not France, that the war they are waging is unjust. The French Communist Party voted in favor of the special powers demanded by the Socialist president Guy Mollet. The trade unions are doing nothing to stop the sending of troops. What are the "possessors of knowledge" waiting for to denounce loud and strong these crimes against mankind's conscience and their universal principles? Where is past proletarian solidarity, what has become of the values of the Enlightenment?

When, the night before I was ready to leave, I tell Si Moussa where my final destination is, he looks at me with unbelieving eyes and says: "But there's no longer any headquarters, no Wilaya 6. Colonel Ali Mellah is dead."

I'm flabbergasted. I don't believe him. There must be some mistake, or maybe it's just a rumor!

"Colonel Boussouf and Captain Telidji wouldn't send me to a Wilaya that doesn't exist! They mustn't be aware of what's happened."

"Well, I sent them a report about two months ago telling them what happened. The entire leadership of the Wilaya was decimated by one of the officers who took charge. The reasons for this massacre remain obscure."

I will learn later on that Colonel Si Cherif (his real name was Ali Mellah), who entered the maquis in Kabylia in 1950 following the breakup of the Special Organization, was charged with organizing the FLN and the ALN in the southern Algiers region in 1955. He was accompanied by other militants from Kabylia, who considered themselves superior to the local Arabic-speaking population. They executed those who didn't obey, lorded it over the Arabic intellectuals, demanded ransoms from the local population, abused their women. The reaction of the soldiers recruited in the region, as well as that of the local population, led to the death of Colonel Si Cherif and his men in 1957, as well as to a terrible hunt for anyone from Kabylia, even those established in the region for years. These exactions were carried out under the leadership of an area chief named Cherif Ben Saidi, who then joined the French army with his men. Ben Saidi misled everyone by calling himself Si Cherif and fought against the ALN until independence.

I show Si Moussa my orders for the headquarters of Wilaya 6 and ask his advice.

"Given the trouble in that Wilaya, we've decided to integrate part of their territory in our Zone 8. We created the

Fourth Region led by a young second lieutenant whose name is Ismet. I feel certain that while you are waiting for new orders you can render him service."

I agree to follow his advice but don't feel familiar enough to ask who decided to integrate the territory of another Wilaya into his. Boussouf, who supervised and approved our assignments, was he aware of the events which led to the disintegration of Wilaya 6?

I address a message to Captain Telidji and inform him of what I just learned and of my decision to continue on to the Fourth Region.

Derdek, Arif, and I take off toward the east with our two radio kits, a group for our protection, some *moussebiline*, and two camels. The headquarters of the young lieutenant are located at Tinegoudham, a picturesque spot in the hills south of the Djebel Amour mountain range.

Tayeb Benyekhlef, alias Ismet, is certainly young, perhaps a year younger than me. Of medium height, he has a voice and the look of a youngster. His eyes are slanted, he appears intelligent though clever and disdainful. When I introduce Derdek and Arif, he raises his head and sketches a smile. They all three know each other from Oujda, where he was a high school student before the student strike, but he acts as though he is seeing them for the first time. I tell him of my assignment to Wilaya 6, my decision to put my wireless equipment at his disposal on the advice of Si Moussa, and then I continue to explain the security measures to be taken, the need for short messages, etc. Benyekhlef remains placid.

When I finish, he asks what happened to my glasses and proposes ordering a new pair. Ten days later they arrive.

Compared to the enthusiastic attitudes of Si Moussa, the
coldness of Benyekhlef is disconcerting, but it intrigues me.
I suppose it concerns first of all Derdek and Arif. They are
also from Oujda but they are of a different social background.
Benyekhlef's father, a high school teacher, is a member of
the local elite, whereas the parents of the two operators are
shopkeepers. As children they were not friends, and I suppose
Benyekhlef fears their criticism. He must know that Derdek
was Boussouf's liaison man and that his parents gave their
home over to the Organization. He is wrong to beware of
them, because they say not a word against him. His young
age, the responsibilities that he exercises in an environment
that he had no knowledge of a year ago, contribute to destabi-
lizing him. Nothing prepared him to lead men who are often
older than himself with a language, an accent, with mental
structures that he never dreamed existed.

I leave the camp with the equipment and Derdek and
Arif. We find a ravine and set up the antenna at the highest
point between two large rocks. I choose the morning session
that starts at ten a.m. The frequency is clear and I hear the
call signal from area headquarters. I recognize Sid Ahmed
Daheur's style of transmission. I hear the call to my station
repeated three times. I hurry to reply and ask whether he
receives me. "Received 4/5." Daheur is as nervous as I am.
The other area operators are receiving me well. My hand is
trembling with emotion. Oujda gets on line and says they are
receiving me 3/5. Derdek and Arif relay each other on the
generator and scream with joy. The event is extraordinary.

Figuig and Oujda must be four hundred kilometers away. No one could have imagined such an exploit.

Oujda has no message for me but Figuig announces mail, messages for the regional chiefs from Captain Kaid Ahmed that had been waiting for transmission. Daheur sends two of the messages and holds the others for the next broadcast. After reading the messages, Benyekhlef sends one in which he mentions the destruction of the electric plant in Laghouat and the bombing of the town's military airport.

Kaid Ahmed uses the network like the telegraph service of a local post office. Not a day goes by that I don't receive several messages from him. They are all called "urgent." Some concern hygiene, food rations, vitamins and proteins indispensable for our good health. Captain Kaid Ahmed has no idea of the conditions inside the maquis. He is probably inspired by a theoretical manual of the French army.

Naturally, this absurd mail displeases the regional chief, who starts looking at me in an unpleasant way.

"Si Ismet, it's my duty to hand over everything that's addressed to you, even my own condemnation to death."

He surely doesn't believe me and reacts a few days later when I hand him his envelope. "Stop these messages. I can't stand them. I have much more urgent problems to settle. We have just arrested two traitors, Messalists from Laghouet. You're going to strangle them."

I remain breathless for a moment.

"Why me?" I say, looking him straight in the eye.

"It's a test of manhood, a test of courage that you have to undergo."

"Clandestinity requires that we not reveal our pasts, but since it's a question of courage and blood, I can tell you that I am the son of a butcher. I strangled a chicken when I was nine and a lamb when I was thirteen. I don't have to provide any further proofs."

My body has tightened, my eyes must have widened. He feels my anger and my determination and must be wondering where this may lead. An instant later, he changes direction.

"And your two colleagues?"

"They are under my command for everything that concerns the radio equipment. I can't give them such an order."

He doesn't back down and decides to force one of my colleagues to take part in the execution, inflicting upon him the most terrifying trauma. As a result, he would wake up in the middle of the night screaming.

"I assure you that they weren't traitors," he would say between bursts of tears.

I try to calm him down as best I can and listen to his horrific story. I learn that the two men dug their own graves singing *Min jdibalina* . . . And that, once tied up, just before being killed, they screamed, "Long live free and independent Algeria!"

Benyekhlef obviously has a problem with authority. He speaks little, he keeps his distance with everyone. He lives in a straw-covered shack that he had built against a rock wall. In order to see him, one has to be announced by the head of the praetorian guards who surround him. The head guard is a real bulldog, a veteran from the French army in Indochina. To get inside I have to double over; the overhead branches stop one from standing straight. It's dark inside but cool.

Benyekhlef listens to the news on a transistor radio and uses a small, low desk for writing his messages.

The officer in charge of liaison and information, his assistant, is from the region and educated. He visits him often and keeps him informed. Judging from the messages he sends, his network is efficient. He was able to get me a pair of eyeglasses in ten days, while I still haven't received any from the signal corps center. The assistant for military affairs lives in El Garda in the Djebel Amour mountain range. The forests, caves, springs, and freshwater streams make it an impregnable fortress.

"I left because I found the noise of explosives unbearable," Benyekhlef tells me. "The French army bombarded us every day, morning and night."

As I'm leaving the hut, I see a horseman arriving. He jumps off his mount and shouts: "I want to see Emir Ismet."

Very alert, the elderly man is wearing a silky burnous, under which is a vest and belt embroidered with gold and silver thread. He hands the bridle to an attendant and strides on in his soft leather boots. The French have shot into his herds and killed about forty of his sheep, wounding some fifty others that his herdsmen hurried to roast. Their chief wants to know what to do with their carcasses. Benyekhlef suggests giving them to the population. The nomads in the region belong to the Chaabas tribe. They roam parts of the southern Algiers and southern Oran regions. They are master huntsmen and took part in the battle of Aflou, which the French journalist from *Le Monde* had covered, reporting that some ten Legionnaires had been killed by shots straight to their heads.

290

Hamou, another excellent sharpshooter, took part in that battle. He's a former policeman from Marseille. Dark-skinned, well built, and with an upper-class Marseille accent, he reminds me of La Cannebière and my stay with the priests of the French Mission. I like his openness and one day tease him: "Leaving Marseille for Tinegoudham is an astonishing choice. I suppose you suffered from the same illusions and believed in the watchwords 'liberty, equality, fraternity.' It was the motto of the Republic and you were a member of the Republic's men in charge of security."

He nods his head and smiles. "I was, and I beat up a lot of demonstrators, especially workers, including Algerians."

"That was part of the job."

"Yes, but we were also uninformed."

"And then?"

"I became informed when I heard my colleagues talking about the 'bastards, the dirty Arabs,' and showing their hate."

His face becomes somber. He places a hand on his head and ends the conversation, announcing, with his delightful accent, "The sun is 'toasting my cigar!'"

Another soldier is also from the other side of the Mediterranean, from Belgium. But unlike Hamou, he spent his time outsmarting the law. He was part of a gang of counterfeiters who also made false IDs for the National Liberation Front.

"I have a friend who was originally from Berrouaghia, who was caught at the Franco-Spanish border with forty-five million phony dollars. He was picked up in a big Citroën despite his soft felt hat. Maybe you know him? Said Saidi, does that sound familiar?" He bursts out laughing and continues: "A redhead with glasses. We called him Rouget. He was a daredevil and belonged to Pierrot-le-Fou's gang."

"I know him. His father knew how to pull strings and got him out of prison. He's outlawed in France. He runs his father's dry goods store across the street from my father's butcher shop. He showed me how to clack-dance."

"It's a really small world."

Yassine Demerdgi, the only doctor in the region, was, prior to the student strike, studying at the medical school in Strasbourg. His hair is light brown, his eyes green, he's dynamic, says what he thinks, is funny. And he wears a large-brimmed huntsmen's hat, unique of its kind. He has a horse at his disposal for trips to the field hospital located at some distance from the camp. He likes to gallop and whips out his gun while doing so, like a cowboy with his Colt in the air, and makes us laugh.

Because, on awaking, my eyelids are stuck together and there is puss in the corners of my eyes, Demerdgi examines me and delivers his diagnosis: "It's not surprising. With your glasses broken and taped together for so long, you contracted trachoma, a disease widespread in the region. Let me see your teeth."

Another examination, another diagnosis: "You have the beginnings of scurvy, but I don't have any vitamin C, nor any penicillin salve or eye drops. In our entire zone, I don't think there's even an aspirin tablet."

Yassine is a complainer, but after sundown, we form a little group and he jokes around.

Alam Farouk, who has decided on the name Omar, is also a student on strike. He's from a school in Meknes and is the base's propagandist. He comes under the authority of a political commissioner with whom he doesn't get along. Very French, he speaks Arabic with the Nedroma accent inherited from his parents. Very light-skinned and balding, he was even taken for a Legionnaire during combat. Someone standing next to him, who knew him well, was able to stop the gun aimed at him.

"I spent a lot of time trying to bring together the tribal heads in my sector," he tells me. "I was proud and sure of myself, so instead of opening the meeting with the ritual saying, 'On behalf of the National Liberation Front and the Liberation Army,' I said: 'On behalf of the National Liberation Army, I open the National Liberation Front...' When I saw those turbaned heads swing around, I realized I'd said something stupid and I said out loud, 'Shit, I just made an awful mistake.' I started over and gave my speech. At the following meeting, they gave me a traditional costume, a burnous and a donkey to travel around..."

Farouk and his superior not getting along, Benyekhlef had him come back to headquarters, where he donned the military uniform and took possession of a submachine gun. However, I do believe he regretted no longer being in contact with the tribes who had nicknamed him Hadj Omar and had sacrificed an animal in his honor.

When they are not on guard or entrusted with a specific task, the soldiers sit around talking and laughing in little groups. Some of them know that I am a wireless operator, because, in order to operate the generator, I had a young soldier assigned to the station. I found them all friendly, helpful. From time to time there would be an incident. The person responsible would be sanctioned, according to how serious it was. Then he has to go up and down the cliff with a bag of stones on his back. A member of the chief's guard follows behind with a cane to stop him from resting. The number of trips up and down can vary. If there's no hill to climb, the punishment consists of running with the bag of stones or sand for a given length of time. I only saw a soldier suffer this penalty once.

When I transmitted a message about two tribal heads sent on mission by Benyekhlef and executed by Bellounis,* he complained: "I asked the Wilaya commander several months ago for authorization to penetrate more deeply south so as to reduce the number of dissidents. At the time I would have been able to capture Bellounis and bring him back in a cage."

"What's the situation now?"

———————

* Mohammed Bellounis, called Olivier (1912–58). Originally from Bordj Menaiel, he organized a maquis of several thousand men for the Algerian National Movement, armed and financed by France. He operated in the region between Djelfa and Bou-Saada, holding up the flag of the colonial power. He was killed on July 14, 1958.

"Now he is cooperating with the French, who are equipping and financing him. He has just organized a parade in Hassi Bahbah near Djelfa. At the head of the parade was a large French flag and a little Algerian one."

Benyekhlef doesn't understand why Messalism has such an audience in the South. He doesn't realize the impact of Messali's house arrests in the region, in 1943 at Reibel (Chellala) and in 1945 at Boghari. I point out that Moulay Merbah, the secretary-general of Messali's movement, was from Chellala. The commitment, the faith in him, the *zaïm*, the guide, has endured. In addition, the secrecy concerning the names of the leaders of the National Liberation Front is not to our advantage.

Shortly after our conversation, another repentant dissident, Driss-Amor, arrives at headquarters. He has come from Oujda, where he met Boussouf. At the head of about one thousand men, he controls the region around Bou-Saada. At first, he had not wanted to be commanded by Colonel Cherif because he didn't accept receiving orders from a man who wasn't from there and whose men didn't respect the customs of the people of the region, who drank and attacked, even raped their women. He then joined Bellounis but didn't get along with him. He later contacted Benyekhlef and joined Wilaya 5.

To contest the authority of a colonel appointed by the Souman Congress is a serious undertaking. To justify doing so by invoking regional arguments is an aggravating circumstance. It's a case for the Central Command and for Wilaya 5 to settle. Driss-Amor went to Oujda for that discussion.

Mokhtar (tallest soldier in back row)
in a war zone, Algeria, 1957.

And he has come back with the mission to root out the Messalists. His arrival provides Derdek and me with a considerable amount of work.

In the evening it is pleasant to join the little group to talk, to discuss the politics of the French government, but not of our own leaders. There is no taboo; political training isn't of any concern to them.

I get along perfectly with Yassine Demerdji. He had been in the north near Ghazouet and the Algerian-Moroccan border before being transferred, for unofficial disciplinary reasons, to this zone. He complains of the captain's incompetence, accuses him of nepotism and rape, and lauds the qualities of the lieutenant, a daredevil who would have been able to stop the construction of the electrified border fence.

Rumor has it that Boumediene said: "Let the French put it up, the electrified line will put a stop to the refugees coming from Morocco." To the east, also according to rumor, a similar order was upheld because the construction of the electrified barrage was undertaken with Algerian workers and enables them to pay their dues to the Organization. Yassine is convinced that the members of the Central Command are unaware of all that is going on, that they should be advised. In my opinion such an attempt would be devastating, would be treated as dissident and a sinister plot.

We leave Tinegoudham and, since the French army is concentrating bombings and other operations on the Ksour

Mountains, our troops occupy the Djebel Amour range, from which we attack the French military barracks and set up ambushes of their convoys. We spread out over the vast empty expanses, camping in a dried-out riverbed or on the cliffs. We hover around a water hole not far from Ghassoul, El Maia, Aïn Madhi, and the hamlets protected by the Organization. French patrols are rare in the region. From time to time planes can be seen surveilling the immense expanses of this extended area.

I set up the station less frequently, but at each contact I have the satisfaction that our headquarters and the other stations in the South are receiving us well. Nevertheless there are some incidents. One day Hassan Boukli, the operator in the region of Aïn Sefra, expresses his anger with headquarters. He always announces his messages as being "of extreme importance" in order to be first to transmit and close down his station. Daheur must have caught on to what he was up to and then applied the normal rules. After the opening call and the announcement of the stations waiting, he starts with the farthest away, which happens to be mine. Boukli imagines that Daheur is favoring me because we are friends. He calls in, attempts to cover our conversation, and then sends a service message that I receive and decode out of curiosity. He reproaches Daheur for having a soft job while he is suffering daily from French attacks.

I send few messages but continue to receive a large number. They are sent to all heads of regions and, in general, are of little interest. All of them end with Kaid Ahmen's order to reply immediately, urgently. Ismet, who is waiting impatiently for his replacement, pays him no mind. Si Moussa, who sends even fewer messages, replies: "received FLN literature. Stop and end."

From time to time I listen to the Oujda station on another frequency than ours. They communicate easily with the stations in Rabat, Tetouan, and Tunis. But it becomes obvious, given their repeated calls, that they find it difficult to communicate with Cairo. Contact with the stations in the interior seems difficult, unless their designated operators haven't yet arrived at their destination. Of all the stations it is obvious that those in the South have worked miracles.

Fall is upon us. Nights are cold. Every morning, the *kachabia* in which I sleep, the sand and twigs that surround me, are wet. We leave the region around Ksar El Hirane near Laghouat with two companies in transit. The presence of these companies, in this flat area, near a strong French garrison, involves a good number of risks. During the day, the sky is gray, the air is hot and stuffy. Toward midnight the wind comes up and soon afterward blows violently and churns up clouds of sand. The guide finds it difficult to orient us without the stars to guide him. After hours of marching, Benyekhlef observes that we've come back to the same point, but the guide refuses the evidence, pretends we are advancing and will arrive at our destination in about an hour. He said the same thing two hours ago. I have difficulty calming Benyekhlef, who wants to kill him.

Daylight has arrived and we are in the middle of nowhere. We have to disperse, hide, and avoid moving around. I'm covered with sand. It's infiltrated everywhere, in my ears, nostrils, mouth, between my shirt and skin. I scratch all over. A few men branch out looking for a water hole. Exhausted, I lie down next to Alam Farouk, who remains seated, and I fall asleep.

For the last six days, Farouk has been fighting a bloodsucker. The doctor tried to pull it out with adhesive tape, to no avail. On the advice of a soldier from the region, Farouk, who is not a smoker, tries to smother the parasite with several *dar'ar* cigarettes. Someone else suggests chewing tobacco. Alam vomits his insides but no bloodsucker.

Those in the know say that after seven days the bloodsucker reproduces an infinite number of suckers, leading to death.

Farouk jokes and says he feels the suckers. Around two a.m. I'm awakened by a cry. Everyone is on alert and I hear weapons being primed; everyone wants to know what's going on.

The bloodsucker has left his throat for his more humid mouth, explains the doctor, and is covered with blood. Rawhide bags, filled with water, arrive soon after. The storm calms but the grains of sand still crack between my teeth. In the evening, two of the companies leave for the North and the headquarters' personnel, reduced to about thirty people, travel east. We camp about fifteen minutes from a water hole. I use the time to give Benyekhlef his mail.

"It seems we have a female *moudjahid* in the area." He raises his eyebrows. "I don't want any trouble. I'll send her to Figuig."

"But there are a lot of young women who have joined the army. I knew some in Constantine. Others have joined in the

Algiers region. *Paris Match* published a photo of Mohamed Amara Rachid in the interior with three nurses."

"All of that is in the North. Here, it's different. One woman surrounded only by men will definitely lead to trouble. I have given instructions for her to be isolated while waiting for her departure."

Sex is a cause of concern. The leaders of the instruction center were obsessed with homosexuality; without naming it directly, they alluded to it, threatening death for anyone caught. Benyekhlef wants to rid himself of the problem by using a radical measure. He confines the young woman but not the two men, Lahbib Chohra and Soufi, whom I find especially pleasant; they are schoolteachers who abandoned their jobs and their families when they found out that they were going to be arrested. They seem proud of their new uniforms and are happy to be with us. Chohra is dynamic and enthusiastic. Soufi doesn't talk much, keeps somewhat distant, like a teacher, but from time to time says something snappy.

The day the three new recruits are to leave, I decide to go to the water hole under a scorching sun. Since we will be leaving shortly, we have been authorized to wash our clothes. I want to shave, brush my teeth, and do some laundry. I see the two men and the woman coming toward me in their bright new uniforms and salute them without stopping. Chohra is carrying a wet garment on his head. About fifty yards farther on, I see a light-colored woman's slip on the ground. I stop and stare like a hungry dog. I see the lace fringes, delicate symbol of femininity. I pick up the silky garment, wave it, and cry out, "Hey, hey." The young woman turns around, signals with her arm, comes back leisurely. I hand over her garment, she looks at me and smiles. We know each other from sight. She's Hannana, who was at the girls' high school in Blida. We often saw each other when out walking on Boulevard Trumelet on Sundays. She takes her garment and thanks me with a *"Choukran"* and goes on her way. The next day, I observe, for the first time since I've been in the ALN, that I've had a wet dream.

When I hand Benyekhlef the message that I have received orders to return to Oujda, he thinks about it a minute, and a little embarrassed, says: "We will be leaving together. My replacement will be here shortly." Seeing that I don't react, he adds, "If you want, we can go back by car."

I smile, think he's joking. He smiles too.

"There's a *caïd* in the region who has a car. I'm sure he'll let us use it if I ask him."

To prove that he's serious, he takes a Michelin map from his bag, lays it out, and indicates the route we would take. I'm flabbergasted. First of all, I see a map for the first time since I've been in the Liberation Army, and second, because I find the audacity of the plan astonishing and tempting.

Benyekhlef says, "We can reach the border in a day and a night. Wonderful, no?"

In other conditions, I wouldn't have hesitated. "I'm not in a hurry to get out, to return to clandestinity. For me, the exterior means being closed in, unable to take advantage of the sun, to run, to scream, to sing..."

"But since you've been called back, why not go by car rather than march for weeks?"

"I'm sorry, but I wouldn't want to take the risk that the equipment and the codes fall into enemy hands."

He puts the map away and says, "In any event, we will leave together."

Is it to confirm our new relationship that he takes a French magazine from his bag and hands it to me? I appreciate the gesture, since I haven't read a book or periodical for nearly a year. He surprises me even more when I give him back the magazine.

"Would you like to write to your parents?"

I have not written to them since I joined the Liberation Army.

"If I write to the family, I'm sure that the village postman, a European, will tell the police or the gendarmes, since they have been looking for me since before I left for Morocco." I hesitate a minute, then add: "But I have a girlfriend in France. I'd like to send her a note."

Curious about my secret, he smiles. I tell him about my trip to the South of France, my stay with the Barthez family, and the after-dinner stories of the little eight-year-old girl before she went to bed. I ask if I can cut out of the magazine that he lent me a little story that might make Françoise Barthez laugh. It's the story of Toto, who takes the exam for his primary school certificate, goes to see the results, comes back home, and closets himself in his room. His mother, anxious, convinces his father to go find out what happened. The father pushes the door open: "So, Toto, what happened?" Relaxed, lying on his bed, the boy replies, "Papa, as long as one's in good health…"

Her parents might not like the moral of the story but I think Françoise would enjoy it.

Taking advantage of our new relationship and mutual confidence, Benyekhlef dares ask a question: "You were surely trained in Oujda. Do you remember the names of the instructors?"

"We weren't trained in Oujda but in an isolated house where we were taken and left at night. I think it was in the Spanish zone. We were totally clandestine, subjected to rigorous discipline and an infernal work regime. Among the trainers, there was a guy who must have been from Laghouat, a former soldier in the French army."

Benyekhlef smiles. "What did he look like?"

I begin to describe Telidji. He interrupts and continues the description: "—dark, of medium height, round face, curly hair, large mouth with pouty lips, a mole on his right eyelid."

"Where did you know him?"

He lifts his shoulders and smiles: "It was me who captured him in Rabat." He lets this sink in before continuing. "Telidji was ready to leave for Poitiers, a new assignment. An Algerian who worked in the Moroccan Ministry of the Interior told the Organization about him. Boussouf sent me to Rabat with a car and a driver to get him to join up with us. I brought him back, a revolver pointed at him all the way."

I'm amazed. Second Lieutenant Benyekhlef, a high school student in Oujda, claims he kidnapped the man who has become captain and commander of the Liberation Army Signal Corps. I'm overwhelmed. Benyekhlef is amused by my stupefaction. Maybe it's true, maybe he's showing off. Whatever the case, I remain speechless.

Benyekhlef is totally distraught. He gives me a message for the area leader in which he threatens to leave before his replacement arrives. During the next day's broadcast, I receive a service message from Daheur asking me to get Benyekhlef because Kaid Ahmed wants to speak to him. I remind the headquarters chief that the instructions are mandatory: only members of the Executive Central Committee have the right to use the speakers and only in case of absolute necessity. The rule is strict, since the speakers are easy to pick up. Our codes might be compromised and, worst of all, our stations pinpointed.

A new message puts an end to my reluctance. "Order: Get station head for phonic communication." I tell Benyekhlef that he must be brief and cautious with his language. I hook up the speaker, shift from the written to the spoken word, and test reception. I am receiving him 5/5 and he's receiving me 4/5. Daheur passes the microphone to Kaid Ahmed.

"Fouf, fouf, fouf. This is Mig Juliet, I'm calling Whiskey Tango. Do you hear me? Your turn to speak!"

"I hear you!"

"Fouf, fouf, fouf, Mig Juliet! The shepherd will be arriving soon. Do you hear me? Speak!"

"I hear you."

"I've sent you underwater glasses. Fouf, fouf! Do you hear me?"

"I hear you."

"Don't worry. See you soon. End."

I am beside myself. It wasn't necessary to use the speakers and the communication was too long. It only takes about seven minutes for us to be picked up and located. As for the coding of the language, the enemy would not need to bring in its specialists to figure out what the "shepherd" and the "underwater glasses" represent!

The next day, before the session, I learn that the replacement has arrived. He is accompanied by two radio operators with a post. They are from the first training class: Hassan Benyekhlef, called Mounir, and Brahim Hamdani, alias Zenaga. Hassan is Tayeb Benyekhlef's brother. In addition to looking like him, he has the same taciturn ways. Brahim Hamdani, on the other hand, is expansive, easy to get along with. He smiles, asks questions. He's short, his hair is wild, he has a childlike look about him and is carrying a machine gun that is almost as big as he is.

It's 10:20 when the soldier who is priming the generator yells, "A plane, a plane!" With the earphones on my ears, I don't hear his screaming, nor see how wild he's become. Between two groups of letters, I yell, "Keep turning, turn!" He has seen a plane. Derdek and the soldier take down the antenna while I disconnect the key and the generator. My assistant throws it into his bag and puts it on his back. He then gives the accessories to the soldier and the two of them run. The plane, a Piper Cub, approaches. I try to remain calm. He circles, comes in lower. I lie on the ground, draw the jute equipment bag over my back to cover me. The plane flies over my head, circles, and comes back toward me. The pilot has seen me. I see his big glasses, his menacing gesture. He flies away. I get up, recover the post, decide not to abandon it. I have left my revolver with my other antenna, the whip, in Benyekhlef's hut. I don't know if he has taken it with him. With the post on my back, I jog to join the column. Yassine, the doctor, who for the last several days has suffered from sunstroke and can't bear the light, is lagging at the end of the convoy. He raises the black band protecting his eyes long enough to recognize me.

"Drop that bag," he says. "We have to keep moving. Run!"

I refuse. He offers to help me carry it. We advance faster, then we see a man lying on his stomach with his arms stretched out.

"Lieutenant," Yassine screams, "take off your tie!"

I am amazed. It's the replacement, Second Lieutenant Abdelghani. His real name is Mohamed Benahmed, he's the only member of the Liberation Army I've seen wearing a tie.

Someone cries out: "The yellow one, it's a yellow one!" to let us know that he saw a T6 plane. At that moment, the plane dives right over our heads. Yassine lets go of the bag, hits the ground. I do the same, just as a machine gun fires at us. The shots hit the ground and trace a line alongside the column. My mouth is dry, I'm afraid. I think of burning the documents. I've been carrying them in a shoulder case that I haven't been separated from, not for one instant, since leaving Figuig. The plane flies off and Yassine and I get up.

"Drop the bag," he says.

"Never!"

"We have to save our skins. Drop the bag!"

"I won't do it unless the head of the region gives me a written order."

The doctor runs to find Benyekhlef, who is at the head of the column. I put the post back on my back, advance as fast as I can. I hear the sound of explosions, speed up to join a guy trailing behind. But, tired, I have to halt.

Yassine and a *moussebel* come toward me. The *moussebel* has a long mustache as white as the veil around his oval, unsmiling face. "Benyekhlef orders you to give your equipment to this brother *moussebel*. He'll hide it. Now, let's go." The solidarity that Yassine has displayed comforts me. I feel better, get a second wind. We join Hassan Benyekhlef and his assistant Brahim Hamdani. They have left their post and the rest of their equipment in the hut of the regional chief, where they found my other antenna.

At about two p.m. we come upon a nurse who was able to flee when the infirmary was attacked. The bombing continues. Then there's a long pause. Benyekhlef summarizes the situation. He points toward the smoking infirmary and says that the French artillery and aviation are convinced that it's our headquarters. The nurse tells us that a Piper Cub flew over them at low altitude, a *moussebel* raised his rifle and fired.

We continue our march until six in the evening. Very far away we can see a column of smoke above the place where the hut and the headquarters had been.

"The bastards! They got my kettle," shouts Alam Farouk laughing.

He tells us that the night before, he had found some dried meat and vegetables in Ain Madhi. He was going to use his talents as chef to prepare "the meal of meals" and had just started cooking when the alert was given.

"The French were informed," says Benyekhlef. "Some civilians gave them information."

It can't be excluded that the open communication by

phone may have helped them locate us; I don't mention this possibility, however. It's sure that the shots fired by the *moussebel* diverted the attack to the infirmary and gave us time to make a run for it.

Mohamed Benahmed must be at least thirty-five. He has not unknotted his dark tie, which stands out against his light shirt. He speaks little, keeps to himself. The heavy mustache and his glasses accentuate his uptight attitude. He deserted from the French army in 1956. While he and Benyekhlef are passing the command from one to the other, I attempt to get my radio equipment back. We decide to pass it along to the radio operators who have just arrived. Benyekhlef gives me a written note authorizing me to make the transfer. I am satisfied and relieved.

Unburdened, I only have to carry my document kit and my bag of dirty laundry. I have no problem keeping up with the march west. Benyekhlef probably regrets having given up his idea of a return journey by car. With two guides, his praetorian guards, Yassine, and Farouk, we are about fifteen men. I am the only one who is not armed.

During the third night of the march, just as the horizon is turning white, we receive the order to stop, sit down, and not budge. We wait for what seems an eternity. We have reached the headquarters of the Third Region and the men on guard have asked for a password. Someone has gone to get instructions and is on his way back as day breaks. He is accompanied by Benbahmed, called Si Moussa, and the two radio operators, Ali Baghdadi and Missoum Ferrah. The regional chief beckons us to follow him. Ferrah calls out to all the soldiers that we encounter: "It's him, it's Amara, he's alive!"

"Everyone thought you were dead or taken prisoner. The soldiers saw us crying. We told them about our past together, our friendship," says Baghdadi.

"When you suddenly stopped transmitting, in the middle of a word, it worried us. The Figuig and Oujda headquarters called you every day. We worried about the codes, all the stations received orders to remain silent."

"We have to reassure Figuig and Oujda as quickly as possible that I've been rescued," I say. "I didn't do it on purpose."

I'm awakened by Ferrah in the middle of the afternoon. Smiling, he hands me a cup of coffee and a cigarette.

"I'm starved," I tell him.

"I thought as much. So you're entitled to a special *méchoui*."

"Stop joking, I really need to eat something. My stomach is aching."

"I'm serious, but you'll have to wait awhile. Two Chamba tribesmen have decided to celebrate your resurrection. They went hunting and came back with two gazelles that they're roasting right now."

The bad news is that in order to reach Figuig, we have to cross the Morice Line at the border. The fence is now electrified from the Mediterranean in the north to south of Figuig. "You are going to cross the frontier tonight and three-quarters of you are going to die crossing the Morice Line," the colonel had warned when we were inducted into the ALN and had a so-called physical exam in Oujda.

The rare civilians we meet on the ten-day march west can tell us nothing about the barbed-wire fence; no one knows whether it's been electrified, if the terrain has been mined either north or south or in between the two grilles of the line. Yassine, who crossed the lines farther north, has expert knowledge of them: "The mines explode at your hip level. It's a diabolical weapon: it mutilates its victim before killing him off. Both the manufacturers and the exploiters are criminals, filled with hate for human beings. To avoid the worst, you have to stay in single file behind whoever leads the group, place your foot where he has placed his, if he has not himself blown up!"

Two days before we reach the border, we camp near a relay station. The person in charge has no information for us, and no insulated scissors to cut the high-tension wires. A soldier bitten by a viper hopes to reach Figuig to be treated. Yassine examines him; his leg is blue and swollen. It should be amputated, but the doctor doesn't tell him so. There is no way of carrying him, no stretcher and no animal; he's condemned to die horribly.

Yassine and Farouk show their solidarity with me; I'll never forget them. Yassine gives me a 6/35 pistol with a chrome chamber, so small it fits into a vest pocket.

"It's a plaything for women," he says. "In Oujda, I'm sure you'll be hospitalized. Ask for my friend Dr. Ghaouti Haddam. He's always dreamed of possessing a weapon, so give it to him. He'll love it. Once he's seen it, he'll inform Zohra, my wife, who's a nurse in his service. You'll meet her and she'll be our *tissal*, our go-between."

Alam Farouk hands me a grenade. "I have enough with my machine gun," he says.

In the afternoon before the crossing, on Yassine's advice, the head of the group of guards finds two long poles. They'll be used to manipulate the electric wires.

We set out as soon as the sun hits the horizon, at a time when the enemy's planes cease their observation flights. Fanning out, we advance just as night falls. We continue in single file. The absence of moonlight, the rapid speed of the march toward what we consider may be our death, make us nervous. My throat is parched.

"We're there, we're there," the person in front of me whispers.

The fence is there, I can make out the barbed wire network. There are two lines of barbed wire set several dozen yards apart. I join the others, listen to the instructions: line up one behind the other, crawl under the wire in the footsteps of the person who precedes you, and then, between the two parallel lines, place your foot in the footsteps of the person in front of you.

When my turn comes, I place my two kits under my chin, crawl as best I can; I feel the barbed wire tear my jacket but not my skin. No thought of stopping. Standing, I march in the footsteps of the guy in front of me and then I join those who have already gone through. We don't know if we set off the alert or where the mines are.

"There must be a road or a trail somewhere," says Yassine. We have to cross it and get some distance away before their patrol arrives.

All the members of our group are safe and sound but we

remain anxious. The fence is not the border. There's a road and a railroad track. We run across both and continue running until we are at the foot of a hill. Exhausted, I trudge to the top. The nervous tension evaporates. Our voices have found their usual keys.

Benyekhlef comes close and points out, to the left, the lights of a village. It's Beni Ounif, where a garrison of the French army is stationed. He points to the right and adds: "That way is Figuig and Morocco." There's less than ten kilometers between the two places.

"*Shsh*," says someone. We hear the noise of a motor.

"The French soldiers are leaving Beni Ounif," says Yassine. "We have to keep moving."

We descend the other side of the hill, rush across a stream. The day breaks. Men wearing djellabas, with some donkeys, are the sign that we're on the outskirts of Figuig. Houses, alleyways take me back to a world I had begun to forget.

My friend Sid Ahmed Daheur is waiting for me to wake up and tell him my story. He then says: "The order to remain silent on the network wasn't caused by your stopping the transmission. Our receiving center picked up an enemy message saying they had captured two ANGRC9 radio kits and killed seventeen 'outlaws.'"

"Unbelievable! They're lying! It's just their propaganda!"

Other news: Boussouf has been named a member of the Committee for Coordination and Execution. Boumediene has replaced him as head of the Wilaya and has been named colonel. Captain Ali Telidji has been promoted to commander. It's surely thanks to the success of our network.

Taken to Oujda and lodged in a house, I'm surprised when Colonel Boumediene and his assistant Commander Dghine Benali, alias Lotfi, come to have lunch with me. I hand the former my kit containing the codes and archives. The colonel seems much more relaxed than when I first saw him. He even inquires about my health and assures me that I will be hospitalized the following day.

He questions me as to the situation inside, listens without interrupting except when I mention the lack of medication, the cases of tuberculosis, the soldier whose leg should have been amputated.

Lofti cuts me off and asks in an acid tone: "How do you know there are cases of tuberculosis and a lack of medical drugs?"

"Because Si Moussa and Dr. Yassine Damerdji told me so."

"First of all, Yassine isn't a doctor, just a medical student. Furthermore, you shouldn't believe what defeatists have to say."

The tone used by this young, well-shaved man, who is looking for an argument, stops me cold. Damerdji is perhaps not yet a doctor but he certainly attended the Strasbourg medical school. Dghine Benali, student at the French-Muslim high school in Tlemcen, would he be jealous? Yassine has served in the North and the South, has crossed the Morice Line three times. Lotfi has never done so. He was part of the team that traveled south to Aflou and which included, among others, Si Moussa, Benyekhlef, and Hamou, the cop from Marseille. Returning to Figuig, he was promoted captain in charge of Zone B and now he is a commander. Talk is easy, he spouts a number of slogans about the need to remain faithful to our struggle, the need to resist enemy propaganda. He doesn't seem to be aware of the conditions in which our soldiers survive in the interior. To speak this way, wearing a brand-new uniform, seated in front of a succulent lamb stew, is indecent. Furious, I lose my appetite and stop listening to him. Boumediene, aware of the situation, tells him to shut up, and for once, smiles at me.

The next day, at the hospital, I weigh in at sixty-seven kilos and measure 1.87 meters. It is confirmed that I have trachoma. An examination of the inner eye reveals that my retina has degenerated. "In two weeks, you'll be back in good health," says Dr. Lazregue. The driver informs him of the colonel's orders: I must not be in contact with other patients, I should remain hidden.

I am set up in a room with a nineteen-year-old soldier who has lost his eyesight manipulating a bomb made locally. His face is covered with bits of black steel, some of which hold his eyelids together. "I'm happy to have some company," he says. "My name is Mustafa, and yours?" Spontaneously, he tells me what has happened to him and says that he can't wait to see again, as the doctors have promised. Seated on his bed, he talks endlessly and surprises me with his gay spirit, his optimism. He has a passion for television advertisements and imagines the musical accompaniment. His favorite clip is a car crashing suddenly, noise let loose; he then breaks in with an ad, in his own voice, for a car radio.

One afternoon, Zohra Damerdji visits me. "I'm your *tissal*," she says with a happy smile as she approaches my bed. I'm overwhelmed by her beauty and have the impression I'm living a fairy tale. She fumbles in her pockets and comes up with two packs of Gitane cigarettes, which she slips under my pillow. She whispers, "Yassine is fine." Then she disappears. I'm moved and explain to my roommate that she is a nurse married to a friend of mine.

A little later, a man wearing the white coverall of a doctor comes into the room. On the heavy side, he looks right and left with a suspicious air. He closes the door behind him.

"I'm Dr. Ghaouti Haddam," he says, extending his hand.

I should have understood immediately, because, despite his serious air, his large babylike face fits Yassine's description. His bright eyes reveal intelligence and mirth.

"It seems you have something for me," he says while checking the temperature chart at the foot of the bed.

I go to the closet, take out the 6/35, and hand it to him. His eyes pop out. He holds the little revolver in his palm, smiles, and says: "If I want to take out an enemy, I'll have to cut into his body and place the barrel into the slit before firing!"

We laugh. He comes back two days later and whispers, "Since you gave me the gun, I've been raising hell with my colleagues!"

Less than a week after entering the hospital, I am suddenly taken out. I protest, but the driver says: "I'm just following orders. The commander told me to take you out right away and bring you to his headquarters."

We leave the town and, for the first time, I see the road to Nador. The instruction center still harbors the offices of the signal corps headquarters. Telidji has his office there. There's been another training session since ours. Telidji, in a bad mood, tries to intimidate me: "You were never taught that one never lets go of his documents, that the codes must never fall into the hands of someone from outside the signal corps?"

"I gave my kits to Colonel Boumediene because I knew I was going to the hospital."

"One goes to the hospital for an operation or when one is dying, which isn't your case," he says, his eyes hidden behind his Ray-Bans.

I tell him about the ophthalmologist's diagnosis in the hope that he'll authorize me to return to the hospital.

"No question of it, and don't forget who's head of the signal corps."

"Commander, I didn't ask to be hospitalized. It was Colonel Boumediene who made the decision."

"Let me repeat that I'm the head of the signal corps."

"I see, and I know that 'discipline is the principal strength of an army!' I could not disobey the colonel. But allow me to congratulate you on your promotion."

Without thanking me, he replies, though less aggressively: "I'm thinking of promoting you to lieutenant."

I lift my shoulders and smile: "My time inside the country has taught me that there's no difference between the skeleton of an officer and that of a soldier."

"Since you mentioned the interior, I can tell you that your friends are softies."

"What friends? Who are you talking about?"

Telidji refuses to say more, but we both know that he means El Hadi Rahal, who was taken prisoner after crossing the Algerian-Moroccan border. He mumbles something, then changes the subject.

"I need you at the command station."

The same driver drops me off in the dark of night at a large house in Oujda. I'm happy to see friends again: Abdelhamid Hellal, Lamine Allouane, Sibawayhi Saker, Taha. Also present are Abdelkader Kharoubi, called Abou Nasr, Nourredine Benmiloud, alias Bensouda, and Abdelkader Bouzid from the first training session. Bouzid is head of the working group and Benmiloud of the operators.

Kharoubi, Saker, and Taha are the night operators of the two ART13 transmitters and receivers and are happy to see their duty reduced from eight hours to six. Being used to marching at night and sleeping during the day, I volunteer for a night shift, either from six p.m. to midnight or midnight to six a.m. The operations room is long and narrow and we sleep and eat in the same room.

Hellal and Allouane do the encoding and decoding of messages. They come under the authority of Benmiloud and Bouzid and work in another room in which the latter two live. It's a room similar to ours but located across the courtyard. The service started by Hellal and Allouane is called "Regulation." Operators enter there only to deposit messages on a high, narrow shelf, the height of which keeps anyone from seeing what is on the decoders' desks. Hellal and Allouane eat with us and spend their free time and sleep with us.

It doesn't take me much time to observe how overlong claustration in a limited space has an effect on human relations. Taha and Saker don't like Kharoubi.

"He's a show-off who pretends he's the best operator in the signal corps," says Saker.

Taha adds, "Recently, he showed a lack of respect for the head of our group, who is, just like him, from the first training session."

Informed of the bad atmosphere, Colonel Boumediene came around, had Kharoubi tied up, and made him ask for pardon, all the while threatening to cut his throat.

Kharoubi is impulsive and can be paranoiac. He is a good operator and receiver. He doesn't understand why operators who aren't as competent have been made instructors, heads of centers or stations in Rabat, Tlemcen, Tunis, Cairo…

"I'm here because I say what I think, I'm not a bootlicker. They want me to change," Karoubi protests.

The two decoders, Allouane and Hellal, don't like each other either. They hardly exchange a word. I have great affection for the two of them, but I can't make them see reason. Could their incompatibility be due to their different social backgrounds? Allouane's father died when he was just a boy and he only attended primary school. But he was able to become a clerk at the Medea law court thanks to the Soustelle promotion, a plan that sought to incorporate Algerians into the civil service. He is excellent at shorthand.

"Amine isn't frank, he's a hypocrite," says Allouane. "With his so-called intellectual gab, he tries to impress us."

Before the student strike, Amine was a teacher. In our discussions, he often quotes favorite poems or sayings, which I like a lot but which annoys his colleague.

As I listen to their complaints, I measure how much we are stifled by our confinement. So I'm not unhappy doing a night shift. I can avoid the prevailing atmosphere and take refuge in sleep part of the day and spend time in the house's small hammam. There's no radio for music or the news, no newspaper or book to read. To avoid boredom, I recite the poems of Verlaine, Victor Hugo, Lamartine, and hum some old, favorite songs. There is also laughter. Each one tells the jokes he remembers.

During my work periods, few stations contact us when I open the lines. I'm not surprised because I too remember never transmitting after dark. The only time I opened my post at night was when a service message ordered all stations to listen to a special frequency for "Le chant des partisans" or for a popular Italian song called "Come prima." That was to test the strength of the transmitter of a national radio that was to become the Voice of Fighting Algeria. Jamming or the choice of frequency rendered the station inaudible.

I never knew why Brahim Hamdani came on regularly during the four a.m. session. It's to him and Hassan Benyekhlef that I gave my ANGRC9. Brahim transmitted from Zone 9, an area created in the former Wilaya 6. He is the assistant to the soldier with the knotted tie, Mohamed Benahmed, alias

Abdelghani. I recognized his way of signaling even before he gave his address. He was alert and brief; he was short, his hair always windblown, his smile, that of a young man, was so drawn as to resemble someone much older. I didn't have time to get to know him in the maquis but the brief exchanges during sessions created a special relationship. Cautious, he minimized the time of transmission of his announcements. He sent few messages, took those I sent, and never came back to ask me to resend any part of a message. He was the perfect correspondent. I hoped his sessions procured him as much pleasure. They put me in a good mood for the rest of the day.

Has he been moving or is he trying to hide from an enemy raid? For three successive nights, he hasn't responded. I increase the number of calls, cover the different frequencies. I am more and more worried. Not bearing to see me so despondent about the uncertainty, Allouane ends by revealing secretly what has happened. My correspondent has been killed. Heartbroken, I no longer want to cover the midnight-to-six a.m. session.

One day, at the Regulation Office, I see the signal corps chief, Ali Telidji, holed up in a corner of the room, wrapped in a *kachabia*, a light brown cap on his head. It's the first time I've seen him since he made me leave the hospital. He looks awful. I attempt a salute and move on.

The next evening, Boussouf and Boumediene arrive, go to the Regulation Office, and order the operator on duty to leave the room. They have something to discuss with the signal corps leader. After their visit, Telidji no longer shaves, remains confined to his quarters. Suddenly, finding a bit of compassion, I ask, "Commander, how is your health?"

He replies stiffly, "Amara, as they say in our neck of the woods, 'When the camel tumbles, volunteers rush in to finish him off.'"

"I don't understand what you're saying."

"Do you see me, at my age, crossing the Morice Line? They want to send me to my death."

What serious fault has he committed? Abdelkrim Hassani tells us that the two of them were on furlough in the Spanish enclave of Melilla. Telidji disappeared, without saying a word, from the café they had just entered and didn't come back all afternoon; he later complained about guards following him. Boussouf and Boumediene wanted to know why he had disappeared in Melilla and threatened to send him into the interior unless he came up with a good explanation. He must have convinced them of his innocence.

Another night, the decoder was sent to hang out in our room because of a visit from Boumediene. He had barely left when the head of the center announced to Saker and me, "Get ready. You're leaving here tonight."

To leave meant trading the military uniform for civilian clothes. Karoubi offered me some trousers that were long enough but too big, Saker contributed a velveteen jacket. I have no idea where we're going and the rule is never to ask questions. But on leaving, the head of the center embraces me and whispers, "It's for a good destination, a new station."

A few hours later, Saker and I are at the training center

in Nador and meet two operators from the first session: Boualem Dekar, alias Ali Guerraz, and Mourad Benachenhou, called Ouhamou. They've come from the maquis, where they manned an RCA post in the region around Tlemcen. They too don't know where we're going. Commander Telidji, whom I see at the center, is happy to keep us in the dark. He adds to the mystery by imitating his superiors.

At nightfall, we're taken to Tetouan and left in an apartment where we meet three operators from the third training session: Mohamed Hamza, known as Abdelkader, Kaoukeb Driss, alias Daoud, Ahmed Fahim, known as Lakhdar, and Second Lieutenant Mohamed Benchaou, who was assistant to Zidane, the German deserter from the Foreign Legion. Benchaou was also from the French army, where he had been a corporal in the signal corps. Teledji comes with us.

He tells me that we will be taking a plane to Madrid and then on to Tunisia. "With those clothes and your Arab face, you won't get by unnoticed," he says.

It's not the first time Telidji exposes his self-hatred, also known as "the complex of the colonized." He proposes buying me a suit. I don't say it, even as a joke, but I'm thinking that even with his outfit, his dark skin, his curly hair covered with brilliantine, he wouldn't pass as Swedish! The head of the Tetouan radio center takes us to a retail shop, but what I try on is either too large or of poor quality. Telidji wants me to take a suit in which I float.

"Two of us can fit in it," I say.

He gives me a dirty look, disdainful. "Don't forget that you already cost the Revolution enough! And we're not going to pay for a tailored suit."

"Commander, I would simply like to point out that I haven't asked for anything."

My remark gives rise to a series of insults. With determination, and without raising my voice, I let him know that I've found a suit that fits: "I can leave in these old clothes and go back to where I came from."

He suddenly changes his tone, wants me to try on a coat too. I try several on and choose the first one that fits me. We then go to a photographer's shop for a photo ID. Three days later, I receive a Moroccan passport: I have become Amara Seddik, born in Casablanca.

Telidji takes a plane with four operators. I join them the next day with three others. He is waiting for us with the front's rep in Madrid. Benchaou, Telidji, and I take a taxi together.

"What do you think of the city?" I ask.

"Madrid is beautiful and its women even more beautiful. You should take advantage of them."

The taxi leaves us in front of a hotel on one of the most elegant streets in the city, Primo de Rivera. Benchaou and I share a large room with a small adjoining foyer. Telidji gives us each three hundred pesetas. He recommends that we not circulate in a large group and gives us the address of the hotel of our other companions, where we take our meals. We're the first customers in the restaurant; Spaniards eat very late. As dessert is served, I put the question, "Does anyone speak Spanish?"

They smile and keep on eating, except for Mourad Benachenhou, who says, "I bought a French–Spanish dictionary and an Assimil book to study Spanish."

Mourad was with the group that arrived the day before. I leave the restaurant with him. Mohamed Hamza joins us and we start walking down the avenue.

"Anybody know whether there's a bordello in the vicinity?" I ask.

"There's none right here but women are on the street at the end of the avenue. It costs two hundred pesetas."

"For the night?"

"You're dreaming!"

We leave the avenue and I see several women on a sidewalk staring at us with smiles on their faces. I'm delighted and yell out: "Wow! But I don't want to spend two hundred pesetas for a half hour or so. I want to spend the night with a woman."

"Stop dreaming," Hamza repeats laughing. "None of them would agree to spend the night with you, even for three hundred pesetas. That's impossible."

I stop, take Benachenhou by the arm, and half joking, half serious, say: "Hamou, you'll be my interpreter. Translate what I say and her reply, that's all. But first of all, how do you say 'how much'?"

The two companions reply at the same time: "*Cuánto!*"

A few feet from there, I go up to one of the women, who had, with a nod of her head, addressed me discreetly. I ask her, "*Cuánto?*"

She wants two hundred fifty pesetas just for a pass.

"I have three hundred pesetas and I want to spend the night with you."

My interpreter, who isn't twenty years old, blushes, hesitates.

"Translate. It's not you making the proposition."

He does it. Dissatisfied, she talks but I don't understand, then turns her back and walks away. My bargaining has become a distraction. Hamza admires my technique when a woman proposes one hundred fifty pesetas instead of two hundred for a pass. We continue walking and find some darker streets. None of the ladies of the night accept my offer and it's getting cooler, there are fewer people around.

After midnight, I begin asking myself if I shouldn't wait until tomorrow night, when a young girl gives me a broad smile. She's wearing a flowered scarf on her head that makes her seem even more attractive. Following the "*cuánto*," I smile without listening to her reply. I make gestures with my arms and my face, and she laughs. I make an attempt at speech and say that I know she's worth many hundred pesetas for a night but I only have three hundred and not a centimo more.

A miracle! She relents. I seal our deal by taking her arm and tell my companions, in Arabic, to note the address of the hotel.

"I'm the groom and you're my witnesses. Follow us to see where she takes me."

Before entering the hotel, I ask them again to take good note of the hotel.

To my surprise, the following morning they are waiting for me nearby. They look downcast.

"Mohamed Benchaou told Telidji that you didn't sleep in the room and the commander is furious," they announce.

"You could have told him where I was and with whom."

They didn't dare, embarrassed or fearful, I don't know which. As soon as they see Telidji accompanied by Benchaou on the avenue, they get out of the way.

"It seems that you're looking for me," I say smiling, ready for a fight.

Teledji spits out, dryly: "Where were you? We can't count on you; you're not serious. A little more and I was going to tell our superiors that you surrendered to the French embassy."

My blood boils.

"You thought that I fought with the Liberation Army and then waited to find myself in Madrid to surrender to the French? As to what I did last night, I spent the night with a woman."

"Not to tell us where you were is not only a lack of discipline but a lack of respect for your superior. It can cost you plenty."

I raise my voice. "There's no superior here. We're in Madrid, in civilian clothes."

The commander takes hold of my arm, recommends that I calm down. The incident is closed.

We stay in Madrid nine days. Telidji refuses to give me enough money to buy a pack of cigarettes. He taunts me, telling me in detail about his evening with a woman he met at the hotel and their time in a nightclub. The guys staying at the same hotel say he's out every night. It seems he has a wad of dollars at his disposal for our use. I will never forgive him for forcing me to pick up cigarette butts in the street.

Fortunately, my comrades invite me to spend time at the movies. They pay my way on the metro, another favorite pastime since there's no limit on how many lines you can take with a single ticket. I convince Hamza to exit at a station called Vantas in a popular neighborhood. The poverty, the sadness remind me of my village on market day. On the stairway at the metro station a child, dressed in tatters, is shivering and selling cigarettes one by one. Not far from there is a grill on a table with someone cooking sardines in the open air. Hamza buys me a sandwich and two cigarettes.

We arrive in Rome after sundown and are put up in a pension. The owner speaks French and seems used to housing Algerians. At breakfast, the commander announces that we will be leaving for Tunis in the afternoon and that we will have lunch at one p.m. He gives us each a thousand liras. At lunchtime, he becomes hysterical because Mourad Benachenhou is absent. He questions each of us, and since no one has seen him, no one knows what to say. Telidji supposes that the group is hiding something from him.

When Mourad finally shows up, Telidji explodes: "So, stupid, I told you all to be here at one p.m. Where were you? What have you been doing?"

Unmoved, Mourad replies with his normal voice: "First I bought a map of the city, then I went to see Saint Peter's Square. I went on foot and didn't realize it was so far from here."

In Tunis we're welcomed by Mustafa Aoul Hadjedj, alias Mahfoud, an operator from the first training class. He is head of the command post of the network installed in a villa in a residential quarter called Le Bardo. Telidji takes me aside the next day.

"We have to set up a listening center in Tunisia. Boussouf accords special importance to this job. We have to put the signal corps' efficiency on display. But we're understaffed, and I will have to assign you to them."

Furious, I feel trapped. He is holding the incident in Madrid against me. By evoking the name of Boussouf he is canceling Boumediene's decision to have me open a station in Damascus.

"I wasn't chosen by Boumediene and the head of the operational sector in Oujda to become a radio operator in a listening station. It's a job for someone who doesn't know Morse well and is incapable of heading up a station. Your decision amounts to a punishment, and I want to know why."

"But no, don't take things that way. On the contrary, it's an important mission that I'm entrusting you with. I know you have a lot of influence in the group and I want the opening of this station to be a success. That's why I need you."

"I don't see why you've decided not to use my skills as an operator. I have proved myself."

"I repeat that I need you to launch this station. Benchaou will be its chief, since he has the experience. As for you, I promise you that once it's launched, you will return to being an operator. Trust me."

Here I am again, locked up. At the Kef this time, not far from the Algerian-Tunisian border. The house is in a courtyard, its ground-floor shutters have been nailed closed. A large room on the second floor has been turned into a listening post with three efficient American receivers and a few typewriters. Next door is the dining room. There is also the chief's room and a machine room. On the ground floor is the kitchen as well as rooms in which the cooks, a refugee couple, and three guards live. Across the way is a small building with two rooms, vaulted ceilings, and no windows; I share one room there with Mourad Benachenhou and Boualem Dekar. Mohamed Hamza, Driss Kaoukeb, and Ahmed Fahim are quartered in the other room with similar cots.

Work begins at six in the morning and ends at midnight. The head of the center has a receiver, we take turns with the two others every three hours. We listen to a list of shortwave frequencies and look for military networks transmitting in script. This type of camouflage, called Slydex, has also been used at Oujda's listening center.

There is a lexicon in which are inscribed words and expressions decrypted with the help of keys using a,b,c's. To find these keys, one has to listen to a number of messages using the Slydex. Two or three of us find the keys that come across most often; we test the letters, words, numbers, and expressions. The word "stop" is the easiest to find. Proceeding with care, we manage to decrypt a phrase. This exercise distracts us part of the day. When the same message is transmitted on another frequency in script, we joke about it because our game becomes useless. But the keys often change.

We also listen in on communications from the prefectures and subprefectures in the Constantine region. They mostly concern the administration, problems not of particular concern for our military. However, the message we don't want to miss is the daily summary of the gendarme headquarters in the Constantine region. Their command center sends Paris headquarters a detailed accounting of the situation in Algeria. This daily information bulletin (BRQ) is transmitted in script and is a mine of information.

The telegrams from the operational networks reveal the presence of Algerian traitors working for the French special services. The information supplied to the enemy is astonishingly detailed. I remember intercepting a message concerning a Liberation Army company that was preparing to cross into national territory. In addition to the precise place it was stationed and the number of soldiers, it included the name of the leader, the type of weaponry, the number of galettes, and the date they planned to cross the border. Four days later, I noted, on the same frequency, the message that summed up the devastating operation launched by the enemy against our unit. I'm sure that neither the head of the company nor its soldiers ever knew that the French army was aware of the planned operation. Every day, we prepare an envelope of at least forty typewritten pages intended for the colonels of Wilayas 1 and 2, as well as the Eastern Base, and give it over to a liaison agent for delivery.

Saturday morning, February 8, 1958, we receive the exceptional visit of Mohamed Lamouri, colonel of the Aurès-Nemenchas Wilaya. He is accompanied by Salah Rajah, his adviser and translator. Lamouri is Arabic-speaking, well educated with university degrees. He understands but doesn't read French. He respects the custom that a visitor doesn't arrive empty-handed, unless it is just to relieve our isolation and thank us for our work. He brings us pastry and cookies.

Salah Rajah leaves us. Lamouri asks if our material conditions are satisfactory, then sips his coffee and says to me: "Your work is extraordinary. The information you provide is of inestimable value."

The conversation is suddenly interrupted by the hurried return of Rajah. "Si Mohamed, we have to leave, it's urgent, extremely urgent," he says, looking like death warmed over.

The colonel returns in the afternoon, his clothes splattered with blood.

"The French have bombed Sakiet Sidi Youssef and a refugee camp. There are many dead and wounded."

A squad of B-26 planes has dropped bombs on a disused mine and on Sakiet Sidi Youssef, a Tunisian village where members of the Red Cross were distributing food to Algerian refugees. A Tunisian school was destroyed and many children were killed. There were more than seventy dead and 150 wounded.

Not long afterward, we received the visit of a deserter from the French army, Abdelkader Chabou. He stayed with us for several days, watched us work, and asked a lot of questions.

"I would never have imagined that the Liberation Army has among its personnel young men as well educated and with a technical level as high as yours," he says to me one day.

To better exploit the data that we furnish, the Military Operational Committee (COM), a body recently created, sends us two young men from the Aurès-Nemenchas Wilaya for training. They are highly educated and very political, and they stay with us for several days. I get along well with them and one day dare ask a question: "At my high school in Blida, I had a supervisor from Khenchela, H'mimi Ait Zaouch, and another from Ain Touta, Lakhdar Gouaref."

"They both joined the army in Wilaya 1," says the man from Batna who had lost three fingers on his right hand manipulating a weapon.

"H'mimi was killed for his so-called involvement in the Abbes Laghrour conspiracy," the second trainee tells me.

I admit that I don't know who Abbes Laghrour is.

"He was an old-time militant of the PPA and MTLD, a companion of Ben Boulaïd. He refused to serve under Mahmoud Cherif, a former UDMA militant, named by the CCE to head the Aurès-Nemenchas Wilaya. He was from Tebessa and was a recent recruit to the Liberation Army."

"Was there any attempt at reconciliation, or a trial?"

"The men accused were tortured and the trial was presided over by Ben Tobbal; the prosecutor was a member of UDMA from Tebessa close to the contested colonel. Seventeen men were condemned to death, of whom two escaped, so fifteen were executed. H'mimi hadn't wanted to submit to the orders of a man originally from the French army."

"Was Gouaref part of the group?"

"No. Last I heard, he's still alive."

I remembered that Ait Zaouche had lent me Malaparte's *Kaputt*.

Once that embarrassing discussion has passed, I am happy to discuss politics, to receive news of people I've known and to learn what's happening in the world. The leader of our operation, given his training and his lack of interest in politics, does not take part in our conversations and is not happy to see his operators associating with and being "charmed" by our trainees.

After their departure, he provokes one or the other of us for nothing, threatens to report us to our superiors. The brotherly atmosphere deteriorates. He has turned us all against him, including myself. After he makes a disparaging, unjustified remark, I react by telling him that I will write to the commander and report the degradation of the situation at the center.

In July 1958 I leave the center for Tunis. The very next day I leave for Tripoli in Libya to head up the station there. The ride in a Volkswagen minibus, which makes the trip between the two cities every week, is unforgettable. I am the only passenger. We depart at daybreak; as we cross the Tunis suburbs, I am aware that I am leaving confinement and control behind. As the sun shines on the surrounding countryside, I feel that I am being transported to new horizons.

The many flags and photos of Bourguiba, and then the stop near Sousse for breakfast, relax me. I talk with the driver, who, discreet, doesn't ask any questions. I am thrilled with the landscape.

"It's more beautiful in Algeria," he says.

During the trip he tells me he is from the Aurès Mountains and that the death of Ben Boulaïd was a tremendous loss for Algeria.

I take in the beauty of the blue sea on the one side and the groves of olive trees as far as I can see on the other. I inhale the air and immerse myself in the décor. Near Ben Gardane, the border post, the vegetation is rare, the sparseness and poverty remind me of the High Plateau region of my birth.

The black stripes on the Libyan custom officials' huts, the uniforms of the officers, the road signs along the road recall the British. I am reminded of the battle of Tobruk and Rommel's Afrika Korps. After his defeat, the British occupied Tripolitania and Cyrenaica, the French took over the Fezzan. It's a poor country led by King Sanusi (Idris I), who is of Algerian origin and attended a *zaouia* in Mostaganem. He preached in Libya and fought alongside Omar Mokhtar during the war against the Italians. Once Libya regained its independence, he became king, symbol, and guarantor of the unity of the Libyan people.

The offices of the National Liberation Front in Tripoli, called the mission, are located in December 24 Street, in remembrance of Independence Day.

I am received by Mohamed El Hadi, the officer in charge, who introduces me to his deputies Kamel and Bachir. From their accent I guess that the first two are from Constantine and the third from Kabylia. Abdelhak, the operator whom I am replacing, greets me and takes me to the end of the hallway, where the room containing the ANGRC9 and the station's radio are located. Young, short, thin, Abdelhak is welcoming and pleasant. He's been assigned to the Benghazi station.

"Maybe you'll miss Tripoli," I say.

"Not at all. To get away from the Eastern Base, to be nearer to Egypt, is a welcome change. My dream is to attend an Oum Keltoum concert in Cairo."

Abdelkak received his training in Ghardimaou in Tunisia at the same time as the second training session I attended. The trainers were Mohamed Said Hakem, called Moh, a paratrooper who deserted from the French army during the Suez expedition against Egypt, and Abderrahmane Laghaouti, alias Laroussi, a technician at Radio Algiers. The trainers and trainees didn't enjoy as good conditions as we had, and Abdelhak retains a poor impression of the Eastern Base and its chief, Colonel Bouglez Amara.

The ANGRC9, though conceived for mobile stations, is easier to use at a fixed station. I don't have to lay it on the ground and kneel with the key tied to my knee. The post here is set on a table with the key screwed to the machine. It is electric and just plugged in. The absence of a generator and batteries, the antenna hoisted on the balcony, transform my working conditions and please me no end. I receive Tunis very well, I'm heard reasonably well by the station in Ghardimaou. Communication with Cairo is not always good. Since the theoretical distance is 150 kilometers, Benghazi and Tunis can serve as transit stations. In any event, there is little mail from Cairo.

In addition to the correspondence of the mission chief, I receive the War Bulletin (BG) from Tunis daily for the press office. It's a long, coded message which I decode with the help of a C2 card, a large checkered board with letters in script in a certain order that changes periodically. The bulletin is based on information our listening centers capture. It is addressed to all Front missions with a radio station.

The press office in Tripoli is headed by an Arabic speaker who has graduated from Al Azhar University in Cairo. His deputy and translator studied at the Zitouna in Tunis and speaks very little French. They can be seen often with an Arabic newspaper or book in hand and keep to themselves; they are considered the intellectuals of the mission. They speak Kabyle among themselves, but do not associate with the bookkeepers, who are also from Kabylia.

I am housed in the same apartment as the latter.

"They're outdated, arrogant, and snobs," says the head accountant.

"The person in charge of the press office exploits his deputy," says another. "He has him draft articles that he signs himself. He spends his time with other journalists or at the radio when he's not reading."

The complaints of the accountant and his two assistants are not really justified. The head of the press office broadcasts on the radio and supplies data for the written press, which, as a result, publishes articles about Algeria every day.

As for the guards and the doorman, they like to remind those who *shab el crayon*, those who work with the pen, that they have been in the maquis and that they are proud to be members of the Chaoui tribe. The first attended the Koranic school and can't show us often enough that he knows how to read and write. I gained their sympathy forever the day I recited a verse of the Koran after he had recited one. We were at the Libya Restaurant, where the mission personnel lunches and dines.

However, behind the smiles and the pleasantries of these members of the different clans, I receive a bizarre feeling with respect to myself. They know that even the head of the mission never enters my office. The antenna on the terrace confirms that I am a radio operator, but no one dares question me as to my training or my job. Both my post and I, myself, remain a mystery; we symbolize secrecy.

In addition to the personnel of the offices, I get to know the Algerians of the *mizrâa*, the farm. They are truck drivers, mechanics, and guards. They spend their days off in Tripoli. Located far from the city, in an isolated region, the farm serves as a warehouse for arms, munitions, and material arriving from Egypt or from Libyan ports.

I often have a coffee or take a walk with a truck driver from Oran or a mechanic from the Aurès. The driver worked in France and speaks French. He was a militant in the Organization and had to leave his family and the country because the police were looking for him. The mechanic joined the Liberation Army in the Aurès Mountains during the period of dissidences. He's my age and is good-looking, light-skinned, with blond, curly hair and green eyes. He attracts attention and is convinced that he is attractive to the European women we see around. He sighs and says, "What a pity I don't know how to read or write."

I don't always understand the deeper reasons that link or divide this small world. The Kabyles and the Chaoui speak Berber but don't always get along. Those from Little Kabylia and the Aurès Mountains are Arabic-speaking and communicate with difficulty in Berber. The three Kabyles from the accounting department have been influenced by the local priests (*pères blancs*) and colonial ideology; they are convinced that the divisions between Arabic speakers and Kabyle speakers are a manifestation of a deeper division between Arabs and Berbers.

I enjoy watching the guards and other illiterate mountaineers walking around in three-piece suits. They have the walk of our peasants but carry on like nouveaux riches or *caïds*, less the cane. Of course, neither they nor I imagined that one day we would be living in a charming city among a welcoming population. In fact, we often mention that privilege. They sometimes forget that they were recently running after goats, sleeping on a floor mat, and didn't have enough to eat; some among them are disdainful of their host population. They imitate the feudals. The worst is that the Revolution doesn't offer another model; it doesn't even propose any thinking on this issue.

In the month of August, I receive the visit of Abderrahmane Laghouati, alias Laroussi, the Algiers Radio technician. He's come to install a hundred-watt Telefunken transmitter-receiver, a large, powerful post conceived for a permanent station. It's made of galvanized steel, is light gray and not the military green of the ANGRC9. Transformed from the simple shelter of a country station, my office becomes more imposing. The antenna, now reoriented, allows me to be heard well in Cairo and Ghardimaou.

Laghouati doesn't know where the unit has come from. He takes his hat off to Boussouf but contests the fact that the signal corps of the Liberation Army was created in Wilaya 5.

I point out that the first operators who served in the interior of the country were trained along the western frontier.

"I can't judge how competent Commander Telidji is, but I'm sure that I'm more competent than Saddar, the technical trainer," he says.

"Saddar owes his rank and his post to the fact that he's served in the maquis."

"But I don't understand why the men from the west dominate the service."

"Boussouf has reasons that are not always reasonable."

He smiles, indicates that he knows what I mean, then informs me: "Boussouf is setting up a network of special service agents in Tunisia just as he did in Morocco. At the head of counterintelligence or DVCR, the Department of Vigilance and Counterintelligence, is Saphar, formerly of the signal corps."

I know Saphar. He was a student in Toulouse. He then took part in the first training session. He wasn't able to take Morse, so he became a deputy when I was in training at Nador.

"I didn't know that he topped the Sherlock Holmes of the Revolution!"

At the end of August and beginning of September, many leaders pass through Tripoli on their way to Cairo. Boussouf shuts himself up in my office, consults his messages. His eyesight is extremely bad; to read he places the page a few inches from his tinted glasses. Relaxed, he is happy to hear my praise for the new post.

I see Colonel Ouamrane in the hall. He extends his hand

to everyone present like a political candidate. He asks me where I'm from. "I've seen a number of people from your town in my Wilaya," he says with a smile on his face.

Another visitor, Benyoucef Benkhedda, whom I meet in front of the building, stares at me and laughs. He asks if I'm not from Berrouaghia, and says, "How is your brother Ahmed?"

I think he's mistaken the name and correct him: "Mohamed! I don't know, I haven't had any contact with the family."

"I remember Ahmed, your older brother, well. We were classmates at primary school in Berrouaghia."

On September 19, 1958, Ferhat Abbas holds a press conference in Cairo and announces the formation of the Provisional Government of the Algerian Republic (GPRA), of which he is president. Boussouf is Minister of General Liaisons and Communications (MLDC). The rapid advancement of Ferhat Abbas troubles me. After all, he is the former president of UDMA and was in favor of integration. He had even denied the existence of the Algerian nation.

The links between Cairo, seat of the GPRA, and Tunis intensify. I take advantage of Commander Telidji's trip to Cairo to point out: "Commander, there is more and more circulation. I really need someone to help me out."

"You're always creating problems."

"I'm not a troublemaker. I've always completed honorably all the missions I've been given."

His unsteady look, which I catch behind his Ray-Bans, is paternalistic.

"You don't realize how lucky you are to be alone on board. If you have someone with you, you'll be responsible for him and it's not sure that the two of you will get along."

"I'm absolutely sure that I would get along with Boualem Dekar. I don't know how his health is but when I left the listening station, he was all in. If you should let him go, I would be happy to have him here."

At the Kef, almost every morning, in the room we shared, Dekar would complain of the nightmares that haunted him. He told me the one that came back most often. He would be at a peasant's house when he was informed of the arrival of French soldiers. He would hide out in a hole in the floor of the hut and listen to the soldiers. All of a sudden he would see a hand holding a grenade enter the shelter. He would scream and wake up.

We got into the habit of laughing about everything. On our arrival at the Kef, Boualem complained of the cold, of the lack of blankets.

"Cover yourself with your tie," I told him. Boualem burst out laughing.

Despite my reluctance, Telidji had obliged us to wear this distinctive sign for our plane trip.

I like his laughter, his frankness, his somewhat naive spontaneity.

Without news of Boualem, I take advantage of a stopover of Boussouf in Tripoli.

"The traffic between Cairo and Tunis has intensified. I've asked Commander Telidji to send me Boualem Dekar, who's at the Kef and who was exhausted when I last saw him. I know I would get along well with him."

Looking tired and thin, Boualem arrives. He complains of the head of the listening center, the atmosphere there, which doesn't stop him from joking, as is his habit.

"I see that you don't have the look of death on you when you get up in the morning," I say one day.

"That's because for the last few days I haven't had any nightmares."

Dekar is ambidextrous. He works the key with his left hand, writes with the right. I took him for left-handed and was amused to see him work this way. As he was passing through Tripoli, Boussouf was amazed watching him work.

"We should teach all our operators to work like you do."

Boualem and I are surprised and disappointed by the arrival of Azzeddine Azzouz, alias Hamid Grindouze, at the wheel of a French car. He introduces himself as the representative of Boussouf's ministry, but finishes by telling us that he belongs to the Department of Vigilance and Counterintelligence. Dekar is on his guard and says: "He's here to check on us."

Mistrustful, we keep our distance even when he invites us to share the comfortable apartment that he rents. He tries to enter our station but I close the door in his face. I suspect him of wanting to break up the friendship between Boualem and me when he invites me to go out with him without my friend. My reticence brings him around to better sentiments.

We talk about our families. He even lets me in on certain aspects of his mission in Tripoli.

He keeps watch on French Embassy personnel and the French oil company reps. I begin to see that he is making contacts: he invites me to lunch at a restaurant outside the city, run by a Swiss and frequented by Americans from the Wheelus base. He's flirting with the waitress, daughter of the owner, who provides him with information on the clientele. He has also been seeing a young Italian whose aunt is the girlfriend of the head of the Libyan police force. He introduces me to two other Italians: the pharmacist in Misurata and her friend Bianca, a student from Italy on vacation.

Between Bianca and me it's love at first sight during a visit to the Leptis Magna ruins in Homs. We go out together as often as possible, fall more and more in love. We are very much attracted to each other, but Bianca is like young Algerian girls: I soon discover that she wants to preserve her virginity. She knows that Algerians are fighting for their independence. Without revealing what my work consists of, I don't hide the fact that I am a member of the liberation movement and working for it. That helps me explain that I can't make any commitment until the struggle is over. She leaves in tears. I keep in touch and with an Assimil book, start learning Italian.

Azzouz introduces me to some Libyan bourgeois. During the Libyan resistance, the Italians decimated the elite. Naturally a new class arose, composed of a new type of citizen who remains attached to their country roots. We're invited by one of them to a picnic in his family's date grove. I taste *legmi*, a fermented drink extracted from the palm tree. I seem to be the only one who doesn't appreciate it. Our host then proposes a mixture that tastes like crushed bedbugs, a kind of whiskey that burns the throat and troubles the mind.

One day we receive a visit from Dghine Benali, called Lotfi. I had lunch with him and Boumediene in Oujda following my return from the interior. He was then commander and has now been promoted to colonel, head of Wilaya 5. I see that he takes as good care of his civilian clothes as he did his new uniform. He is wearing a dark summer suit, shirt, and silk tie. He has not changed. He spends a lot of time with the mission head and Libyan personalities and makes a good impression with his knowledge of Arabic and French. When he has free time, Azzouz takes him shopping. Benali wants to buy some things for his wife. He's recently married, though keeps it a secret. I have to admit that after several conversations, I find him less severe and sure of himself. He asks about the country, talks of his admiration for Mustafa Kemal Atatürk and the leaders of En Nahdha, including Djamel Eddine Al Afghani. When I talk about Leptis Magna, he insists on going there, the only leader of the Revolution who has expressed interest in visiting Roman ruins.

Since the creation of the GPRA, the chief of mission has the rank of ambassador. He's an old-time militant of the PPA and MTLD, Arabic-speaking, former owner of a restaurant in the Lower Casbah. He spends most of his time in discussion with the city's personalities seated under the arcades of Omar Mokhtar Street or at the Al Mehari Hotel. He accuses Azzouz of damaging Algerian-Libyan relations and informs Boussouf of Azzeddine's friendship with the niece of the Tripoli police chief. Azzouz is transferred to Beyrouth and I am called back to Tunis without being told why.

"I've named you head of the Eastern Region Administrative Service," Commander Telidji announces.

Mistrustful, I ask what that imposing title stands for.

"You'll supervise the future technical instruction center of the signal corps, a welcome center for operators undergoing medical treatment or convalescing, and you will receive the money to pay their living expenses and bonuses from the ministry accountant. You will be housed in Douar Chott with the head of the network command and the chief operator. A chauffeur-driven car will be at your disposal. In addition, you're promoted to warrant officer."

He looks me over and waits for my reaction. I laugh and shrug my shoulders.

The car, an old 403 Peugeot, travels along a road between, on one side, a smelly lake, and on the other, the train tracks of the Tunis–La Goulette–LaMarsa line, known as El Trino. My driver is from Ain Beida and speaks with a Tunisian accent. After the village of Douar Chott, he turns down a dirt road and stops in front of a two-story building in the middle of an unmowed field. "Si Rachid and Si Mansour live there," he says, pointing to a house next to the larger building.

I met Mohamed Sefardjli, alias Mansour, in Tetouan, where he was in charge of the signal corps station. He heads the National Transmissions Center (CTN) located in the larger building, but I don't know Mohamed Benamar Hakiki, called Rachid. He supervises the coding center. They were both trainees in the first class. They've added a cot in the room they share but don't look particularly happy to house me. They display no hostility, but they stop talking when I appear. The atmosphere gradually improves and we end up becoming friends and cohorts. On the other hand, from the first day on, I'm welcomed by Sibawahli Saker, alias Yacine, and Abdelhamid Hellal, alias Amine, buddies from our training class and from the Oujda command post.

My friendship with Hellal dates from Nador. Our friendship and confidence in each other developed when I was stationed at the command post in Oujda. It was Hellal who secretly told me of Dekar's problems. They had been friends and colleagues at the Moulay Abdallah School in Casablanca. In Douar Chott, where he is head of the Regulation Office, he asks me whether I would like to write to my family and confides in me that he knows a grocery store run by a man from Djerba who agrees to pass along mail. I refused to do so when Benyekhlef made a similar proposal in the maquis. To mail a letter to my family from Tunis could be harmful for them, but I think of Bianca. She'd be so surprised. Or maybe she's met someone else...I would be desolate but at least I'd know where our relation stands. Bianca replies quickly, says how happy she was to hear from me. She writes at least once a week. Her letters are so gay, sensitive, and sincere that I feel like I've received balm on a wound.

The news from the interior is awful. The office of psychological action, a specialized agency of the French army, has invented some diabolical methods to force our militants to reveal the names of other militants, to spread suspicion among the leaders of the Liberation Army and bring about their destruction. Ferhat Abbas has circulated a message to the heads of the different Wilayas to cease executions. There have already been some 780 executions of men for so-called treason. Another calamity: the Challe Plan and the massive mobilization of all human and technical means by the enemy are like a steamroller. Going from west to east, the French army is massacring the population, bombing and burning houses and harvests. Some 2.5 million civilians have been placed in internment camps. Eight thousand hamlets have been burned to the ground. Dispersed, the units of the Liberation Army are in areas that are insecure, deprived of the supplies and food normally supplied by the people.

After four groups trained in Morocco, Boussouf, minister of general liaisons and communications, has created the Center for Technical Instruction of the signal corps at Fondouk Choucha, a suburb of Tunis. It is now beginning operation in a former caravansary. There are about fifty trainees well outfitted with new uniforms, Pataugas, and soldier's caps. They talk normally and are not forced to lower their voices and watch their backs, as we were in Nador. In the dormitory are bunk beds, the classroom is spacious. There's an infirmary, a sports field, and a small cell for punishments. The trainers have offices and rooms for workshops.

The main difference between this fifth class and those trained in Morocco is the diversity of the trainees' origins and the excellent quality of the trainers. Those at Fondouk Choucha are all from Algeria, the eastern Wilayas, and the Algiers region. Many of them have come through the maquis and have been soldiers. From the countryside or from the city, they are from every sector of society. The parents of the trainees are living in refugee camps.

Some of the instructors have been in the maquis. They are competent, teachers without resentment of their more educated students. Laghaouti, a radio technician in aviation, was working at Radio Algiers when he decided to join the Liberation Army. Abdelhamid Benalmadjat, a teacher from Khroub, transported arms between the Algerian-Tunisian border and the Wilayas. The sound instructor, Mohamed Said Hakem, alias Moh, is, like Commander Telidji, a former noncommissioned officer of the French army. However, Hakem deserted between Port Said and Ismailia during the Suez invasion in November 1956.

I can't believe my eyes when after lunch I am approached by a student trainee: "Do you recognize me?"

"Of course. Hamid Bencherchali! You, here!"

A student at Duveyrier high school, Hamid is from the Blida bourgeoisie. His family owns a cigarette factory, Noralux. He is three years younger than me.

"Do you remember my cousin Moustafa?"

"The eldest of the family."

"He was killed in battle."

I remember he was just finishing his studies when I was beginning. He ran with a group of "in" students who associated with Europeans. They spent their time flirting with girls, on weekends they went to dances at the Orient Hotel. It was the era of an American dance music called swing.

"His three brothers are in Tunis, but since I've been at this center, I've lost contact with them."

At the high school, Hamid and his cousins looked down upon the boarding students with their black coveralls and snubbed those of us from the South. They called us "*Guebli*," a condescending term.

Another man interrupts us: "Do you recognize me?"

"Sure, you're Abdelkrim, Mohamed Nabi's cousin. I would never have thought I'd see you in uniform! How did you manage to get from Berrouaghia to this center?"

"After my uncle Miliani was executed and my cousin Mohamed arrested, my father and I had to get out of town. My father is working in a refugee camp and I'm here in the training class."

Abdelkrim is seventeen. Like Hamid and the other trainees, he arrived at the center at night, in a covered truck, not knowing where he was heading. I know the method, it was tried out in Oujda and since has constantly been used. It begins with "Discipline is the principal strength of an army. Execute an order, complain later." From this follows "Obey the rules of clandestinity, the code of secrecy and mystery."

The rigorous discipline imposed during the course and the communal life is difficult to endure. The trainees coming out of the maquis bear claustration with difficulty. Some complain, others stop talking, withdraw. Many of them resort to Dr. Frantz Fanon's psychiatric service. Their comrades sometimes laugh and call them "Fanonized." Dr. Fanon has set up a "day" hospital where the patients arrive in the morning and leave in the afternoon. There are more and more visits to the hospital. Patients in convalescence or treatment are received in an elegant mansion in Megrine, a residential neighborhood.

I realize how much being constantly closed in is detrimental when a soldier stops me in the courtyard and whispers, in tears, that milk is coming out of his breasts. He is beside himself. I give him a bit of money and an authorization to leave the center. I ask the nurse to make an appointment with a psychiatrist and, in addition, give him the address of the local bordello.

Thank heavens, I can, with certain comrades, secretly of course, go out for a beer at a little grocery store run by someone from Malta, in a quiet street in Douar Chott.

One afternoon in the Avenue de Paris I bump into Pierre Chaulet. I haven't seen him since I stayed with his parents and visited him in Algiers. He tells me about his arrest and his deportation from Algeria in 1957. His sister Anne-Marie spent a little over a month in prison and was tortured. She is in Paris for the moment and visits Salah Louanchi regularly at the prison in Fresnes.

Pierre is a pneumo-phthisiologist at the Ernest Conseil Hospital and member of the editorial committee of the main publication of the Revolution, *El Moudjahid*. He has set up and runs a documentation center for the Ministry of Information and invites me to come visit. He introduces me to the woman in charge, Monique Laks, and two of her coworkers, Nadia Oussedik and Zine Mokdad. I look over the bookshelves covered with books on Algeria and North Africa. There are also newspapers from France and Algeria. The tranquility, the atmosphere of the place, the desire to read and find out what is going on in the world incite me to come back. I read the press, the files, and the specialized documents put out by the center and chosen for me by Monique Laks. This charming and discreet young woman is Parisian, the daughter of a taxi driver. Her companion, Michel Mazière, is a deserter from the French army who refused to fight in Algeria. He is from a middle-class family from northern France and is studying economics at Tunis University. Monique is studying sociology. They are living in a very modest apartment, and even though they find it difficult to make ends meet, seem happy. They are passionate about politics, as I was before joining the Liberation Army. Michel is especially critical of the French Communist Party, holds against the party their vote of special powers for Guy Mollet's government, its agreement for communists to be enrolled in the army in charge of repression in Algeria, and its condemnation of deserters. His activist friends refused to aid him when he was hiding out in Paris.

I discover Marx, the history of the workers' movement, Lenin and the Russian Revolution. I read John Reed's *Ten Days That Shook the World*, Trotsky's *My Life*, and measure the extent of my ignorance. Monique insists that I attend the night course in economics that she is taking for her sociology degree. Enthralled with the course, the atmosphere, the relationship between the students and the professor, I am encouraged by Monique and the professor to sign up on a regular basis.

I don't tell them that I have come in secret and that my superior would never give me authorization to enroll. Monique doesn't realize that I have also been frequenting the documentation center secretly. I decide to try to obtain Boussouf's authorization. His cabinet director is absent and the replacement happens to be someone who was at my high school in Blida. I ask him to make the request and insist that I will be attending the class only in the evening. Two days later, he communicates the answer: "The minister refuses because that would create a precedent."

Bianca, on the other hand, wants to come see me. Tunis is rife with Algerian agents in civilian clothes. The minister of the interior has his agents and Boussouf has his Mobile Brigades. Some keep watch on the signal corps men in particular. To befriend a foreigner or to be seen in a foreigner's company makes one suspect, even possibly suspect of treason. When I tell Pierre and Christine how embarrassed I am about a visit from my Italian girlfriend, they offer to house her. When Bianca arrives, I tell her that I can't be with her much of the time. Our meetings are limited to a few hours a day in the Chaulets' apartment in Franceville. Happy, though resolved to wait for us to marry, she asks questions about our future life as a married couple.

"Would you like to have children?"

The question makes me laugh, it's so far from my preoccupations. "Of course, lots."

"How many?"

I reply without thinking, "Twelve, enough for a soccer team, with one replacement."

She gets red in the face, stares at me, then kisses me.

"That's a lot!"

"Well, then, half as many, just enough for a basketball team."

She agrees and seems happy.

Pierre and Claudine invite us to a restaurant in La Goulette. It's the only time I go out in public with Bianca. She only stays for a week and she leaves Tunis convinced of our future together. Pierre and Claudine were extremely nice. I would have wanted to spend evenings with them, but sleeping out ran the risk of my comrades in Douar Chott informing our superiors first thing in the morning.

There exists such a climate of fear and disdain in the signal corps that anything can happen: from the telling of tales to the invention of them. In my opinion, this behavior originated with a first shock that I have already mentioned: during the first operator training class, in August 1956, the trainees were obliged to take part in the strangulation of two young patriots accused of wanting to desert. That event not only traumatized those present, it also contaminated relationships among members of this army corps for the duration.

In January 1960, a new GPRA is constituted. Ferhat Abbas retains the presidency, Boussouf becomes minister of armaments and general liaisons. The ministry (MALG) is located in a residential section of the city a stone's throw from the magnificent Belvedere Park. It's a large residence of three stories at the corner of two rarely frequented streets. Surrounded by a garden and a man-high wall topped by a decorative iron railing, it has three entryways. The main entrance is on Parmentier Street. A stone-covered alleyway leads to the two swinging panels of a glass door into Boussouf's and his cabinet director Khalifa Larousi's offices. A soldier, wearing a *kachabia* to hide his gun, guards this doorway. In a street perpendicular to this one, another man discreetly keeps watch over a large barrier that forces cars to stop, as well as access to the third door. The kitchen and offices surround a large covered patio. Torsaded columns support the gallery that runs along each floor. I often visit the accounting office on the ground floor to pick up the money for the functioning of the centers. It's headed by Said Bayou, former goalkeeper of the Blida Muslim Sports Union.

Each time I visit, I meet Lamine Allouane, my companion from Nador and Oujda. I am also surprised to find my childhood friend Abdelkader Boukhari. He's in the general services and is free to move around. Thanks to him, I meet Louenes and Lakhdar Lamari, both from Berrouaghia. They are living in a very dirty room in Bab Souika, awaiting a scholarship for study. However, the Wilaya 4 colonel having lost all authority in Tunis, they don't know what will happen to them. Being neither Kabyle nor Chaoui and not from the North Constantine area, they feel abandoned. Victims of regionalism in the offices on rue Saddia in Tunis, they are kept twiddling their thumbs in their nasty room.

Lakhdar says that after joining the maquis, he took part in a gathering of high school and college students near Chrea.

They camped in that region for about a month. Abane Ramdane, Mohamed Amara Rachid, and some other leaders lectured every day before sending them to the Wilayas of Algiers, Kabylia, and the South as political commissars. As for Louenes—he's small and has a large head and very large, mobile eyes—he tells me his fragmented story. Since he was only fifteen years old and no one wanted the responsibility of taking him into the maquis, he decided to act on his own. He left the village (he probably hadn't yet begun to shave) in the direction of Mont Gorno, the mountain to the east of Berrouaghia. He questioned shepherds and peasants and finished by being taken under the wing of a *moussebel*, auxiliary of the Liberation Army, who put him in touch with some freedom fighters. When he was introduced to Colonel Ouamrane, he refused to return home. After a short period of adaptation, he began showing his courage by cutting the throats of traitors. In the same spirit, he volunteered for a commando that took part in particularly dangerous missions.

Traversing half of Algeria, crossing the electrified barrier, and arriving in Tunis only to vegetate in a lousy studio and be abandoned by their leaders, they are close to a state of depression. Thank goodness, they are finally sent to Cairo, where Louenes is put in high school and Lakhdar obtains a scholarship to study in Bulgaria.

The fifth training class of radio operators finishes and a sixth starts up in Nador. The center in Fondouk Carolina is getting ready to welcome the seventh class. I decide that the signal corps can get along without me. They now have graduated hundreds of trainees of different categories. I think about how I can achieve my objective and be done with this routine work. So, one day, when I visit the accounting office, I hang around the patio of the ministry, in discussion with Allouane and a member of the studies office, Ahmed Bakhti, alias H'mida, when Telidji appears.

"What are you doing here?" he says with a sour tone.

"I was just seeing the accountant when I ran into these brothers."

"You shouldn't be hanging around here. Get a move on and get back to work."

I control my desire to slug him. "Commander, I don't permit you to speak to me that way. Furthermore, I don't want to remain in the signal corps. Three years, that's enough. You have many operators now and the work I'm doing is of no interest."

He pales and remains speechless for a moment. "Okay, if that's the case, I'll send you into the interior. I hope that this time, you won't come back."

To send me into the interior means crossing the Morice or the Challe barriers, the supreme threat. Telidji isn't the only superior ready to use this threat to get rid of men they don't want around, who refuse to bend to their wishes. He imitates his superiors, who used the same threat when he was suspected of having taken advantage of a furlough in Melilla to contact the enemy.

I spurt out: "Go ahead! I'll leave tomorrow, but with a gun, without a radio post. Do you remember, it's thanks to the southern region that you won your promotion. I won't let you do me in a second time."

He shakes his head and says with a threatening air: "I'm going to a cabinet meeting. You'll hear from me as soon as the meeting is over." Then he takes off for the minister's office.

For weeks now, rumors have been circulating about a reorganization of the ministry. It will be discussed at a meeting that brings together the various directors, including Telidji. It lasts three days and when it's over, I'm on the patio with the same friends. Telidji comes toward me with a bright look on his face.

"Amara, thanks to me, you are going to work in the minister's cabinet." He waits for me and my friends to show some recognition.

Convinced that he has given in, I say, quite detached, "That's good news."

He walks away, grumbling.

Assigned to an office under the minister and his cabinet director, I find myself with Bakhti and Abdelaziz Maoui, whom I met in the house in Oujda when we were waiting to be taken into the Liberation Army. We share an office and I begin a new life.

My childhood friend, Abdelkader Boukhari, offers to put me up in an apartment situated on Bourguiba Avenue, in the center of the city, on the fifth floor with an elevator. He shares rooms with Ahmed Bakhti, who sleeps in the dining room. I set up a cot on the other side of the table. Boukhari has a big bed and a large armoire.

Work in the ministry means arriving at eight a.m. and leaving at eight in the evening. Entering and leaving must be discreet; that is, groups must be small, not more than three people at a time. Meals are at strict times, morning, noon, and evening. The cook's assistants set up tables with benches in the courtyard. About forty people eat there. Drivers and secretaries mix with cabinet members and workers from the different departments. The atmosphere is pleasant, even if affinities and antipathies exist. I don't feel out of place in this environment.

The main work of this new office is the writing of a monthly report for the members of government. It's a synthesis elaborated from the reports of the different directors of the ministry and sent to the members of government. The reports are presented to us after they have been censored by the minister and his cabinet chief. Obviously, the Revolution has many paradoxes: a former French prefect authorizes himself to decide what Ferhat Abbas, Belkacim Krim, Ben Tobbal, and other leaders can or cannot know.

The plan for the different sections of the synthesis varies little. The data supplied by "honorable correspondents" and suggestions from foreigners favorable to our cause often make the work interesting. People in Parisian circles, French civil servants, are the sources of documents. A leader of the Fourth International, Michel Raptis, called Pablo, proposes creating an armaments factory in Morocco. I discover with pleasure, from a report sent by our correspondent in Constantine, that Dr. Jean Le Bail is helping him. He's a Frenchman whom I recruited. I am happy to see that Jean Le Bail continues to believe in our common future in an independent Algeria. I imagine that Vandevelde also maintains his commitment to a free, just, and fraternal Algeria.

The writing of the monthly synthesis requires three or four days' work. The rest of the time, Maoui, Bakhti, and I read the Tunisian and French press delivered every morning and evening by Alam Farouk, the former propagandist whom I got to know between Laghouat and Aflou. He assists Tahar Debagha, a former student at Blida High School, in a library that has been set up on the second floor. Contrary to Farouk, who maintains his openness and good humor, Tahar is rigid and taciturn. To make fun of him, we call him Malreux, after André Malraux.

Nicknames are rampant and remind me of high school. Boussouf is called "The Bigleux," Khalifa Laroussi is "H'na-fez," an untranslatable term that evokes something unpleasant. Abdallah Khlef, alias Kasdi Merbah, is "the Buddha"; Abdelkrim Hassani, alias Ghaouti, is "Baby Cadum"; Saddat Senoussi, alias Moussa, is "Tchombe." At the head of the DVCR is "Sherlock," whose open humor I appreciate. At the head of the counterintelligence brigade are "Bab's" and "Briquet," who patrol in a car and are still kids with a juvenile aspect and Moroccan accents.

Since I've been deprived for so long, I devour all the newspapers that the documentation section delivers. The "week of the barricades," during which Pierre Lagaillarde, former student at Duveyrier, distinguishes himself, fascinates me. Lagaillarde is the personification of the racism I encountered in Blida for eight years. The French of Algeria shoot at the half million French soldiers who have come from France to protect them. They defy the head of state because he has talked openly about "self-determination."

Three weeks after Lagaillarde has given himself up and

the barricades erected within the university have been taken down, the press announces the arrest of Frenchmen who have housed, transported, or assisted activists of the National Liberation Front in France. They are worker priests, like those I was received by in Marseille, progressive Christians, intellectuals who have broken with the Communist Party, and others. Francis Jeanson, who worked with Jean Paul Sartre at *Les Temps modernes*, was the originator of this network. This is bad news, but it is revealing of the courage and determination of people ready to disturb the conscience of French men and women. My hope is for them to descend into the streets. After six years of atrocities inflicted in their name, the passivity, the silence of the French is unbearable.

I read the interview given to *France Observateur* by Boussouf. He thinks that the government of free Algeria will introduce an agrarian reform. The journalist asks how profound the reform will be, and Boussouf provides the example of a member of his family who owns thousands of acres of land and concludes "It's too much." I feel his reply insufficient and say to Bakhti: "Did you see that Boussouf finds that the feudals have too much land? He's for limiting their estates, but not for redistributing the land to those who work it."

Disdainful, Maoui responds, "You and your Marxist ideas, you should keep your mouth shut."

Suddenly I feel coming from the bottom of my soul and my childhood, the fighting instinct, the bottled-up violence, the hate accumulated because of injustice, humiliation, and frustration. I jump up and stand in front of him with my fists ready.

"If you're a man, repeat what you just said."

Bakhti jumps in between us and pushes Maoui, uncomprehending, his face drained of color, toward the door. I let out a bunch of insults against the feudals from Morocco, the reactionaries who are hiding out, the second-class Frenchmen (Algerians) from Morocco, those who are in wait for the moment to strike. Bakhti laughs and waits for me to calm down. Then he goes out and finds Maoui in the accounting office, brings him back, and reconciles us.

I continue to correspond with Bianca, although I write less than she does. In her letters, she tells me about her daily routine, her relationships with her sister Aurora, her parents, her friends. She talks of what she feels, her dreams of our life together. I don't want Boussouf to discover our correspondence through one of his numerous agents who swarm around the city and the administrations. I can't bear hiding from my future wife my real identity. I finally request an appointment for personal reasons. He receives me. I tell him outright, calling him by his wartime alias: "Si Mabrouk, I have come to speak to the militant. I don't wish to keep to myself, or for you to be told in some other way, what I have to tell you. In Tripoli, I met a young Italian who was on vacation…I have told this young woman that I can't marry her before independence. All I'm asking you for is the authorization to continue to write to her."

"There's nothing wrong with this. But before giving you my reply, I would like to see her letters and, if you have one, a picture of her," he concludes after listening to me without interruption.

I am about to get up and go when the courtyard door opens and Colonel Boumediene enters. Boussouf looks insistently at his watch and says roughly, "It's only now that you arrive?"

The colonel's face turns red as a beet. He doesn't say hello to me. I walk out.

Boussouf, the militant to whom I addressed my request, entrusts Khalifa Laroussi with communicating his negative reply. With a tired voice, he begins with a weak speech, paternalistic and pseudo-revolutionary, in which he invokes a drama, Corneille's *Horace*, and then asks me "to sacrifice the love of a woman for the Revolution." Sick, with my heart in my stomach, I get up to leave.

"You can count on me," I say, shaking the weak hand that he tenders.

The little consideration that I have for the man is gone for all time.

Naturally I have been careful not to give Boussouf the address of the grocery store where both Hellal and I receive our mail. I continue to write to Bianca. The idea of visiting her secretly in Naples occurs to me when the minister grants a bonus for clothes, followed almost immediately with a two-week furlough. My decision is taken. I obtain a visa at the Italian consulate and buy a round trip ticket on the *Tyrrhennia*, which sails between Tunis, Palermo, and Naples. I don't want to be absent for more than a week. The day before I am to leave, I run into Hamid Bouchakji, alias Younes, who is in a hurry to get to lunch before the end of the service.

"So we're going to Italy," he says, smiling but not stopping.

"How do you know?" I say weakly.

"Never mind. But don't worry, bon voyage," he laughs, while running to lunch.

Bouchakji is the assistant to the director of vigilance and counterintelligence. He probably read my correspondence with Bianca. We have known each other since Casablanca, where we were both members of the FLN economics commission.

Bianca is waiting for me at the dock. Happy, she cries with joy, mixes up French and Italian. Enchanted, moved, I am on a cloud, feel ready to defy the universe to keep my Bianca. She has reserved a room for me in a pension close to the one she lives in. She can come to my room but I can't go to hers. She can't wait to show me her city; we visit her favorite places.

Nationalistic, I compare the superb bay of Naples with that of Algiers.

"Did you know that the capital of my country is called Algiers le Blanc—la Bianca?"

She laughs, thinks I am joking. She is used to my calling her "My Bianca, my dove." I practice my Assimil Italian, I hum some songs. She never stops complimenting me. Stimulated by her encouragement, I yell out one day, in a crowd, my fist raised, *"Italia farà da sè!"* (Italy will do it alone!), Garibaldi's words, the father of Italian unity.

She listens to my political speeches, raises her head, stares at me. When I stop bothering her, she asks: "Do you love me? Tell me that you love me."

"I love you with my very soul, I will love you all my life. I promise you that we will get married as soon as Algeria is independent. We will have as many children as you wish."

She can't imagine that with this trip I run the risk of death for desertion or espionage for a foreign power. I can't give her a greater proof of my love. Telling her about it would require so many explanations and would worry her even more.

The night before I leave, we have dinner in a charming little restaurant overlooking the bay. I order cannelloni and a special Chianti. I am in seventh heaven.

"Will you accept that our children be baptized?"

"No, we should wait until they have attained their majority. They will decide what they want to do then."

Obviously, I had thought about this question. I don't know how much longer the war will last nor what I will do in independent Algeria, but I know it will not be difficult for me to have Bianca accepted by my family. One thing that I can't envisage, however, is taking my children to church to be baptized.

There follows a conversation with Bianca where our two visions of the world confront each other. Whereas she is afraid of being excommunicated for not respecting the tenets of her religion, I want to give our children religious instruction that will allow them to choose a religion—or even abstain from having one. After all, the idea of one God has not always existed. Monotheism is a recent discovery in the history of humanity. Mankind has had a multitude of gods. They have venerated pharaohs, stones, trees, spirits, and in some places continue to do so. I feel our children should know there are agnostics, atheists, who deserve our respect. Intolerance is dangerous, and I insist on this theme with Bianca.

"I respect your religion. I learned when I was very young to respect Jesus. I will willingly accompany you to church, but don't ask me to baptize our children because the pope demands it."

"It's not just the pope but my religion that demands it. You can do that for me."

"I'll do everything for you, including risking my life. You are the love of my life. I love you as I've never loved anyone. I don't know how to say it nor how to prove it. I want to keep you and I'll fight to do so. Think about us, our happiness and that of our children. Religion must not destroy our love."

She breaks out weeping, wipes the tears from her cheeks, sniffs softly. The low lights, the space between tables, the ambient noise, makes us invisible to others. My heart bleeds. I grab Bianca's hand, hold it tight. I have no more words, my head is empty. I watch the flame of the candle as it dies.

Outside, Bianca's chagrin gives way to a flood of tears. She cries her heart out, chokes, taps her foot on the sidewalk, appeals to the Virgin in Italian. I take her in my arms.

"Stop crying. It hurts me so."

Brokenhearted, I no longer have the strength to argue, to tell her that in my opinion, religion separates people. Christians have fought their religious wars, Muslims have too, between Shiites and Sunnis. Europe has sent Jews to concentration camps and furnaces to die.

After a sleepless night and some last supplications, I leave Bianca to her dogma and take the boat, sad, defeated. Naples, Palermo, Tunis, the crossing is gloomy. The pleasure, the enthusiasm of the first crossing give way to depression. During the stop in Palermo, the sight of porters, of small-time crooks, of beggars relieves me of my lethargy and I remember Algiers's harbor. I wander around the streets until the middle of the afternoon. When I return to the boat, I leave the city with the impression that I am abandoning tremendous deception and disillusion in Italy.

Very unhappy, Bianca tries to safeguard our love and the dogma of her faith. I tell her that I have been raised in the Muslim religion, that I have memorized a quarter of the Koran. I feel that, like other religions, Islam includes a large part of the irrational. Above all, I can't bear dogma. I write her that I wish religions would introduce more rationality and freedom of thought into their faith. Bianca continues to ask me to understand her. The painful misunderstanding cannot continue indefinitely: I decide to break it off.

At the ministry, General de Gaulle's call for "the peace of the brave" finds little echo. The provisional government meets and deliberates for two days. With the two delegates sent to Melun is Mohamed Benamar Hakiki, an operator from the first training session with whom I shared a room in Douar Chott. After a secret meeting at the Elysée Palace with the leader of Wilaya 4, the head of the French government wants to know if we are ready to give up. The meeting was a failure, but my friend won a nickname: Rachid Melun.

The signal corps national center is transferred from Douar Chott to the top floor of the ministry. The Megrine welcome center is closed and the training center in Fondouk Choucha is set up in a large farm near La Marsa, where the ninth session has begun. With the new recruits, the signal corps has now trained 959 technicians (operators, coders, repairmen).

Mobilized by the French Federation of the FLN, students arrive in great numbers at the Didouche base, a military base abandoned by the Allies not far from Tripoli. The director Khalifa Laroussi is sent there and put in charge of training. Seventy young men from the information division and some of the new recruits prepare files on economy, oil, military questions, and the Morice and Challe electrified border barriers.

The office the interim cabinet directors occupy has just been raised with the addition of several steps. Boussouf doesn't want more than one minister or colonel at a time to use this office and Khalifa Laroussi uses his authority to sit in there and read the documents that are deposited. In fact, Boussouf is rarely present in the ministry and when he is, he doesn't sit in this office. He prefers an armchair near the glass entryway or a seat at the far end of a long table that the government uses from time to time. Boussouf doesn't write except for little notes. He dictates his instructions, then checks them. Despite his disastrous eyesight, with his nose in the page, he reads all the reports, orders summaries of voluminous documents. His elephant memory serves to retain a smattering of political culture and surprises his more educated visitors. It also serves to intimidate his colleagues and the top-level civil servants of the provisional government, accompanied by insinuations as to their private lives. He knows who drinks, who is sleeping with whom. He himself doesn't smoke, doesn't drink, but it seems he has married secretly. To be sure that the secret is well guarded, he chose as the officiant someone who is both a civil service officer and religious officer: President Ferhat Abbas. Thanks to the information concerning Algerian officials that the multitude of agents gather, he has a file on everyone. Mine contains Bianca's letters. His long experience of clandestine life, since the 1940s when he was in the Special Organization, has heightened his mistrust. Boussouf compensates for his poor eyesight by vigilance and Machiavellian methods. He doesn't hesitate to eliminate those who threaten his power, and he knows how to force people who can be useful to him into obedience. On the other hand, he is capable of extreme courtesy and, since becoming minister, that is, a public personality, he has learned to match his shirt and tie with his suit. So we see him less and less in the ministry. He navigates between the Didouche base, in Tripoli, and the arms factory that the European Trotskyists have set up in Morocco. This is a project imagined by Michel Raptis, alias Pablo. After its creation, the first weapons tested, including mortars, were very satisfactory. He travels in friendly countries to buy arms and equipment and to contact leaders in advance of the September session of the United Nations.

From July 26 to August 1, 1960, the fourth congress of UGEMA takes place in Bir el Bey, a suburb of Tunis. I attend the closing session, at the Trade Unions Hall in Tunis. In front of a full house, Ferhat Abbas denounces the claim that Algerians are not apt for science, a prejudice used as a pretext to close the doors of leading universities and institutes to them. His arm raised, addressing the delegates, he says: "And you have destroyed this myth. Every day we see the tangible proof of this incontestable truth: there is no superior race, no inferior race. For the last six years, the Algerian Revolution has trained more technicians than the colonial regime has in 130 years of occupation."

In the crowd leaving the hall, I am accosted by a former student from Aumale high school, Tahar Boutmedjet. He looks exactly like Mehdi Ben Barka, leader of the Moroccan left. He tells me that he is working at the Ministry of Social and Cultural Affairs. I tell him: "I want to begin studying again, but I don't have my records and diplomas with me. I have a Libyan passport in the name of Amara Seddik and would like to register at the University of Tunis in sociology."

"That's no problem. Come to see me at the ministry."

"But unfortunately, I have another problem. In Algeria, I was enrolled in law. The faculty of letters requires a first year of general studies. I don't want to waste a year in a course that has little to do with what I want to study."

"Don't worry, we can fix that."

Within the week, Boutmedjet gives me an attestation with my borrowed name and a false general studies certificate. The enrollment office of the university accepts my papers without the slightest objection and enrolls me for economics and sociology. I realize that I will never be able to take advantage of the degrees that I receive in such conditions. My only desire, my deepest desire, is to learn, to gain knowledge. Shortly thereafter, Benmiloud tells me secretly that Boussouf has decided to send signal corps personnel to the Soviet Union, and asks whether I am interested.

"I want to study industrial pharmaceutics," I reply. "It's a specialty that will be needed."

"No, it's for engineering and telecommunications."

"Then I'm not interested. I refuse."

Members of the first five classes are sent for training in the USSR and in China.

I meet Pierre Chaulet at the documentation center.

"Would you like to come to dinner this evening? Annette Roger, whom you have certainly heard of, is coming."

"Of course, she was arrested about a year ago. I remember a journalist called her a 'red doctor' and another treated her as an underling of the FLN Marseille. The French press gave her a thorough drubbing."

"She's a highly competent scientist, a former resistant and dissident from the Communist Party. At the time of her trial, she was pregnant. When she was allowed to leave the prison to have her baby, she escaped and left France under cover."

Annette Roger is a beautiful woman, with green eyes, her red hair pulled up into a chignon. Wearing a Chanel suit, she resembles the lovely women photographed for *Jours de France* and fashion magazines. Gay, talkative, she looks straight at me, tells us about looking for a place to live, about her children whom she misses. She lives in a small house that belongs to the hospital, is looking for something more comfortable. She talks about Paton and Michel Martini, who hold open house at their place at the hospital, and makes fun of the various people who spend time there drinking and making and remaking the Revolution in the dining room. It's "Martini House," laughs Pierre.

Annette Roger speaks of her work team in Marseille. A specialist in epileptology and the electroencephalogram (EEG), she has opened an office in the Neurology Department for Tunisians. Once a month she goes to the Algerian-Tunisian border to provide consultations at the refugee camp. She talks a lot, but I listen to her with interest and sympathy. I admire her courage and the devotion of this woman who has sacrificed family and professional life for her ideas, for the independence of Algeria. She tells us of an incident at a Communist Party cell meeting: when she attempted to obtain their support for the Algerian cause, a trade unionist insisted that "the Algerians are rabbit stealers." Her amusing stories of her time in a laboratory of the USSR Academy of Science reveal her disillusions. Just before leaving she asks me from where I come.

"From Berrouaghia, the heart of Algeria," I say with a smile.

She has me repeat the name of the village, attempts to pronounce it but doesn't succeed. She bursts out laughing, then proposes to give me a ride home. Flattered, I follow her, reply to her questions. In front of the building, Avenue Bourguiba, we continue talking, politics and so on. I take a gamble and invite her for lunch the next day. She accepts.

I take her to Chez Eugene, a little Italian restaurant in the Sicilian neighborhood where two men with eyeglasses play the violin during meal hours. It's Bachti's, Boukhari's, and my secret place. Not being sure, I nevertheless ask my roommates not to step inside the apartment during the afternoon.

Annette doesn't refuse to have coffee at my place. We go directly to bed. She lets herself go, vibrates with pleasure, calls me her "Greek pasture." Happy to take possession of a perfect body, an uncommon person, to let go voraciously, I feel of Herculean strength, ready to start over, for eternity. Relaxing, I listen to her sweet words. She gets up and goes to the bathroom, leaving behind an enormous wad of hair on the pillow.

"What's that?" I ask.

"A postiche, fake hair."

I've heard of it but have never seen it.

The political situation is evolving. General de Gaulle hasn't succeeded in his maneuvering. The Constantine Plan that was supposed to constitute a third force with which to achieve integration has been a flop. The reception at the Elysée of the Wilaya 4 leaders, the false encounter in Melun last June, have proved that he was on the wrong road. The army and the front remain active both inside and outside the country. The French army, to whom he has given carte blanche and great means, has not been convincing: it has deployed 1.3 million soldiers these last five years, with equipment from NATO, has placed over two of the nine million Algerians in concentration camps, and has practiced torture on a scale unknown before.

Abroad, the image of French grandeur is tarnished, diminished. The Americans and their NATO allies are asking France to take up its responsibilities and to supply the military contingents deployed in Algeria. At the United Nations, a majority is asking for a debate on the Algerian question and is no longer considering it an internal French question.

After having evoked, four months ago, a peace of the brave and leaving weapons on the doorstep, de Gaulle is now talking about the future Algerian Republic. The solution to the Algerian problem has become existential, since part of the French army is for a French Algeria and is ready to eliminate him. An officer has said, as reported in a weekly magazine:

"We are convinced that France's destiny is playing out in Algeria...If nothing changes, France will succumb. We want to stop the decadence of the West, the advance of communism. De Gaulle is bringing France to ruin."

It's at the breaking point. Generals, whom de Gaulle calls the *quarteron*, have taken power in Algiers and threaten to debark in France. The army is divided. De Gaulle reacts by multiplying concessions during the secret encounters taking place in Switzerland between the French delegates and the Algerian government. Like a seething volcano, on December 10, 1960, demonstrators pour out of Clos Salembier, a popular neighborhood, and march toward Algiers, yelling, "Muslim Algeria!"

Until May 1961, the sociology course, centered on the works of Georges Gurvitch, is given by a professor who was sent to Tunis by Gurvitch because, each year, Gurvitch himself chairs the jury that awards Tunisian graduates the equivalent of a French degree. However, in the middle of May, it is announced that Raymond Aron will replace Gurvitch, who is ill. Annoyed, Gurvitch's disciple gives a series of classes devoted to Raymond Aron and his thought. I have never taken more notes. In June I pass the written exam and am admitted to the oral. Raymond Aron is seated at a table on which there are slips of paper folded in four. He politely asks me to choose one of them. I choose "Are there laws in History?"

"Go sit down. You have ten minutes to think about the question."

Are there any laws in History? I have never thought about it. I jot down a few ideas inspired by the notes taken in class. I look for some way to link them to the subject. As an introduction, I improvise some jargon about science, its basis (postulates), and theorems, without forgetting the role of experimentation. I make some allusion to various polemics and interrogations that refuse to designate as science the studies of sociology, ethnology, and other social sciences, as well as humanities.

After a few minutes I begin to wander; but, thank goodness, Aron interrupts me and says: "That's good. It's better than your dissertation. Another question, do you think sociology can be helpful to Tunisia, given the present state of things?"

"Of course. To accompany its development projects, Tunisia requires social studies."

"You are Tunisian, aren't you?"

"No, I'm Algerian."

Suddenly his face softens. "Ah, you're Algerian," he says, separating the words. "Algeria will also need sociology and men like you..."

I listen to his words concerning the negotiations taking place, the economic future of Algeria, but think about the reality of the moment: the Secret Army Organization (OAS) and their more and more murderous attacks and the unrelenting support of the Europeans for them, which compromises a common future. I don't dare attack his optimism. He thanks me; extends his hand to shake mine, and says with a large smile, "Good luck."

Admitted finally, I am proud of having defied the man who refused to permit me to study, even if the degree I receive will never be of any use to me.

On July 6, 1961, President Bourguiba demands that France evacuate the Bizerte base. Demonstrations, organized by the Neo-Destour, break out all across the country. The French government responds by sending seven hundred paratroopers from Algeria. Convoys of buses and trucks loaded with volunteers converge on Bizerte from the four corners of the land. Three days of battle ensue, exceedingly bloody: 700 Tunisian dead, 1200 wounded. Twenty-four French dead.

On July 28, the Algerians request the cancellation of the Lugrin conference because de Gaulle is vacillating. He is suggesting a partition in which the Europeans will be settled in Algiers and Oran and the surrounding fertile land. He wants to detach the Sahara from Algeria and name an Algerian collaborator. It would be an emirate that would join with the surrounding countries. As soon as the conference closes, the GPRA convokes a National Council meeting on August 9–27 in Tripoli.

A net separation is apparent between the fighters from the interior and those they accuse of being soft and wanting to cooperate with France. The leaders of the Liberation Army want to fight on until total independence is achieved. Abbas is replaced by Benyoucef Benkhedda.

The real reasons for this replacement have their source in the history of the Algerian national movement. Despite his maneuvering, de Gaulle has accepted Algerian independence. The problem on the Algerian side is to determine which political personalities will lead the remaining negotiations and take power in independent Algeria — in other words, bring things up to date. As of 1954, the leaders of the First of November felt they had to bring about a united front; differences of opinion had to be left aside, forgotten. As we near independence, here they are again. The road each individual has taken is decisive. Ferhat Abbas is not an example. For a long time, he was for assimilation, before accepting an independent Algeria in association with France. He only joined the FLN in 1956. Benkhedda, the new president, Saad Dahlab, Ben Tobbal, Boussouf, Belkacem Krim, are all old-time members of the PPA–MTLD and represent a guarantee for the fighters inside the country. Because he led a delegation to China, Benyoucef Benkhedda is called "Chinese" by the French media. They insist on his Marxist tendencies and his interest in the Chinese and Yugoslav models. In the first press release of his government, he excluded association with France. De Gaulle, in a press conference, has stated that if Algeria secedes, France will remain in the Sahara.

I meet Pierre Chaulet at the documentation center. He tells me that his mother has come to visit his little family and invites me to spend the weekend with them in their country house in Bordj Cedria. I haven't seen Suzanne Chaulet for five years. In July 1956, when I was being looked for just before the general strike, Pierre's parents had put me up. The mother has the same smile, is as sweet, and has the same sense of hospitality. She moves me deeply. She is accompanied by Suzette, Christiane, and Yves. The girls and the boy have grown up. The girls are pretty; one resembles the mother, the other the father. Like Anne-Marie, Suzette has inherited the grace and charm of their mother; the lovely lines of the faces of Christiane and Yves have been inherited from their father. Intimidated, they all watch me, reply politely to my questions.

Sunday, Pierre drives us in a big rental car to Hammamet; then to Nabeul to the potters' market. Attracted by the festive atmosphere, the abundance of products, the bright colors, his mother spends time in the shops, in front of the displays. She buys some gifts. She names those for whom she is buying, consults the children, then all of a sudden she turns to me: "And you, aren't you buying anything?"

"Who for?"

"Your mother, for example."

I laugh and shrug my shoulders. "I haven't given or received news of the family since my departure from the house five years ago. I'm not going now to send a piece of pottery by mail from Tunisia and take the risk of compromising them."

Madame Chaulet stops smiling and finds her authoritative voice: "Choose something. I'll pay for it and will see to it that it reaches your family in Berrouaghia."

My mother will tell me much later that the priest dropped

off the vase at the butcher shop and said it was from "your son." That's how they knew, at long last, that I was still alive.

In Tunis, the traumatic events of Bizerte don't stop the inhabitants from going to the beach. Annette Roger, who has found a house at Dermech, has rented a bungalow at the foot of the Sidi Bousaid cliff. Our ties have grown stronger. She shows her affection; I try to do the same. I go to the minis- try every morning, Annette does her time at the hospital or at the border. We meet at the end of the afternoon. From time to time she comes back with Parisians who are activists for Algerian independence. They are sent by her friend Marceline Loridan. Alain Landau, a neurosurgeon, and his wife Nicole arrive in Tunis on a UNESCO mission. Annette takes them to the border refugee camps, has them visit the orphaned children's houses; they have been traumatized by the war. And Alain is horrified by what he sees. Rather introverted, he speaks little. On the contrary, Nicole is expansive, curious about everything, and wants to see it all. She works in publicity, for an agency associated with the radio broadcasting station Europe n° 1.

Jean-Pierre Sergent, Marcel Loridan's partner, visits the bungalow with Regis Debray, who is from the École normale supérieure in Paris. Jean-Pierre is exuberant, optimistic, full of life and ideas. Regis reminds me of Alain Landau; quiet, calm, observant, he listens to us talk about the present and the future.

The regular visitors to the bungalow are our friends Monique Laks, Michel Maziere, and Leyla Vekili, a Turkish journalist. In our discussions a recurrent theme is the permanent revolution and how to clear Africa of neocolonialism. The chaos instigated by the imperialists in the Congo so as to kill Lumumba is revolting to us. With the poverty and ignorance in which the Belgian racists have maintained the population of the Congo, the chef d'oeuvre of the civilizing mission of the Christian and European worlds has been accomplished.

In our vision of a free Africa, the Algiers–Cape axis plays a fundamental role. The struggle of the Algerians for their independence and the South Africans against apartheid represent the same combat. South Africa has industrial strength and an advanced proletariat. Algeria doesn't lack resources and has enormous potential. The victory of the African National Congress (ANC) in South Africa will eradicate white power in Africa; we are convinced of it. With the continent freed, the revolution will take on the tasks of economic and social development. Priority will be given to the fight against illiteracy, tribalism. If we do not do away with these horrors, African unity will be a disaster. Taking into account the arbitrary fixing of the borders of these new states, we are faced with the problem of nationalism. The general impression is that in Africa the principal preoccupation is tribalism. Our main discussions are about the idea of the nation. Stalin's definition is satisfactory for some. I think we have to go beyond it with strong regional regroupings whose institutions must be defined and established with the participation of the people. Without this element, any union will be for the benefit of a minority allied with and manipulated by the imperialists' economic interests.

It's the beginning of December 1961. I am just finishing breakfast on the patio of the ministry when Benmiloud, who is the acting director of the cabinet, calls me into his office.

"Do you have a passport?" he asks with a mysterious air.

"Why do you want to know?"

I know Benmiloud from my time in the command block in Oujda. Just when I was leaving, he whispered in my ear that I had been chosen to open a station in Damascus. He knows what happened afterward.

"You're going to Cairo with Boussouf and a delegation led by President Benkhedda."

I laugh out loud. "You're joking! You know I'm not an ass-kisser."

"No, no. Krim and Dahlab are on this trip. They are there to strengthen the delegation. Boussouf definitely wants you along."

"I don't understand his sudden interest in me. I didn't ask for anything and I'm fine here."

"Stop being so stubborn, and furthermore you'll get the chance to meet Nasser and see Cairo. Do you have a passport?"

"Meet Nasser? A dictator who put all of Egypt's democrats and progressives into concentration camps in the desert? I would just like to see my friend Boualem Dekar."

"I'll tell Boussouf all that, but in the meantime, go get your passport."

I show him the passport that doesn't contain the Italian visa.

It's the first official trip of the new president of the GPRA. In addition to Benkhedda and Boussouf, the delegation includes Ben Tobbal, minister of state, Abdelkader Maachou, cabinet director of the president, and me. On the plane, I am seated next to Maachou. In his way of looking at me from behind his dark glasses, his way of walking through doorways ahead of me, I imagine that he thinks I'm Boussouf's eyes and ears.

Maachou belongs to the category of Algerians terrorized by the files kept by Boussouf on everybody. In their investigations in town, agents dissimulate their function by saying they are members of the signal corps. In the minds of those who think they are well informed, this confusion is never-ending. I attempt to talk to him, but he barely replies and turns his head toward the window. When we fly over Libya, he asks suspiciously, "You're here as what?"

"It's certainly not to carry the suitcases of these guys."

Vexed and angry, I turn my back to him and decide to stop speaking to him.

The sun is going down when the plane lands. The president and his two ministers get off first. My neighbor follows them. Surprised by the projectors, the flashes, and the hoard of journalists, I see the vice president of the United Arab Republic, Mohieddine Zakaria, welcoming President Benkhedda at the foot of the gangway. Confronted with the elegance and imposing allure of Zakaria, I think of the crease in my pants that I placed under the mattress last night to iron them out.

I avoid the lights, the crowd. Someone from protocol

tells me to get into a black American limousine in which Ben Tobbal is seated. The cortege takes off, leaves the airport surrounded by motorcyclists and the sound of sirens. I have never had the slightest conversation with Ben Tobbal. He observes me turning my head in every direction and breaks the silence just as we are crossing an immense square.

"Do you know Cairo?"

When I say no, he smiles.

"That's Maidan Al Tahrir, Liberation Square. Cairo is a very beautiful city and the people are gentle and gay. They're civilized."

The cars stop in front of a palace where a multitude of employees and servants welcome us, nodding their heads. Our rooms are upstairs. Dinner is served on the ground floor under the vigilant eye of a head waiter. As we leave the table, I catch up with Boussouf.

"We'll be staying how many days? I would like to get Boualem Dekar's address."

"Don't worry, you'll have time to see him. The radio station is in the embassy. Get some rest and we'll see tomorrow."

Breakfast is served in the room. I taste some exotic fruit. At the foot of the staircase I join Benkhedda, Boussouf, our ambassador in Cairo, Ali Kafi, and Maachou. We're waiting for Ben Tobbal. The president is impatient. Boussouf whispers to me that the minister of state spends considerable time in the bathtub because of a skin disease. I take advantage of the wait to ask: "Is the embassy far from here? How can I get there?"

"This morning we're going to meet Nasser and you are coming with us," he says with a smile.

"But I have nothing to say to him."

"I know, but it's a chance to see him. Come with us, you won't regret it."

Journalists and photographers are waiting for us in front of the presidential palace. My underground reflexes are at work and I remain off to the side. In the small chamber next to the president's office, the head of protocol questions Maachou, who comes over to me.

"What's your function?"

I extend my arm toward Boussouf, who is looking my way: "Go ask him, he must know."

Boussouf comes over and asks what's going on.

"Si Boussouf, the head of protocol wants to know the titles of the members of the delegation."

Boussouf signals to the head of protocol to come over and tells him: "He's my assistant."

The head of protocol nods and goes away. Boussouf pats me on the back.

We enter Nasser's office. He is standing, welcomes Benkhedda and places him to his right, Ben Tobbal to his left. Boussouf and I are placed next to Benkhedda, Ali Kafi and Maachou across from us. Nasser sits down, we do the same. At ease, his upper body straight, Nasser smiles broadly. With his back slightly curved, his face pale, Benkhedda smiles stiffly.

Nasser's first words are "How are the brothers in prison in France?"

He mentions no names and I don't believe he is thinking only of Ben Bella. He hardly listens to the reply and, with a strained air, begins a serious and persuasive speech: "Our Syrian brothers have just separated from the United Arab

Republic. I have to say that I wasn't in agreement for a precipitated union. I tried to dissuade them by explaining the complexity of the plan. I am harassed by Egyptian citizens who ask me to intervene in their private lives. That said, the decision of the Syrian leaders will not take away from the feeling of brotherhood that links the two peoples."

Nasser then enumerates the Egyptian economic projects that have been carried out, smiling optimistically.

The voice of Benkhedda is not as strong. Leaning toward the rais, he gives an account of the negotiations with the French government and concludes: "The essential point of disagreement is the Sahara. France wants to detach it from Algeria. For us, giving in to them is out of the question."

Without the slightest hesitation, Nasser states categorically: "It's for you to decide what to do. We will support you whatever you decide."

He gets up. The meeting is over. Smiling, he takes Benkhedda by the arm, takes us slowly through a series of large ceremonial rooms. In front of the dining room are Ali Sabri, Mohieddine Zakaria, and another man whom I don't recognize. As I shake the man's hand, Boussouf intervenes and says: "May I introduce you to Fathi Dib, a man you have to watch out for. He watches over everything we do."

I laugh, Fathi Dib also laughs.

"Don't listen to Si Boussouf."

I know his name. He is head of the *moukhabarate*, the secret police.

Very elegant waiters welcome us, bending low. Nasser tells a number of jokes and finishes by relaxing Benkhedda. Of the two Egyptian ministers, Ali Sabri is the more talkative.

As tall as his president, he has a strong personality. Mohieddine Zakaria seems more refined but withdrawn.

At the table, Nasser brings up the problem of the unity of the Arab nation. He casts a distracted look at the head waiter, who is dressed in a dark outfit, and at the two waiters in white who present a large fish on a serving platter. He is once again somber, insists on the need for unity to escape Western domination. He thinks the community of language, religion, and culture must be accompanied by solid state structures resulting from a long process of negotiation.

"That's what our Syrian brothers have not understood," he concludes.

In the evening, I attend a dinner hosted by Benkhedda for the Chinese ambassador in Cairo. Ever since his trip to China in 1958, he has been presented by the press and French wire services as a pro-Chinese Marxist. Surrounded by Ben Tobbal and Kafi on his left, Boussouf, me, and Maachou on his right, he is seated across from the Chinese ambassador, accompanied by an interpreter in Arabic, another in French, and two councilors. Benkhedda expresses his satisfaction at being received by the representative of a great friendly country, evokes the ties of friendship between the Chinese and Algerian people, the agreements signed during visits of members of our government. He thanks the People's Republic of China for its unfailing support for the struggle of our people and its humanitarian aid to our refugees. The ambassador in turn thanks the president for his invitation and the friendship between the two peoples. He expresses his admiration for the Algerian people and their fight against colonialism and imperialism. He esteems the support given by his country as natural, asserts that China will always remain at the side of fighting Algeria. Following the solemn statements and the beginning of the meal, the conversation covers a variety of subjects between the president and his guest. Not very long ago, incidents broke out on the border between China and Nepal. Ben Tobbal raises the problem: "I know that brothers Lenin and Mao Tse-tung condemn imperialism, but I wonder why China has attacked Nepal, a small, poor nation."

Calling Lenin and Mao Tse-tung "brothers" makes me want to laugh. Benkhedda stiffens, puts his hand in front of his mouth, and says in Arabic in a low voice: "Let it drop. Change the subject."

Boussouf explodes: "Let him talk. You think you're the only one who knows how to talk!"

Horrified, I'm ashamed. The few illusions that I have concerning our political leaders are gone. During the luncheon with Nasser, only Benkhedda had spoken; Boussouf and Ben Tobbal had remained silent, as had Ali Kafi, the colonel, and the ambassador. I know their schooling didn't go beyond the primary school certificate, but I was unaware of their mentality. They remain filled with childish reactions.

Colonel Nasser and his companions know how to read a military map. The colonels of our army are incapable of doing so. Obviously, guerrilla warfare is not conventional war, but the colonels who let the enemy build the electrified fence along the border certainly had a short view.

The next morning, Boussouf tells the attendant to put a limousine at my disposal to take me to the embassy. Surprised to see me, Dekar bursts out laughing and yells to the Algerians present in the entrance hall: "This is the vice minister of arms and general liaisons!" Then, turning to me: "I didn't recognize you in the photo because your back was turned."

"It was to trick the enemy," I say laughing.

"Here, everyone thought it was Omar Oussedik and the radio and the newspapers had made a mistake."

"There's no mistake. Amara Seddik is the name on my passport. I'm the first vice minister for a few days. Don't scream it from the rooftops."

We have a good laugh. Dekar is obviously as happy as me with this encounter. I want a change of atmosphere and a visit to Cairo. Boulem takes me around the elegant neighborhoods to see the swanky shops and cafés, then alongside the banks of the Nile. We have lunch in a restaurant where I discover Egyptian cuisine, its dishes made from lima beans and chickpeas. We leave the restaurant and go to the pyramids. The majesty of the spectacle is breathtaking.

I then visit the apartment that Dekar shares with another operator.

He takes me to a friend's, who has invited some women over for the evening. His friend has the *baouab*, the concierge, pick up and deliver the evening meal; he makes some phone calls while I relax and watch the sun go down over the city. The guests soon arrive, two attractive young women. Leila, stocky but svelte, is olive-skinned and is wearing a blouse through which we can surmise firm breasts. She smiles, repeats my name, and makes a sort of bow. Isis does the same and extends her hand. She is taller, also svelte, has light skin, green almond-shaped eyes, and curly hair that falls to her shoulders. They both try their French on us, laugh a lot. I ask them questions and listen to their charming accents. Leila wants to be a civil engineer and will finish her studies in three years. Isis hopes to get a degree in architecture in about the same time. Without my prompting, they declare that they love Algeria and Algerians, admire Djamila Bouhired and the *moudjahidate*. Nasser's politics seem fine with them, giving them a chance to study and hope for a future that their parents would never have dreamed of under the former regime.

At the end of the meal, our host raises the volume of the music. Leila accompanies the voice of Chadia and swings her long black hair from left to right. Like a spring, Isis jumps up, spreads her arms, and begins to belly dance. Leila gets up to dance too, clapping her hands, shaking her torso, her stomach, her body. Enchanted, I let my imagination take flight to Samia Gamal and Tahia Carioca, the famous belly dancers whom I have seen in Egyptian movies. It's all a dream. Alternating songs and dances, the lovely ladies seem as happy as I am. At the end of the evening, I leave them with regret.

Boussouf informs me that President Nasser has put his plane at our disposal for our trip back to Libya. "The Egyptian authorities demand that someone from our delegation inspect the plane before we take off. Can you do that?"

I break out laughing. "Me, inspect a plane? I don't know anything about planes."

"They insist, but it's only a formality. Go ahead, make believe, that's all."

A limousine takes me to the military airport. While the

driver hurries to open the door for me, a captain and a lieutenant stop and salute. The captain points to the plane, an Antonov. I board with his colleague.

The remaining members of the delegation arrive, without Ben Tobbal, who is prolonging his visit with his wife. I notice that Maachou is boarding the plane with an enormous round purple box.

"Is it a gift for your wife?"

"No, it's a hat for the president's wife," he replies, embarrassed.

We land in El Beida, the new administrative capital of Libya. To put an end to the antagonism between the cities of Tripoli and Benghazi, the federal government has settled in El Beida. We are welcomed by the minister of public transport, who takes us directly to the office of the prime minister. A simple welcome, informal talk, and an ordinary lunch. Benkhedda and Boussouf go into the prime minister's office. The minister of public transport, Maachou, and I wait outside.

Since Maachou is sulking, to break the silence, I talk to our host about my time in Tripoli, of the situation of Algeria and the intransigence of the French.

"I'm sure Algeria will be independent," he says, "but I am worried about its future."

"What do you mean by that?"

"You know our king was Algerian born, so I wonder if once independent, Algeria shouldn't join us."

I can't believe my ears. Ignorance, naïveté, hegemonic temptation, or imperialism? I choose ignorance.

"I would point out that our government is provisional, but the fervent wish of the Algerian people is a republic."

He has nothing more to say, nor do I. The waiting is eternal, in the midst of a heavy cloud of cigarette smoke. Boussouf, Benkhedda, and the prime minister end their talk and we take the plane to Tripoli, where we find Idriss I, king of the Libyan Federation.

We spend the night in a residence for special guests. Ahmed Bouda, our ambassador in Libya, who demanded that Azzeddine Azzouz be recalled, represents the counterespionage branch, and joins us. Boussouf, with his phenomenal memory, remembers that my dates with Bianca figured in his report concerning Azzouz.

We return to Tunis. One evening, on leaving the ministry with Lamine Allouane, I find myself face to face with Cherif Belkacem. I haven't seen him since Casablanca, in other words for five years. We sit down at a table upstairs in the Café de Paris and begin by exchanging news about our mutual friends. Then Cherif, who is stationed in Ghardimaou at army headquarters, talks about the crisis between the army and the GPRA.

"It seems in Ghardimaou, the soldiers receive political training," I say with a mocking tone. "And it seems that the courses and lectures require everyone to speak of the struggle of the masses and not the class struggle. That must be Kaid Ahmed's idea, the great theoretician."

"He pretends to be a great theoretician, but there are people like Mendjli and Boumediene who are more serious and determined to defend the people and the Revolution."

"Uncultivated men," I say sharply.

Allouane and I got to know Boumediene during the signal corps training program. He gave us rudiments of military training, but does Cherif really know him?

"Of course, he's the only man who has a vision of the future of Algeria. There is no one else."

"You're joking or what?"

"Not at all. You don't realize what's going on. Things are very serious, and each one of us has to decide where we stand and choose his camp."

"Well, I'll tell you, my choice is made. I've undergone Boussouf and his system for five years and, no question, I will not commit myself to a clan led by a man even more mediocre than him."

Cherif tries to get me to change my mind but I'm determined. We leave each other on good terms. Once alone, Allouane, who followed the conversation without intervening, says: "Cherif didn't expect your reaction."

Cherif Belkacem and the army heads forget that the sophisticated weaponry (among which are 75 mm recoilless canons) that the army along the borders now deploys is the work of Boussouf. Boumediene has entrusted the use of this equipment to deserters from the French army (DAF) whose behavior is equivocal. In addition to obtaining the modern arms and enrolling the heads of the signal corps and counterespionage agents in training courses abroad, Boussouf has also been active in training pilots and frogmen. In Oujda, a brass band is rehearsing in a stadium in preparation for a parade in Algiers. In his confrontation with the army staff, he has taken Kaid Ahmed off the delegation at the negotiations in Evian and replaced him with Colonel Amar Ben Mostefa Benaouda. A former member of the OS, he was arrested in 1951 and escaped from prison in Bone (Annaba) along with Zighout Youcef.

As the negotiations progress, the system laboriously built by Boussouf starts to crumble before falling apart altogether after the cease-fire. Men he brought out of nowhere to become the foundation of his power have let him down, the most famous being Boumediene, whom he placed at the head of the army and who now commands tens of thousands of *moujahidine* placed along the borders. Knowing that "power comes from the barrel of a gun," Boumediene invents an alibi to neutralize it: he reproaches Boussouf with not having managed to convert the GPRA to the army leaders' views. They are wispy views that will allow him to take power after independence. Despite powers of observation and his gift for judging men, Boussouf discovers to his detriment that he cannot penetrate the mind of the student from Al Azhar. Khelifa Laroussi and "Baby Cadum" Abdelkrim Hassani, to whom he has confided the operation of the Didouche base in Tripoli, load up the files and documents in trucks and join the other camp. In the west, Larbi Tayebi, another of his creations, turns his coat. However, Boussouf is not discouraged. He orders the ministry personnel to wait until August to enter Algeria.

Despite his faults, Boussouf remains the man whose balance sheet is exceptional. No president or minister of the GPRA can claim to have carried out his mission with such success. On the other hand, how can we forget the climate of suspicion that he entertained, his use of force, and his taste for conspiracy? He is a man who does not hesitate to carry out his convictions and his projects to their limits, even the most terrifying, including assassination, in particular of Abane Ramdane. After these harrowing years of the country's history, it is time to look squarely at the men involved.

The crisis between the GPRA and the army persists. The leaders of the Wilayas become arbitrators. The Algiers region Wilaya declares its solidarity with the GPRA and takes in former members of the Wilaya from Tunis: Azzeddine, Boualem Oussedik, Ali Lounici. Charged with taking over the command of the Algiers autonomous zone, they are confronted by Yacef Saadi and his men from the Casbah, who have been contacted by the other clan. In favor of neutrality, they invent, among others, a slogan devoid of meaning: "The only hero is the people."

As for the French army and security forces, they no longer control the entire country. The OAS reigns in the cities and villages and benefits from the massive support of the Europeans, who are all armed . . . The army gives orders to them daily with pirated broadcasts and has no difficulty in having them participate in "concerts of pots and pans" against the curfew or to provoke enormous bottlenecks in the streets. The prospect of an independent Algeria makes the Europeans go crazy. The separation between the communities is filled with bloodshed. But the advance of history is ineluctable. A cease-fire is finally declared for March 19, 1962, putting an end to eight years of war.

The day after the cease-fire, the political prisoners from France arrive in Tunis.

I manage to get an appointment with Ben Bella, who was in prison with my brother Mohamed. Ten years after having seen him at the prison in Blida, I find that Ben Bella has the same look, although he seems more accommodating. He listens to the account of my experience in the ministry, my analysis, and doesn't interrupt me except once to say that he hears poorly and that I should speak louder. He listens and lifts his head, furrows his eyebrows at times. At the end of my story, he thanks me, then adds with a troubled air: "The information received since I've been let out and what I just heard confirm that the situation is serious."

He then deplores the divisions within the leading bodies; he doesn't speak of the GPRA nor of the army or the CNRA and cites no names.

"I can assure you, however, that the Revolution is in danger," he concludes.

After his remarks I leave him. Gone is my last illusion. I feel that he will not be capable of facing the immense tasks awaiting him. I learn, the next day, that he has left Tunis for Tripoli. The race for power is within his sights. And the crisis is exacerbated.

According to a rumor, Boussouf counts on stopping the members of the ministry from returning to Algeria before the month of August. This is confirmed. I decide to take my freedom and to return home on Independence Day. I let Annette Roger know; she agrees with my decision and proposes going by car.

To cross the frontier, you have to have a refugee card delivered by the FLN base, which comes under the Ministry of the Interior. The base is on rue Sadikia; I go there secretly and obtain a document with my real ID. The paradox is that Annette Roger must renounce her real identity because she is still being looked for. She gets a card with my family name and chooses Djamila as her first name.

Two days before our departure, I confide in the interim cabinet director, Nourreddine Benmiloud, that I have decided to leave. Surprised, he stops smiling. "You're crazy or what? The minister has decided that we should remain here for two months after the proclamation of independence."

"He can decide what he wants. I didn't sign up for the Liberation Army to serve Boussouf. I chose to die for the liberation of the country and to see our flag fly over our land. I'm going back."

"Don't be foolish. Boussouf is going to deliver individual booklets to each one of us and wants to sign them all himself. You have to wait until he comes back to Tunis. I'll try to get an exception for you."

"Thank you very much, but I don't need any documents to return to my country."

"You're wrong. This document will serve later on for your pension."

"Listen, I didn't decide to fight to get a pension. We are lucky enough to be alive, unwounded, and to return home. Don't speak to me of pensions."

"I repeat that you are being foolish. You might be considered a deserter."

Mokhtar, Berrouaghia, Algeria, 1962.

"Because I will have deserted the exterior for the interior? You aren't serious!"

Benmiloud lowers his head, is pensive. He knows how determined I can be. I first knew him at the radio command center in Oujda and, although we're not intimate, our relations have always been friendly. An hour later, he comes to find me in my office and takes me out into the hall.

"Here, I've taken it upon myself to give you a proper document. It can always be useful. But don't tell anyone."

On the morning of July 1, I return to one of the voting offices in rue Sadikia. I cast my ballot for independence. Annette Roger is waiting for me at the wheel of her Fiat 1100. We head for Algeria! A few kilometers from the border, fearful of the presence of French soldiers, I take the wheel and a deserted secondary route. Suddenly I see a forest of barbed wire held up by pickets: the macabre Morice and Challe lines. I see an opening in the wire we can go through and slowly start, my heart tight. There is nobody around. I speed up without addressing a word to Annette. My emotion is so intense. On the roofs of the huts our flags are flying. I slow down, point to a hut: "Look at the flags. Now I'm certain that Algeria is independent!"

Annette laughs, speaks of her impressions. I feel that the apprehensions, the fears are disappearing. I take to the main road where a *moujahid*, a gun hanging from his shoulder, signals me to stop. He's the first soldier we've met since arriving in the country and the first control on the road. I present the car's papers, my driver's license, and the refugee cards. I get out of the car to point out the sticker on the car windshield and explain what it signifies. As I approach, I see that the soldier is looking at the car's papers upside down. My blood boils. "Go get the person in charge or at least someone who knows how to read."

He gives me back the papers and waves me on. I go back to the car, shut the door with a bang, and say grimly: "Ignorance out of the barrel of a gun is preparing us for bitter tomorrows."

Acknowledgments

For their recognition of Mokhtar's book as a document to be read and hailed, for their contributions to its publication, and for their friendship, I would like to thank profoundly: Karim Ainouz, Andrea Brazzoduro, Janet Brof, Zeynep Celik, Bell Chevigny, Montserrat Daubon, Madeleine Dobie, Allison Drew, Judith Gurewich, Selma Hellal, Amara Lakhous, Gloria Loomis, Nadia Sariahmed, and Adam Shatz.

Map of Northern Algeria

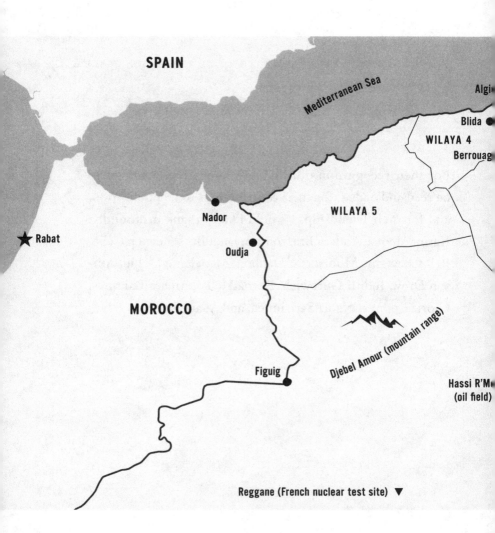

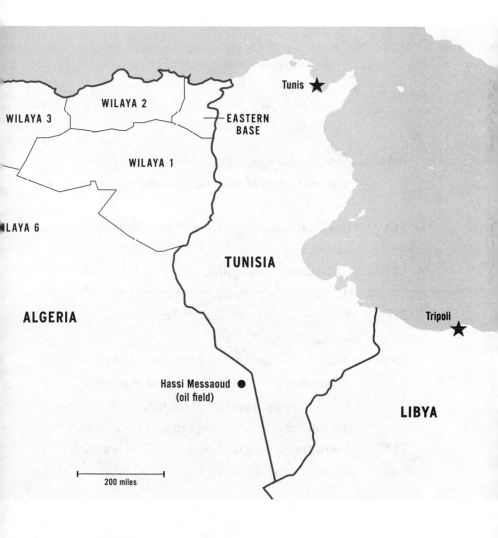

Acronyms

AJAAS Algerian Association of Youth for Social Action (Association de la jeunesse algérienne pour l'action sociale)

ALN National Liberation Army (Armée de libération nationale)

CCE Coordination and Implementation Committee (Comité de coordination et d'éxécution)

CEP Primary school certificate (Certificat d'école primaire)

CNRA National Council of the Algerian Revolution (Conseil national de la Révolution algérienne)

CRUA Revolutionary Committee for Unity and Action (Comité révolutionnaire pour l'unité et l'action)

ESMB Berrouaghia Muslim Sports Star (Etoile sportive musulmane de Berrouaghia)

FLN	National Liberation Front (Front de libération nationale)
GPRA	Provisional Government of the Algerian Republic (Gouvernement provisoire de la République algérienne)
MNA	Algerian National Movement (Mouvement national algérien)
MTLD	Movement for the Triumph of Democratic Freedom (Mouvement pour le triomphe des libertés démocratiques)
OAS	Secret Army Organization (Organisation de l'armée secrète)
OS	Special Organization (Organisation spéciale)
PCA	Algerian Communist Party (Parti communiste algérien)
PPA	Algerian People's Party (Parti du peuple algérien)
SOB	Berrouaghia All-Sports Association
UDMA	Democratic Union for the Algerian Manifesto (Union démocratique du manifeste algérien)
UGEMA	General Union of Algerian Muslim Students (Union générale des étudiants musulmans algériens)
UJCAS	Union of Constantine Youth for Social Action (Union de la jeunesse constantinoise pour l'action sociale)

Algerian Leaders

FERHAT ABBAS (1899–1985) Head of UDMA, a moderate nationalist organization that joined the FLN in 1956. First president of GPRA, provisional government in exile. On independence was president of Constitutional Assembly. Outspoken political personality placed under house arrest by Ben Bella in 1965 and by Boumediene in 1976. Married Marcelle Stoëtzel in 1945.

CHERIF BELKACEM (1930–2009) (nom de guerre, Djamel) Close collaborator of Boumediene, active in 1965 coup d'état against Ben Bella. Held several ministerial posts.

KRIM BELKACEM (1922–70) Served in French army during Second World War, known as sharpshooter. In 1947 accused of murder, sentenced to death by French courts in 1947 and 1950. Went underground, organized armed group in Kabylia.

Head of Wilaya 3 at outset of war. Minister of defense, later foreign minister of GPRA. Chief negotiator with France at Evian, March 1962. Opposed Boumediene, was accused of attempt on Boumediene's life and sentenced to death in absentia. Was found dead in hotel room in Frankfurt.

AHMED BEN BELLA (1916–2012) One of nine "historic leaders" of FLN. Captured by French in 1956 when plane carrying Algerian leaders was forced to land in Algiers. First president of independent Algeria, put in place and then removed by Houari Boumediene on June 19, 1965. Spent fifteen years in confinement following coup d'état. Married Zohra Michelle Sellami, journalist, in 1971, while under arrest. Lived in exile (1980–90).

MOSTEFA BEN BOULAÏD (1917–56) In French army during Second World War, received the Croix de Guerre. Founding member of FLN, one of six men who launched independence war in 1962. Killed in action.

BENYOUSSEF BENKHEDDA (1920–2003) Pharmacist, second head of Algerian provisional government in exile. From same village as Mokhtar Mokhtefi. Longtime militant for independence, was colleague of Abane Ramdane. After open statement, also signed by Ferhat Abbas, calling for new constituent assembly, placed under house arrest by Boumediene (1976–79).

LARBI BEN M'HIDI (1923–57) One of six men who launched the Algerian Revolution on November 1, 1954. Initially commanded Wilaya 5 (Oran region), then headed Algiers region. Was captured in 1957 by French paratroopers, tortured, then killed by French General Aussarasses. Execution was masked as suicide.

LAKHDAR BEN TOBBAL (1929–2010) Member of PPA and OS Special Organization, which preceded FLN. Held several ministerial posts in GPRA. Opposed Ben Bella, was arrested after independence.

HOUARI BOUMEDIENE (1932–78) (nom de guerre; birth name Mohamed Boukherouba) Studied and received military training in Egypt. Colonel, head of ALN at independence. Second president of Algeria, author of coup d'état that overthrew Ben Bella in 1965. Married Anissa El-Mansali, lawyer, in 1973. Died while still in office.

ABDELHAFID BOUSSOUF (1926–80) (nom de guerre, Mabrouk) Central figure in war for independence. Member of group of twenty-two that founded FLN. One of three *B*'s (Belkacem Krim, Ben Tobbal, and Boussouf) behind execution of Abanc Ramdane, leading political personality of wartime struggle. Minister of armaments and general liaison of GPRA, responsible for creation of signal corps and military intelligence that emerged as pillar of independent Algeria's military regimes. Became businessman following independence. Married secretly during the war.

SAAD DAHLAB (1918–90) Longtime militant, jailed by France in 1945–46. Created *El Moudjahid*, served as foreign minister of GPRA in 1961–62. Following independence, founded publishing house.

MESSALI HADJ (1898–1974) Known as father of Algerian nationalism. Arrested by Vichy and later by French postwar governments. Founded series of political organizations but was rejected as lifetime leader by nationalists who launched war for independence. Created MNA, the Algerian National Movement, which fought and engaged in armed struggle against FLN and ALN. Married Emilie Bousquant, French feminist.

SALAH LOUANCHI (1923–90) Longtime militant, member of Muslim Scout movement, later head of press section of FLN federation in France. Imprisoned in France from 1957 to 1962. Married Anne-Marie Chaulet, FLN militant.

ABANE RAMDANE (1920–57) Political personality who spent years in French jails, often called Architect of the Revolution. Organizer of Soummam Congress, which declared political power determinant over military and the "interior" over the "exterior." Executed by Boussouf and collaborators in 1957. Death was originally masked as "killed in action" but later confirmed by Ferhat Abbas. Married to Izza Bouzekri, FLN militant.

Glossary of Arabic Terms

Allahou Akbar God is the Greatest

'ammi paternal uncle

baba papa

bach adel deputy of a cadi or judge

bachagha dignitary in the Ottoman colonial administration and later in the French administration

bey ruler of a beylik in the Ottoman era

beylik Ottoman province in Algeria before the French conquest

bismillah grace; literally, "in the name of God"

burnous loose, heavy, wool cloak with hood

cadi judge

caïd functionary in the Algerian colonial administration

chahada Islamic testimony of faith: "There is no god but God; Mohamed is the messenger of God"

chahid martyr

cheche long cotton veil or turban

chorba soup

choukran thank you

derbouka percussion instrument

djellaba long, loose-fitting garment worn by both men
and women

djoundi (pl. djounoud) foot soldier of the Algerian Liberation
Army (ALN)

Ennidham the Organization, specifically the National
Liberation Front (FLN)

essalam aleïkoum greeting or farewell; literally, "peace
be upon you"

fatiha first sura or chapter of the Koran

fellagha derogatory term for an Algerian freedom fighter;
literally, "bandit"

fez cylindrical felt hat with tassel

fidaï (pl. fidayin) urban guerrilla

gandoura lightweight garment with short sleeves for sleeping
or lounging

gembri primitive lute

guebli derogatory term for a person from rural Algeria

guessâa round wooden dish

hadith saying attributed to the Prophet Mohamed

hadj (fem. hadja) someone who has been on pilgrimage to
Mecca; also, term of respect for an older person

halal permissible according to Islamic jurisprudence;
specifically, ritually fit to be eaten

hammam bathhouse

haras ranch for horse breeding

hizb political party

ijtami'ou military call to attention; literally, "gather together"

imam Islamic spiritual leader; priest or pastor

imma mother

inchâallah God willing

istaâd stand at attention; literally, "be ready"

isti'mar colonialism

istiqlal independence

istrah at ease (military term)

kachabia thick, hooded cloak with sleeves

kadi judge

kanoun law

kouloughi child of a Turkish (Ottoman) man and an Algerian woman

mabrouk congratulations

Maghreb Northwest Africa

mahakma court administering Muslim law during French colonial era

marabout holy man, denigrated by orthodox reformists

marhaba welcome

mazhar orange blossom water

méchoui animal roast, often whole animal

mechta hamlet

medina historic neighborhood in North Africa; literally, city or town

mihrab niche in mosque wall indicating direction of Mecca

Min Djibalina national anthem; literally, "From Our Mountains"

mokhazni Algerian serving in French army contingents called makhzens

mouderes Arabic teacher

moudjahid (pl. moudjahidine, fem. moudjahida, fem. pl. moudjahidate) militant or freedom fighter

moukhabarate Egyptian secret police

moussebel (pl. moussebeline) civil auxiliary of ALN

mtourni renegade

muezzin person calling to prayer at a mosque

nif honor or pride; literally, "nose"

Reguibet southern Algerian tribe

rfiss semolina and date dessert

sarouel traditional baggy trousers

Si title of respect preceding a name

sunna practices and sayings of the Prophet Mohamed

tlssal go-between

ulemas *or* **olemas** (singular, 'alim) scholars of Islamic doctrine and law

watani nationalist

watania nationalism

Wilaya administrative division

youyou ululation

zaïm supreme leader or guide

zakat yearly almsgiving, one of the five pillars of Islam

zaouia Islamic institution serving as monastery, school, hostel, and shrine

Zitouna mosque in Tunis, and one of the first universities in Islam

MOKHTAR MOKHTEFI, born in Algeria in 1935, joined the National Liberation Army (ALN) in 1957. Trained as a radio operator, he worked as the head of a communications unit during the Algerian War. After independence, he became president of the General Union of Algerian Muslim Students and went on to study sociology and economics at universities in Algiers and Paris. After living in France and publishing several books on North Africa and the Arab world, he moved to New York in 1994. He died in 2015, and his memoir, *I Was a French Muslim*, was published in Algeria the following year.

ELAINE MOKHTEFI was born in New York City and raised in small towns in New York and Connecticut. She lived for many years in France and Algeria, where she worked as a translator and journalist, and is the author of *Algiers, Third World Capital: Freedom Fighters, Revolutionaries, Black Panthers*. She is the widow of Mokhtar Mokhtefi.